CW00370135

MY KIND OF
AMERICA

MY KIND OF AMERICA

JEREMY POOLMAN

BLOOMSBURY

First published 2000
This paperback edition published 2001

Copyright © 2000 by Jeremy Poolman

The moral right of the author has been asserted

Bloomsbury Publishing Plc, 38 Soho Square, London W1D 3HB

A CIP catalogue record for this book
is available from the British Library

ISBN 0 7475 5311 4

10 9 8 7 6 5 4 3 2 1

Typeset by Hewer Text Ltd, Edinburgh
Printed in England by Clays Ltd, St Ives plc

For Thomas Wolfe, who taught me (amongst many other things) that you can't go home again; and for Simon Williams, who gave me that most precious of gifts, his time.

I must write it to know it

Eddie Reno Jnr

Author's Note

When, as a twelve-year-old Jacksonville schoolboy, I walked out of the Roxette Theater on the corner of Maple Street and Vine, so leaving my parents with (I used to imagine) a lifetime's worth of searching, it was – and would remain for all these years – an act without explanation. Indeed, it is only now, now that both my father and mother are dead, that I feel it appropriate to speak out. Hence the following. Hence my sitting here in this big old house – sitting here at this window overlooking the lake, my ears tuned as ever for the sound of footsteps on the stairs, and my thoughts – for the first time in years – drifting back to that twelve-year-old boy. Of course, that today is Clare's twelfth birthday (or perhaps I should still call her Isabelle – at least until the papers go through) is no coincidence. Nor is it a coincidence, I suppose, that it was this very morning I learned that the 2005 Academy of American Photographers Lifetime Achievement Award is to go (posthumously, of course) to my father, and that I, his loving son, will be asked to collect it on his behalf.

Talk about irony.

Or maybe not.

Perhaps it's entirely appropriate that I should be there – that it should be me standing in the spotlight and smiling – seeing as how it was me, and not those pictures of Eisenhower or Elvis or Richard Nixon, that was his real – his greatest – achievement. I mean, what greater success could a photographer hope for than to produce an image so like the original that scarcely a soul could tell them apart?

But I'm running ahead of myself here. Before all that – before I begin – I should just like to post a warning to all those who will dismiss what follows as *only a work of fiction*. Yes, it is fiction – but it is also true. As somebody once said, you can always find the truth of a man in the lies he tells. Well, these are my lies. Honest they are.

Part One

THE KEY

Eddie

I

People said it was some kind of madness that made Eddie Reno quit his job at the K-Mart and, at the age of sixty-two, attempt to recover what had once been his life. It was, people said, the same kind of madness that, years ago, had persuaded poor Clare Summerfield that stepping off of the Seven Mile Bridge into the clear Gulf waters with her pockets full of rocks was the thing to do, and it was noted, by those who had a memory for such details, that both tragedies occurred at the same time of year – in early fall, between the summer hordes drifting north from the Keys and the snowbirds in their RVs flying south. Some even speculated that it was this season's general drift to such melancholy coolness (and how, they said, it got into your bones) that was responsible now and had been responsible then. This, however, was an explanation which others thought way too simple. To them, the timing had to be more than coincidence; to them, Eddie's walking out on the deli counter when he did after nearly seven years (and there'd been three years before that, don't forget, in men's fashions) was some kind of reckless but nevertheless planned act meant to honor the gruesome anniversary. To them – if not to Eddie – there was a neatness about it (it was, after all, ten years near as dammit to the day since the body had been washed up way down in Key Biscayne) that was surely far beyond the reach of chance. Indeed, such was the talk that fall, and so persuasive the logic that had Eddie the master of some devious but as yet impenetrable plan, that soon pretty much everyone believed it. Everyone of course but Eddie. Oh, for sure, later, when all that would happen had happened, when the ghosts that would rise up and so nearly finish him had drifted away and the season turned again, leaving the debris of summer strewn once again on the land, even he'd come to see patterns in things – connections – that hitherto he'd been blind to – but only later. At the time, there was just now – not forever. At the time, no woods existed in his landscape, only solitary trees.

Take the day, for example, when it all began.

It was a day – a Tuesday – much like any other. In fact, it was a day so like every other day lately that it might just as well have been a Monday or a Wednesday or any other day for that matter. If it was planning to be a special day, it was giving no clues. It began (as every day these days began) at six-thirty, with a click on the nightstand and the usual slap like tiny hands clapping of the numbers flipping down in the window of his clock. A second, then the radio-tape started hissing and soon the voice of Jimmy Buffett filled the room:

> *Livin' on sponge-cake*
> *Watchin' the sun bake*
> *All of them tourists covered with oil.*

He turned in his bed. *Jesus Christ.* Every morning he meant to change the tape – swore he would – and every morning when he woke his failure to do so was just sitting there on his chest like some big old weight, pressing down on him, until, every morning, whether he wanted to or not (and he did not), he was thinking of all those other things that needed doing that he just never seemed to get around to and probably never would. Like a mailbox that needed fixing to its post before it dropped clean off, and a seventy-eight Toyota Supreme that was not so un-supreme that a half-hour's work on the plugs wouldn't fix it. Not to mention a whole host of other things that, though he tried every morning not to think about, just plain refused not to get thought about until they had him hanging hopelessly onto sleep even though sleep had already fled.

He reached out a hand, killed the tape. Slowly, he opened his eyes. Everything was blurry. For a moment he lay still, not bothering trying to focus (he knew too well what he'd see when he did), his limbs heavy, suspended in that limbo that lies between dreams and the day. His throat was dry, his muscles as stiff as some corpse's in a grave. Again, all night (as every night lately), he'd been standing in his dreams halfway up an outside iron staircase at a Spanish-looking house someplace way down in the Keys. He'd been leaning out, now and then smacking at the bugs as they landed on his skin, and sweating, all the time peering through a bough of shimmering leaves at some people gathered and talking round a swimming-pool. Though their voices were muffled by the thick dripping trees and the stifling heat, and their words were indistinct and faces obscured, every night he knew who they were and what he must do. Which was? Well, photographs, of course. Take photographs. But, as ever, stuck, an old man on the staircase, he couldn't move. Every night he tried to push off with his legs, tried to raise up the dead weight of his camera, but every night it was like he was standing in quicksand on paralyzed legs, and all he could do was stand there helpless as the voices drifted off and in time were gone. In the silence then, every night, came the blasting of a shotgun, then the sliding of cats in the bushes below, the rising buzz of bugs in the trees.

And no pictures. Just that dull empty feeling that comes from opportunities missed. Just that twisting in his stomach, burning low like last night's whiskey; and then, every morning, this lurch into light, this slow coalescing into shapes of the cracks in the plaster overhead, this intimate whispered censure of things left undone.

Like the car.

That mailbox.

Like that letter – *Dear Edward* – composed a half-hundred times but unwritten still in more than a half-dozen years.

He pushed himself up; the thumping in his head told him *no*. He reached out, found his pills, unscrewed the top – all thumbs – set a couple on his tongue, drew his tongue back, swallowed hard. Then he lay back down, listened to the sounds of the morning rising up through the floor – the clattering of bottles, the angry snarl of Angelia's ancient hoover – and was lying there still when the clock buzzed for seven.

2

E ver since that dark and disappointing spring of nineteen sixty-one, Angelia Huelos, former Miss Cuba, had been waiting for the Big Man from Havana to come bowling down the street and into Awful Arthur's Bar and Grill. For thirty-five years, in expectation of his arrival, she had not spent a day without a pistol tucked snugly into the waistband of her skirt, or a night (including that night whose pleasure and pain would lead to the arrival of her daughter) without its reassuring presence beneath her pillow. Not for one second in all those years had the weapon – a thirty-eight Magnum with a solid-steel case – left her side – nor would it, she had sworn, until that deed on the day of liberation was done.

This morning, as every morning, hearing footsteps from the apartment overhead, she stepped into the shadows and fingered the pistol's polished handle. One bullet, she knew, and her nation would be free. She cut her breathing and listened. The footsteps grew louder then fainter. The running of water, then the slamming of a door. Slowly, with an assassin's deliberate care, she withdrew the pistol from her waistband. She froze at the creaking of stairs. For so long she'd been waiting for this moment, and now at last it was here. From her hidey-hole, scrunched in between the phone-booth and the cigarette machine, she studied the top of the stairs. First, a pair of scuffed brown shoes appeared, then the legs of a pair of pants, blue check, the pockets of a coat, then a hand clutching keys on a ring. Silent, deadly, she raised up the gun. She sighted, taking aim, crossing the wires on Castro's cigar. She drew a shallow breath. 'So, comrade,' she said, spitting the words out in a low mean hiss, 'you feelin' lucky today?'

Eddie Reno felt his spirits sink. He raised his hand against the flaring of the window. 'Angelia?' He heaved his eyes around the room, squinting in the blue morning light. Every morning it was the same. Every morning she came at him from a different direction, practicing the stealth that she knew would be required when the day of liberation arrived.

Outside in the street, a car backfired. In the bar, Eddie Reno felt his

6

heart-rate rise and fall. 'Angelia?' he said, feeling suddenly weary and every year of his age. 'Look, for God's sake –'

From somewhere then, the click of a hammer drawing back, the faint sound of breathing.

'*Jesus*, Angelia –'

And then suddenly there she was, stepping out of the shadows, a barmaid, a beauty-queen, a middle-aged gunfighter and mother-to-be. She was scowling. 'You're late,' she said.

Eddie sighed. 'I'm not late, Angelia.' He glanced at the Michelob clock above the bar, then back. 'Look. Seven-thirty. Okay?'

She lowered the pistol, cocking her head to one side and still scowling. 'What's the matter?' she said.

'What do you mean, what's the matter?'

'Something's wrong.'

'Wrong?'

She slipped the gun back into her waistband and shrugged. 'Angelia can tell,' she said.

Eddie Reno let his eyes close for a second; he was back on that iron staircase, his camera hanging heavy in his hands.

'Eddie?'

He opened his eyes. The camera, the stairs, the voices round the pool drifted off.

'What?'

'Is it that Papa? Is he botherin' you again?'

He shook his head. 'I have to go.' He moved toward the door. Footsteps behind him, then a hand touched his arm.

'Eddie?'

'What?'

'You want me to speak with him?'

He sighed. 'He's dead, Angelia. Hemingway's dead. He's been dead for thirty years.'

The grip on his arm was light but firm – a mother's grip. 'So it *was* him,' she said.

'I have to go.' Eddie Reno pulled away, pushed through the door, stepped onto the street. Despite the early hour, the street was baking, the sidewalk and the highway beyond pale as bleached bone. He stood still for a moment, blinking like a child in the light. Across the highway, the parking-lot outside the Babies By the Sea Birthing Center was already busy, the warm air off the Gulf filling up with the sharp sound of voices. Eddie squinted, watching as a great rotund woman maneuvered herself up and out of a beat-up station-wagon, her hands gripping tight to the door, her shoulders heaving with exaggerated breathing, her belly bloated with life. He followed her with his eyes as she moved unsteadily across the parking-lot and in through the center's double doors.

Suddenly heavy-hearted, he stood watching for figures in the window. None came. A minute passed, then he turned away and walked slowly down the alley that ran between the bar and the Tasty Trash JewelMart, heading for his car and another day on the slicer, pausing only to peer without hope into his mailbox.

3

The package – a white padded bag, the kind with fancy stitching along the end seams – was doubled-up and jammed inside the mailbox – in fact, jammed so tight that in his efforts to remove it the whole mailbox itself finally came away in his hands. He stared at it with surprise, then disgust. Unseen except by three gulls on a wire, he breathed a heavy sigh. 'Well, of *course*,' he said sourly to no one in particular. He waggled the wretched post. The brackets he'd been meaning for so long to replace were hanging limp and leering, the bolts twisted and rusty. The whole thing was way beyond repair now and would need completely replacing. He kicked it, but without conviction (although still nearly knocking it over), cursing as he did so his own hopeless self.

It took some tugging (he had to grip the mailbox between his knees and pull like crazy as if he were prizing a swollen cork from a bottle), but finally the package came free. Setting the mailbox beside the post, he turned it around in his hands. The writing was deliberate in style – almost childlike – his address just a series of neatly formed loops. He turned the package over. There was no return address. He drew it up close to his face until it was barely six inches from his nose and squinted at the postmark. It was smudged and indecipherable. Gripping the thing in his left hand, he pulled on the stitching with his right.

Later, in the days and weeks ahead, Eddie Reno would remember with great clarity the moment when first he reached his hand inside the padded envelope and the tips of his fingers touched the book's rough-textured covers. Again and again, as if that moment in the sunshine on a Florida street were itself the very source of his final chance at freedom, he would find himself, like some bemused but grateful pilgrim, returning to it, reaching out just to turn it around in his hands, so as to study it from every angle and in every kind of light, so as to touch and caress it, so as to confirm once again that it really *was* real – that it really *had* existed – and that this new chance at life wasn't just some dream come from nothing. Indeed, in the days and weeks ahead, that moment when he first withdrew the book from its envelope – when he first held it up to the light, first turned its delicate pages – would come to be a moment so familiar as to become, in time, almost overfamiliar – a moment so often seen as to be quite unseeable afresh, and consequently one which, ironically perhaps, would come to be as invisible as the words on a page of a book too often read, or the line of a melody too often heard.

But that, for now, was all in the future. For now, there was just the crispness of that moment first seen – the harshness of that street, the heat of that sunshine, that clock on a wall somewhere ticking slowly down, the pages of that book, that spidery secretive hand.

He closed the book carefully (he could hear its binding crack like the crack of old bones), then opened it at the first inside page, aware as he did so of a faint musty smell – that same smell of genteel decay that clings to the furniture of long-shut-up houses months after their opening for the season. It gathered in his throat like dust. He cleared his throat and drew the book in close, studying the first carefully formed words. The ink with which they had originally been formed was faded now to a pale watery brown – brown the color of ancient dried blood – its tones a little darker at the tops of loops and the ends of strokes where the writer's pen had pressed more heavily or lingered longer. Set quite apart from the main body of sloping prose, these first words – *A Personal Account of Travels to the Dakota Territories, by Matthew R. Princeton* – were large and bold, and easily deciphered at a glance. Not so what followed. Eddie squinted hard, his eyes raging at the fancy curls and disguising loops, but could make out barely one word in ten. For sure it was some kind of journal (there were dates and capitaled place names scattered throughout), the prose every now and then broken by short columns of figures or annotated drawings which appeared at first glance to be maps. Slowly, page after page, then three at a time, then five, ten, until, finally, no wiser as to the sender's purpose (nor, indeed, the true contents of the journal – if that was, indeed, what it was) than he'd been on first opening it, he reached the end and closed the book. He turned it in his hands, studying the binding, the spine. The cover was pale blue, much stained. He shook it gently, half-expecting some note of explanation to fall free. None came. He shook the padded envelope, peered inside. Nothing. He checked the address again. It was his alright – *Mr E. Reno, 321 Tarpon Street, Islamorada Key, Florida* – so no mistake there. For sure whoever had sent it had meant it for him. But why? And who? He shook the book again, this time a little harder. Still nothing. Finally then, shaking his head as if illustrating his confusion for the benefit of an audience, he slid the book back into the envelope and made his way slowly down the alley to his car.

*   *   *

Irene was already halfway through mincing that day's budget beef when Eddie showed up in his overalls at the counter.

'You're late.'

'I know,' he said. 'Sorry. Something happened.'

'Mr Frampton wants to see you.'

He opened the hatch, closed it behind him. He pulled a pair of surgical gloves from the dispenser on the wall and snapped them on. All the way in the car he'd been trying to think of someone he knew who might send him a book, but there was no one. These days, he didn't even know anyone who used the mail.

A finger poked his shoulder. 'Hello? K-Mart to Eddie?'

He looked up.

'You okay?'

'Okay?'

'You look like you swallowed something nasty.' Irene laid a hand gently on his arm. 'This something – was it a bad something that happened?'

Eddie shook his head. 'I don't think so,' he said.

'You don't think so?'

He shrugged.

'Well, what was it, honey? Did that Cuban crisis go crazy on you again? She been flexing those missiles of hers again?'

Eddie thought of the package – of the book – lying in the trunk of his car. It was stupid, he knew, but he couldn't stop the feeling – hadn't been able to all morning – that somehow it was waiting for him, and also that – like some scar on his body – now it was here, it would never go away.

'Honey?'

'What?'

Irene shook her head, whistled through her teeth. 'Honey, you sure are in some strange kind of place today.'

'Sorry,' said Eddie. He looked down, smoothed the gloves' fine rubber on the backs of his hands.

'Sorry?'

He looked up. 'I guess it's just –'

'Just what, honey?'

It's just that somebody I don't know but who for sure knows me sent me a book and I'm scared and I don't know why I'm scared, I just am, okay?

'Eddie?'

He tried to raise a smile. It rose hard as if weighted with the dead weight of stones. 'Nothing,' he said. 'It's nothing, really.'

Irene cocked her head. 'You sure now?'

'Sure.'

' 'Cause it sure don't look like nothing.'

'I'm sure,' he said.

'Okay,' said Irene. Then she turned away, sighed a heavy sigh, and flicked the switch on the mincer.

4

As a child and as a man, Eddie Reno had always hated mysteries. The unknown, the unseen, had always made him nervous – so much so, indeed, that the first time his father shut him up in a cupboard and pretended to saw him in half he screamed so loud (and was so frightened by his own screaming) that half the women in the audience at the Sanborn Auditorium in Pampa, east Texas, started screaming too, with the consequence that – in one case – a baby was born nearly two months prematurely right there and then in the stalls.

'Mr Reno? Are you listening to me, sir?'

'Pardon me?' said Eddie. The child, he recalled, had later died of complications in the hospital.

Mr Frampton sat back in his chair. 'This,' he said, waving a thin, bony hand vaguely before him, 'is *precisely* what I mean.'

'Pardon me?'

'This . . . this . . .' He screwed up his pale face, searching for a word. 'This . . . *vagueness*. This *inattention*.' He leaned forward. 'I mean, honestly, look at you.'

Eddie looked down. There was blood already on his white coat; his hands were bloated and blue from the chill of the freezers.

'Take that collar, for instance. Would you say, Mr Reno, that that collar was a K-Mart collar?'

Eddie fingered the collar. It was worn at the edges, the cardboard inside peeking through.

'And that tie!'

He felt for the tie. There was none. He looked up.

'Precisely, Mr Reno.' Mr Frampton shook his head, held his look of disdain for a second (he was a man who liked to make his point and to have that point acknowledged), then dropped his eyes to the folder on his desk. 'I see we were late again this morning.' He looked up. 'Trouble with the car again, was it?'

Eddie shrugged.

'Hmm,' said Mr Frampton, looking down again. He drew a finger down a column of names, then along to a figure in a box. 'That's three times this week,' he said. 'Four times last. And the week before that –' he paused, turned back a page '– twice.' Pushing back in his chair again, he closed the folder. He smiled a mirthless smile. 'Do you see my problem, Mr Reno?'

Eddie nodded. Mention of the car had made him think again of the book in the trunk. 'Mr Frampton,' he said. 'Can I ask you something?'

'What?' said Mr Frampton brusquely.

'Well, if somebody sends you something in the mail – a present, say a book maybe – do you think it'd be possible to find out who sent it, if there's no return address?'

Mr Frampton frowned. 'I beg your pardon?' He'd a look, for a second, of bewilderment in his eye; this hardened, however, in no time to one of pity – the pity of slaughtermen for the fate of dumb animals. 'Look,' he said. 'Mr Reno. You've been with us now –' He glanced down at the folder.

'Ten years,' said Eddie. The look was shaming. He cringed.

'Pardon me?'

'Ten years. I've been with you ten years.'

'Quite. Ten years.' Mr Frampton blew a sharp stream of mint across his desk. 'Wow, that's quite a time, isn't it?'

Eddie shrugged. The look was a look – contempt for something worthless, disdain for something harmless – he'd seen so many times; it was a look that for years now had not had the power to touch him.

Mr Frampton leaned forward. 'Mr Reno?'

For years until now. But why now? What suddenly had changed? He thought of the book in the trunk of his car, felt again its eyes somehow upon him.

'Mr Reno?'

'I'm sorry,' he said. He shifted in his seat, tried to focus. 'What were you saying?'

Mr Frampton cleared his throat. 'I was saying, *Mr Reno*, that ten years is a long time, is it not?'

Eddie felt himself nodding. It was as if the book was staring at him, scrutinizing him – as if it was waiting for something, expecting something of him.

'And it's easy after so many years to just let things drift, to let standards slacken. Do you think you've been letting things drift, Mr Reno?'

'Drift?' said Eddie. It was like the book's coming was some kind of test.

'Drift, sir. Drift.' Mr Frampton narrowed his cold eyes. 'You're not listening to me, are you, Mr Reno?' He leaned forward, dropped his voice to a hiss. 'You're not hearing what I'm telling you – are you?' He shook his head, straightened up. 'Well, Mr Reno, I can tell you you'd better start hearing what I'm saying and fast, or things will have to change, okay? Do I make myself clear?'

Eddie stared at the young man's pale face.

'Mr Reno?'

'Yes,' he heard a voice saying.

'Good,' said Mr Frampton. He stood. Outside, in the parking-lot, a car revved its engine; inside, in the office of the store's assistant manager, Eddie Reno felt rising that panic at a mystery he'd first felt as a child, felt again that cupboard's closeness, smelled again the sudden stench of his fear.

'So?'

'So what?'

They were sitting – the two of them, Eddie and Irene – at a table in the canteen.

'So what did he want?'

'Who?'

Irene snorted. 'President Clinton, of course. Who do you think?'

Eddie shrugged. He was staring at the mound of mashed potatoes on his plate.

'Well?'

He looked up. 'Nothing.'

'Nothing? He must have said *something* –'

He laid the fork down, pushed the plate aside. 'Irene,' he said, 'can I ask you something?'

Irene shrugged. 'Sure.'

He paused.

A hand snaked across the table, covered his. 'What's wrong, honey? Is it Mr Frampton? Did he say something to you?'

Eddie shook his head. The hand gripped his fingers, squeezed them tight.

'Eddie? Are you okay?'

'Do you ever get scared?' he said.

'Scared? Of what?'

He shrugged, looked down.

'Honey?'

He looked up. 'I don't know.'

'You don't know?'

He shook his head, turned away. On the wall across the canteen, the Green Bay Packers were lined up, five rows of them, each one of them tanned and confident, squinting without care in the harsh southern sun, each one of them bursting with life and youth.

'Eddie?'

He turned back. 'What?'

Irene was studying him.

'What is it?'

'You know what I think you need?'

'What?'

'Fun.'

'Fun? What do you mean, fun?'

She sat back, folded her arms. 'Well, precisely,' she said. She screwed up her nose. 'I mean, just look at you.'

'What's wrong with me?'

She shook her head. 'Tell me, just exactly how old are you?'

'Sixty-two,' said Eddie. 'Why?'

She leaned forward, hung her face before his. 'Is that all? I thought you were a *hundred* and sixty-two, the way you've been acting. Honey, don't you want to do no more living?'

'Living?' said Eddie.

'Oh Jesus,' said Irene. 'Man, we really got some work to do on you.'

5

O f all the bars in all of the Keys (and perhaps in the whole state of Florida) everyone knew that the only place a man could get married, drunk, divorced and buried all in one night was at Sol and Roxie's Green Turtle Inn two minutes off of Highway One on the ocean side of Key Largo. And, of course, everyone who knew *that* knew, also, that Sol and Roxie served the best damned snapper that anyone could ever recall, and that, consequently, if you weren't a big fish-eater going in, then you would be for sure coming out, and you wouldn't be coming out (if you ever came out at all) until dawn.

Irene snapped the clasp of her handbag with intent. She shot Eddie a glance. 'I thought you said you wanted to have some fun?'

Eddie felt himself wilting.

'Well, do you or don't you?'

Four bars in three hours he knew was three bars and two hours too many. He closed his eyes tight, opened them. Everything lurched, steadied. How he'd managed to steer the car all the way from the Pig's Breath Saloon (or was it the Pink Porpoise?) and then park it in the Green Turtle parking-lot without hitting anything (at least anything that he knew of or could remember) he couldn't for the life of him imagine. He stared at his hands, watched them gripping the wheel. He couldn't feel his hands.

'Well?'

He shrugged. 'I guess,' he said.

'You guess?'

For the last hour all he'd wanted was to be home safe in his apartment, to be lying back in his Rest-A-Matic armchair and squinting out between his feet at his flickering TV.

'So?' said Irene.

'So?'

'So are we going in or not?'

He screwed up his eyes, looked out across the parking-lot. The Green Turtle Inn was bathed in a pale pink light, the thumping of its music reaching out through the still air and rattling the Supreme's ancient muffler.

'Okay then?' said Irene.

Eddie tried to raise a smile. 'Okay then,' he said.

It was a fight to get through but they made it at last to a booth in the corner. Eddie slid himself in, looked around. The place was seething with sweat and bodies, the air so smoky it was hard not to squint, the music (from Rickie Scallop and His Seafood Serenaders) so loud he could feel the bass rhythm in his kidneys.

Irene nudged his knee beneath the table. Eddie turned. She was saying something, her lips moving, the words lost in the smoke as soon as they were uttered.

He leaned forward. 'What?'

'I SAID DO YOU WANT A BEER?'

Eddie shook his head.

Irene frowned.

'I don't feel so good,' he said.

'WHAT?'

He sighed, suddenly exhausted at the effort of even talking. 'I SAID I DON'T FEEL SO GOOD.'

She leaned forward, took one of his hands in hers. The palms of her hands were lightly abrasive, roughened from work. 'What's wrong, honey?' she said. 'You wanna get some air?'

Eddie nodded. He could feel his gut churning, that familiar dull ache in his shoulder.

Irene pushed herself up and out of the booth. 'Okay?' she said.

'Okay,' said Eddie. Then, with a hand still gripping his, he let himself be pulled up and onto his weary feet, let himself be led through the swirling heaving crowd like a very old man or a very young child.

6

For his seventh birthday, Eddie Reno had received from his parents the only gift he'd ever really wanted. Oh for sure, for a while, he'd really, really wanted that bike, and that balsa-wood model of the USS Constitution had been something he just couldn't live without. In the end, though, his desire for these and other things had cooled, leaving him, every time, with just the longing for that one perfect, unreachable, so out-of-the-question gift that suddenly, on the morning of his birthday in that fall of nineteen fifty-two, had so miraculously arrived.

'You sure?'

It was a day, a morning, a miracle of providence to which, in recent months and weeks, he'd often in dreams returned. In his dreams, again and again, he'd felt that cool weight in his hands, the smoothness of its brushed-metal contours.

'Eddie?'

Again and again, he'd peered at the world through that tiny frame of glass, again and again heard the solid heavy click-clunk of a shutter.

He looked up. Irene from the K-Mart was standing before him and frowning, her head framed by a canopy's tight twisting vines. 'Sorry?' he said. Within the vines, like stars set in a night sky, hung a string of Christmas lights – pink flamingos, green palm trees, white and ocher sea-shells.

'Are you sure you're okay, honey? Do you want me to fetch you some water?'

He raised a hand, rubbed it across his face. For a moment he'd been standing again in that cool morning kitchen, his father watching him, smiling, as he buried his head in his mother's sweet-smelling dress, felt the tenderness of her hands on the back of his neck.

Irene said something he didn't catch. She moved away. Eddie watched her crossing the verandah, weaving her way between the busy tables. A sudden blast of music then as a door opened and closed. He turned back. Way off, beyond the verandah, way out across the Gulf's black waters, the lights of the Keys were strung out hard and clear, the only marker between the sky and the sea. He sat back. He closed his eyes. The darkness coalesced into sunshine and the past.

He is standing in the yard, the weak autumn light folding over his sneakers. You comin'? says a voice; a car door slams hard. The growl of an engine and he's watching the storefronts flicking by, the bunting so bright against the graying sky. A walk dodging puddles and he's standing on the sidewalk, jostling in the crowd, waiting in the rain for the President. Hey! says a voice; someone points; he cranes his neck to see, lifts up the weight in his hands, squints, drops the shutter, as a car passes by. The sounds of a scuffle and he turns. Fists are flying, boots cracking bone. A man is sinking, arms and legs flailing; then the air is filled with sirens, and tears, then the silent disinfectant of a hospital foyer at noon.

Irene set a beer and a bottle of Perrier on the table.

Is there anyone at home, son? says a voice, fading.

'Look, I got you one anyway.'

He looked up.

'It's okay, you don't have to drink it if you don't want to.'

A fly, he remembered, there was, tapping on the skylight above him, searching for a way out.

'Eddie?'

She pulled back her seat, sat down.

'What is it, Eddie?'

He shrugged. Her face, in the low light, was all shadows and years. 'Nothing,' he said.

'Nothing?'

Another shrug. 'I was just thinking is all.'

'What about?'

Have you a mother, son? Is there a telephone at home?

'The President,' he said.

'The President?'

'Eisenhower.'

'Eisenhower? Jeez, Eddie, what the hell you been thinking about *him* for?'

'Did you know he never owned a car?'

'What?'

'Did you know he spent thirty-five billion dollars building all those interstates and he never once owned a car – not once? Did you know that?'

Irene shook her head: no, she didn't know that.

'Well, it's true. He told me himself.'

'Eisenhower?'

'Uh-huh.'

'President Eisenhower? You met President Eisenhower?'

Eddie nodded. 'He got right down on his haunches, hung that great melon head with those buggy little eyes in front of me and said, "Son – you know what?" "What?" I said. "Well," he said, "I'm gonna tell you a secret?" "Okay," I said. "Can you keep a secret, son?" he said. Well, I said that I could. And then he told me.'

Irene was studying her beer, turning it around on the table.

'What?' said Eddie. 'You don't believe me?'

'I believe you,' said Irene. She looked up.

'What?'

'Ah, nothing,' she said. She looked away. A breeze was picking up, drifting in across the water. 'Eddie?' she said.

'What?'

She looked back. There was something in her eyes – a look of distance, or sadness, maybe. 'Can I ask you something?' she said.

Eddie shrugged.

'Well –' She paused, gave her beer another turn on the table. 'Well, I was thinking.' Another pause, another turn. She looked up. 'About Clare?'

'What about her?' said Eddie.

'Well, I was thinking it was strange how she had the same name as your wife.'

'Strange? What do you mean?'

'Nothing, I suppose.'

Eddie looked away.

'And then I was thinking, you know, if she hadn't of died –'

'Well, she did.'

'I know, but if she hadn't of –'

'Look,' he said, 'aren't you cold?' It was true: the breeze was stronger now. It was shifting the lights in the vines overhead and whipping spray like wet dust from the surface of the water.

'No,' said Irene, 'I'm not. Are you?'

Eddie pushed himself up. 'Yes I am. You want to go?'

'Go?'

'As in leave,' he said.

'Look,' said Irene. 'I'm sorry, okay? I shouldn't have mentioned her.'

'It's okay.'

'It's just, well, I know how you felt about her and all, and I know it's that anniversary time again . . . I know all that, it's just, well, I know too – believe me I do – that you can't just go on blaming yourself forever –'

Eddie pulled on his jacket.

'Well, can you?'

Zipping it up, he said, 'Did you know he let me take his picture?'

'What?'

'President Eisenhower. That day when he came to call. I just asked him straight out and he said okay – right after he told me about his never having had a car of his own. "Okay, son," he said. "Where do you want me?" and then he just stood there in front of the grate like he was just some regular person come to call.'

'Eddie?'

'Couldn't get him to smile, though – Lord no. He did nothing *but* smile all the rest of the time – except of course when he was talking about Daddy and saying what a hero he was and all – standing up for America and all that – but as soon as he saw that old camera – bingo! – all frowns and stern-looking. I guess he felt like he had to look presidential or something.'

'Eddie?'

'What?'

'You want to come back with me tonight?'

'Why?'

'Why? Because I want you to.'

'I can't,' said Eddie. A hand found his.

'Yes you can.'

He withdrew it.

'What's the matter?'

'Nothing,' he said.

'Is it Clare?'

He shook his head. Irene shrugged.

'Okay then.'

'What does that mean?'

'It means okay then. Maybe it means to hell with you.'

'Well, that's nice.'

'It wasn't meant to be.' She looked up, her face suddenly pale, her lips blood-red. 'I thought you said you were going?'

'I am.'

'Then go.'

'You don't want a ride?'

'No,' she said, 'I don't want a ride.'

'Okay,' said Eddie. He turned, felt the heavy weight of eyes on his back as he moved between the tables. He reached for a handle, twisted it, pulled. He stepped into the music and the smoke.

Awful Arthur's Bar and Grill was in darkness when he turned his key and pushed on the door. He flicked on a light above the bar. Whether it was the driving or the sea air or Irene or all of it was hard to say, but he was sober now and he didn't want to be. Bad luck when you're drunk is bad judgement when you're sober. He filled a shot-glass full of whiskey and drained it, then again. The whiskey spun to his stomach, burning.

Avoid alcohol. Do not operate heavy machinery. He poured a third. He closed his eyes. For a moment he was back on that sidewalk, then standing at a graveside in the rain. He opened his eyes, drained the whiskey. The scene lingered, faded, was gone.

7

Dear Mr Reno,

Despite extensive enquiries, William Tennessee and Partners have to report that no trace can be found of your son. Due to the negative likelihood of this situation changing, I have to inform you that regrettably we will no longer be working on your behalf. I enclose our amended invoice, and look forward to receiving your remittance within twenty-one days.

Yours sincerely,
James L. Bank
President

Eddie Reno woke suddenly at four, his sheets cool with sweat. He lay still for a moment, then reached over, flicked on the light. The room swerved, settled. He listened to his breathing, squinting up at the plaster on the ceiling.

No trace can be found.

He swept his brow, pushed up on his elbows. His breathing slowed; he lay back.

As is the way with dreams, it had all – the letter, his own increasingly inept searching – been as true in the moment of dreaming as the truest-sounding, most persuasive stories. And as is true, also, of dreams generally, now it was gone, it was, suddenly – in the instant of waking – as distant and yet as familiar as the lives of relatives lived out in other centuries, the details of which are known only from the moment of a single photograph.

He closed his eyes, willing on sleep; but sleep would not come. All that came was the usual parade of early-morning faces, of places and voices gathered in from the corners of his and others' lives: his father, smiling, sweating, accepting applause and bowing in his shiny stage suit; the President, frowning hard, standing stiff as a mourner before a grate; the blast of a shotgun in the trees; Clare Summerfield, dancing, doomed, her dress swirling up around her waist, her hair turning as she turned in a slow auburn arc. These faces and others – Irene also, and his son of course, always his son – passed by and were gone, until those that replaced them grew more and more distant as his grasp upon them weakened, and their voices drifted off to just echoes, then nothing, like the voices of those leaving growing faint across a field.

When he woke a second time it was close to five, the sun already reaching like hands around the blinds. He lay still for a while, listening idly to the hissing of cars on the highway, pushing back any thoughts of the day ahead. It would come soon enough without his help. He thought of Irene. He turned onto his side. *To hell with you, Eddie Reno*. His squinting, straining eyes edged their way around the room. Not once in seven years, it came to him now, had he ever thought of Irene as being a person with a life beyond the deli – of having a life of her own beyond its overlapping with his. Not once had he ever – for one single moment – pictured her, for example, at home frying lamp chops on a barbecue or crying at some movie or holding the hand of an unequal lover. Not once in seven years. In all that time he had given her not one single thought, except to think her shallow, except to mock what he'd seen as a life without substance, a coward's life, a life lived entirely on the surface, a life lived in fear of the depths below.

The chinking of bottles rose up from the bar. He pushed himself up. His body was heavy, every pound like two pounds. He reached for his glasses, slipped them over his ears. The room cleared, drew suddenly into focus. He thought again of Irene, and it struck him – as his eyes scanned the room, scooting over his TV, his books, the pile of unwashed clothes – that it was his that was the life, now, lived entirely on the surface – that it was he, not she, who was shallow and fearful of the deep.

He closed his eyes tight. From the bar came the clattering of a hoover, the scraping of chairs on the floor. He lay back for a moment, just listening, just trying not to think, just trying above all not to remember. *To hell with you, Eddie Reno*. He opened his eyes; Irene dinked away. He stared at the plaster on the ceiling; he listened to his own shallow breathing.

He was studying his face in the bathroom mirror, trying to figure out if he could get away just for once without the bother of shaving), when, at a shade past six-thirty, the package caught his eye in the glass. It was sitting propped up against the wall on top of the cistern, its stitching bright red in the light. He turned, frowning, then crossed the room, paused a moment, picked it up. It was funny, but he couldn't for the life of him remember having fetched it last night from the trunk of his car. He opened the package and pulled out the book. All he could remember was gripping the wheel real tight driving home, then the whiskey, then the wallpaper spinning as he climbed the stairs, then squinting at his keys in the darkness.

He sat on the edge of the tub, staring hard at the book. He ran his hand lightly across its rough cover. He looked up at the sound of a click, then Jimmy Buffett:

> *Livin' on sponge-cake*
> *Watchin' the sun bake*

He pushed the door to with his foot. His heart was thumping. Then, opening the book slowly like a man half-expecting some unpleasant surprise, he drew a deep calming breath and turned to the first page.

Matthew

8

He writes with the care and constriction of an invalid, his twisted hand moving slow across the page. He pauses, lifts his pen, cocks his head like a bird, listening. Voices rise from the landing, a sharp screech of laughter, then the slamming of a door. The thin walls shiver, the lamplight flickers, sending shadows dancing like black ghosts around the walls, then settles. He looks down again at the page. *A Personal Account*, he reads, *of Travels to the Dakota Territories*. He crosses the T's and dots the I's. He sighs, sets down his pen. He closes the book. He is tired – too tired to begin tonight. Besides, there is, as yet, nothing more to write. His journey west to the frontier is, as yet, still just dreaming. He pushes back his chair, rises. He stretches, arching his back. He crosses the room and lies down on his bed. He listens, drifting, to the sounds of the house.

For months (for maybe years now, he can't remember) he has lived two lives: one, this life of the whorehouse, of photographs and flyers, of breakfast alone and dinner in the quarter; the other, the life of his future lived in dreams. He turns on his bed, turning his head away from the lamplight. Shadows fall, unseen, across his face. He closes his eyes, wonders again, as sleep comes to claim him, whether if by imagining a future – by giving it colors and shapes – you are making it more real and so drawing it nearer, or whether, by living it – by having lived it, even in dreams – you are clothing it already in the shroud of the long-dead past. Or whether, in the end, a man can do nothing but wait for what's to come, just as a lamb, unknowing, waits for slaughter, or a prince in his robes for coronation.

9

J ust exactly how Matthew Robert Princeton, at the age of twenty-nine, came, in that cool and distant fall of eighteen seventy-five – ten years after the war that had so scarred him – to be living so far from his Arkansas home – to be living, indeed, in one airless room upstairs on a landing at Miss Eliot's whorehouse on the corner of Lafayette and Vine in, this, the city of New Orleans, was a mystery, for sure, to all but himself. Not even his twisted, mangled hand – the curious way, as a consequence, he lifted his fork to his mouth as if he were aiming to stab himself in the eye – had ever drawn more than a knowing, unpitying glance – for why would it? In a city drowning beneath the weight of broken limbs and scarred minds, a busted hand is nothing. And – make no mistake – the city, in those days since that great and most uncivil war, was such a city – a place not without hope but without hoping, a port at the end of the Mississippi river that could just as well have been a port at the end of the world.

'Hey, you in there, soldier-boy?'

It was a place where nothing rested, not even in sleep, a city burning day and night, devouring the hours like some fiendish machine.

He opened his eyes.

'Hey, soldier-boy.' A rap on the door, a woman's voice, a negro's. 'You hidin' in there?'

His eyes were sore. Again he'd barely slept. He turned in his bed away from the door, let his eyes shutter down.

Another rap, harder.

'Are you hearin' me, soldier-boy?'

He drew a shallow breath. 'What is it?' His voice was muffled.

'What it is, *mister lieutenant sir*, is you got yourself a visitor.'

'A visitor?' He turned his head on his pillow, opened his eyes to a squint.

'Ain't that what I said?'

He pushed himself up, locked onto his elbows. His head was thumping. 'For *me*? Are you *sure*?'

'What?'

'I mean, what did he say?'

'He didn't say nothin' – 'cept his bein' a friend of yours from your little white war – that and how he's been ridin' all night which for sure must be the truth 'cause he sure looks like shit –'

'He didn't say a name?'

From beyond the door, a great heavy sigh. 'No, he didn't give no name and I didn't ask. To me he's just one more Yankee soldier is all.'

'A Yankee soldier?'

This time a snort from the landing. 'What's the matter with you? You got some repeatin' disease or somethin'?'

'So he didn't say anything? Nothing at all?'

'Jesus Lord. Ain't that what I said?'

'And you're certain he's a soldier?'

'Certain? What do you mean, am I certain? You think I don't know no Yankee soldier when I see one? Jesus Lord, you think it weren't no Yankee soldier that burned down my house and gave this grateful nigger her freedom?'

'Alright, alright,' said Matthew. Slowly, he pulled back the blanket, set his feet on the bare wood floor. Despite the open window, the room was thick with the smell of sweat and chemicals.

Another rap on the door.

'So is you comin' down or what?'

'I'm coming,' he said.

' 'Cause either you's comin' down or he's comin up, 'cause for sure he ain't stayin' where he's standin' right now, smellin' like he does –'

He pushed himself up and tramped to the door. He opened it a fraction, peered out. Josephine was moving slow down the stairs, her bulk swaying this way and that, the sweat dancing on the back of her neck.

'Josephine?'

'That's my name.'

'Did you tell him I was here?'

She paused on the lower landing. Her heavy shoulders rose and fell in a shrug. 'Maybe.'

'What do you mean, maybe? Did you or didn't you?'

She set a hand on the banister, twisted round. She was breathing hard. 'What I *mean*,' she said, 'is I told him *maybe* – maybe you was in and maybe you was out. Said I'd go see. Said I'd climb these stairs again like I got nothin' better to do.'

'So he doesn't know?'

'Know what?'

'That I'm here.'

She shrugged.

'And he won't?'

'Are you askin' or tellin'?'

'I'm asking.'

Josephine cocked her head, half-smiling, revealing for a moment the child before the chains. 'You askin' nicely, soldier-boy?'

'I'm saying please, Josephine.'

Another shrug, then a voice calling harsh from below and the child fled. She turned away.

'Josephine?'

Then turned back. 'What?'

'So will you tell him I've gone?'

'You mean will I lie?'

Matthew nodded.

Josephine shrugged.

'Then you will?'

She screwed up her face in a disbelieving scowl. 'You mean you ain't heard?'

'Heard what?'

Another smile then, but a different, mocking smile. 'You mean,' she said, 'you ain't heard about the black man? You ain't heard about your new Yankee brother?' She set her hands on her hips, held her head back, looked down her nose in disgust. 'You mean you don't know after all this time that a nigger can't do nothing but lie and that's the truth?'

Matthew opened his mouth to speak, but – not for the first time – could find no words within.

'Well?' said Josephine. 'You tellin' me you don't know that?' She held his eye for a second as if something had passed between them that had not in generations past been forgotten and would not be so by those yet to come, then cast it away – as she, once, had been cast – with an insolent turn of her head. At once she turned back. 'You's nothin',' she whispered, hissing. 'You's shit.' Then again she turned away, slammed the door, and was gone.

Matthew stared at the door, feeling numb as if he'd been punched. In a while he crossed to the window, looked down at the crowds below, just in time to see a horse drop exhausted in the street, then a man step forward and with a look close to glee pull a pistol from the holster by his side.

IO

The shot split the heavy air, sharp like a crack of summer lightning. The horse bucked, suddenly blind, spilling its brains in the dirt street. A group gathered, staring dumbly down at the still-sweating corpse. The executioner holstered the pistol, stood a moment, looking down at his work, then turned away, still smiling, and in a moment was gone, lost like a thief in the crowd.

Enter and exit Mr James Monkton Webb: killer of horses. A man with a humorous and ironical story, he smiled at a woman who followed him with her eyes. He raised his hat, walking on. Horses and people. Sometimes in his mind it was hard to tell the two breeds apart. He turned down an alleyway, dipped into the shadows, cutting his breath. He waited, listening hard, aware of the beating in his chest. He fingered the pistol, so smooth in its holster. Footsteps – a woman's. He smiled. Some days these days every day was like Christmas. Some days these days he could barely contain the joy in his heart.

He counted to ten (sometimes it was twenty, sometimes more; today, though, he felt unaccountably impatient), then stepped from the shadows and whispered his greeting. The woman – as they always did – smiled. She nodded; he nodded, enjoying the game immensely. She stepped toward him, teetering on her heels. Some days it was all he could do not to laugh.

'You see this, Mr Princeton?'

It was noon. Matthew turned away from the window, squinted into the gloom of the upstairs front parlor. 'Pardon me?' he said.

Miss Eliot sighed. 'Mr Princeton, sir,' she said, 'I do believe you are sickening for something. Are you sickening for something?'

'Ma'am?'

She replaced the gilt frame on the mantel. Within the frame was a single lock of hair, artfully arranged in a graceful curl. She turned back. 'No, sir? Are you telling me you feel perfectly fine? That you've not fallen victim to Mr Steep's river fever, or some such gruesome ailment? Because, Mr Princeton, sir, if you *are* telling me this, then perhaps you could tell me also why you persist in paying me – your employer – such scant attention – why, indeed, you persist with this staring out of my window when I'm addressing you as if there were a carnival passing below. I mean, I may be old, sir, and I may have lost that which only time alone can steal – namely my beauty, which was not, I assure you, an inconsiderable thing – but I believe I am still due the courtesy of attention. To wit, sir, your eyes upon mine when I am speaking. Now, do I make myself clear?'

'Yes, I'm sorry,' said Matthew. He paused. 'It's just –'

But Miss Evangeline Eliot raised an imperious hand, so halting further speech like a New York City cop stopping horses in the street. In silent motion, then, she pointed to one of two high-backed velvet chairs that stood before her on the hearth. Matthew sat as directed; Miss Eliot remained standing.

'Now, sir,' she said, picking up a small lacquered box from the mantel, 'are you quite comfortable? Would you care for a bon-bon?' She opened the box. A tiny click, then 'Who Will Be My Darling – Will It Be You?' spun out into the room as delicate and fine as the finest Charlotte lace.

Matthew shook his head. His eyes were heavy from barely sleeping. He felt his eyelids falling. They opened abruptly at the snap of the music-box.

'No, sir? Very well.' Miss Eliot replaced the box on the table beside her. She paused a second, letting her eyes linger on the box's polished surface as if she were turning something over in her mind; then she looked up, fixing her gaze upon him with that surgeon's sharpness, that cynic's purpose known well to all those – men and girls – whom weakness or bad fortune or loathing of self and the desire for oblivion had brought to her door. 'Sir,' she said. Another pause, the faint trace of a smile. 'Would you say that you are content in your position?'

Matthew twisted in his seat. 'Ma'am?' The sweat was cool on the curve of his spine.

'Would you say, Mr Princeton – *Lieutenant* Princeton – that our arrangement with regard to the pursuit of our mutual satisfaction is still one with which you are happy? And that you wish that arrangement to continue?'

Matthew looked down at his boots. They were scuffed and dirty.

'Well, sir? Can you not speak?'

He closed his eyes. Oh weariness, weariness. Sometimes its weight seemed to settle on his shoulders so heavy it made him want to stoop; sometimes he felt its arms around him, gripping his chest and squeezing tight, as if it aimed to force from him all the air in his lungs, as if it planned to leave him floundering like some beached and dying fish, gasping for life. He drew a long shallow breath. 'Miss Eliot,' he said. He opened his eyes, looked up.

Miss Eliot was watching him, her head half-turned to one side as if to facilitate the proper hearing of special words. 'Yes, Mr Princeton?' she said. 'You were saying?'

Matthew held her glance a second, then looked away.

'Mr Princeton? Has some cat got your tongue? Or can I take it from your silence that you do wish to serve me still as I have served you?'

He shrugged. Her gaze as ever was acute, all-seeing: it could pick out – he could swear it – the very emptiness of his soul.

'Well, do you or do you not, sir?'

'*Yes*,' he said, the word just a whisper.

She arched forward, cupped her ear, the better to detect a man's shame. 'Sir, you will have to speak up –'

'Yes,' he said again, 'yes, yes.'

'Splendid,' said Miss Eliot, her face rich suddenly with a full-bloom smile. The smile, however, froze and withered as she lifted an envelope from the table beside her. This she held out before her between finger and thumb as if the envelope or its contents were the disinterred corpse of some rancid pesky rodent. 'Perhaps, then,' she said, a coolness now in her voice, 'you would explain to me why – if you do wish still to reside in my house as you claim, sir – why the governor of this great and glorious state of Louisiana – who, as you are certainly aware, is a personal friend – did not receive from you – and, therefore, did not receive from *me* – that which he requested, and, instead, received *these* –' She tossed the package into Matthew's lap.

Matthew stared at the envelope. He didn't need to look inside to know its contents: pictures – men, not the usual girls – shattered men with blank, hopeless faces; limbless soldiers, a corpse lying ragged at the river's edge – the gratuitous misery of a nation's finest manhood gone to hell.

'Well, sir? Do you have an explanation?'

He sat still.

'Sir? I am waiting –'

He shook his head. 'I don't know,' he said.

'You don't know?' Miss Eliot grabbed the envelope, tore it open, spilling its contents all about her on the hearthrug. 'You *don't know*?' She dove down, hung her rouged and powdered face before his. 'I'll tell you what you don't *know*, sir: what you don't *know* – what you cannot seem to *grasp* – is that you are here – beneath my roof, eating my food, breathing my air – because I allow it and because you belong here. And why do you belong here? Well, sir, for the very same reason that my girls and my gentlemen belong here – because, sir, this is a *whorehouse* and you are a *whore*, and the best, most reliable, kind of whore at that – a cripple whore who's grateful for the lash, a grotesque person who so disgusts himself that he'll welcome any chance to open himself up and show the world just how disgusting he really is, just how putrid are his insides and how badly he deserves all the beatings he gets. *That's* why you're here and *that's* why you'll stay – and you'll do as I tell you. And why will you do that? Well, *mister* lieutenant, sir, *mister* Yankee soldier, you'll do that – you'll do what I tell you – because if you don't then you know you're back out in that sweet forgiving world where you just might meet with a little understanding or – the good Lord forbid it – a trace of human tenderness – where you might just get what you know a piece of shit like you don't deserve. And you don't deserve it – do you?'

Matthew screwed up his eyes as the sudden soft touch of fingers on his cheek, on the flesh of his ear, on his neck below the hairline made him flinch.

'Well, do you, Mr Princeton?'

He arched away but the fingers followed him, tracing the sinews of his neck, rounding his collarbone and on, undoing the buttons of his shirt and sliding down through the sweat and the heat until they dipped beneath his belt and had him in their grip and he tried to cry out in joy at the pain but he couldn't cry out – couldn't make a sound – until the fingers, the hand, withdrew, smeared themselves on his cheek and were gone.

A minute, then, passed.

He sat still.

'Mr Princeton?'

In his own private silence, he listened with despair to the beating, the life-pumping of his heart. He felt a breeze cross his cheek from another, other time and he opened his eyes, fearful of the coming of the past, longing in that moment for that numbness, that nothingness, that unknowingness, that comes to some men only in death and only then if life has been sneaked away with a magician's sleight of hand in a moment of divine inattention.

'Are you listening to me, sir?'

He looked up, tried to focus. Miss Eliot was back at the mantel. He looked up, tried to focus, the gilt frame, the lock of golden hair, once again in her hand. She was staring hard. 'Well, sir?' she was saying.

Matthew frowned.

'I was asking if, sir, you had an explanation.'

He raised a hand to his cheek. His cheek was dry. He felt the front of his shirt; the buttons were fastened right up to his neck, a light choking pressure pressing in on his throat.

Miss Eliot sighed. '*Really*, Mr Princeton,' she said, 'this gross in-attention really is most insulting –'

He looked down at the package in his lap, watched his fingers run their way across its smooth surface.

'Well, sir? Have you nothing to say?'

This is a whorehouse and you are a whore. He looked up.

'Are you certain you don't require the attentions of a doctor? Should I ring for Mr Steep?'

He felt his head moving, heard a voice saying no.

'Well then, as you appear quite unwilling to provide any kind of reason for your extraordinary and ruinous behavior, let me just say this: once more, sir, and you're out of here – do you understand me? Displease me once more, sir, and you will find yourself once again in that gutter from whence you came, and I warn you, do not expect a second rescue, as there will be none. Do you understand, Mr Princeton?'

'Yes,' said Matthew.

Miss Eliot smiled a hard and shallow smile. 'Well, then I need detain you no further, sir – except to say that the governor – being a personal friend and all and a Christian – is, I understand, generously prepared – as am I, sir, this one time – to overlook this unfortunate error – on the understanding, of course, that he receives at once that which he originally requested.' She paused, set her eyes sharp upon his. 'Now, sir,' she said. 'Do we understand each other?'

Matthew nodded. He sat still a moment, then, blinking hard, tried to push up. His legs were heavy like a corpse's. He pushed again. Once up, he stood swaying, certain sure he would fall, but he didn't fall; instead he crossed the room, heading for the door and its cool brass handle, moving slow like a convict crossing a yard.

He was standing on the landing outside his door, trying hard to focus on his keys, when he froze at the touch of a hand.

'Matthew?' A whisper.

He turned.

'Did you tell her?'

'Clare?'

'You didn't – did you?'

'Tell her what?'

This is a whorehouse and you are a whore.

'You know. About the baby. *Our* baby.'

He shook his head. 'I have to go,' he said. A hand touched his. He pulled away.

'Then you didn't?'

'No, I didn't.' His fingers found his key, twisted it free on the ring.

'Matthew?'

'What?'

Silence.

'*What?*'

Just a young girl's shallow breathing.

'I love you.'

'I have to go.'

'Matthew?'

He stiffened, fumbling with the lock. The hand again, the curl and pull of fingers on his sleeve. 'Do you love me?'

The key found its place, turned.

'Matthew?'

'Yes,' he said. The door swung in.

'Really?'

You are a whore.

'Really,' he said and he stepped inside and closed the door sharp behind him, aware as he did so – as he had been for so long now – of the deceiving power of love and of lies, and how, in such gloom, in such times, in such a city, they can appear so indistinguishable as to seem nothing more than just the entry-site and exit of the same bloody weeping wound.

12

B arely once, in the thirty-two years that thus far had constituted his brave or, perhaps, foolhardy life, had James Monkton Webb, latterly captain of cavalry, United States Army – a man decorated, indeed, for his bravery by the great stupid genius President Grant himself – barely once, in all those years, had he ever smelled a horse he hadn't wanted to shoot, or seen one riding by that wouldn't, in his opinion, have made a much better use of the world's remaining equine resources if it hadn't been shot, skinned, dismembered and boiled – thus providing a man with not only the pleasure, which was not inconsiderable, of dispatching such a mean and perverse creature, but also, thanks to its otherwise useless hide, the rudiments of a greatcoat for use in foul weather – not to mention a whole bunch of nutritious and satisfying steak suppers, and a skeleton's worth of glue. In short, James Monkton Webb, of the Monkton Webbs of Sonora, California (ironically, perhaps, or, perhaps, not surprisingly, given the contrary reaction of a son to a father, a family of ranchers – horses, naturally), was that perversest of creatures: a cavalry officer who couldn't stand horses. Which is not to say that he hadn't the skill with them, for he had (by eight, he could saddle one and ride it in the direction of his choosing; by twelve, he was jumping the fences that bordered the ranch and riding all the way alone to the ocean); no, sir, the skill he was born with – plenty of it – but not the love. Not that he hated them either – at least not to begin with. The hating, like the hair on his face, like the desires he never would understand and could never resist, would come later. No, to begin with at least, horses, to little James Webb, were just a part of the world, like fences were a part of the world, like the way his father's wife was a part of the world and the way she used to caress him to sleep. They were just there (as God had made them, the Reverend Winters was always saying in that mean nasal whine of his, clutching his pale hands together before him in that way he had that made you think he had some kind of creature trapped in there that was trying to get out) – just there like her hands were just there, rough like the rough hide of horses, and her smell of sweat always there

37

in the air like their smell. No, he thought nothing special of them, until one day when he was maybe fifteen – until the day they started thinking of him.

It was Christmas Day or maybe a day in the middle of summer, he could never remember. All he could remember was the tightness of his belt, the way its buckle dug into his flesh, biting. It was a new belt, he would always recall (a new buckle), a gift (as everything, wanted or not, is a gift to a child) – in this case a gift from his father and his father's new wife. Although nominally a joint gift, it was she, he knew, who had chosen it – not he – and she who would demand that he wore it. Touching its leather that day, the tips of his fingers running smooth across the buckle's cool pleasing surface, he could see in his mind's eye her reddening face, feel in his stomach the warmth and the wetness she hid in the darkness within the tumbling sourness and dampness of her skirts.

But back to that belt. It was tight, was the point, like a noose is tight around a neck, which is what he was thinking, standing there that afternoon (or was it morning, or early evening? – again he couldn't say), gazing up at old Jube's thieving corpse as it twisted slow in the kind of breeze you couldn't feel if you were living, his flesh all the time turning bluer behind the brown with every twisting, his eyes bugging out like maybe he could see something only dead folks could see – something real scary like some wild and vicious beast that was headed this way with the taste in its mouth for blood.

Anyway, all those years ago now, he frowned, studying the man's bulging features, then he turned away, following the line of the nigger's staring eyes. He squinted hard. Nothing. He turned, back. 'So?' he said. He cocked his head. 'What is it you's lookin' at, nigger?' But the nigger said nothing; he just went on twisting in that breeze like he was rocking to some lullaby that only he could hear. James scowled at the man's dumb insolence, screwing up his face like he'd seen his daddy do – even reached up with his daddy's old stick, poking the body's swollen feet, then again, harder, until the stick's sharpness split the graying flesh, creating a wound from which no blood escaped. 'Well?' he said, and he frowned again, harder this time, cupping his hand to his ear like he'd seen old and deaf people do, listening out for the faintest of whispers. But none came. All there was was the creaking of the tree, the taut labor of the rope, the bulging of old Jube's eyes as they stared sharp at something way out across the land.

But at what?

James had turned then, squinting hard. It was a mystery. All there was, besides the land itself – besides the fences and the horses and distant copse of trees – was the house, sitting squat in the hollow, its stack like a finger pointed up toward heaven and its slow-rising, slow-turning smoke.

He turned back, cocked his head, skeptical. 'Is it the house?' he said. But old Jube was saying nothing.

'Well, is it?'

The nigger just seemed to be smiling.

James scowled. '*Jesus*, Jube. You can't just say a thing and then quit talking. It just ain't *fair*.' He shook his head weary like he'd seen his daddy do, then raised the stick, poking again at the soles of the dead man's feet. 'Jube?' he said. Nothing. He poked again, though this time with little conviction. Clearly, old Jube had said all he was planning to say. (He never had been much of a talker.) James stood for a moment, wrestling with the scrag-ends of thoughts in his head, then, turning away and not looking back, he returned the way he'd come – across the fields and over the fences, past the sullen, grazing horses – heading for the house and the silence now that he knew lay within it, all the time beating the hard ground with his daddy's old stick as he went.

A lifetime, then, passes, and he's back down on his haunches in that New Orleans alley again, gazing, questioning like a bird, into the woman's smiling eyes. Unseen, he purses his lips. It's a funny thing, he thinks (funny peculiar, that is, not funny ha-ha, although the laughing will come later), how they always end up smiling – how it's always as if they can hear a joke that he can never hear – and how, everytime when it's over, he just wants to lie down and sleep, so heavy with melancholy and the weight of the past does he feel.

So he closes his eyes; again, a lifetime dinks away and suddenly – without warning – he is walking, a boy again, barefoot across those fields, toward the body in the house – just thinking, walking hard, until suddenly, without warning, he feels on his shoulder the sweet condemning breath of his daddy's favorite mare, and her eyes upon him, huge and dark, like the dark condemning eyes of a wrathful God.

13

T he following, from the *Maynard County Sentinel*, dated April 25th 1861:

The black man's tragedy

It is the sad duty of the editors of this newspaper to record that the people of Maynard County will be waking this morning to the news that one of their finest sisters has been slain. It is our sad duty also to record for the sake of history the events and circumstances of this tragedy – for, make no mistake, it was a tragedy, and no less so for being one that this newspaper has long been predicting. Which is not to say that we take any satisfaction today from having been proved correct. Indeed, far from feeling such pride as might be excusable in other circumstances at the accuracy of our prediction, we at the *Sentinel* can today, in truth, feel nothing but contrition for our failure to expose fully the wanton wickedness of those gentlemen in Washington, whose steadfast refusal to acknowledge those truths which by all men of sound mind are today held to be universally so – truths which recent events herein described can only serve to underline further – namely, and principally, that the negro, though he may be, generally, a species in want of industry, is not so lazy by nature that he will not seize the chance, when such a chance by circumstances is offered, to wreak havoc upon not only the property, but also the persons, of those, his superiors, whose only wish is to see him maintain that position into which God in His wisdom saw fit to place him.

Yes, readers, fellow Californians, fellow believers in the liberty that is every American's birthright, it is the position of this organ that the responsibility for the murder, during her husband's absence on a state-wide drive for recruits, of Mrs Robert S. Webb by the negro Jubal lies not with the wretched negro himself (for, like a dog given access to a pantry, knowing no better will eat until sickness overcomes him, so a negro slave, given hopes of his freedom, will be thereafter useless for work and, indeed, a threat to his betters, so unreasonably excited will he have become) – no, that responsibility lies squarely with those whose stated intention it is to attempt to make equal that which the good Lord Himself did not design thus, and, because of whose actions, this present state of turmoil exists in our country. In short, then, the tragic events of the last several days illustrate once again that it is the black man's tragedy that he should have been persuaded, through the meddling ignorance of others, that he has somehow been denied that to which he is entitled – and, consequently, it is the tragedy also of the white man. For, as the country heads for war, it is the master and not the servant who will suffer. And how, you ask, do we know this? Well, readers, for the truth of this statement we need look no further than little James Webb, a now motherless boy, whose distress was so complete that he has quite lost all reason – a boy, indeed, who was found only yesterday morning wandering in the fields with the blood of his father's prize mare on his hands and stories so fanciful in defense of the murderous negro that his father had no choice but to have him placed in the county's care until such time as the wounds of his experience have healed. It is for you then, dear James, that we at the *Sentinel* say: Enough is enough! It is for your sake and for the sake of all our children that we hereby declare: To arms! To arms!

14

Those first weeks of war, being as they had been, with God's delicious irony, the first weeks of spring, had had about them that season's gift of lost strength regained, of celebration, of *at last* – of the land's blinking awakening from winter's long and bitter occupation. In the west as in the east, on those clear early mornings in Arkansas and Virginia and Georgia and Maine, with the sum of a nation strolling gaily toward slaughter, blossom and boys' talk sounded the season's bloodless victory – for victory, then, was in the notion of victory – in the sound of its syllables, the craven softness of its touch. War, in short, in those first weeks, was all grand talk and cymbals. *At last*, people said, peering out across their land and squinting in the sun's rising light, expecting any minute – half-hoping for, half-fearing – the Devil's righteous army. But, of course, in those first weeks, that army never came, and so carbines and muskets – so proudly shouldered, so cleaned with such love – were returned to their sleeping in the corners of rooms, and uniforms, so pressed, their buttons gleaming so, worn only in the fields to be bleached in the sun.

'Same again, buddy?'

But it would come, that army. Of course it would come, was coming. Indeed, even as the blossom was falling from the trees, so were the first martyrs at Manassas Junction, their faces contorted in ghastly surprise, frozen suddenly – for the first and last time – in that knowledge of death that can never be known by the living and may only be shared by the quiet stare of corpses.

But past – all that was past now. Surely all scars now were healed. Matthew nodded, winced at the sharp chink of bottle on glass. Two whiskeys and already he was drunk. He reached out like a blindman, turned the glass slowly with the tips of his unfeeling fingers, watched the thick golden liquid moving sullen like oil.

'Say – ain't you that fella from Miss Eliot's that makes them pictures?'

He lifted his eyes, squinted hard.

'What?'

'Them pictures. Ain't you that fella?'

'Nope,' said Matthew.

The barman frowned a minute, then shrugged, moved off down the bar. From across the room somewhere came a hard shriek of laughter; Matthew huddled up closer, drained the whiskey, felt its burning in his throat, laid his head for a second in the crook of his arm.

When he woke, perhaps a minute had passed, perhaps an hour. He rubbed his eyes with the flesh of his palms. From his hands, his fingers, came the bitter stink of bromide. *Do not expect a second rescue, for there will be none.* He laid his hands on the bar like a pair of gloves, tried to focus on them – tried hard – but could not.

'Hey –'

They were blurry – everything was blurry. Everything except that which was sharp – and what was sharp, eternally – what was always clear, always in the light, even in the unlighted dark – was that figure who walked always a pace behind, whose breath was always cool on his neck – that other, distant self – that self betrayed – the son, the brother, the father – all that once, in that other life, in that other world, he had been and would never be again.

'Hey, mister –'

He blinked hard.

'You drinkin' or what?'

He pushed away from the bar and onto his feet, aware as he did so of something sharp-edged – a package – rustling in his pocket. He reached in his hand, pulled it out, stood swaying, squinting hard, as everything moved around him in a slow swirling arc. He closed his eyes tight, opened them. For a second all was light – a bright, white blinding light, so bright that he had to shield his eyes – then the light flicked away, like a candleflame caught in a draft, and all again in an instant was darkness, blackness, as black as the river at night . . .

'Hey, mister – you sick or something?'

There were voices – so distant – all around him, then hands, the curve of fingers, gripping tight to the flesh of his arms. They pinched; he pulled away, stumbled, tumbling, a pain seering through his hand at the sound of breaking glass . . .

Silence, then – the howling silence of dreams. He blinked hard, his head level on a cool level surface. He snaked out his tongue, caught the salt tang of blood, heard the pulse like a clock in his head, felt the river easing over him, felt it lift him and cradle him, felt it rock him in its arms and carry him away, felt it turning him over and drawing him down, felt its cool embrace, saw the fishes bright as flame, heard the whispered conspiracy of time's slow changing tide.

Libbie

15

My name is Elizabeth Bacon Custer. I stand before you on this the last afternoon of the year nineteen hundred and eight, a testament to the persistence of Mr Irvine here, who – as you will all doubtless be aware – is the captain of this fine vessel. Captain Irvine, I have discovered, will not – as the current fashion for clever talk has it – take no for an answer – a quality which, I imagine, sir, is as useful in the career of a sailor as it has always proved to be in that of an army man. That being so, I have, however, to report to you all that when this gentleman first approached me with the idea that I might say a few words to you today on the subject of the life of the general, he met with a rebuff quite as sturdy – if I may perhaps take the liberty of flattering myself – as any encountered by the hostile Indian on the frontier – as, not having been trained as was the general in the art of public speaking, I felt myself then ill-equipped to do such a subject the justice it deserves – without, that is, the opportunity for contemplation and revision which my pen has long provided; and besides, were I to have accepted such an offer, I would feel myself thenceforth honor bound, being, as I am, a democrat – and an *American* democrat at that – to accept all other similiar offers, of which, honesty compels me to reveal, there have been – and remain – many. Indeed, wherever I go it seems such requests are seldom long absent. Why, only a few days ago, I opened my humble door to find the very Tsar of Russia himself standing before me as bold as you like, the snow still on his boots and a chain in one hand minted from – I am told – the purest silver, to the other end of which was attached a genuine living and breathing bear. Well! Imagine, if you will, my surprise – not only at the sight of such a wild and vicious creature reclining in the hallway of St Petersburg's finest hotel, but when, a moment later, while I was still recovering from the shock, His Majesty himself bade me receive the animal as a gift from the people of Russia – and from himself personally – as a token of gratitude for the contribution to the world of the late lamented general, whose life and achievements, it seems, have reached further and more widely than even I, his grieving wife, had imagined.

But I digress. I was speaking, was I not, of the good captain here, and of my reluctance to address you today. Well now. As my presence here before you indicates, I have had cause, in the last several days, to change my mind. There was, of course – as I have, I believe, mentioned – Mr Irvine's quite admirable perseverence, although, if I am being honest – and I hope I shall be, for what do we have if not honesty? – it was far from this alone which provoked my change of heart. No. Gentlemen and ladies – fellow Americans – something happened on board ship yesterday afternoon that I had scarcely thought possible – and it was this, finally, that persuaded me to break my silence.

And this was?

In short, gentlemen and ladies, it was the presentation before me during the hour following luncheon – in the form of a young lady's question – of evidence, finally, of what I have long suspected is the greatest threat to our nation's health and future well-being – America's growing forgetfulness and ingratitude toward those whose lives were given in her service.

And the evidence?

Well. As I said, it was a question put to me by a young lady – the daughter, no less, of one of New York's most well-regarded financial families – in response to another's speculation – speculation that the general – had he not been an army man – would have made perhaps the finest of naval commanders.

'The general?' said the young woman. 'And who would that be?'

Well, of course I and those around me were rendered for the moment quite speechless. Finally, it was the captain here who was able first to gather his breath. 'Who?' he said. 'Why, General *Custer* of course!' At which point, the young lady set upon her face a frown of such concentration that it seemed she was attempting to withdraw from her memory not the events of barely thirty years gone, but those of several centuries ago, until, finally, she said, '*Custer*, did you say? Wasn't he the fellow that went charging after Indians and got himself killed and all those that followed him?'

Oh yes, yes, gentlemen and ladies, I know what you are thinking, for I thought the very same myself. How, I thought, could a young lady from such a fine family know so little of one of her nation's greatest sons – and, indeed, care so little for the truth? Well, my friends, I don't know. I suppose it is just the way of things these days – to dismiss from the present all that has happened in the past.

Well, perhaps so. But let me tell you this: that as long as the good Lord has the grace to put breath in my body, then that breath will be used to tell the truth of what happened on that day to my husband, to fight as he would have fought for honor and for truth, however hard and however lonely the fight.

So. That is why I am with you this afternoon, and why, with your permission, sir, I shall begin my remarks by telling you a little of the general's background, so that what is to follow will not simply be the shout without the whisper, or the flesh without the bone.

But first, sir, a request. That young lady. Could she be found, and her presence requested? I should like her to hear and to remember. I should be grateful for the attention of her eyes upon mine when I speak.

16

S o then, if we are all settled now, I shall begin.

The general – as God, from the beginning, surely decreed he would become – was born on the morning of December fifth eighteen thirty-nine, in the small Ohio town of New Rumley. Now, for those of you among us too young to have been alive then and too young therefore to have stood witness, you must remember that America, in general, in those days – and, perhaps, Ohio in particular – was a land as unlike that which we recognize today as could be. In those days, she was a youthful land – a land – indeed, like the young boy who would, as a man, do me the honor of allowing me to become his wife – unshackled as yet by the grave responsibilities that were destined for them both, and which, today, weigh so heavily on the conscience of the nation. In short, then, she was a child, still, with a child's boundless hope – but also a child's want of discipline –

But wait now.

Already – even here – I see with that word that the late Mr Benteen is with us. He and, of course, the late Mr Reno. And I see already in some of your faces the mountain I must climb here this afternoon if I am once again to defeat the lies of those two now deceased gentlemen whose only purpose in life – and now in death – has been, and is, it seems, to attempt to dishonor the reputation of the general and in so doing disguise their own cowardice and failure. *He had no discipline*, they say. *Mistakes were made*. Well, indeed. It is true that the general did make mistakes – in number, two. He was surely mistaken in agreeing to lead two men of such low and base character, and then mistaken in believing that, regardless of that character, they would – being soldiers, however poor – perform a soldier's first duty – that of following to the letter a superior's orders, regardless of their own personal conviction. But of course this they did not do, and they know they did not do it, which knowledge accounts for the bitter nature of their false recollections.

But I see I am already deflected from my purpose.

So.

Where was I now?

Oh yes.

The early life of the general.

Well, at the age of nine, my husband was apprenticed to a cabinet-maker in Cadiz, before his parents, deciding that such an occupation was beneath a boy of such obvious and outstanding abilities, sent him to live with his sister in Monroe, Michigan, where, in 1856, he began teaching school. It was here, before the gaze of those eager to learn and those – like himself – eager to advance themselves from their modest beginnings, that he first employed those qualities of leadership so necessary for an officer of cavalry on the plains – qualities now so gratuitously dismissed as a fanciful confection by those today and in the thirty years since the general's passing who wish for their own personal reasons to tarnish his memory. Of course, what such persons fail publicly to acknowledge (although, of course, they know it to be true) is that no one but a man of the highest qualities could possibly have made of the Seventh Cavalry – a regiment, indeed, at one time so poor and unregarded that the only employment for which it was considered fit was as chaperone to the President's mother's horses – that no one but such a man could have made of something so sickly that which it has, in the military as well as the public mind, become – namely the healthiest, finest and most revered regiment in the long and glorious history of the United States Army –

But I see a raised hand. You have a question, sir?

About *what*, sir? You will have to speak up. Remember, sir, I am an old lady now –

The *bear*, did you say? What *about* the bear, sir?

No, sir, to my knowledge the creature does *not* have a name. Now, if you will permit me, I was saying –

I beg your pardon, sir? You suggest I name him *what*? Well, really, I do believe your humor is misplaced. Indeed, I would be grateful, sir, if you would kindly refrain from providing us this afternoon with any further examples. In fact, if you cannot be quiet, sir, I will ask Mr Irvine here to have you removed. Do you understand?

Good.

Now, with your *permission*, I shall continue.

First, though, let me say a word of reassurance to the ladies. Some of you, I see, are alarmed by this sudden gentle pitching. Well, please do not be. I'm sure Mr Irvine here has everything under control – do you not, Mr Irvine? Mr Irvine?

Oh, now the lights. Could somebody turn them back on?

Hello?

Oh my Lord. What was that? Did anybody hear that? Hello? Can anybody hear me?

17

The following, from the *New York City Tribune*, dated January 1st 1909:

SHIP FEARED LOST!
**Financier's son and a bear
among those feared drowned!
No word since 6pm!**

Grave news reached these offices last night of the probable loss of the SS *Liberation* during the storms that are now approaching the nation's eastern seaboard. It is understood that no wireless communication has been received from the vessel since six o'clock last evening and speculation is growing that the ship, whose complement – passengers and crew combined – is thought to be in excess of three hundred, has perished in turbulent seas. Amongst the passengers on board, we believe, was Mr Nathan B Zeitezmann III, only son of Mr Nathan B. Zeitezmann II, Chairman of the board of Zeitezmann Industries, owners of the *New York City Tribune*. The young man had been on a motoring tour of Europe before returning to New York to take up a position on Wall Street. His father, we understand, is currently at his Long Island home, where he is awaiting news. Our thoughts and prayers go out to him and to Mrs Zeitezmann at this time.

Also believed to have been on board the ill-fated *Liberation* was – bizarrely perhaps – a genuine four-hundred-pound Russian bear, the property, it is understood, of Mrs Elizabeth Custer, who was returning to the United States following a prolonged vacation overseas. The bear – a gift, we understand, to the widow of the former general from no lesser a personage than the Russian Tsar himself – had been given (so reports have it) accommodation amongst those passengers traveling steerage, for whom, it is said, the creature provided much-needed distraction during the long voyage.

More on page 3

18

'Sir, there is a telephone call.'

Just as the lights were going out on board the SS *Liberation* so were they coming on all over Long Island. All over the Island, streetlamps flickered on as if woken from sleep by the afternoon sky's sudden gloom; while in houses all along the Atlantic shore, from Bishop Point to Oyster Bay, butlers and maids moved as if one through darkening hallways and mute shadowed drawing-rooms, their hands reaching out, practiced fingers twisting switches, so illuminating in a second all that that morning and deep into the still heavy-aired afternoon had been hiding, crouching forgotten in the darkness like those animals – is it dogs? – who can sense what is coming when we cannot. Suddenly, then, at that moment of electrical connection, Chinese vases appeared, preening, self-satisfied, aware in that instant and for all time of their incontrovertible value, and marble, so polished that to walk upon it was to walk upon the surface of some still frozen lake, laid bare in reflection those French chandeliers imported from Rheims or from Strasbourg in crates made of cedar and stamped '*Exceptionel*', and those mirrors, gleaming, themselves reflecting others and on and on, until everything real – everything that fingers could trace or a hand caress – seemed lost in a moment in a palace of sparkling dreams.

'Sir?'

The old man on the jetty appeared not to have heard. He was standing a little stooped, as if his shoulders were bearing some invisible weight; his hands pushed deep into the pockets of his dinner-jacket. He was staring out across the darkening bay, his back to the glowing mass of the house, to its light spilling out across the neatly manicured lawns.

'Mr Zeitezmann, sir? Should I have them call again?'

All that was visible in the gathering gloom was a single light, shining green and constant, way out across the sound.

'Mr Zeitezmann?'

The old man half-turned. 'Who is it?' he said.

'A gentleman, sir.'

'Which gentleman?' His voice was muffled in the moist air.

'I couldn't say, sir. Sir?'

'Alright. Just ask for the gentleman's name and tell him I'll telephone him presently.'

'Very good, sir.'

The old man withdrew something from his pocket.

'Sir?'

He paused in the act of lighting a cigarette. 'Yes, Robert, what is it now?'

Robert crossed the last of the glistening grass and climbed the two shallow steps that led onto the jetty. The wooden planks of the jetty seemed oily and treacherous in the dirty yellow light, so he moved with care, heel to toe on his patent leather shoes, the rug folded double over his arm. He paused at the jetty's end, a pace behind his employer.

'Sir?'

'I've been thinking, Robert,' said Mr Zeitezmann.

'Sir?'

He turned; in profile, he'd that look of some stooped and balding bird that, even as a younger man in business out west, had had those who'd felt certain they'd been cheated by him but couldn't figure out quite how address him (in his absence) as the Vulture.

'I thought you might be cold, sir.'

'Cold?'

Robert advanced cautiously, the rug held out before him like a bullfighter's cape. This he slipped without permission around the old man's shoulders.

'Sir?'

The old man crossed his arms on his chest and drew the rug in tight.

'I was thinking about that light, Robert.'

'The light, sir?'

He nodded out into the settling gloom. In that moment, as if cued, the light winked off and then on again. He turned. 'Did you see that, Robert?'

'I saw it, sir. Sir?'

A faint sigh, barely audible. 'Yes, Robert?'

'About that telephone call?'

The flare of a match. 'I believe I told you to take down a name.'

'Yes, sir.'

'Well?'

'Very good, sir.'

Robert turned, made his way slow back down the jetty.

'Robert?'

He paused on the second step, one foot sinking into the wet grass. 'Sir?' he said. His shoes, it occurred to him then, would need polishing again. The thought made him weary.

'If it's the President, you can tell him that I have nothing further to say.'

'The President, sir?'

'Just do as I ask, will you, Robert?'

'Very good, sir.'

He stood a moment, squinting down at his shoes, then out disapprovingly at the water-logged lawns. Then, in a moment of inspiration unwitnessed by his employer, he slipped off his shoes and socks and, hitching up the legs of his pants, started out across the grass, arching the soles of his feet as he went, aiming for the bright blaring silence of the house.

He had his suit off and was sitting in his undershorts and vest, warming his feet by the fire in the downstairs parlor, when he thought he heard a cry. He lowered his heels cautiously onto the cool flagstone floor and turned his head, listening.

Nothing. Just the roaring of the fire, the tap-tapping like children's fingers of the rain on the window. He sat still a moment longer, then raised up his feet once again, once again splaying out his toes before the warmth of the fire, feeling, once again, the blasphemous stroking of his flesh by the flames.

19

W hen Robert woke the next morning it was to the faraway jangling of a telephone. He sat up. The fire was out, the grate all ashes and dust. 'Clare?' he said, rubbing his eyes with the calloused flesh of his palms, remembering only at the sound of her name that Clare, of course, was dead – had been dead now for nearly twenty years, killed by a speeding train on the tracks outside Brentwood.

He closed his eyes tight, opened them. For a moment – as ever in the moment of waking during those years since the call – all that had been (and all that hadn't) spun around him like dust-mites in a shaft of summer sunlight, twisting and turning in their usual drowsy dance – until the telephone jangled again (it seemed urgent this time, as if it were annoyed at having so far been ignored), and what had and had never been his life dispersed, leaving only what, through the casual passage of time, it had somehow in his absence become.

He pushed himself up, padded barefoot through the morning gloom of the parlor and down the narrow hall to the telephone. Here, pausing only a moment to gather himself, he unhooked the receiver and pressed it to his ear.

'Yes?' he said.

'*Hello?*'

The voice – a woman's – sounded faint, like a voice heard calling from across a misty field.

'Yes, madam?' Unseen, Robert pushed up on his toes a fraction – thus drawing his lips so close to the contraption's funnel mouthpiece that he could feel the warmth of his own breath and his nose could pick out individually the smell both of the telephone's enameling and the bare base metal beneath it. 'This is the Zeitezmann residence. Who may I say is calling?'

'*Calling?*'

'Yes, madam. Could I please have your name?'

But the line went dead, as it did so often these days. Carefully, he replaced the receiver, turned, and padded back down the hall and into his room. Here, he stood for a moment and considered himself in the mirror (in those twenty years he reckoned he'd aged thirty, until he looked more like sixty now than fifty), wondering idly what he'd do if all the stories were true; then, with the casual precision of a surgeon preparing for a stint at the operating table, he removed from his chest of drawers the socks, underwear, collar and shirt that behove a man in his position, and proceeded to dress for the day.

20

Always a balance in everything; always a night for a day, a winter for a spring; always a death for a life.

'Mrs Zeitezmann?'

It was with the Devil's own irony, or, perhaps, at least, with his flare for melodrama, that the death-call when it had come – *Oh, Bobby, it's Clare, she's dead* – had come at the very first moment of life for Nathan Zeitezmann III. Indeed, so precise had been the timing that, just as the high-ceilinged cream-pillared mansion was echoing to the baby's first strangling cries, so was it, too, in that very moment, filled with the intimate and unexpected knowledge of death. It was the kind of irony – at once grotesque and beautiful in its perfect balance – that for some will recapture that lost rapture of faith, while, for others, it will mark that faith's end. For Robert, however, it had meant both. For him, the events of that day all those years ago now – those cries both at death and of life – had confirmed not only what he'd suspected and longed for – that there *is* a greater being – but also what he'd feared – that that being, though real, is a callous one, heartless, compromised and eternally damned.

'Mrs Zeitezmann?'

So, consequently, for twenty years, he'd scarcely heard of a coming without searching for (and, most often, finding) a going – barely woken to a morning without seeing already in the dawn skies the first tell-tale traces of dusk.

He rested the breakfast tray on the palm of one hand and tapped again on the door with the other.

'Mrs Zeitezmann?'

He turned the brass handle, eased the door inward.

The room was in darkness, the air thick with breathing. As he had most every morning since Annie's departure for a position at a house in Westchester County, he set the tray down with the *chink-chink* of china on the table behind the door and crossed to the window. The drapes were heavy and operated by a taut golden cord. This he pulled gently; the drapes parted. Suddenly, as if it were some vast body of water that had long been held back behind a dam now spectacularly and unexpectedly breached, the morning's light flooded in, tumbling and cascading, coursing over the carpet and the stuffed arms of chairs, rising then like a tide and submerging the vast, ornate, golden ship of a bed.

Robert settled the cord still against the wall. He paused for a moment, squinting out of the window. Way off, beyond the storm-battered gardens and debris-strewn lawns, the figure of Mr Zeitezmann stood alone on the end of the jetty. He was looking out across the gray morning waters, standing motionless as if mimicking the flat sleeping stillness of the Sound, his arms hanging straight by his side as if he felt himself a young man again with a fortune still to make standing lookout before the vast rolling plains of the west. To Robert, in that moment, he had about him – even at such a distance – that look of desperate vigilance that comes to a man whose only hope resides now in the near-hopeless.

He turned his head at a rustling sound.

'Nathan? Is that you?'

He stepped away from the window and crossed the room. He paused a few feet from the end of the bed. He cleared his throat. 'It's Robert, Mrs Zeitezmann.'

'Robert?'

'I've brought you your breakfast. Would you care for it now?'

From the canopied gloom of the bed came a terrible sigh.

'Mrs Zeitezmann?'

'Where's Annie?' she said.

'Annie's gone, Mrs Zeitezmann.'

'Gone?'

'You asked her to leave, if you remember. She had disgraced the house.'

For a moment, then, silence. In the distance – perhaps too far away to really hear – the gentle slapping of water against the jetty.

'Robert?'

'Yes, Mrs Zeitezmann?'

Again silence. The tapping of a fly against the window.

'Is there any news?'

'No, madam.'

He turned away, moved toward the door.

'Robert?'

He lifted the tray. 'Yes, madam?'

'But . . . but there is *hope – isn't* there?'

'Yes,' he said, 'there's always hope.' He paused, thinking suddenly of Clare, of that train, of that voice on the line – *Oh, Bobby, it's Clare, she's dead* – of its whispering low like the voice of a sinner confessing.

'Then he's alive?'

Always a balance in everything; always a night for a day, a winter for a spring; always a death for a life.

'Let us pray for it, madam,' he said, aware as he did so that to pray for one life is to pray for the death of another, and that though to pray for a drowning is surely a sin, that that sinning is just bartering, just trade with the Devil or with God or whomever, just the fair exchange of that night for that day, that winter for that spring, that death for that life.

21

S he came to him on the afternoon of the third day. All morning he'd been clearing the gardens of what was left of the storm's debris and stacking all the broken branches ready for burning in the brazier beyond the poolhouse, and he was just heading down across the south lawn to wash his hands in the clear waters of the Sound when he noticed her standing there at the water's edge in the shadow of the jetty. She was standing half in the darkness and half in the light, her head tilted to one side, her dark eyes watching him with a stillness and an ease that made him feel she'd been watching him for some time.

He paused a minute, squinting into the sun. It was a strange thing, but, though for days now he'd been expecting her (ever since news of the ship's probable loss had reached the house), now that she was here he could scarcely believe it. He let go the rake, heard a light thud as its handle hit the still-dewy grass.

'*Bobby?*'

He raised his hand, shielding his eyes. Now she was here it made suddenly certain – suddenly real – all that he'd dreamed of and all that others had feared.

'*Bobby, what is it?*'

He frowned. In his mind's eye he saw the face of a young man he loved distorted with fear, heard his gasping for air, watched his pale fingers loosening their grip on a rail, then sliding, disappearing, beneath the bubbling surface of a dark evening ocean.

He lowered his hand. He heard a voice say 'Clare?', felt in his throat that word's vibration.

'*I'm here, Bobby, I'm here –*'

He stepped toward her, heard the folding of the grass beneath his feet, felt the thumping in his chest of the heart he'd thought broken and finished, and was nearly within reach of her – nearly touching that flesh whose absence for so long had so haunted him – when a sudden look of fear in her eye stopped him dead.

'What is it?' he said. 'What's the matter?' He reached out a hand, but she stepped back, away, and, in that moment, all that had been suddenly certain – for real – became uncertain once again – once more in the balance – as the tide of God's world or the Devil's, having turned, turned again.

22

'Sir?'

To the casual observer (if, given the circumstances, one can imagine such a thing), that moment in the dark night in the middle of the oil-dark sea when the *Liberation*'s generators unexpectedly started up and her lights – for six hours dead – suddenly winked on, illuminating the ocean as the lights of a Christmas tree will illuminate a late-winter parlor, would have seemed for sure nothing less than what it was – which was? Well, a miracle, of course – the work, surely, not of engineers alone, but of the hand of some forgiving and benevolent God – that moment the moment (could it be anything else?) when a ship of lost souls was returned to the world – the very moment when a ghost-ship and those riding it came back from the dead.

To a casual observer, perhaps – but not to Mr Irvine – not to a captain of forty years' experience. For him, for now, there was only the great God of science – that and, of course, the immovable, inexorable will of man.

He turned stiffly from his instruments at the sound of a light cough. 'Sir?'

Lately – since, really, Southampton and the start of the voyage – he'd been feeling a chill in his bones he'd not felt before – this and an old man's stiffness in his fingers that made gripping his binoculars now a particular trial.

'Yes, Mr Parr?'

Unseen, he flexed his fingers as best he could behind his back.

'Well –' Philip Parr, at twenty-three the *Liberation*'s youngest officer, was standing red-faced and sweating, his chest heaving: indisputable evidence of physical exertion, the appearance of which was, in the view of Mr Irvine, hardly becoming in an officer of the Blue Star Line – let alone a gentleman.

He shook his head. 'Have you been *running*, sir?' he said.

Unable to stop himself, Philip Parr bent over, dropped his hands to his knees and started coughing.

Captain Irvine turned away, back to the sweep of the instruments on the bridge. 'You are aware, sir,' he said, 'are you not, that the practice of running on this ship is, for an officer, forbidden? That, sir, such conduct is guaranteed to produce in women and children feelings of distress – of panic, even?'

Philip Parr straightened himself up, managed a breathless yes he was aware, but in this case –

'This case?' said the captain. 'And what, pray, is special about this case?'

'Well, the chief said to tell you –' Lack of breath forced a pause, during which – much to his surprise – Captain Irvine discovered that somehow, in the darkness and confusion of the last six hours, a decision about his future – a decision he'd long delayed – had finally been made.

'Said to tell me what, sir?' he said. 'Will you speak up?'

'That, well, it was a miracle –'

'A miracle?'

He frowned. For weeks now – months, really – he'd been wrestling with it, and now, from out of nowhere, it seemed it was settled: come New York and the end of the voyage he would offer his resignation. It was an offer that he knew would (though with regrets, of course) be accepted.

'He said you should go take a look for yourself. He said he'd never seen anything like it –'

Indeed, already, in his mind's eye, he could picture the future as clearly as if it were already set: days spent sitting silent on the front porch or down by the sea, his greatcoat wrapped around him and a scarf wound tight around his neck to keep out the chills.

'Sir?'

He shook his head. He flexed and straightened his fingers. *And silence*, he thought, *in the future there will always be silence*. He drew a deep breath and set his eyes sternly on the young man's face. 'Sir,' he said, 'there are no miracles. There is only what is possible and what is not.'

'But the chief said –'

He let his eyes close for a moment as a weariness overcame him, and for a moment, then, he was lying on a bed somewhere just staring at a wall, just listening to the regular beat of his pulse.

'Sir? Are you well, sir?'

He opened his eyes; the image fled in body, though the shadow of course remained. 'Yes, Mr Parr,' he said. 'I am quite well, thank you. Now, if there is nothing else?'

'But, sir, the chief –'

He sighed. 'The chief, sir, as you know, is – aside from being, of course, a fine engineer – by origin a Frenchman, and, consequently, prey to that nation's weakness for hysterical delusion – a weakness which, I fear, in this case, has become all too apparent –'

'But —'

'But *nothing*, sir. The ship was broken; she is now repaired. Those are the facts. Furthermore, I would be grateful – that being the case, as it surely is – if you would pull yourself together and return to your duties. You do *have* duties, I believe – do you not?'

'Yes,' said Philip Parr.

'Yes?'

'Yes, *sir*.'

'Good. Now, run along, if you please, and perform them!'

Philip Parr stood a second, eye to eye with his captain, then turned sharply away. Captain Irvine watched him go; then he, too, turned away. He crossed to the windows, laid his fingers on the narrow brass sill and stared out with foreboding at the deep, black, starless night.

23

Nearer my God to thee
Nearer my God –

For six hours they'd been drifting, unable to steer – an unlighted vessel prey to the fickle, shifting will of the ocean. And for six hours, unable to communicate with a soul in the lighted world, the *Liberation*'s living cargo – passengers and crew alike – had been as lost in the world as it is possible to be – their position unknown even to themselves, their fate as unknowable, as unseeable in the darkness, as the moment when dusktime turns finally into night, or the last breeze of late summer into the first chill winds of early fall.

For Libbie Custer, those hours of darkness that for some had been hours of fear or duty had been a time of stolen peace, of quiet solitude. For her, it had meant – for a moment at least – the suspension of her duty of public remembrance, and – as for fear – well, the last she'd known of *that* had been forty years ago in the breathless heat of the plains, when her fingers, now so stiffened with age, had been younger and more supple and her voice so clear that – even despite her premonition on that terrible day – it was *hers* that had risen effortlessly above the voices of the other officers' wives as they'd stitched with such care, with such wasted love now, their American quilt – *her* breath, raised in song, that, fittingly perhaps, had, above all others, been, consequently, the most absent, the most stilled, at the sudden sound of tapping on her door.

She opened her eyes. The tapping came again. For a moment, though she squinted hard in the sudden light, she was back once again with the ladies in that stifling front parlor, then looking up on a whim from her work, at that fine dust on the windows, at the empty parade ground and the vast plains beyond. For a moment again, she was turning her head at the sound of heavy boots on her newly polished floor, then, standing, a general's wife, watching three soldiers looking down, away, as awkward in their manner as first-year cadets called up before the commandant.

65

'Ma'am?'

Then one of them – Mr Middleton, the post surgeon – was stepping forward, his lips moving slow beneath his whiskers, his crooked teeth stained yellow with tobacco. *Ma'am, the Far West has arrived*, he was saying. *There is terrible news –*

Another tap on the heavy cabin door.

'Ma'am? Are you there? Mrs Custer?'

She'd known it, of course, felt it in her heart since rising that morning. That morning, sitting in her cramped and narrow sewing room, gazing out across the dusty plains to the blue distant mountains and the vast empty sky beyond, she'd had the sudden sense of something coming – of something bad that would change things forever – and when, at noon, she'd seen the Indian women sifting dirt beyond the fort's perimeter, seen how it settled gray as ashes at their feet, she'd been certain of it.

An unseen hand rattled the cabin's brass handle. There was breathing beyond the door, a voice calling out once again across the years.

'Mrs Custer? It's Nathan. Nathan Zeitezmann.'

In that moment, with her fingers stilled like a skeleton's in their intricate work, she'd been certain like never before of something having ended and of something longer – something so, so long – having begun, of a sudden rootlessness, an unnerving loss of balance.

'Mrs Custer?'

And she'd stood then, aware of the blood running slow in her veins, and had been standing there still when the ladies and their talk had been filling up the house down below. She'd turned, caught herself in the looking-glass looking back, seen the face she'd always feared – the gaunt face of a widow – and heard the screams and the hooves as they pounded the earth, watched the rising of those rich golden locks and the flash of that knife, then that bloody weeping skull, then the silence of time passing, then those awkward frightened faces, Mr Middleton and his sour whiskey breath.

She stared at the door, watched the slow-turning handle.

Be assured, ma'am, he did not suffer. He was found untouched save by death.

She let her eyes close.

'Ma'am?'

A lie: she'd always known it. She'd known it in her heart – had had it confirmed every night since in her dreams. In her dreams, every night, her own golden boy, her Autie, had been lying naked on some desolate rise somewhere, just a pale, broken corpse, his beautiful blue eyes staring out like a child's up to heaven, his flesh that was her flesh slashed and torn and growing cold as the shadowed earth beneath him, his heart that was her heart ripped with bloody hands from the gaping cavity of his chest . . .

'Ma'am?'

And all, now, for what? For it all to be forgotten? For the truth to be perverted by cowards who'd looked on from afar whilst others – those with honor, with courage – had fought and died?

'Mrs Custer?'

She opened her eyes. The tapping was harder now, insistent. Slowly, she rose, stood a minute, aware only of the ship's gentle swaying, only of that last smile, only of those last words borne away on the back of some long-distant afternoon's breeze.

Another tap, another rattle of the handle. 'It's the captain, Mrs Custer. I just heard him talking –'

Remember, my darling, dance with no one but me.

'He says something's happened – something real bad –'

She blinked once; the breeze, the dust of summer, that smile slipped away.

'Mrs Custer?'

'I'm here,' she said, 'I'm here.'

'Then you'll come?'

'Yes,' she said wearily, 'I'll come. You go.' She stood a minute, listening for footsteps; then, when they were gone, she crossed to the foot of her dressing table, from the fine polished surface of which she retrieved an old silver locket cast in the shape of a heart. This she turned in the light, but, of course, did not open. For forty years, its contents had remained unseen in the darkness, and so forever would it remain, a single lock of golden hair sealed – forever young – in a moment of the past.

James & Matthew

24

When, one cool early morning in the late fall of eighteen sixty-two, with a year of that distant eastern war having passed, the Summerfield Institute for the Treatment of Fever opened its doors and let loose upon the world the grave and upright figure of James Monkton Webb, the world, for sure, wasn't ready. But then the world, back then – at least that *part* of the world – had other things on its mind – namely death and its most efficient creation – and, consequently, seemed either not to notice or not to care that one more madman had come to join the party. Which is not to say, of course, that it wouldn't *come* to care (no, on the contrary, a gallows in Medora would in time see to that) – just that, for now, for then, a facility for the letting of blood was what was required if a man were to be accorded the grace of anonymity – an ability, which, as we shall see, little James Monkton Webb (or, now, not so little, for he was fully six foot, and a good-looking man) had in full, though, as yet, raw, measure, and one which he would come to develop with the aid of all the natural guile and heartlessness of any true artist.

But that, on that morning, was all yet to come. For then, there was only the clang of those gates and the final turning of that key behind him – just that breeze in the trees and those crisp brittle leaves at his feet, just that dirt road leading left and leading right, just the future, unknown and unknowable, stretching way out before him, twisting and turning then disappearing from view like a river lost in trees.

'Well then?'

He stood, his back to the gates, looking first one way then the other. He frowned.

'So where *is* you goin'?'

For weeks and months – indeed, ever since his father, now dead, shot through the head at Fort Henry, had permitted his imprisonment – all he'd thought of was this moment, but now it was here it was not at all what he'd expected. With a sigh, he set down his old beat-up carpet-bag and slipped his hands into the pockets of his pants. He tipped back his head and gazed up at the sky. 'I don't know,' he said.

'What you mean, you don't know?'

The sky was a flat pale gray, the light diffused with no visible sign of its source. He lowered his head, looked once again about him. It was a funny thing – and foolish now it seemed – but, come his release, he'd expected, at the very least, some feeling of having been returned to the familiar, and he'd assumed (why, now, he couldn't for the life of him imagine) that, as soon as those gates closed behind him for the last time and he was finally free, he'd somehow know exactly what to do and where to go – that, just as his razor had been returned to him that morning and his daddy's hunting knife, so would that piece of him that he had long been aware of by its absence – that is, that part of him that acted as some kind of compass, the part that existed in others (he knew this to be true, for he had seen it – seen the unwavering righteousness and self-knowledge of other men) – the part that would give him direction and that clear, unambiguous knowledge of a purpose.

'Ain't you gonna go see your daddy like you said?'

He squinted hard at the thick copse of trees straight ahead, tried to make out what manner of country lay beyond.

'Well, ain't you?'

But the trees were too dense to see. He shrugged. 'Maybe,' he said.

'What you mean, maybe?'

'I mean maybe I will and maybe I won't.'

Cleaver Wilson frowned hard, confusion twisting his pale flabby features. He was gripping the bars of the gate like a monkey in a cage, his face pressed up tight, his fleshy lips splayed, exposing blackened teeth. 'But you *said* you was *gonna* –'

Just then a flock of birds rose cawing from the trees, black as tacks thrown up against the pale autumn sky. James watched them circling in confusion, then settle again.

'Say, Jimmy –'

'What?'

'Well, has your daddy really got all them horses and stuff?'

'My daddy's dead.'

'Dead? He ain't dead. You said –'

He frowned. *The boy is hysterical and cannot be calmed. For his own sake, and for the sake of his father, he must be subdued –*

'Jimmy?'

He half-turned. 'What?'

'About them horses –'

The truth is the boy is a danger to himself and to others, and must, for the present at least, be restrained.

' 'Cause I mean if you *was* and he *has* got that real fancy spread you's been talkin' about, then how come you's still standin' here talkin' to me?

How come you's not sitting by now on some real shady porch just drinking your mama's lemonade?'

Cleaver rattled the gates; James started.

'Are you listen' to me, Jimmy-boy?'

He looked up. For a second, again, he could feel the straps tight across his chest, hear the whispering of voices in a hall.

'I mean, Jimmy-boy, if it was *me* what was gettin' free, well man, I'd be gettin' me some pussy right now, 'stead of standin' there starin' at them leaves –'

Did you see the child's eyes? Did you see what he's done? Do you think it's some kind of madness handed down?

'Say, Jimmy?'

He blinked, again.

'Talkin' 'bout *pussy* –'

The leaves at his feet blurred then sharpened, as the voices drifted off and the thin leather straps around his heaving chest loosened. He squinted at the pig-like grinning face between the bars. '*What?*' he said. Unseen, in his pocket, the shaft of his daddy's old hunting knife was cool against the flesh of his palm.

Cleaver Wilson drew his tongue across his stumpy teeth. 'Well, I was thinkin' – 'bout that step-mama when you done her – when you stuck her with that knife of your daddy's, well, did you take a look-see at what your daddy'd been gettin'? Did you lift them old skirts and get you a peek?'

The shaft of the knife was ribbed, the blade as sharp as a blade could be.

'Well, *did* you, Jimmy-boy? Did you give that old whore what she wanted?'

He touched the edge with his finger, felt the stinging, living pain of parting flesh, then the slow, seeping warmth of his blood. He smiled.

'I knew it!' said Cleaver Wilson, his face richly flushing as he threw back his head, exposing his throat and laughing – laughing so hard, indeed, that it wasn't until the blade had completed its arc and was glinting blood-red in the afternoon's light that he felt something changing, something coming to an end and something much darker beginning. He stepped back, his eyes flaring, raised his hands to his neck to stop the flow. But the flow would not cease, for it flowed like a river, and he, in that river, could do nothing but drown.

25

A nd so it was that James Monkton Webb – for so long a boy – became a man.

By which I mean what?

I mean, of course, that his was the freedom now of which all men secretly dream: that freedom from the censure of conscience that comes only from the spilling of others' blood and plenty of it – that lifting of the stifling burden of compassion that only its confronting and defeating can bring – that liberation from the expectation of heaven that comes only from wallowing in sin.

And oh how he laughed as he walked away! How he opened his arms as if in receipt of some perverse benediction, as, taking the road neither left nor right, he moved through the trees, feeling, as he strode on, that crisp crack of death in the leaves beneath his feet and the cool of the slow dying year on his face. Oh how he smiled as he tripped and nearly fell, but recovered himself just in time to hear the whisper of voices beyond a hedge, coming from some artfully sunken road, like voices drifting up from some newly covered grave.

He froze in his step, for all the world a living, breathing corpse. He listened with the care of a burglar at a door.

Nothing.

Then something.

Voices.

The grinding of wheels in the dirt.

He held his breath, crept forward, crouching, peered out through the baffle of leaves. Below, so close he could have reached down and tweaked the ear of the driver, sat a man and, beside him, a woman, the pair of them riding an old beat-up buggy, drawn by the skinniest of horses. On her lap, the woman, whom James could see (even from such an unusual angle) was blessed with some beauty, held a child who was nursing at her breast, her pale exposed flesh made paler by the rich dusty blackness of her dress. *But I don't understand*, she was saying, as they passed slowly by, and she turned to her companion who, though dressed in the blue of a soldier, had nothing martial in the set of his face.

He was, James thought, perhaps a man of modest property called up reluctantly to serve – or even some lowly sort of gentleman. There were, after all, the stripes on his shoulder of a captain of cavalry, and, pointing awkward and stiff from his belt, a gleaming new sabre. *You must try*, he was saying. *There is fighting to do and the Union needs men –*

Then, apparently unseen, the buggy and its cargo moved on, drawing with it, as if by some invisible but, nevertheless, physical means, the gaze of the watcher behind and above them in the hedge. Soon they were gone, snatched away for the moment from his view, just as he was moved beyond the range of their hearing. He stood, brushed the leaves from his knees and from the front of his shabby and disgraceful woolen jacket, then picked up his carpet-bag and dropped down with some grace to the road.

He was smiling when the driver heard his call, his arm raised high in the friendliest of greetings. The buggy slowed to a stop; the soldier dismounted, careful of his sabre and unwatched by his companion, whose wife's and mother's eye was on the futures of her husband and her child, and not on the present.

'Hello, stranger,' said the soldier, to which James replied most heartily in kind. He had about him (the soldier) the look of a dutiful man, which pleased James immensely. He was pleased, also, when he shook the man's hand to find it not only cool and dry but firm to the touch – the sort of hand, indeed, that a man, were he choosing, would choose.

'I was wondering,' said James (he was smiling that smile of his – the one that made folks think him kind and, perhaps, a little simple), 'about this road's destination –'

'The road?' The captain of cavalry turned and squinted away down the road, as if he were trying to imagine its end. 'Why,' he said, 'you keep on this road, friend, and it'll take you just as far as you could ever want to go.' He paused, turning back. 'Keep going, in fact, and your feet will get wet in the *At*lantic Ocean.'

At this James smiled. The soldier, it was clear, was a humorous soul – one of whom, in another life, perhaps, or, perhaps, in another world, he might have in time made a friend. For now, however, this life and this world being all that he had, he just kept his own counsel and that smile upon his face – even when, later, with the dusk rolling in across the land like a tide, and a melancholy so rich and so heavy seemed to press down upon him, making his breath come short and labored, all he could picture, as he drove, was the soldier's smiling face and that of his wife (oh, she was certainly pretty) set in terror beyond, and between them the restful, now forever-sleeping form of their child.

26

'Hey, buddy, you alive?'

And so it was, back then, that little James Monkton Webb became a man, and that man became a captain of cavalry.

Matthew opened his eyes. A face, blurred and wheezing, was hanging close to his. 'I'm alive,' he said, surprised by the distant sound and at the same time the nearness of his voice. He squinted hard against the light. 'Who are *you*?'

' 'Cause you sure don't *look* it –'

He tried to sit up, but gave up at the jabbing of pencils in his eyes. He raised a hand and swept it across his face. His face felt as foreign to his touch as would have the surface of the moon. He drew his eyes into reluctant focus. The face – a man, unshaven – was frowning, emitting pity and the strong stink of whiskey in equal measure. 'Where am I?' he said.

'You don't remember?' The face drew back, the head shaking, disapproving but somehow still kindly.

Matthew moved his head, *no*.

'You sure now? You sure you don't recall how one minute you was lookin' to drown yourself in a whole barrel of whiskey, then the next you was hollerin' and swingin' them fists of yours and cussin' like I don't know what –'

Matthew screwed up his eyes and tried to remember, but all he could remember was Miss Eliot and her parlor – just the look of disgust in her eyes, just the thickness of photographs gathered in an envelope – just that, then nothing –

'Say, you want I should fetch you somethin'?'

Just an absence, a nothingness, just that vacancy that somehow exists without the slightest knowledge of itself that he'd seen in the still staring eyes of corpses. He opened his eyes, turned his head. The man (a barman, he supposed, from the smell of his breath and the apron drawn tight around his belly) was sitting at a beat-up table, turning the pages of a newspaper, every now and then raising his right hand to his lips and licking the tip of his first finger to facilitate the pages' turning. On the table beside the newspaper sat a glass of copper-colored whiskey and, beside that, a brown paper package.

The governor, Mr Princeton, is a personal friend and a Christian –

The barman raised his hand without raising his eyes, licked the tip of his finger and turned another page. Matthew watched him, watched the gathering of his brows as he leaned a little forward and let slip from his lips the faintest whistle of surprise. 'Well, Lord have mercy,' he whispered low beneath his breath.

'What is it?' said Matthew. *And he will receive, without delay, that which he is expecting –*

The man looked up. 'Pardon me?'

Matthew pushed himself up. Perhaps it was the sudden movement – the sudden shifting of pressure in his head – but in that moment he felt himself once again leaning over a bar, the smell of wood and polish as strong in his nostrils as the smell of the excrement of horses, then the strange close-up sound of cursing in his ears. 'Nothing,' he said. He drew a shallow, rasping breath. He looked to the backroom's grimy window. 'What time is it?'

'Six – maybe seven?' The barman, still studying his paper, shook his head, his face swept for a moment by the wriest, most disbelieving of smiles. '*Custer*,' he said.

'What?' said Matthew.

He looked up, closed the paper. 'Would you believe,' he said, 'that those idiots in Washington have gone and given him the Seventh?'

Matthew frowned. 'Custer?'

'Custer.'

'Jesus,' he said, and he closed his eyes. His head was suddenly pounding again. He opened his eyes. 'You sure about that? You sure it's Custer?'

'By decree of the President, by way of the great and wise wishes of General William Tecumseh Sherman.'

'When?' said Matthew.

'Right now,' said the barman. 'Right this very goddamned day.'

27

'I don't believe it.'

'Well, it's true.'

Matthew pushed himself up, stood, unsteady. The room spun for a moment, then slowly settled. Custer. It was a name he'd barely considered in more than a decade – one, indeed, that seemed, now, so lost in the past that it scarcely seemed to make any sense in the present. He swept a hand across his face. 'Jesus,' he said. 'You mean he's still alive? You mean some well-meaning God-fearing hero hasn't shot the son-of-a-bitch yet?'

The barman filled his glass from a bottle on the table, then raised it in ironic salute. 'To the general,' he said. 'May he rest in pieces.'

Matthew sat back against the arm of the beat-up leather settee. 'You sound like you knew him,' he said. He felt suddenly more weary than he'd ever felt before. 'And you *look* like you survived. That some kind of miracle, you reckon?'

'I reckon,' said the barman. There was something, in that moment, in his voice that was different. Matthew squinted, tried to see from his look what it was.

'What is it?' he said.

The barman looked up. 'What?'

'You look like you ain't sure.'

'Sure?'

'If you survived.'

He shrugged. 'I'm here, ain't I?' He raised the glass, took another drink, then lowered it, circling it between his knees with the tips of his fingers. 'Antietam,' he said after a while. He flicked his eyes up to meet Matthew's. His eyes were a clear pale blue, made paler and bluer by his heavy grizzled face. 'I guess you heard of it.'

'I heard of it,' said Matthew. In his mind's eye, suddenly, he saw corpses lying still on a single muddy road leading to a beat-up wooden bridge.

'Yeah, I know,' said the barman.

'Know?'

He paused, circled the glass some more, watched the whiskey ebb and flow slow as oil.

'Know what?' said Matthew.

Another pause.

'Know *what*?'

The barman sank the whiskey, set the glass on the table. 'I coulda had him,' he said.

'Who?'

'Your pretty-boy general.'

'He ain't mine.'

He looked up. 'He *was*.'

Matthew said nothing. The corpses had been piled three and four deep, every one of them shifting in the summer heat with a livid suit of flies.

The barman smiled. "Fact, I coulda had you too. You and that captain of yours.'

'What?'

'Yep. I knew I'd seen you someplace before, and now I know where.'

'I don't know what you're talking about.'

'Sure you do. I never forget a target. You and that captain were standin' right next to Colonel Goldilocks, just holding his horse like a good little boy.' He raised up his arms, left arm extended, the palm of his hand flat, fingers curling, while his right he held crooked, the hand a fist at his chin, first finger curled tight around a make-believe trigger. He closed his left eye, sighted with his right.

'You're crazy,' said Matthew.

Then he squeezed on the trigger. 'Two shots,' he said. 'Boom-boom and it's bye-bye Mr Last-In-His-Class, and bye-bye Mr Pictureman.' The barman lowered his rifle. He was smiling still. 'Still say you're alive, Mr Pictureman? Still reckon you're breathing?'

'Look, I'm going,' said Matthew. 'I'm obliged to you for your help –' He crossed to the desk, reached for the package of photographs. A hand caught his wrist, twisted it.

'Well, do you?' said the barman. His breath was close-up, sour as an undershirt left to rot in the sun. ' 'Cause if you do, then you know who to thank. And it ain't your precious lover-boy.' The hand twisted harder; Matthew tried to pull away, but could not. 'You know who it is you got to thank? Well, do you?'

'I guess you,' said Matthew. The pain was bleeding like some drug up his arm and into the hollow cavity of his chest.

'You guess right. And you know *why* you're still breathing – you and that fancy piece of shit?'

Matthew shook his head.

'Well, let me see now. I guess I *could* say, Mr Lieutenant, sir, that maybe at last I'd had enough of all the killing. I guess I *could* say that after sittin' in them trees for so long just watching you Yankees comin' on and on, that I'd finally gotten sick of the blood, of the piles of stinkin' bodies, of the hunger and the no boots and the marchin' all night with nothin' in my stomach but fear and whiskey – I guess I could say all that. But I won't – no, sir. And you know why?'

Matthew closed his eyes tight at another twist and turn.

'*Because*, Mr Pictureman, it wouldn't be right. You see, the truth is I wasn't sick of killin' you Yankees at all – in fact, I coulda gone on and on – I coulda sat in that tree just makin' me a bigger and bigger hill o' blue – and I woulda done – was plannin' to, startin' with you and that asshole Custer – if I hadn't in that very moment run clean outta shot. Yeah, that's right. It was luck, Mr Yankee soldier, just luck. I had yous two sighted, and two minutes before or two minutes after I'd have blown off both your heads and made that hill just a little bit higher – but I didn't. Instead I just pulled on that trigger, heard the click of that empty chamber – and you know what?'

Another twist and Matthew opened his eyes as the hand on his wrist suddenly released its grip. He stepped back; the room swayed, everything blurry through his tears.

'Well?'

'What?' he said.

The barman sat back on the desk, turning away, one hand on the packet of pictures, the other reaching for his whiskey bottle. He filled up the glass, raised it in a toast. 'Well, I can tell you right now I ain't sorry, 'cause lookin' at you I can see you's dead anyhow, and shootin' you would just have been a waste. In fact, I'd have been doin' you a favor. Oh, for sure you'd have been dead – but *real* dead – real peaceful maybe – instead of bein' dead but still somehow kinda livin' like you are right now. And well, as for the general, I guess he's got his comin' anyhow where he's goin' –'

'What do you mean?' said Matthew.

The barman sank his whiskey and smiled. He leaned forward, shaking his head and his eyes wide, as if he were talking to an idiot or a child. 'Well now,' he said, 'you don't really think Mr Sitting Bull's gonna just be sittin' around and smokin' some peace-pipe when the general comes a-callin' now, do you? And you don't think Mr Crazy Horse ain't gonna get a mite crazy when old Long Hair rolls up and says *Howdee, now I'm takin' all you got*? No, sir. I reckon those boys are gonna have them a fine time with your general and his blue-coated savages, maybes even get themselves a whole new set of ventilated clothes and some new boots to wear. In fact, you know, if I had any kind of energy left, which I don't, I might just have been tempted to take me a little vacation up onto them plains just to catch me a little sport – 'cause, man, it sure would be somethin' to see, don't you reckon? It sure would be some kinda sight, huh, soldier-boy?'

Matthew reached forward, snatched the package, stepped back. His heart was pounding. 'You're crazy,' he said.

'Well, maybe I am –'

He crossed to the door, aware of eyes sharp as arrows in his back. He reached for the handle, twisted it, pulled.

'But at least I'm *alive*. At least I ain't walking round half-dead already and lookin' for a bullet to finish the job –'

'*Oh, just shut your mouth, just shut it –*'

'At least I'm still breathin', soldier-boy –'

He stepped into the bar and closed the door hard behind him. He stood a moment, aware of the dangerous thundering of his heart. *I never forget a target.* He swallowed hard; his mouth was dry.

'Say, fella, you okay?' said a voice – the barman. He was back behind his bar now as if he'd never left it, polishing a glass and smiling.

Dead but somehow kinda livin'.

Without speaking, without looking, then, left or right, Matthew set out across the bar-room, the package gripped tight like some shield against his chest, heading straightaway for the door, for the street, for air.

He was rounding the corner of Meterie and Duvalier when a shot that sounded like it came from just behind him made him jump. He turned, scanned the crowds, he was sweating hard. 'What was that?' he said to an old man walking by. But the old man just shrugged and kept walking. Matthew squinted through the sweat, but could see nothing – just the afternoon crowds rolling onward like a river, swirling this way and that, ebbing and flowing through the pale autumn shadows and the slow-dying light.

28

Today, should you take that excursion as suggested and visit what was then the governor's mansion – should you pay your six dollars and take your place in the line – then you'll visit, now, a museum – a white-pillared, two-storied, clean-swept mausoleum – whose manicured lawns and cool marble halls speak only, now, in whispers – and, only then, to those lonely foolish souls whose ears are turned away from the uneasy, unsettling life of the present toward those comforting, distant-echoing voices of the past. To them – to us – to *you* – where, now, the exhibits stand – the glass cabinets filled with browning indecipherable letters, with anonymous pairs of yellowing gloves (gloves too tiny, surely, for any but the tiniest of human hands), will stand again, will live again, all that stood and all that lived before, and you will stand – as I stood, that distant summer – cradled in the arms of the dead but still living, mesmerized by their voices, their cool breath on your cheeks, until the pages of a dozen or more guide-books are turned and the tour moves on and refreshments are taken, and lives, for a moment suspended, are returned to the present from whence they came, while the past slips away before the acrid stink of diesel and the click of camera-shutters, and slinks back into shadows just to watch, wait and breathe.

'I've a delivery for the governor.'

But that was now; this, now, is then.

'A delivery? What delivery?'

Matthew held up the package, at which, with that supercilious and disdainful look of flunkies everywhere, the governor's new first assistant frowned.

'Pictures,' said Matthew. He was jumpy still and sweating from his walking, his mind free-falling still from the barman's recognition.

'Pictures? What pictures? The governor mentioned no pictures –'

I coulda had you too. He sighed, felt the breath leave his body, knew the effort required to replace it. 'Look,' he said. He closed his eyes, sucked in a mouthful of the moist, heavy air through his teeth. He opened his eyes, opened the envelope, withdrawing halfway the first picture of the set, exposing for a moment Clare's head and naked shoulders. 'So now,' he said, 'does the governor get his pictures or not?'

The governor's first assistant stepped involuntarily back as if an invisible hand on his breastbone had pushed him and hard. For a second, he looked to Matthew as if he might faint; but then, clearing his throat as if he were preparing to sing, he recovered himself. He held out a tiny, white-gloved hand.

Matthew shook his head.

'I'll take them,' said the governor's first assistant. 'You can go now.'

'Uh-uh,' said Matthew.

'What?'

'I'm supposed to deliver them personally.'

'Personally? Why?'

He shrugged. 'Instructions from Miss Eliot,' he said.

'Miss who?'

'Eliot. Miss Evangeline Eliot. Runs the whorehouse down on Vine?' He stepped forward, aware acutely of the workings of his legs – of the muscles and sinews all working together. 'Know it, do you?'

The governor's first assistant opened his mouth, but evidently could find no response. Instead he held the door wide, and was standing there still – still mute, still white-faced and motionless – as Matthew gripped the package and stepped inside.

29

Mr Jackson J. Leap, then governor (but not for long, there being, on that very afternoon, moves afoot to have him impeached and disgraced – and not before time, believe me) of the great and glorious state of Louisiana, was – as anyone knew whose vote he'd snatched through falseness and lies – a philanthropist, a moralist (of the crusading type, oh yes), and, above all, of course, a family man.

All of which was news not only to his staff, but also, and particularly, to his family. To his family, particularly, Mr Jackson J. Leap was a shit of monumental proportions – a man, indeed, so lacking in those altogether positive qualities normally associated with role-model success as a husband and as a father (let alone a state governor), that even his dog (of whom he'd been genuinely fond) had in time grown so testy (and sometimes downright vicious) whenever his master approached, that the governor had had to take him out to the back lawns one early spring morning and, with regrets, shoot him – an event (the only one that anyone could remember) the sadness of which had brought tears to the button-eyes of his rubicund face and that familiar shake to his liver-spotted hands, the only remedy for which had been (as ever) another game of Hunt the Oyster with Miss Jefferson, his secretary (now *there* was a woman), followed by his usual midday – of course medicinal – quart of Tennessee rye.

Which is not to say he was *all* bad.

Well, come to think of it, he pretty much was. In fact, just about the only redeeming feature (if thus it could be called) of his generally repugnant nature was an overweening and grossly sentimental attachment to his not inconsiderable collection of native western cacti – to each specimen of which (and there were many – over one hundred) he'd attached a name, and to which, on that, now, distant afternoon, he was attending with a small jug of water and a tiny silver spoon purloined from the kitchens, when his communion with the spiky things was interrupted by a knocking on his oval-office door. He paused a second, then – deciding to ignore whoever it might be – went on with his probing and watering.

Another tapping, this time louder.

He straightened up, glared harshly at the door, as if it was the door itself and not some person beyond it that was guilty of disturbing his work. 'Who is it?' he said sharply.

'A delivery,' said a voice he half-knew.

'A delivery? What delivery?'

'From Miss Eliot.'

Which was enough to have him set down his fine silver spoon and the tiny china jug and make his wheezing sweating way across his office to the door, through which he squinted with the aid of a magnifying peephole. 'Oh, it's you,' he said. He opened the door a fraction, peered out. 'Well?'

Matthew held up the package. The governor reached out a chubby hand, grabbed it, ducked back and slammed the door. He listened for footsteps receding, his mind racing with lascivious expectation. When none came, he sneaked a look through the peephole. The young man was still standing there in the hall, his features distorted by the fish-eye lens, the pallor of his face made more acute – more sickly-looking – by the darkness of the rings beneath his eyes. He had the intense staring gaze of a blindman or a corpse. The governor frowned. He was impatient to get to his pictures – to one special set in particular. He squinted harder, blinking away the sweat. 'What the fuck you want now?' he said. Already he was stiffening in the swamp of his undershorts. 'I ain't payin' you again if that's what you're thinkin' – no, sir. In fact you're lucky I paid you up-front in the first place, 'cause I can tell you you wouldn't be gettin' one single friggin' dime from me now, not after all the trouble and distress you caused me –' He drew back, wiped the sweat from his face with the end of his egg-stiffened necktie, then peered out again. The young man was still just standing there – looking, in fact, like he wasn't ever planning on moving again. The governor sighed. This was just typical of the people. You give them all you've got – your time, your money, the best years of your life – and are they grateful? No, sir. Instead, what do they do? Hang around all the frigging time is what – just whining all the time and sticking out their grubby little hands – and always without ever having the good grace to know when to leave. Jesus Christ. Didn't they think that a governor – a *governor*, for Christ's sake, not just some pen-pushing ass-wiping mayor or some lowly piece of shit like that – might just have some calls on his valuable time? Did they think he could just stand around waiting all day until they graciously decided to come by? No, sir. He frowned, tried to think, tried to calm the rising pressure of the blood in his veins. He peered once again through the peephole – still there – and was just drawing breath to launch the threat of reprisal by means of his own personal firearm (a gift, so he claimed, from Vice-President

Johnson himself), when a thought quite as cool and quite as deadly as that pearl-handled Colt forty-five lodged itself spiteful as a bullet in his gut.

Blackmail.

Oh shit.

He swallowed, heard the sudden click of fear in his throat. He closed his eyes, tried to gather himself. *Calm down*, he told himself, but himself wouldn't listen – instead he felt that sudden familiar trickle in his pants. It was weird, but, still, everytime was like the first time – the threat of a threat and bingo he'd piss himself. He swallowed again, though his mouth was dry. You'd think by now – after so many threats, so much soiled underwear – he'd have learned; but no, everytime was the same. The same sudden leap of fear, the same sudden evacuation, then the same tired routine – the bargaining, the trade of hollow threats, and in the end always the same bloated corpse floating face-down in the river, then a night – sometimes two – of bad dreams and heavy drinking. He sighed. Sometimes the whole damn cycle of things seemed so never-ending. And sometimes – just sometimes – he felt like maybe he should quit – let somebody else carry the heavy burden of high office for a while – although always, in the end, he knew that was *his* duty and he must carry on, for the sake of his people, for the sake of the state and the sake of the nation.

He drew a deep breath, preparing himself for the battle to come. He reached out a hand and had just turned the handle when the door, propelled by the dead weight of the pale sickly boy, came swinging right in at him quite of its own accord, striking with malice the bridge of his nose and breaking it, and so causing him, howling, to step back in haste and lose his footing (which was never so sure at the best of times) and tumble with a strange kind of grace right into the arms of a great spiky cactus called Patty.

'Ah *Jesus*,' he said, trying at once unsuccessfully to rise, his voice struggling like a child's through the blood and sudden tears. 'What the fuck you do that for?'

But the boy wasn't saying. He was out, lying still, for all the world as still and cold as the coldest, stillest corpse.

30

I t was a curious thing (although by no means unique) that while Matthew's star had been falling (and surely it could fall no lower, being as it was now barely sky-borne at all), there had been all the time in the arc of its descent the back-to-front image of its rising.

Not, of course, that he could see it then. Then, out cold on the governor's floor (with the governor himself looking down, disgust and bewilderment playing tag across his rouged and bloated face), all he could see was all that ran feverish in his dreams – dreams the details of which would die in the moment of his waking, but whose spirit, of course – as with all dreams – would shadow and, so, alter his life.

Nor, of course, could he see the eyes (besides those of the governor) that were fixed upon his slumbering form from beyond the French windows, nor the handsome, solemn face in which they were set; nor, indeed, could he see the pistol still warm from a killing in the streets, nor the cool grace of death that hung like a cloak about the watcher's shoulders and gave to him, ironically perhaps, the sense of a ghost or a man in a slumber so deep that he might never rise from it, except in the too-late neck-breaking moment of his death.

But that death – that creaking of a rope, the sudden drop-slam of that Medora trap-door – was, for James Monkton Webb, yet to come (although the time for it was counting down); indeed, for now, for then, as he stood obscured by the governor's shrubbery, all he could think of was his newly revealed life ahead, and how, now, with what he'd recently learned (the news about Custer – like Custer himself – was not a thing easily silenced), the future was calling him as he'd always known someday it would, and with specific direction – *go northward*, it told him as he'd always dreamed it would – northward to the plains and beyond, to the red man and the killing grounds, to the chance of a destiny – a purpose in things – he'd begun to think lost – to a future squandered in the everyday squalor of life.

He stepped back from the window as the governor looked about him. He held his breath, held a beat, sneaked a glance. The governor was staring down at the body and frowning, then nudging it, uneasy, with the toe of his boot. He looked up, his nose streaming blood, at the sharp sound of tapping, at the twist of a handle, the creak of French doors. 'Who's there?' he said, shielding his eyes and squinting into the light. 'Why, it's me, sir,' said a voice that was new to him, and he stepped back in sudden fear as a figure silhouetted against the harsh noon light stepped toward him. 'Who the hell –' he started, though in his heart, in the saying, he knew the question's answer. 'Oh Lord,' he said, half a prayer and half a curse, 'oh Lord, oh Lord,' for he knew in his heart as he heard the hammer click that the long-delayed hour of reckoning was finally upon him and that all those he'd cheated and all those he'd ruined would soon now – in the blink of an eye, in the crack of a bullet speeding forth from a chamber – be standing before him, ready at last with their pitiless judgement and their cool, steely knives.

I t is simply a matter of record (and something that need not detain us here) that the Leap family – a bruised wife and three small damaged children – when they heard of the governor's murder, did precisely and collectively just as their family name suggests they might. In other words, they lept. At first it was shock (indeed, many years later, Mrs Leap – by then Mrs Summerfield, wife of the millionaire designer of the Summerfield cattle-grid – was often heard to say that the news when it came shot through her body like a dose of the new terror electricity) – although such leaping thanks to shock soon gave way – in private at least – to regular sessions of jumping for pure joy at such a sudden and unexpected release.

'Say, what you got there, man?'

But this story is indeed *another* story and – as I say – need not concern us here. What *does* concern us (or should, if you've been paying attention) is the reacquaintance in the poor governor's office of Matthew Princeton and James Monkton Webb, former soldiers of the Union, and how, consequently, from that moment onward, their futures (like their pasts – although one of them hadn't known of such a link, but would soon) would be inextricably linked – a link, indeed, only severed by the blasting of a shotgun and the burial thereafter of a corpse – still warm – in the warm dusty earth.

'Just a body is all – you got a problem with that?'

But that was yet to come. For now, there was just a soldier – a captain of cavalry, no less – and a body slung over his shoulder like something thieved from a slaughterhouse slipping out through a freshly cut hole in the (now late-) governor's fence and into the cowering back-streets of the city.

James adjusted his burden (it was already getting heavy – heavier than he'd expected) and, with a free hand, dipped into his pocket and withdraw a silver coin. This he tossed into the gray rebel cap of the drunk propped up against the fence. He stared down with purpose into the man's rheumy eyes. 'You ain't seen nothin' – right?' he said.

The drunk squinted. 'Right,' he said, half-choking on the word, his whiskey-sozzled mind already forgetting the soldier and his burden as already in his twenty-eight years he'd forgotten so much.

Tell a big enough – bold enough – lie and most (sometimes all) will believe you: it was this theory of existence that had so informed little James Monkton's life – both during his incarceration and later on in Mr Lincoln's army – and one that, now, years on, he discovered applied in some circumstances to the most improbable, the most physical masquerade of all. He discovered, in short, that, in the city of New Orleans in the year of eighteen seventy-five (or perhaps any year, for it's *that* kind of city), if you carry a body (to all appearances a corpse, remember) through the afternoon streets and you carry it with enough gusto – with enough belief that what you are doing is no more remarkable than, say, a hotel porter carrying some fancy lady's calfskin valise – then your boldness will likely be rewarded with invisibility – people seeing, as they do, only, really, what they want to see – people being, as they are, as willfully blind to the awkward, the challenging, as one lover to the faults of another.

Thus it was that James was able, with his living, sleeping burden, to make his way unremarked through the stifling streets to the door of Miss Eliot's whorehouse on the corner of Lafayette and Vine, where, shifting the weight of his burden, he rapped with his free hand on the heavy paneled door. At once (as if the sound of his knuckles on wood had all along been expected, had all along been the unspoken cue for sudden action), a narrow shutter in the door flipped up, revealing a pair of squinting negro eyes.

'Yes?'

James bent at the knee, leveling the eyes with his. 'I have a delivery, ma'am,' he said. He smiled. There was a lightness in his voice now, for he felt suddenly, unaccountably – standing there on the street as he was, his arms full, the hair at the back of his head all mussed-up like that of the little boy he so often felt himself still to be – the humor and absurdity of his – and of all – life.

'What delivery? We ain't expectin' no delivery?'

Indeed it seemed, right then – this life-thing – the most absurd thing in all creation – as pleasurable, certainly, but at the same time as futile as trying to catch and hold moonlight in your hands.

'Ma'am,' he said, 'I'd sure be real grateful if you'd open the door. A man sure can be heavy to hold when he ain't helpin' none.'

The dark negro's eyes scanned the body through the slit, then flicked up, settling on James's pale face.

'Don't I know you?' she said.

'Ma'am?'

'Ain't I seen you someplace?' Then the eyes narrowed, memory returning. 'Oh *sure*,' she said. 'I know you. You's that asshole Yankee soldier got me climbin' them stairs on some chicken-shit errand, ain't you?'

'That's me, ma'am,' said James. He smiled his most accommodating smile.

Josephine shook her head. '*That's me, ma'am*,' she hissed, mimicking. A pause, breathing.

'Ma'am? Is everything alright?'

'Jesus Christ.' The shutter slammed down.

'Ma'am?'

Frowning, James reset his burden and was just raising up his free hand to knock once again, when a key was turned with a clunk in a lock and the door opened inward on a rich purple hall.

He undressed him in the gloom, removing shirt, socks and pants with the sensuous care of a lover. These he folded and placed on a chair. He stood then, unseen, above the pale and low-breathing body, gazing down, rich with the sickness of longing, on that body's gentle rises and falls.

32

When at last he woke, it was to a world turned entirely on its head – to the familiar recognizable but inverted, to a smile become a frown, to the darkness of noon and the thick heat of midnight.

'Welcome back, lieutenant.'

He blinked hard, again. The upturned face lowered, looming, teeth white as stripped bone, breath as delicate as the soft touch of fingertips.

'Can you hear me?'

He let his eyes close.

'Well, can you?'

The voice drifted, faded, was gone.

Silence.

'Lieutenant?'

The sharp crack of rifle-fire, far off but growing nearer, and then the color returns, bleeding in across the land, water-coloring his dreams, unfreezing as it sweeps, animating the past. The past, again, lives; the years like the leaves of a calendar fall away; he is a boy again now, upright but dozing in the coolness of a chapel, caressed into sleeping by the preacher's solemn words.

'Lieutenant?'

Always the river, child, and the smell of the river. And remember, child, there is nowhere the river cannot find you, for it winds through our lives and runs through our blood. It creeps through the earth, bleeding into the roots of the very things we eat; thus it is inside us always, and we cannot escape it. It carried us blind from the source and will carry us in the end all the way to the sea. It is life, child. It is death. We are nothing.

Not in so long have the voices come – not for years the blackness of the chapel, the cool of Cooper's Creek running spinning like silver through his stick-like spider's legs: none of it, not for years – not the horses restless on the eve of battle, not the orchard in summer filled with peaches . . .

He stirs in his dreams at a sound.

A shriek.

In his dreams, his eyes open. Sweating hard, he raises a hand to his face. His hand is bloody: jagged bone, twisted sinew. The blood is rising red through his shirt like ink through a blotter; he watches, distant, fascinated, as his life drains away, until soon he is spinning, turning slow on the surface of the clear cooling creek, then sitting once again with his brothers on a hard chapel pew.

Always the river, child, and the smell of the river.

The wheezing then of the chapel's ancient organ and his brothers rise as one and he rises; they sing and he turns to watch them sing – to touch them – but there is nothing now to touch but that which is absent, for his brothers already are spirits, their lives already lost though they are breathing still, their paths already set, their steps already counted to that bloody sunken road.

'Lieutenant?'

From far off – way off – the call of a bugle; between his thighs the heavy nervous sweating of a horse.

'Can you hear me?'

He turns; beside him, horse and rider – *Captain Webb at your service, sir* – and fifty others are facing down the skeleton trees and beyond them that slow-running creek, the general, his yellow locks curling in a dance about his shoulders, shielding his eyes from the sun as he watches – as they all watch – men die. *Steady, boys* goes the call and all for a moment – for the longest ever moment – is steady – a moment long enough for the longest of last prayers, long enough for the voices of the long dead to rise, for the fleeting return of a mother's still longed-for caress or her call to supper across dusk-heavy fields – long enough for a life to be led, reviewed and found wanting, for the future – now so precious – to be that life's only saving; and long enough, in the end (for it is the end for many, and the many know, so otherwise, unaccountably, do they feel, in that moment, the cool hand of peace), for the rising and sudden falling of the general's shining sabre to last (or so it seems) the whole length of a second life, and then –

Go, Wolverines!

– and all suddenly is pounding, heavy hooves and wild hearts until at its height, at the blasting of muskets and the clashing of steel on steel, all sound drops away but the pounding of blood and once again there's the chapel and there's sun streaming in through the windows, and the voice of the preacher droning on and on, lazy in the heat, until a sharp spear of pain breaks the spell and there's blood all red and pumping and his brothers again, their heads thrown back and throats exposed, singing and singing but all the time silent and staring like corpses –

'Hey, lieutenant. It's me, sir. It's the captain –'

Oh yes, the past lives, in dreams and in daylight, and in daylight and in dreams it is always victorious, the past, always swirling over us as we fight to breathe, always holding us close, always drawing us down and down.

Eddie

33

'**Y**ou're late, Mr Reno – *again*.'

'Late?' He looked down at his watch. His watch was absent. 'It's nearly *noon*, for God's sake –'

'Noon?'

Always the river and the smell of the river.

Sneering, Mr Frampton shook his head. Eddie looked up, his mind still half-lost in the journal. It was true: the sun was already high in the sky, the mall's parking-lot already filling up with Labor Day shoppers.

'Well?'

It is life, child. It is death.

'Mr Reno? Are you listening to me?'

Outside Dunkin' Donuts, a woman in a grubby beige coat was scolding a scrawny child, grasping him by the shoulders with one hand and slapping his backside with the other. The child, once struck, stood silent for a moment as if disbelieving the evidence of his senses, then suddenly a great wailing cry filled the air.

'Mr Reno?'

Eddie turned back to Mr Frampton. Mr Frampton's narrow face was in shadow, though pale nonetheless – as pale as if the blood that ran through his veins was neither red nor thick like his own, but thin, like water – as thin as the blood he'd heard described many times during Blood Week on *Doctor Mel's Cable Surgery*. 'I'm sorry,' he said. He squinted hard, tried to concentrate.

'You're *sorry*? Is that it?'

But it was no good. In the hour or so since he'd closed it, for some reason all he'd been able to think of was the book. Sitting at the lights outside Taco Express, then gridlocked on the bridge, though he'd tried to dismiss it, tried instead to figure what on earth he would say to Mr Frampton, his mind had been filled with nothing but the image of an old-time preacher in his pulpit, and a tiny southern church, and the nation, a hundred years ago and more, on the very brink of civil war.

Mr Frampton set his hands on his hips and shook his head. 'Mr Reno,' he said with an oh-so-weary sigh, 'I told you – did I not? – what would happen if you failed in the future to mend your ways with regard to your time-keeping? Well, let me tell you, sir, I did. Indeed, sir, I recall being somewhat explicit as to the consequences of any such failure.' He paused, looked away for a second, out across the parking-lot, then back. 'Tell me,' he said. 'Mr *Reno*.' He smiled his most practiced, most patronizing smile. 'What *exactly* is your problem?'

'Problem?' said Eddie.

Another pause, another smile. 'I mean,' said Mr Frampton, 'forgive me, but, well, I'm wondering right now how it's possible for a man such as yourself to have lived for so long and yet still be so stupid.' He shrugged, shook his head as if such a bizarre conundrum had him completely foxed. 'I mean, maybe it's me, but, frankly, I just don't understand.' He thrust his head forward, menacing. 'I mean,' he said, pulling his lips back in a taunting, weasel sneer, 'perhaps you could help me, Mr Reno. Perhaps you could give me some *direction* on this matter –'

Eddie said nothing – there was nothing in his head but the diary and its violence.

'Well, in that case, sir, let *me* give *you* some direction. Namely, sir, I'd be obliged if you'd follow me outside –'

'Outside?' said Eddie.

'Where, from then on, wherever you go is not my concern. Do you understand? Mr Reno?' Mr Frampton frowned. 'I said, Mr Reno, do you understand?'

34

'What did you say?'
'I think I broke it.'
'Broke what?'
'His nose.'
'His *nose*? Whose nose?'
'Or maybe I killed him. Jesus Christ, Irene. Maybe he's dead –'
'*Dead? Who's dead?*'
'I mean, he did land awful hard –'

Unseen in back of the K-Mart's deli counter, Irene Bonikowski closed her weary eyes. 'Look,' she said, 'for God's sake, Eddie, will you just calm down?'

A pause, breathing.

'Okay.'

'Good. Now just tell me where you are, alright?'

'I'm in a phone-booth.'

'Okay. Good. Now where exactly?'

'Outside.'

'Outside? What do you mean, outside?'

'In the parking-lot.'

'The parking-lot? You mean here – right here?' She crossed the deli store-room and peered out of the window. People were milling about, running this way and that. One hand still clutching the phone, she cupped the other to the glass, squinting out. 'Jesus Christ, Eddie, what the hell's going on?' Then a wailing sound turned her head. 'Is that an ambulance? Can I hear an ambulance?'

It was an ambulance alright – and not before time. It screeched across the parking-lot between rows of parked cars, sirens whooping, lights flashing, coming at last to a halt outside the K-Mart's main entrance.

'Irene?'

'Jesus Christ, Eddie. What the hell did you do?'

A pause.

'Eddie?'

The doors of the ambulance opened out, pushing back the crowd. A pair of orange-suited paramedics forced their way through, dropped to their knees either side of a body lying still on the ground.

'Oh God, I don't know,' said Eddie.

'You don't *know*?' Irene squinted harder, trying to see. The figure – a man – had his face obscured. The back of his head was glistening, his hair wild and matted.

'Irene? Are you there?'

Carefully then, one of the paramedics turned the body's head, revealing its bloody features. Irene gasped. The gasp traveled swiftly down the line.

'Irene? What is it?'

'Oh Jesus, Eddie –'

The body's nose was twisted, the eyes closed tight.

'Irene?'

'Mr Frampton?' she said, for a moment disbelieving the evidence of her eyes. 'You *killed* Mr Frampton?'

In the phone-booth across the parking-lot, Eddie Reno felt his heart skip a beat. 'Dead? He's dead? Oh my Lord!' Suddenly, then, all the strength seemed to drain from his body, loosening his bowels and the grip of his fingers on the phone. The phone clattered against the side of the booth and swung free. He stood a while then, staring blindly at the phone-booth's polished chrome. His heart suddenly was thumping, the blood pounding loud in his ears.

Later he wouldn't remember how, but somehow he found himself moving as if in a dream between the endless rows of cars, unaware of the slap of his soles on the hard concrete ground. *You killed Mr Frampton*. He paused in the shade of a beige RV. His chest was heaving, his head spinning with the words. He raised his palms to the sides of his head and tried to think – tried to remember exactly what had happened, but it was all some kind of a blank. One minute he'd been standing there in the noonday sun, watching Mr Frampton's narrow lips opening and closing like some newly beached fish, then the next . . . well, the next, here he was, a killer clutching his head in the shade of an old beat-up trailer, his ears full of ringing and his pants full of well, Jesus, one hell of a mess –

'Hey, mister.'

He raised his head. His head was level with the RV's rear window, his eyes with those beyond the glass of a small freckle-faced boy.

'What do *you* want?' he said.

The boy gave a sharp nonchalant shrug. His cherub's face was resting in his hands, his hair slicked down, a red and white striped bow-tie set large and level beneath his chin. His eyes were the clearest blue, their candor quite shaming. Eddie looked away.

'Hey *mister* –'

Far off, way beyond the parking-lot and the highway, the clear warm waters of the Gulf were rippling smugly in the sunshine. *You killed Mr Frampton.* He looked back. It seemed amazing in that moment that the world was still turning just as it always had, and that people – despite what had happened, despite what he'd done – could still be lying quite happily on a beach, every one of them quite oblivious to such a terrible dark deed – that they could still be reading the same paperbacks they'd been reading yesterday, still be licking ice-creams as they'd done yesterday, still be worrying themselves as before about the sun's harmful rays, when all the time, less than a mile away, a man had been murdered, and he – the murderer – was suddenly on the loose, suddenly at large.

The boy clicked a catch and slid the window aside. From out of sight, he reached down and fetched up a large glass jar. This he held out unsteadily, his fingers gripping hard, his hand shaking with the weight. 'You want a M&M, mister?' he said.

It is life, child. It is death.

Eddie stared at the jar. The boy shook it, rattling the bright-colored candy within. 'Well?' he said. '*Do* you, mister?' Dream-like, Eddie raised up his hand, watched it feed itself into the jar. His fingers found the cold, hard candy.

It is life, child. It is death. We are nothing.

And what was amazing also (*is* amazing, for surely we all feel it) was (and is) the touch like the touch of hands reaching out across years, the finger-tip tracing of other lives upon ours – lives long finished and distant – a vague sense of the curious synchronicity of things – the unsuspected echo in *this* present of *that* past – that sense of connection with what has gone before that makes some turn in confusion to God for explanation, while others turn away to look within themselves for clues. For most of us, either direction is fruitless and any connection with the past (if such it is) dies with its birth and so never lives to tell us its secrets of what lies ahead; for others, though – those lost, those falling, those like Eddie whose grip on life circumstances have loosened – that voice is stronger, that voice is alive – *was* alive that day and would continue to live, until a moment on a hillside overlooking a river when fear of losing the very last of his life would excite his grip, and the siren voices abandon him and drift away, searching for another soul to haunt.

'Hey, mister – you sick or something?'

It is life, child. It is death.

For now, though, that voice was just waking (it was the voice of a preacher for now, but there would be others) – its face like the face of some cold, golden watch just beginning its mesmerizing arc, just testing its subject, just measuring his hearing like a doctor with a tuning fork, just sizing him up, just waiting, just watching.

' 'Cause you sure *looks* sick –'

Eddie blinked hard, shook his head. 'I ain't sick,' he said, 'just a little –'
He paused, trying to figure out just exactly *how* he felt, just exactly
what it was that was wrong with him. Then a smell from below rose to
meet him, reminding him.

'Mister?'

Oh Lord, I shit my pants.

'You ain't gonna *c*ollapse – are you?'

I'm a murderer and I shit my pants. He tried to straighten up. His
undershorts squelched. 'I guess I had an accident,' he said.

The boy shrugged. ' "Accident's gonna happen," my daddy says.
Ain't nothing a person can do about it.' He withdrew the glass jar, put it
back where he'd found it. Again, he sat up, set his elbows on the back
shelf and his chin in his hands.

'Well, I guess your daddy's right,' said Eddie.

The boy nodded. His daddy, he said, was a Christian.

'What?'

Always the river and the smell of the river.

'Uh-huh.' Then he sighed, seeming suddenly weary and so much older
than his years. 'Yes, sir, he *sure* do believe in Our Lord Jesus Christ, my
daddy. Says he's coming for sure. Says he'll be here in time for
Superbowl Fifty –' Another sigh. 'Of course, Mama thinks he's crazy
– says he thinks more of Jesus than he does of her. Say, mister – what
you planning on doing anyway?'

'Doing?' said Eddie.

'About your accident.'

He looked down. The dark stain was spreading, the smell growing
ever more pungent. He looked up. The little boy, like the little boy who
sometimes appeared in his dreams, was gone. But then, in a minute,
unlike the little dream-boy, he returned, carrying now a pressed and
neatly folded pair of gray-colored slacks. These he held out through the
window as before he'd held out the glass jar.

'What's this?' said Eddie.

'My daddy's pants,' said the boy.

'What?'

'Well,' he said, 'my daddy says a man don't need what he don't need,
and I don't reckon he needs no six pairs of pants.' He shook them.
'Don't you want them, mister?'

Eddie held out his hands. 'Are you sure?' he said. 'Won't your daddy
mind?'

The boy shook his head. 'I don't reckon,' he said. 'Why, only last
night he was saying we should all of us be practicing what he's
preaching –'

'You mean he's a preacher, your daddy?'

The boy shrugged. 'Sort of.'

'Sort of?'

'Well, he don't do no *regular* preaching –'

'You mean like in a church?'

'No, sir,' said the boy. 'He don't never preach in no church no more. He says preaching in church is like pissing in a men's room – it ain't gonna fertilize no lemon trees.'

'So where *does* he preach then?'

The boy stuck out his hand, pointing over Eddie's shoulder. Eddie turned. All there was was cars and more cars and bustling crowds and, beyond them all, the mall.

'In the mall?' said Eddie. 'Your daddy preaches in the mall?'

'Dunkin' Donuts,' said the boy. 'My daddy's got a contract with God. Says God directed him in a dream to preach the evil of donuts. Says the donut is the Devil's instrument.'

'*Donuts?*' said Eddie and he turned back just in time to see the boy slide the window closed, hear the click of its catch. The boy raised his hand in a strangely pious-looking wave before disappearing into the RV's gloom and shadows.

Well.

Eddie stood a moment, looking out across the parking-lot to the highway and the ocean, aware as he did so that something had changed – something had shifted – in the world. Oh sure; the ocean was still sparkling in the sunshine as ever it did, and the sky, as ever, was blue – but there was something else, something more, something different now. But what? He squinted hard, tried to make it out, tried to see in the faces of those passing by what exactly it was – or at least find there some acknowledgement that they saw it too. But there was nothing in their looks – just laughing, just talk. He turned away, and it was then – in that moment of turning – that it came to him what it was. The difference was simply that now he was alone – *really* alone – and not just in his mind. The difference was that now, for the first time, he was a fugitive from others and not just from himself. The difference was that now, for the first time, he was really on the run.

35

W ell, of course he couldn't go home – not now, and probably
never. (God knows he'd seen enough *Rockford Files* and
Streets of San Francisco to know home was the *first* place
they'd look.)

Okay then.

He tried to think.

Where *could* he go?

He looked down at the gray-colored slacks, searching in their folds
for some kind of a plan, but no kind of a plan would come. All that
would come was an uneasy shifting in his stomach and a cool whispered
voice in his ear.

On the run, on the run, Eddie Reno's on the run.

The whooping of a siren raised his head. Far off, way out across the
sea of glinting cars, an ambulance was making its way through the
drifting crowds, every now and then slowing to a stop, then moving off
again. Eddie squinted, watching. The ambulance turned left beneath the
parking-lot's arch, headed out at last into the traffic on the highway. He
followed its progress as best he could until it was gone.

He closed his eyes, again tried to think. Again, nothing. Jesus Christ.
All he could think was, *How on earth have I gotten to this? How on
earth did I come to be standing here in the sunshine in some Florida
parking-lot with blood on my hands and shit in my pants?* Jesus Christ.
God knows it was a mystery – and surely not a part of *his* life.

He opened his eyes just to check.

Oh, it was *his* life alright.

He raised a hand, pressed his palm against his forehead. A plan, a
plan, he must have a plan.

He lowered his hand.

Okay then.

But what?

He turned then at the sharp sound of laughter, feeling as he did so a
squelching down below.

Okay.

Stay calm.
Stay calm.
Breathe slow.
First he had to get out of these pants.

Thank God the men's room on level two was empty. He shuffled into a stall, bolted the door and dropped his pants. Oh Lord. The stink was extreme. Screwing up his nose and trying not to breathe, he slowly, reluctantly, set to work.

It wouldn't come to him of course until way, way later, but the upside of all this – the positive charge to all this negative – was there all the time with him in that stall, and working hard. And it was? Well, that carelessness, of course, that liberation, that can live only when all that's been hoped for has finally, irrevocably died – that peace that can breathe only in the rarefied atmosphere of the absence of hope . . . Yes, it was all there, all the time – all that is necessary for a man to sustain himself – there, but for the moment (and for a long while to come) invisible. For now, for then, there was just him, moments later, standing alone in that men's room, squinting at himself squinting back in the mirror, a sleepwalker's look of disengagement in his eyes.

On the run.

He screwed up his eyes so tight it hurt, and was met in that moment of darkness with the sad smiling face of the only woman he'd ever really loved. She had her head cocked to one side, her dark eyes studying his own for clues. *But I thought you'd be happy*, she was saying, *I thought it's what you wanted*.

He opened his eyes. The bright lights flared. He felt himself suddenly unsteady. He leaned forward, gripped the edge of the sink. From somewhere, through a wall, a baby started crying.

She'd chosen to tell him as he'd sat on the verandah that morning all those years ago polishing his lenses and preparing his film for the day's work ahead. Crossing barefoot from the screen door and letting it bang behind her (she always let it bang, said it pissed off the bugs trying to sleep in the trees), she'd stood behind him, looking down, watching him, watching his breath cloud the tiny hidden mirrors and thick-coated lenses, and then suddenly (as if she'd just thought of it) she'd said there was news. 'News?' he'd said, not looking up, and then she'd told him: a boy, she was certain.

The men's-room door hissed open; a fat, sweating man in a stained linen suit stepped in and said *Howdee*, already unzipping his pants as he heaved his unwilling bulk toward the urinals. Eddie pushed himself up, reached down to the cold fawcet, splashed his face.

A boy, I'm certain.

He crossed the room, pulled down the towel and buried his face.

We'll call him Edward, I thought, after you.

'Say, you okay there?'

He lifted his head. The fat, sweating man was standing beside him, his face shadowed by concern.

Eddie nodded.

'You sure now?'

'Sure,' he said. Trying a smile, he lowered his hands from their grip on the towel and made his way unsteady across the room. A hand reached out, found the door's cool metal handle. He pulled, stepped out, felt the whooshing of air on his face. In a moment, then, he was walking, moving this way and that, just drifting here and there with the crowds.

How come, a while later (how much later he couldn't have said, as his time then was dream-time and recognized the tyranny of no clock), he found himself standing in line at a newsstand he had no idea: he'd just been walking – been carried along – and now here he was.

He shuffled forward, caught himself looking a young boy in the eye. The boy had orange hair and was scowling. 'Well?' he said.

'Eh?' said Eddie.

'Jesus,' said the boy.

Flustered, Eddie looked down, picked up the nearest magazine.

'Six twenty-five,' said the boy.

Eddie reached into the pocket of his pants. The feel of the pockets was unfamiliar, tighter. He felt for some change. Nothing. All there was, in the right-hand pocket, was what felt like a small piece of card. This he pulled out, held up to the light.

'Hey, you payin' for that or what?' said the orange-haired boy.

The card, in plain black letters on white, read simply:

Ms CLARE VOYANT
225 Hope St
Lives Transformed
Amex/Visa/Diners

The boy leaned forward. His breath was rich with the stink of mustard. 'Hey, I said six twenty-five, mister,' he said.

Eddie looked up.

'And sometime today, okay?'

Then down again at the card. *Lives Transformed.* He swallowed hard. His mouth was dry. *Ms Clare Voyant.* In his mind's eye, then, he saw her face again – that cocked head, those dark, unhappy eyes – felt again, beneath the hesitant touch of his hand, the shallow rising of a belly filled with promise, with hope, with life.

36

That day, those hours, that moment on the verandah, so long ago now – days, hours, a moment, surely, from another's life. So long ago now, and so lost – the truth of it – in the cruel distortion of a lifetime's echoes; as foreign, now, as words whispered low in the indecipherable language of dreams.

A dream, now: yes, that was it, and he stood in the parking-lot, in the sun once again, and, once again, he dreamed it.

The creak of wicker; the soft slap-slap of her bare soles on the wooden verandah; the sweet scent of jasmine in the air.

He half-turns, meaning by it that he knows she is there and that he loves her. She breathes, so quiet, drifts her fingers – just the tips, mind – through the hair above his collar, then down across the cotton on his back. Unseen, he closes his eyes. Far off (or so close he feels he can feel the beating of its heart), a dog barks, is silent. Just the silence, then, with its intricate, calming web of delight, then –

Honey, I've got some news. Special news.

He draws a breath, feels the creeping of the heavy, moist air as it fills his lungs. *News?* he says.

Yes, she says. *A boy*, she says. *I'm certain of it*, she says.

He opens his mouth to speak – to say *something* – and sure enough the breath rises through his throat, but no words come, and it spends itself, useless, floating out and away.

Then it's later that same day, and he's standing on an outside iron staircase, half up and half down, squinting through his camera at his subjects sitting lazy round a pool.

Hey, Papa, says one, *ain't you got no tequila?*

Click.

A moment preserved, as the great man turns his head, smiling gruff, already in that moment looking out from the covers of a million magazines.

We'll call him Edward, I thought, after you.

He squints harder – then click, and again, as he tries to crop, to unremember, what he said.

Which was?

Well, nothing, of course – just silence – just words gagged by sudden panic, then there's the squeak of his own rubber soles on the polished verandah, then the banging of a screen door left to swing, then the quick-down-the-steps-and-not-looking-back, then the turning of a corner, then the stepping breathless and heaving into shadows.

'Eddie?'

And then?

Then he's standing on that staircase, squinting down at that pool, his youth, his promise, draining sharply, suddenly away in the face of this new unasked-for burden.

'Eddie Reno? Is that *you*?'

A punch, light, on his arm then, and he turned his head in the sunshine, turning away as he did so (for the moment at least) from the deep-shadowed memories of that day.

He stared hard, taking in the man's features, trying to place them somewhere in his life.

'Say – don't tell me you don't remember!'

'Well –' he said, and in that moment of speaking it came to him.

'It's Davie, Eddie! Davie Cohn!'

And so, unseen within his chest, his weary heart sank.

Davie Cohn, long-ago K-Mart employee, men's fashions, reached out a hand, slapped Eddie on the shoulder. Eddie winced. Davie Cohn, he recalled, had been famous for his slapping – indeed, infamous – his slapping – when applied once to Mrs Curle in bedding – having led to his dismissal and a suit for assault heard finally (and successfully) in St Petersburg.

'Look, I'm sorry –' said Eddie, stepping back.

'Sorry?' Davie Cohn stepped forward, glancing this way and that; then, dropping his voice as if he feared being overheard, he said those words for which, in the end – along with his slapping – he'd been famous, and for which, in the end – along with his grossly inappropriate behavior (slapping of course) in a Florida courtroom – he'd been sent to the state penitentiary for a period not exceeding two years.

'I have to go,' said Eddie, turning away.

'Go?'

And then he was walking, moving hard, unseeing, through the lines of shining cars, then running, his old-man's chest heaving, along past the men's room and the First National Bank, then out through the parking-lot's great gleaming arch.

37

He ran, that day, until he thought he would surely die, then he ran some more. He ran out past the Dairy Queen and Marky Mark's Muffler Shop, then over the scrub where once, years ago now, the Coronet Drive-In had stood, and where, once, he and a girl whose name was long gone now had kissed in the back seat of his father's Studebaker. He ran on and on, turning this way and that and looking over his shoulder like the hero pursued in some movie, quitting only when his knees buckled under him and he stumbled, tumbling to the hard ground, where he lay, face-down, gasping, his heart thumping, his eyes closed and waiting for the blow from behind that any minute would surely come. Reaching up, he covered his head. He clenched his raging muscles and waited.

And waited.

Nothing.

He waited some more.

Still nothing. Just the pumping of his blood, just the smarting of his cheek on the cold, biting ground.

A sound, far off – a siren, fading – then silence.

Slowly, easing onto his back, he opened his eyes.

At first there was nothing to see in the gloom. Then, like figures emerging from some dense, dark mist, he made out the shape of some trash-cans by a wall, then the bars on a window, then the great hulking carcass of a car with no wheels. Turning his head and looking straight up, he found the sky was still blue, although it seemed a million miles away now – just a narrow lighted strip caught between the blackness of the alley's rising buildings. He tried to sit up, but a sharp, searing pain in his head forced him back. He closed his eyes, tried to think where he was – tried to think *who* he was – but nothing would come – nothing but pain and confusion. *It is life, child. It is death*, whispered a voice in his ear, and a shiver moved over him like the fingers of a ghost. *It is life, child. It is death. We are nothing.* For all he knew, he *could* have been dead; for all he knew, this alley, this darkness, those trash-cans, that window, those bars, might simply have been what all along had been waiting for him – all that for so long now he'd known he deserved.

But then something alive scuttled over his ankle, and he knew in that moment he was not dead, but living – that, while God was in His heaven (or in hell, or in between), he – Eddie Reno – was still here on earth, still breathing, still cursed with the blessing of life and memory, still able to fear, to feel pain and to lie, still able to struggle, to rise and to fall.

He lay still another moment, then again pushed up. This time, resting on his elbows, he looked around.

The alley was dark and unknown to him. For sure, in all of his years, in all of his lonely wanderings as a child with his old-man's magic show – before his camera had taken him way across country – he'd never once, he knew, been this way – never even known it was here, and so close to all he *had* known – just a stone's throw, indeed, from the drive-in and his Uncle Nate's electrical store – so close, in fact, that it seemed impossible now that he *hadn't* ever seen it – but he hadn't. He twisted, straining, looked back the other way. There was nothing to see – just the alley going on and on and disappearing in the end into shadows. He closed his eyes, tried to think – tried to figure what to do – but his thoughts wouldn't stick – everytime they just seemed to slip away, leaving him breathless and grasping. A breeze touched his face like fingers. *On the run*, said a voice, *Eddie Reno's on the run*. He opened his eyes. *Oh my God*, he thought, *oh my God*.

It was an effort, but somehow – half-rolling – he managed to get to his feet. Unseen then by a soul, he stood stooped and swaying, looking this way and that, his actions like those of an actor illustrating uncertainty for the benefit of an audience. In the end, heavy-limbed like a man underwater, and careless of the tears in the knees of the donut-man's gray-colored pants, he just started walking, his arms hanging down by his side, just raising his scuffed shoes as high as was necessary, and no more.

It was a strange thing, but when, moments later, Eddie's eye caught the street-name – Hope Street – at the end of the alley, it came to him somehow as really no surprise. In fact, it was almost as if something inside of him had been expecting it. Anyway, he just stood there looking up at the words – at the letters high up on the pole that were scarcely visible beneath the grime, aware as he did so of some vague sense of things shifting, breaking down and reassembling – of some strange kind of alchemy in the air.

38

Ms Clare Voyant, retiring vice-president, no less, of the Florida Collective of Professional Soothsayers, had (as you'd expect) been expecting him. Indeed, she'd been standing behind her door awaiting his arrival for nigh on an hour now, and, consequently, she was not at all pleased. In fact, truth to tell, she was angry – being kept waiting always made her angry, reflecting as it did not only the casualness with which others regarded the value of her time, but also the (these days) creeping inaccuracy of her own predictions. Indeed, only yesterday, she'd gotten so mad (having predicted to perfection the winner of the three forty-five at the Jacksonville Raceway, but not, alas, until four-fifteen) that she'd hurled her entire collection of *Weird But True Magazine* clean across the room, out through the open window and into the alley, where, still, this afternoon, it lay scattered at Eddie's feet as he studied his card and squinted at the number on the door.

Reaching up a hand, he tapped lightly.

The door opened inward at once, revealing a small lobby of spectacular gloom.

'Yes?' said a voice.

'Miss Voyant?'

'*Ms*,' said the voice. 'Can't you *read*?'

'Sorry,' said Eddie.

From within came a tiny hiss and click, then the glowing orange eye of a lighted cigarette.

'Look,' said Eddie, 'maybe I should go –'

The cigarette flared. 'Go? Where you gonna go?'

He frowned. 'What do you mean?' He was squinting, trying to make out a face through the darkness and the smoke.

'What I *mean*, Sonny-Jim, is where *you* gonna go where *they* ain't gonna find you? *That's* what I *mean*.'

Eddie felt himself flush. He swallowed hard. His mouth was dry. 'But how –' he started.

'How what?' said the voice. It was full of mocking. 'How do I know? How do you *think*?'

'I don't know,' said Eddie.

At which point, Ms Clare Esther Voyant, sixty-six years old and counting, stepped out of the shadows, so revealing herself in all her bizarreness. Eddie gasped. 'What is it?' she said. She looked down, considering herself with evident pride. 'Have you never seen a woman in track-pants before?'

But it wasn't the track-pants that had made Eddie gasp – and she knew it. No, sir. What it was – what it *always* was – was the three brightly colored South American macaws she had perched upon her person – one on either shoulder and one sitting square on the top of her head.

'Jesus Christ,' said Eddie.

'And Mary and Joseph,' said Ms Voyant.

'Eh?'

'Jesus, Mary and Joseph,' she said, touching the breast of each bird in turn with the tips of her fingers, like a priest making his devotions before an altar. Then she flicked her eyes left, then right, then up toward the top of her head. 'There now,' she said, smiling. 'Say hello to Mr Reno, will you, fellas?'

It turned out of course that the birds weren't real; or, rather, that they were *real* alright, they just weren't *alive* – hadn't been, in fact, in over a year now – ever since the unfortunate incident with Sheriff Baker and that cattle-prod on the bridge.

'Now then, first things first.'

It was an incident Ms Voyant had tried to forget (as, indeed, had Sheriff Baker's widow Valene), but without success, for not even the comforting attentions of Mr Chope, the county's finest taxidermist, had been able to banish from her daydreams those terrible screams or the looks of disbelief on the faces of passers-by.

'Mr Reno?'

'Pardon?' said Eddie.

'I *said* first things first.'

However hard he tried, he couldn't take his eyes off the birds: they'd seemed like they'd been watching him all the way up the narrow stairs, and now, in this richly, absurdly cluttered room illuminated only by the dim light of candles, they seemed to be watching him still – and with a distinct malevolence of eye.

Ms Voyant gave a dry and theatrical cough. 'Mr Reno?' she said.

Eddie blinked. The eyes of the top bird (was it Mary or Joseph – or even Jesus? He couldn't remember) seemed to blink right back at him, winking knowingly.

'I was *saying*, Mr Reno, that first things must come first.'

A finger poked his ribcage. Reluctantly, he slid his eyes down, settled them a moment on Ms Voyant's outstretched palm.

'Well?' she said.

Eddie frowned. Even staring at the woman's fingers – even *counting* them, then again, for distraction – he could still feel the birds' eyes upon him, still feel them black and burning into him, still feel their leering gaze as they picked their way slowly and with an undertaker's infinite care across the barren broken landscape of his life, across the debris of his botched and irredeemable past.

'Mr Reno?'

'I'm sorry?' he said. 'What is it?'

A weary sigh, a curl of the fingers. 'It's one hundred dollars the hour, Mr Reno – *that's* what it is. Okay?'

'What?'

'Cash up front, if you please. No personal checks. No credit. No bartering except by prior arrangement.'

'*How* much?'

Ms Voyant frowned. 'Of course,' she said, 'if you have no *interest* in what is to come –'

'Oh but I do!' said Eddie. 'I *do*!' He reached inside his jacket, tugged out his wallet.

'I mean, Mr Reno, if a mere few dollars is too much to ask for a *genuine* glimpse of the future –'

'No, no, please –' Then he was pulling, fumbling – all thumbs – at his money, then watching it tumble beyond his grasp to the floor. 'Oh Lord,' he said, stooping, kneeling, scooping up all he could find in the gloom, 'oh Lord, oh Lord, oh Lord –'

39

'Seventeen dollars? *Seventeen* dollars? Are you *serious*?'

It was all he had (at least, all he could find in the gloom) – that and a ticket-stub for *Alien: Resurrection* from the SpaceCity multiplex in the mall.

Ms Voyant shook her head, causing as she did so her ghastly stuffed trinity to bounce drunkenly this way and that. '*Really*, Mr Reno,' she said. She sighed. There was a weariness suddenly in her look, in the curving slope of her shoulders. 'Tell me,' she said, 'do you think I spent seven whole years studying nights with the Great Albertini just so as you could come here and insult me with your seventeen dollars?' She stepped closer, her eyes as black in the gloom as the eyes of her birds. 'Well, do you?' she said.

Eddie shook his head. He looked down. He felt weary too – worn out from running, from thinking, from struggling to be.

'Mr Reno?'

And all he wanted to do right now was just lie down and sleep – just drift on and on, unknowing, unfeeling, uncaring. He let his eyes close.

'Jesus H Christ, I'm *talking* to you here –'

In his mind's eye, suddenly, he was wide awake and staring, sitting again, in that moment, in the counterfeit dark of some afternoon movie-theater, his eyes looking into *her* eyes (they were so huge, way up on the screen, and dark – as dark and sparkling as the darkest and starriest of nights in the Keys), his heart thumping so hard it seemed certain any second it would burst.

'Well? Have you nothing to say?'

Another poke in the ribs then and he opened his eyes. The image flicked away.

'I'm sorry,' he said. He looked down at the money. 'It's all I have.'

You're not human. You're just a construct.

Ms Voyant screwed up her face. 'You mean like in the *world*? Are you telling me you don't have like some kind of savings?'

'Savings?' said Eddie.

'Yeah, savings. Look, aren't you listening to me?'

You're just a construct. You're not human. It had been then, sitting in that movie-theater, that the quite amazing resemblance had really struck him (there'd been something in the way she'd said the words – something, too, in the way she'd turned her head) – struck him so hard, in fact, that, for a moment, sitting in that movie-theater, he'd thought it *was* her – that somehow she'd not died in those treacherous waters off the bridge after all – that somehow, against all the odds, she'd survived and made it to the bank, and then, somehow (God knows how) all the way across the country to California and the movies, where she'd changed her name (for which he couldn't blame her – he'd have changed his too if he'd thought it would have done any good) – in fact, changed her whole life, and all because of *him*, all to get away from *him* and his foolishness and his lies.

'Well, don't you?'

'What?'

Another sigh. 'Have any *savings* –'

But then, of course, the lights had come up in the theater, showing up his sad fantasy for what it was.

He shrugged. 'I guess,' he said.

'You *guess*? Don't you *know*?'

And then, that day, walking back to his car, he'd felt so alone (not only a son gone – walked away – but a wife, too, and drowned, for God's sake, *drowned*) – so alone that, sitting behind the wheel, he'd tried to think what it is people do – that thing they do with a length of rubber tubing and an engine left running – but nothing would come and in the end he'd just given it up as yet another failure – just another thing never done and not even attempted.

'Would that be like in a bank?'

He squinted at the woman's moving lips.

'A bank, yes,' he said.

And then, that night, sweating in bed, he'd had the first of a whole series of scary dreams – dreams of running but getting nowhere, of being chased through the bowels of some dark and dripping space-ship by something terrible he could never see but knew was there – dreams that had only, in the end, ceased when other dreams had risen up and overtaken them – vanquishing dreams whose power had come from their not really being dreams at all, but memories, the truth of which could only have been recollected in the second-hand safety of sleep – memories of a day so distant as to seem like a day from another's life, whilst being, at the same time, distant enough to gain now a clarity in his vision – memories of words that, once uttered, were forever irretrievable, then of driving like a maniac but arriving too late – always too late – then of standing, helpless, looking down, searching the water for any sign of life, whilst knowing with a certainty of heart that all life was extinguished – never, in this life, to return.

'Jesus,' said Ms Voyant. 'Are you sure you're a resident of this planet?'

'Planet?' said Eddie.

'Planet earth.'

'What?'

She snorted. 'Oh, just forget it.'

'Forget it?' He frowned. 'But I was hoping, I was counting on –' He stopped abruptly at the raising of a hand.

Ms Voyant sighed. She looked away a moment, then back. 'Oh Lordy,' she said, 'I must be crazy.'

'Crazy? You mean –'

Then she shook her head, as if finding her own actions scarcely credible. 'Okay. Let's just call it a special rate, shall we? One day only.'

'Special rate? How much?'

Another sigh, a brief weary closing of eyes. 'Sixteen-fifty.'

'Sixteen-fifty?'

'Plus fifty cents tax for aliens.' Then she stepped up so close Eddie could feel her warm breath on his chin. 'Do you think you can manage that?' she said. 'Do you think you've got a future worth that?'

40

'I was a *what*?'

They were sitting moments later, the shades drawn, around a circular velvet-draped table, at the center of which, set on a stand of dull ebony, sat a chipped and grubby crystal ball.

'You heard me.'

Eddie yanked back his hand from Ms Voyant's tender grip, drew it up close, squinting hard at his palm. 'You're crazy,' he said, 'I don't see no *horse*.' He looked up.

Ms Voyant leaned forward; she was shaking her head. 'I didn't say *any* horse,' she said. '*You* was a *special* horse. Matter of fact, you was just about the most special horse there's ever been –'

'Jesus Christ,' said Eddie. He looked again at his palm.

'I mean the Kentucky Derby ain't nothing to sneeze at –'

For sure the woman was a fruitcake – even crazier than he'd first thought. Nowhere in the lines that seemed just so random on his palm was there anything even faintly resembling a horse. He looked up. The woman was staring at him – but blindly, like she was maybe in some kind of a trance. 'What is it *now*?' he said. He squirmed in his seat. Her stare was stark and disarming; it was like she could see something telling inside of him – something really unusual – something shocking even to her. He pulled his eyes away, looking hard at the weave of the moth-eaten cloth, tried to think of other things for distraction – of the warm embrace of his Rest-A-Matic armchair, of the life-preserving click of the lock on his door – but his eyes wouldn't stay pulled away; no, as if with a life, a will, of their own, they rose up and once again lost themselves within hers, losing him as they did so his old-man's fevered grip on the blind of the present and tumbling him with the graceful arrowed arc of a diver down into the shallows and deeps of the past.

Matthew & Eddie

41

Matthew woke from a fevered dream of angels to find the hands of an angel upon him. They were cool hands – as cool as the water in some shady summer creek – their touch as gentle as the gentle touch of a lover's words whispered low in the secret darkness of the darkest and most secret night.

'*Matthew?*'

He went to open his eyes, but found they were were already open. He frowned: how long had he been awake? How long had he been dreaming, his eyes opened wide upon the world?

'*It's morning, my darling. You're safe.*'

Safe? He turned his head. His head was as heavy as a boulder. The face – a girl's – before him now was pale – white like the pillars of some rich southern mansion – her lips a muted red, eyes green, hair dark and gathered in, sprung behind traps and straining to escape.

'*Darling? Can you hear me? You've been sick but now you're well. Are you alright, my darling? How do you feel?*'

With an effort so costly it was nearly beyond him, Matthew worked by proxy the muscles in his arm, watched as a distant hand rose, saw its fingers curling, felt the sharp cool of a clasp, felt it give way beneath his touch, then knew in a moment that fearful pleasure a drowning man feels, as the scented locks flowed all about him and over him, covering him, taking him down and down.

The next time he woke it was noon of the following day. He pushed himself up, looked around the room. For a moment, he had the strangest sensation – the feeling that everything in the room – all that was so familiar – had been stolen in his absence and replaced by a complete set of absolute replicas just to fool him. He closed his eyes, opened them, squinted through the gloom. The noon-light was muffled as ever by thick faded drapes, the air, as ever, heavy with breathing and the sour stink of chemicals.

Slowly, he turned his head.

The girl was breathing low beside the bed, leaning forward, her arms folded before her on the covers, cradling her sleeping head. Her hair was back in its clasps. Unseen, Matthew frowned. The smothering touch of her hair on his face: had he just dreamed it? He couldn't remember. He swallowed hard, let his eyes trail their way across her sleeping form. *Clare*, it came to him: this was her name. And then it came to him who she was and who – before his very eyes – she was every day becoming. His eyes drifted down to her belly, to the new and tiny heart beating frantic somewhere in her skirts. *Do you love me?* He swallowed again; his mouth was dry. *Will you love us now that we're two?* He turned away, heard in his ears the deafening rustle of his sheets, his pillow.

It had been in this very bed that the child had been made – the result of an unequal passion that, in one, had devoured all fear of the past, and, in the other, all thought for a while of the future. It had been, then, just a moment, but one which, now, was lengthening every day, reaching out with its tiny slow-forming fingers and grasping at the flesh of his future, pawing him and raking his skin, until mornings these days he'd wake with a jolt to the sharp sound of crying – surely a baby's tears – only to find that the tears were his tears, those cries his cries, and the thumping in his chest not the calm beating heart of a father-to-be, but the panic of a child still lost in the forests of youth.

A knock on the door.

'Lieutenant?'

He opened his eyes. Indeed, these days – these mornings – all he could think of was escape – of running and running and keeping on running until the cries that were his cries were so far behind him and buried so deep that nothing again could ever raise them.

Another knock, harder. The girl stirred but didn't wake.

'Who is it?'

'Lieutenant?'

'I said who is it?'

The brass handle turned, the door easing inward. Matthew pushed himself up. His head was spinning. He squinted at the blue-suited figure, at his bright-polished sword, at the whiteness of his gloves, the blackness of his boots. 'Who are *you*?' he said. 'What do you want?'

At which James Monkton Webb, former captain of cavalry, smiled, then at once dropped that smile in favor of a frown. 'What I want, sir,' he said gravely, 'is you, sir.'

'Me?' said Matthew. 'What do you mean? Who the hell are you?'

'I,' said James, 'am your escort and your guide.' He stepped forward, was pleased by the clip of his boots on the boards. At the bedside, he bent stiffly at the waist, glancing for a second with disfavor at the girl. 'We must leave,' he said softly. 'At once.'

'Leave?' said Matthew. 'What are you talking about?'

'A man, sir, has been killed. And not just a man, sir – but a *governor* –'

'*Killed?* Look, who the hell –'

'And another, sir, is sought for his murder.'

'*Murder?*'

'Murder, sir.' James Monkton Webb drew his face close to Matthew's. ' 'Tis a capital offense.' His face was pale, his eyes quite as pale and as blue as the palest and bluest of winter skies. He smiled. 'Sir?' he said. There was something in his eyes of the stillness of death, a coolness in his breath like the coolness of the grave. 'Are you hearing me, sir? Are you understanding what it is that I'm saying?'

Matthew opened his mouth to speak – to say something – but for a moment nothing would come. All that would come was the sound in his ears of those sharp baby's cries and the touch of those fingers, the drag of those chains.

'Sir,' said James, 'the matter is pressing. We must leave, sir, within the hour.'

'Leave?'

'Or the hangman, sir, will have you.'

Matthew closed his eyes a second. 'Where?' he said.

'North,' said James, smiling, then he said it again, tasting the word and finding it as good as if its sound on his tongue was the very sound of salvation itself.

42

'South? Why south?'

Ms Voyant shrugged. '*I* don't know.'

'What do you mean you don't know?'

'Look,' she said, lifting her eyes from the grubby crystal ball, 'I just read 'em, okay? Don't mean I have to understand 'em. *It* says south, *I* say south. *It* says a goddamn pink tutu, *I* say a goddamn pink tutu.'

'A *what*?' said Eddie.

'Jesus,' said Ms Voyant. Wearily, she sat back, pulled off her opaque green eye-shade. 'Look,' she said. She rubbed her eyes. Her eyes were red and tired from her squinting. 'You asked me to tell you what I see and what I see is you heading south, okay? Why, I do not know – nor, for seventeen dollars, do I care. For all I know you could be heading down there to Mexico or someplace just to rendezvous with your alien brothers, or maybe just 'cause you's fixing to buy yourself one of them little bitty dogs that ain't no bigger than some big ol' rat. Anyways, whatever it is I do not know and I assure you I will not lose no sleep over wondering. Now, do I make myself clear?'

Eddie nodded.

'Well hallelujah,' said Ms Voyant.

'It's just –'

She held up a pale palm, stopping him dead. 'Just *nothing*, Mr Reno.' She leaned forward, tapping her chest with the tip of her finger. 'This sooth, Mr Reno,' she said, 'ain't saying no more – okay?'

'Okay,' said Eddie.

But then she paused, a look of unease settling onto her face. 'Except maybe one thing.'

He looked up.

'Except maybe to mention the fact – and God knows why I'm mentioning this fact 'cause I sure don't owe you nothing – that you ain't exactly gonna be traveling alone.'

'I'm not?' Eddie felt his stomach lurch. 'Well then, who –'

She shrugged. 'I don't know,' she said. 'I didn't exactly see his face. He was carrying a piece, though – I saw *that*.'

'A piece?'

She sighed. 'A firearm, Mr Reno. A shooter.' She frowned. 'Of course he's trying to look like he ain't, but he ain't fooling nobody. No, sir. And you don't need to be no expert to tell it ain't no pea-shooter neither. Say, you alright?'

'A *gun*?' said Eddie, his pulse suddenly racing. 'He's carrying a *gun*?'

' 'Cause you sure is looking real pale.'

Suddenly, he could feel his insides shaking – wobbling this way and that like some big old plate of jello.

'Of course, I guess I could be wrong –'

'*Wrong*? What do you mean, *wrong*?'

Ms Voyant sighed, spreading her hands on the table before her. These she considered, palms up, as a melancholy distance crept into her eyes. 'I mean I ain't *really* been myself lately –'

'You mean he maybe ain't got no gun?'

She looked up. 'Oh no,' she said, nodding, 'he's got a gun alright.' She paused. 'It's just –'

'Just what?'

'Well –'

'Well *what*?'

'I don't know.'

'What do you mean, you don't know?'

'Well, it don't make no sense.'

'For God's sake, *what* doesn't make no sense?'

'I mean, something just don't *look* right.' She frowned. 'I mean him wearing that head-dress and all –'

'*Head-dress*?' said Eddie. '*What head-dress*?'

'And whooping and hollering like that.' She squinted hard, as if trying to search out the truth of something. 'I mean, I seen some strange old things in my time but this is just about the strangest.'

'You're crazy,' said Eddie.

Ms Voyant shook her head. 'No, *he's* crazy,' she said. 'Least that's what they *call* him –'

'*Who*?'

'Why, the soldiers, of course.'

'Soldiers? What soldiers?'

'Well, the general for one.'

'General? What general?'

'General Custer.'

'*Custer*? What the hell's *he* got to do with anything? He's been dead for a hundred years!'

Ms Voyant shrugged.

'Jesus,' said Eddie.

For a moment there was silence. In a while he pushed himself up from the table, crossed the room to the door and pulled on his coat. He twisted the door's handle, paused, looked back. Ms Voyant was sitting still, her shoulders hunched forward, a strange look of absence on her face. She turned, as if drawn by his attention. 'I ain't crazy,' she said, 'and you ain't alive.'

Eddie frowned. He said, 'What do you mean, I ain't alive?', although he knew what she meant. He knew it deep down, but had known it for so long that the knowledge now had worn smooth and so slipped from his grasp, leaving him empty and forever disengaged, content like a sleeper with the void.

43

The illusion was magnificent – everyone – even the newspapers – said so. It was, truly, a trick beyond trickery – the kind of trompe-l'oeil that trumps not only the eyes but the mind into the bargain, and makes an audience as one start to doubt its very sanity.

And the name of that trick?

Well, *Custer's Last Stand*, of course.

And Custer? Just exactly who *was* it wearing that inaccurate blue uniform (surely everyone *knows* he was dressed on that day in light tan, not that ghastly army blue), and carrying that shining sabre? Just exactly who *was* it peering out, blinking, from beneath those flowing locks? Why, a boy in a man's role, of course – none other than little Eddie Reno, only son of the larger Eddie Reno, that man whose name arched lively and with the confidence of a nation possessed of the A-bomb across the side of an old Buick truck, not to mention the backdrop hanging limp in the warm air upstage in some theater in some town or some city, or in the middle of somewhere that in truth was nowhere, except to those fools standing, hands in pockets, their eyes raised in simple wonder at the lights and the fizz.

Not to mention that voice.

'*Hey, Custer – you in heap big trouble!*' it would holler from some place way off-stage, sending chills like tiny arrows not only through the hearts of those watching (who, oftentimes, could scarcely contain themselves, the combination of cheap beer and cheaper sentiment being the loosening agent that it is), but also through that doomed heart of the general himself (in the person of Eddie Junior) as he waited heroically on that rise (in reality a tarpaulin draped over a half-dozen orange crates) for what inevitably, every night, was his fate.

Which was?

Well, slaughter, of course, as every schoolboy knows – one man and his command cut down in hot blood (the details of which were mercifully kept from the audience by a cunning use of sweeping lights and shadow), their bodies mutilated so bad that not even God in His heaven would know them. And all this for two dollars (discounts for veterans) – but not *just* this, no, sir – for there was more, and – oh boy! – *what* a more!

But how *could* there be more? What could possibly outshine the glorious nightly death of such a hero? What indeed!

Well!

RESURRECTION is what – nothing less! He dies, oh yes, but it sure ain't the end – no, sir! No, sir, indeed, for death (as it says in the Bible someplace) is only the beginning – just the treacle through which every soul must wade if it is to find its way clear to the kingdom of heaven.

And so it was at this point, every night, at a little after nine, that beat the magical, unbelievable heart of the show – for it was here, every night, before whatever audience had gathered, that General Custer, late of the glorious Seventh Cavalry, would rise like an angel, sailing up quite unaided toward heaven, there to claim his celestial reward.

But how did it work? How was the miracle achieved?

In essence it was all (as, surely, is everything) a matter of timing and preparation. Indeed, without either of these essentials it would for sure have been a bust – winding up most likely like that whole fiasco of *Daniel Boone and his Unsinkable Canoe* that just plain refused to do anything *but* sink, with the unfortunate and distressing consequence that Eddie Junior nearly drowned one time on that stage up in Buffalo and surely would have done had it not been for a doctor named Rude who'd leapt from the audience and revived the poor boy with a series of severe (though, as it turned out, judicious) assaults on his narrow, heaving chest. All of which, of course, is beside the point (except insofar as it illustrates the precarious nature of the whole magic business) – the point being General George Armstrong Custer and his rising from the dead, and how precisely this was achieved.

So then.

The trick.

Firstly, to say the means by which it was achieved were cunning would be greatly to underplay them, for, not only did the combination of the inflatable pouches invisibly secreted about young Eddie Junior's person (made especially from the double-strength rubber employed by the army for use in its weather-balloons), and the inflating of same on cue with excessively noxious quantities of pressure-bottled helium (by means of a thin piece of tubing fed up a trouser-leg from canisters hidden entirely from the audience beneath the draped tarpaulin) – not only did this cunning (and, surely, entirely unique) combination cause the body of the newly deceased general to swell as any corpse left to rot on some hillside surely will, but also thereafter (following continued surreptitious inflation) to rise with that grace given only to the righteous at the moment of their ascension into heaven. Up and up that blue-suited man-boy would rise, his elevation accompanied every night by gasps of amazement from the audience – both men and women – until, his having risen just as far as the theater's construction would allow, the spotlight that had hitherto been following his progress upward would be flicked off and the figure plunged into darkness, thus ending the evening's performance – for everyone, that is, but Eddie Junior himself, who, floating still on the ceiling, had to wait for the theater to clear, and for his father, then, to rescue him by means of an air-gun equipped with a Chinese Army night-sight and some mostly accurate shooting. Indeed, only twice was Eddie Senior's aiming ever off (both times – ironically enough – at the SureFire Auditorium in Spruce, Kentucky); for the most part, three shots would be followed by the gleeful hissing of escaping air and the slow graceful drifting of a boy to the ground.

'Hey man, you got a dollar for a soda?'

All of which, now, as he sat staring over his wheel in that parking-lot, seemed as foreign to him and yet at the same time as familiar as a flower pressed in youth within the pages of a book discovered only and by accident in old age.

He turned his head and the eyes within it from their blindman's study of the K-Mart's stuccoed features.

'Hey man –'

Knuckles rapped hard on his window. This he lowered.

'Yes?'

'Well, do you?'

'What?' The man was smelly and unshaven, the frayed collar of his shirt dark with sweat. Eddie squinted, tried to figure what on earth it was he wanted. 'I'm sorry?' he said, but then the man just walked away, cussing hard under his breath. Eddie watched him move slow between the cars and disappear in the end beneath the arch.

He turned away, hands still gripping the wheel. He let his eyes close.

It was a strange thing, but only maybe twice in thirty years had he thought of that illusion – of Custer and an oversized suit packed tight with balloons, of the gasps of the crowd and his rising to the rafters – and only then when his drinking had become so severe that his resolution crumbled, and the past – for so long and so studiously denied – crept out from wherever it was hiding to stand before him, laughing at him and gripping him though he tried to squirm away –

He opened his eyes. The parking-lot – though still full – was striped now with shadows, his hands on the wheel losing shape in the gloom.

Hey, Custer – you in heap big trouble!

He gripped the wheel tight, felt for a second again that sickening sensation of rising he'd felt as a boy, and for a second, then, he was hanging in the rafters, scared of such a height, but fearful too of the inevitable descent.

A noise or something turned his head toward the arch. The arch now was in shadow, the day already failing. Beyond the arch, beyond the highway, beyond the low rooves of the Honeysuckle Motor Motel with its giant gaudy neon-lit bloom, the ocean was sparkling still, though there was something now of the falling flare of fireworks in its gaiety. Eddie turned away as a coolness beyond that of the afternoon's breeze overcame him. It passed over his forearm and settled on his brow like a kiss from a stranger or the whisper in some dark room that time is running out. He reached forward (heard the squeaking of the car's leather-look plastic seats), watched his fingers twist the keys, heard a click, then again, then the engine as it turned, caught and fired. *I see you going south. I just call it as I see it.* He sat for a moment, just listening to the engine's sullen growl. *A firearm, Mr Reno; it ain't no pea-shooter.* Then, entirely disengaged, he watched a boy far off in blue shorts and a bright crimson vest turn the heel of his sneaker on a can of Dr Pepper, heard the hissing like gas escaping as the can sprayed its contents high into the air with the grace of release in a curving rainbow arc like the curving earthbound arc of a diver.

He pulled on his seatbelt and touched the gas; he watched the car moving, saw it head beneath the arch. Go south, he thought. Must go south. He waited for a gap in the traffic. Then, twisting the wheel, he set out on his journey.

Heading north.

Part Two

THE BEAR

Libbie & Robert

44

Remember this.

A lie: she'd always known it. She'd known it in her heart – had had it confirmed every night since in her dreams. In her dreams, every night, her own golden boy, her Autie, had been lying naked on some desolate rise somewhere, just a pale, broken corpse, his beautiful blue eyes staring out like a child's up to heaven, his flesh that was her flesh slashed and torn and growing cold as the shadowed earth beneath him, his heart that was her heart ripped with bloody hands from the gaping cavity of his chest . . .

'Ma'am?'

And all, now, for what? For it all to be forgotten? For the truth to be perverted by cowards who'd looked on from afar whilst others – those with honor, with courage – had fought and died?

'Mrs Custer?'

She opened her eyes. The tapping on the cabin door was harder now, insistent. Slowly she rose, stood a minute, aware only of the ship's gentle swaying, only of that last smile, only of those last words borne away on the back of some long-distant afternoon's breeze.

Another tap, another rattle of the handle. 'It's the captain, Mrs Custer. He's saying you should come at once –'

Remember, too, Nathan Zeitezmann III – and remember Robert's long-dead Clare (she who died on those Long Island tracks so long ago now); remember their drifting in and out of life, one for the other and back again. But, above all, remember Libbie, remember her alone in her cabin on that storm-battered vessel, and remember that single lock of her dead husband's hair, then that knocking – urgent, insistent – on her door, then the footsteps receding, then her own following.

Remember that, then this.

How the ship was a maze, how she turned left then right, then again, then back – how, instructions followed, she found herself – a miracle – edging down an iron staircase and into the sweating stink of steerage.

'Mrs Custer? Are you alright?'

Then how she stood, an old lady, correcting, beneath her skirts, the gentle sway of the ship. 'Yes, thank you, Mr Zeitezmann,' she said. 'I am quite well.' As a girl, then as a wife, she'd always known a great and easeful sense of balance. 'Now,' she said, 'what was it that was quite so urgent?'

'It's –' Nathan paused.

'Yes?' said Libbie. There was about the young man's features now a look of anxiety – sweat on his brow, his face flushed.

'It's, well, it's the bear, Mrs Custer –'

'The bear?'

'It's, well, *escaped* –'

'Escaped?' Libbie frowned. Only once during the voyage had she thought of the creature – and only then in a dream. In her dream, the bear had been pacing around her whilst she stood – a captive – her wrists and her ankles bound tight with a bugler's satin cord.

'Mrs Custer?'

And then, suddenly, it had reared up, high on its hind legs and, with hands strangely human, pulled off its head, revealing inside the head of a man – a savage, dark-skinned, scowling creature, fearsome with sharp and pitiless eyes.

'Mrs Custer?'

She frowned harder, pulling her weary eyes into focus as the memory of that dream faltered, was gone. 'Escaped?' she said. 'But how is that possible?'

At that moment – as if cued by the sweep of some invisible hand – a great roar rose up, echoing through the corridors, followed on its heels by screams and the strange unmistakable sounds of panic and distress.

Nathan Zeitezmann shook his head. He looked away, along the empty corridor, then back. 'We must hurry,' he said. But he didn't move.

'Nathan?'

'The captain said to inform you at once –'

She reached out a hand, found his. His fingers in hers were narrow and sharp like tiny sticks, his palms wet with sweat. 'Nathan?' she said. 'Are you alright?'

Another roar, another scream.

'Nathan?'

His fingers tightened.

'Which way do we go?' she said.

'Go?' said Nathan.

'Come on now,' said Libbie; then, moving past the young man, his hand still in hers, she led him along through the dark and narrow corridors, with every step moving closer and closer, with every turn deeper and deeper and further away from the light.

45

'*S*o do you like it, my darling? Shall I wear it when we're married?'
When Robert woke to her voice at the first sign of dawn it was not a return from the nourishing absence of sleep, but an escape from the sweet, choking prison of dreams.

'*Shall I wear it when I'm old and our baby is grown?*'

He stared at the cool shaft of light on the ceiling, lying still as a corpse or a corpse-to-be as it lies alive but still as death, bound by desire as strong as ropes on the tracks outside town.

'*See how it shimmers like silver in the light. Do you see, my darling? Do you see?*'

He closed his eyes, but closing his eyes was no good, for the bleeding of dreams into day had begun, and her absence, now, become just a dream.

Slowly, he sat up. He looked about the room with a stuttering sweep of the eyes. All was as familiar and yet as foreign as ever it was these days, the room like a room known only from a photograph, or a place familiar only from the detailed description given by another.

His eyes rested a moment on the papers on his desk, then slipped to the legs of his chair, to the carpet. The carpet was striped with the morning light, the light folding over the graceful arch of a pale, naked foot.

'*What are you lookin' at, Bobby?*'

The foot turned slow on the carpet, was joined by a second. They were as pale and pink as the feet of a little child, though the toes were painted a bright, lascivious scarlet. Robert felt himself stir with desire. Slowly, he raised his eyes, felt the blessed embrace of the dress's white satin folds, ran his eyes with the touch of a blindman's fingers across the inclines and dips he knew so well. His eyes stung with tears as his mouth grew dry, as again, again, he longed for more than he'd ever really known, longed again, again, for the simple grace of breathing on his cheek, for that benevolent, forgiving numbness that those who know know as love.

'*Oh, Bobby, oh, Bobby –*'

He raised up his arms, reached out, reached out, and – miracle of miracles – she came to him, moving over him, sending him deep into the deepest of her crimson shadows, whilst all the time warming his old and battered heart with the warmth and unspent youth of her own.

Later that morning he was down on his knees, lighting the fire in the Chinese sitting-room, when he heard the voice he knew to be that of Mr Zeitezmann raised, far off in the empty house, with a lightness and melody he guessed to be that of a parent's joy. Lowering his tongs, he sat back on his haunches a minute, listening, the twin tongues of pity and relief curling and twisting like serpents around his ears and over the crown of his head. It was news from the ocean, he knew it, news of a ship's and a son's unexpected safety. He sat a moment longer, then resumed his work. Soon enough, he thought, the man would know that the news was a lie just sent to torment him. He poked without reason at the fire. Soon enough, he thought, and he thought then, again, of his own love's return, of the miracle of redemption, of the sheen of white satin drawn taut across the rising of a belly, and of the power of dreams to do and undo, to make right what for so long had been so wrong.

46

The bear was obvious by its absence, its presence somewhere in the bowels of the ship made certain by the trail it had left in its path. There were broken chairs in the great steerage hall and tables upturned, and clothes torn and shed in haste, and a body lying face-down, stripped of all clothes as if by a valet, the flesh ripped and torn, innards spilling out in such gray profusion that it seemed impossible to those watching that such a billowing mass could ever have been contained within the pale slight form that lay silent as if sleeping before them.

Captain Irvine (who had his cap held before him in his hands as if he were a large child steering an invisible automobile) was shaking his head – disbelieving, perhaps, or perhaps just denying the plain evidence of his senses. Beside him, and a little behind, First Officer Philip Parr was staring wide-eyed at the back of his captain's bullish neck, as if it were the neck and not what lay beyond it that had him in a trance.

'Captain Irvine?'

Only the captain turned at the sound of voice and footsteps. He considered the approaching figures with the blankness something like that of a sleepwalker – the rustling of a stiff dress, the sharp click of heels. He raised a heavy hand, palm out, halting their progress.

'Madam,' he said. 'Please step no further.'

Libbie squinted through the sudden brightness of the hall's stark electric lights. There were blue-suited men standing here and there amid the chaos as quiet as mourners, their heads bowed, whilst others were down on their haunches, sifting through the debris and whispering low. And all the time, so central to the hall that it seemed it must surely have been placed there with the aid of some means of measurement, lay the still, bloodied, seeping corpse, and – leading from it, away toward the furthest recesses of the hall – a trail of scarlet markings that were clearly the work of beast, not man.

Captain Irvine cleared his throat. Heads looked up at the sound, attention gathered. He straightened his back, raised his eyes to the cream-painted pipes that ran like thick bloated veins across the ceiling. A minute's pause, then he began.

'Gentlemen,' he said gravely, here closing his eyes – an aid, perhaps, to concentration, 'the situation is – as you will understand – a grave one, and one for which, as your captain, I accept full and unconditional responsibility. A man has been killed; others, mercifully, were spared and able to flee for their lives to other decks, and for this we are grateful. However, it will be clear to you all that the problem is far from over, for the perpetrator of a young man's brutal death remains at liberty. In short, gentlemen, that creature hitherto thought merely a harmless mascot of a foreign land is at large somewhere within the bowels of this ship, and must be recaptured before more damage is done. To this end, I have ordered the limited distribution of rifles from the armory, and seek, now, from amongst you, volunteers. Make no mistake, gentlemen, the work will be arduous and not without danger, but it is work that must be done.' Here he paused, stood a moment still, and there settled upon him then a quality of silence known to all those bereft whose bereavement still has in its shining coat of newness the harshness and sharpness of some newly minted coin.

'Captain Irvine?'

He turned, and in that moment of turning what was new grief became old, became a thing not upon him but within him, as settled and as permanent as the very organs – the very blood – that gave and sustained him in life. He drew a hand across his face. 'Madam,' he said. His face was pale and drained. 'Madam, I had hoped to spare you this.'

'Spare me?' said Libbie. She stared beyond him to the corpse. The corpse had the look now of something hiding – just a series of rises and falls obscured beneath the folds of a greatcoat. 'Had he a family?' she said.

The captain nodded. 'A family, yes,' he said, straightening then and setting his cap with much care upon his head as if his actions had been cued by that sequence of words. He drew a breath, then a second. 'His mother and I were his family,' he said, and then, with an economy of gait that the years had forced upon him, he crossed the steerage hall and was gone.

Josh

47

'*His mother and I were his family,*' he said, and then, with an economy of gait that the years had forced upon him, he crossed the steerage hall and was gone . . .

Oh, how strange to write these words now. How strange, given all that, recently, has happened – given how today – March third, nineteen ninety-eight – is the first anniversary of my own daughter's passing, of my own half-death, and the start (for now – at least retrospectively – does it seem) of that which I am pleased to call my recovery.

But how do you recover? How does anybody? How can it ever be more than just living, just breathing and not thinking? And how, ever, will I break up the stillness that sits heavy in this room, or shout down this silence that stifles me now and squeezes the breath from my lungs, forbidding any movement for hour after hour?

And then there is she – gone now too. Oh, how I wish she would come to me now, as easily as I have her come to Robert. How I wish she were standing before me now, smiling once again in that shimmering satin dress. Oh, how I wish I were not writing this, but living it again. But then perhaps I am. Perhaps dreaming is living, and living really dreaming. Perhaps if I just close my eyes the past will live again, return again, and she will be before me again, her bare feet set together in that shaft of spring sunlight, her hand on her belly and her words – *I thought we'd call him Edward, after you* – as soft again as the touch of her fingers on my scalp . . .

Perhaps.

Perhaps not. Perhaps I am really here in this crumbling Montana motel – perhaps my life really is as it seems. And perhaps my story of Libbie and Robert and Nathan really is all that's keeping me from that trip I must take – perhaps, after all, I am only as good as that which I create, as the lives that are lies that exist only on this rising pile of pages beside me.

But hey.

This is getting me nowhere. Davie'll be by soon for our usual evening game, so I'd best get ready. He hates it when the table's not set, the cards not ready for shuffling.

But first I think a shower – wash the tidemark of another day's waiting from my flesh. Then maybe a drink to set myself up. Just a small one, before Davie gets here.

48

Well, it's gone eleven now and I'm sitting here feeling like a fool. I mean, the table's all set (has been for over an hour now), the cards all fanned out in that way that Davie always says makes him think of Spain (which, incidentally, is a place he's never seen except on some cable show) – but where is he? God knows. Usually by now he's sitting there smiling out from under that cap of his, holding up his cards with both hands like he has to grip them tight to stop them floating away, his feet tapping out some tune that he says is *Hill Street Blues* or *LA Law* or something, but which, quite honestly, could be anything. Not that I'd say so, you understand, as I always reckon any man who'd spend the greater part of his day sitting up on the roof of his mama's old motel taking pot-shots with a bent-barreled hunting rifle at any truckers unfortunate enough to happen by on the Bozeman–Bismark highway is not the kind of man I'd argue about pretty much anything with. Which is why, I suppose – now I come to think of it – he always seems to win these games of ours; I mean, it's not that I don't *try* – because, believe me, I do – it's just that, well, there must be something inside of me – that same self-preserving bit that I guess is in all of us – that stops me trying too hard in case I do go and win and, consequently, find myself peering down that old bent barrel and thinking my last thoughts, which, I can tell you, would not, right now, be pleasant ones. I mean, Jesus. Two hours I've been sitting here now – two hours wasted that I could have spent working on my book, which, incidentally, is already way overdue.

So then.

Get back to it – now that I have the time – is what I should do. And I will. It is, after all, what I'm here for. However, before I do, there's a couple of things I feel inclined to mention about this place – things which, up until this evening, have really been bugging me, but which, due in main part to these past hours during which I've had nothing much to do but think, I think I have finally figured out.

Firstly, there's this business of the cable. Up until tonight I just couldn't figure how come such a dead-beat out-of-the-way place like this got itself wired up in the first place, it not being exactly anywhere close to the beaten track – but then I thought *Custer* and it all made some kind of sense.

You know, thinking about it now, it's amazing what that man is responsible for. I mean, not only did his martyrdom just down the road here a hundred-odd years ago once-and-for-all seal the fate of the very first Americans to walk this earth, but he also (indirectly at least) made it possible for a writer like me to sit here as I did last night in this, the Last Stand Motel, drinking beer from this old chipped glass while watching *Dougie Howser, MD* on TV, and then (even more bizarrely) Jack Clayton's *The Great Gatsby* – both dubbed, if you can believe it, into what sounded to me like Japanese.

How so?, you say. How come it's all down to the mad, bad general?

Well, it all (coincidentally, I suppose) has to do with how I came to be staying here in the first place – which, like so many things in life it seems, was just the result of random chance.

But let me start at the beginning – in a minute or so. First, let me fill up this glass – let me get to that numb, floating place where I can talk but I don't have to listen. I mean, I have, after all, heard it all before – and, besides, I am – am I not? – after all, a drunk – and what does a drunk do best but drink?

49

Okay then – I'm here now.
So.
My life.
Are you listening?
Okay.
Well.
Here – as they say – goes nothing.

Now, as far as the early part of my life is concerned, suffice it to say it was really rather normal – or as normal as being raised in America can ever be. My father beat me and my mother drank – or maybe it was the other way around, sometimes I forget. Anyway, childhood was survival, and I survived. *That* I survived – that I had someplace to go when the beating and the drinking felt like they would surely overwhelm me – I see now as something of a miracle. It was like God or somebody, having placed in my way so much that needed escaping from, felt some kind of guilt or something and gave me the means of that escape – by placing, just about a hundred yards down my street, the Roxette Theater on the corner of Maple and Vine.

Now, although the actual first picture I ever saw at that theater was of all things called *Paradise Hawaiian Style* starring Elvis Presley, it was the second that really did it for me. Looking back on it now, of course, casting Robert Shaw as Custer is nothing short of ludicrous (too big, too blustering, too Irish) – as indeed, from the point of view of what actually happened on that bright summer's day in eighteen seventy-six, was the whole picture. (But then, of course, whoever went to the movies for the truth? And who but a fool would ever think they'd found it?) Anyway, whatever, that picture did something for me – took me away, I suppose – and started something in me that is still in me today. Still, today, when I sit in some movie theater and the lights start going down, I cannot escape the feeling that I'm safe, that that darkness has made me invisible and that, if I stay so perfectly still, I will never get found out – never feel that hand on my shoulder, never hear again the crack of that belt, then that whoosh as it swept through the air, and never smell again that sweet sickly cocktail of whiskey and vomit, and maybe – if I sit real quiet – so quiet I can hear my heart beating in my ears – when the movie's over and the lights go up, maybe they will only go up in the theater and not within me, leaving me then forever and ever in that clear, ordered world where everyone knows – but nobody cares – that all life and all love is faking and where a man exists only in those moments of light, and where the darkness that comes with the darkness of night is nothing but that numbness that those who know know as the numbness – the nothingness – of death.

But hey.

It seems too much whiskey (or maybe not enough) is making Eddie here a sad, weeping boy.

I suppose the point of what I'm trying to say is that ever since that afternoon at the Roxette I have never been able to shake off my fascination with this arrogant, sentimental, brilliant fool, Custer (though, believe me, I've tried) – particularly the feeling that without understanding him I will never truly understand this nation of ours – how we came to be here and how we came to survive, and how, in the end, chances are we'll continue to survive – at least until there's nothing left out there to conquer but ourselves – until we find ourselves standing in the glare of that sun, then, appalled by the terrible un-American silence, we turn on ourselves and the nation is done.

Or not. Or whatever.

I don't know.

All I *do* know is I can't outrun him, just as he in the end couldn't – didn't want to – outrun his own death. Everywhere I turn these days, more and more, he is right there in front of me, that pistol in his hand and that final beatific man-child's smile on his face – and those eyes, clear and blue that have known from childhood the scene on that day: the hard, baking ground, the smell of fear in horses and men, the terrible silence of knowing, then that howling tide, rolling closer and closer, tiny and glinting and growing ever larger, ever nearer, until, so close now, a moment of peace comes over him in that moment of death, and he raises his face to the sun, feels its burning, hears again as if for the first time the running over stones of that cool Ohio creek, so far away now, but so close, so close –

But hey.

I digress.

Back to the real point of all this.

Me.

Here.

Now.

Call it just coincidence, call it synchronicity – call it what you like – call it fate, whatever, but that I should wind up here – amongst the ghosts of Crazy Horse, of Sitting Bull, of the son of the Morning Star himself – spooks me, I can tell you. So what if they were just actors – just pretending – so what if it was just a movie – so what if NBC or CBS or whoever was paying them all to set out from here every morning and some evenings – paying them to dress up, paying them to speak the words – *his* words – and paying them, finally, to live on or die – so what. No matter. His spirit is here – they felt it, I know, as I feel it. He is here with me now in this room, just as he was all those weeks ago when I turned off that highway and drove through the dust, aware as I did so of his voice in my ear, urging me on and on . . . until Davie shot out my nearside front tire, so inviting me to stay here while I'm working and waiting on the time for the final part of my trip.

All of which reminds me.

Jesus, will you look at the time?

Nearly three now and the book's got no further. Still the bear is roaming in the bowels of that ship, and still Robert is waiting on that shore. And Clare? *His* Clare, who – like mine – died so long ago now, but who – unlike mine – died alone? Is she really returning from the dead? Will she, if Nathan is imprisoned by death, be released to live? I must write it to know it. I must write it now, and not think of myself – not think of my Clare and our girl – our Grace – burning together in the furnace of her daddy's automobile.

So.

Watch me begin again – watch me step back to step forward.

Watch me.

Watch me.

Libbie & Robert

50

'**W**atch you? Why? What *exactly* are you planning to do?'
'I'm volunteering.'
'Volunteering?'
'Yes, ma'am. I'm set on it.'

Libbie studied the young man's face. It had nothing, now, of that careless youth and gaiety always captured in the New York and Washington papers. Now, there was a light sheen of sweat on his brow, reflecting the muted glow of the cabin's electric lights. He swallowed hard, straightening his back.

'It's my duty,' he said, his voice betraying the faintest tremble.

'Because of your father?'

He blinked away the sweat from his eyes. 'No, ma'am,' he said.

'Then why, sir?' said Libbie, though she already knew the answer – had heard it before, many times.

'*Because I'm a man.*'

She looked down at the gloved hands set neatly in her lap. Unseen, on the third finger of her left hand, she felt suddenly the presence of her wedding ring – of the diamonds and emeralds set in purest Dakota gold.

'Mrs Custer?'

She looked up and, for just a moment, saw in her mind's eye the distant face of that long-ago preacher – the blackness of his hair, the pallor of his skin, his voice as he whispered, '*Miss Elizabeth, are you ready?*'

She frowned as the face of the preacher faded, was replaced by that of a young man who seemed to her scarcely more than a child.

'Ma'am?'

She closed her eyes, searched the darkness for the features of that other golden boy. '*I am ready, sir,*' she heard herself whisper, '*I have been ready all my life.*'

'Mrs Custer? Are you quite well?'

She opened her eyes. For a moment the scene lingered: the stiffness of her grandmother's dress, the smell of such flowers she'd scarcely thought existed, the men in their uniforms, so grand and so stern, the steel of their sabres so sharp, so bright and bloodless, all as still in their ranks and quite as immovable as the elm and the oak standing sentry in the garden on some windless summer's day.

'Ma'am?'

She blinked; the scene shifted, was gone. She lifted her chin, just as Miss Stoop – mistress of deportment – had taught her long ago. 'Yes, sir,' she said. 'I am quite well.' She studied the young man's face. 'It is you, sir, I fear, who may be suffering some malaise.'

'*Malaise*, ma'am?' Nathan Zeitezmann frowned. 'On the contrary, I assure you, ma'am, that I have never felt more . . . *alive* –'

'Nevertheless, sir, I believe you are sick.'

He shook his head, felt as he did so the pumping heart in his chest, the clammy coolness of his sweat-soaked shirt. 'Ma'am, I assure you –'

'You are sick, sir,' said Libbie. 'Depend upon it.' Then, gripping the arms of her chair, she pushed herself up, stood swaying gently with the gentle rocking motion of the ship, her ever-youthful heart suspended like a child's in a cradle of old and weary bones. She reached out a hand, laid the tips of her fingers on the young man's sleeve. 'Nathan,' she said – her voice scarcely more than a whisper – but, as if commanded by another voice come from deep within him – a reckless and persuasive voice urging him on and on toward some beautiful and treacherous river – the young man stepped back, pulled away. He shook his head, then again and again, shaking it hard like he was trying to expel from it something that would not be expelled. He gritted his teeth hard and closed his eyes tight. 'I am going,' he said, spitting the words out like they were too hot or too sharp for a man to easily swallow, 'and I'll thank you, ma'am, to keep your opinions to yourself.' The eyes opened. Libbie dropped her hand. The look within them was the look of some kind of madness – the look a man finds in the moments before death or a woman before the birth of a child – a look known to all who have stood beside that river and felt that rising tide sweeping in from the ocean. 'Come back,' she said, though she knew it was useless, for she knew that, while a woman is driven to act from the inside, and carries all of the world within her, a man is neither solely led nor followed – but both – and, consequently, spends much of his life in puzzlement, standing, paralyzed, just waiting for the strongest voice of fear to goad him on. 'Very well,' she said, withdrawing, watching as the young man turned away and crossed the cabin to the door. Here he turned back. The sweat was like tears on his face. 'I'm not *afraid*,' he said, his voice rising from his throat, querulous and blustering as a boy's, 'I'm never *afraid*.' Then he turned away again, and in a moment was gone.

That evening, at a little after nine, Libbie woke with a start from a deep and dream-filled sleep. Her heart was racing, her breath coming hard. In her dream there'd been screaming – the terrible screams of children and men. She sat up, slow and with care. She turned, squinted out at the deep, black night. There were stars, but no moon – no way to tell where the falling sky ended and the ocean in its blackness began.

51

Today, should you pay your six dollars (four dollars for minors, veterans go free) and take a tour of that white-painted, grand-pillared house overlooking Long Island's Oyster Bay, you will find no trace, amongst the artefacts preserved in the high-polished cabinets, of the wedding one summer of a butler and his lover – no tarnished forks or crumpled napkins, no thumbed and yellowing invitations. You will search in vain for some plaque in the garden denoting the place where their vows were exchanged, and find – however hard you look – no reference to that day in the five-dollar guide-book, or words of exposition on the ten-dollar (fifteen-dollar deposit) audio-tape. Neither in English, nor in French, nor Japanese, nor, indeed, in a dozen other languages, does history record one breath of the lives of Robert Jackson or Clare Laura Summerfield – but then, of course, all history is fiction – all remembrance being, as it is, so partial as to reveal less of the past itself and more of the hearts and minds of those remembering today.

So then. What *will* you find in that house?

Well, you will find Jay Gatsby in his pale-yellow suit, and a blustering Tom Buchannan sweating hard; from the posters, too, and the stills, you'll find Daisy and Jordan gazing down at you, one misty-eyed, remembering the past, the other hard and cynical, calculating some future. And all around you you'll find props and mementos from that movie shot nearly thirty years ago now within these very walls, and in the garage, that fateful yellow roadster, its fender still dented, still red with Myrtle's blood. All this you will find – all this fakery – but nothing of Robert and nothing of Clare. And why? Well, because they were nothing – except, of course, to themselves – except, of course, to each other, to whom they were everything.

Everything – even in death.

Death.

No frontier so final, and yet none so easily breached by memory, by faith, by fantasy. Especially for a man like Robert, who never could grasp its finality, whose conscience never would let him accept it as an end of things, who'd never stopped looking, though he knew in his head but not his heart it was hopeless, who'd never once paused in the turning of his head at the clip of distant footsteps in the night or the echo of voices calling out across the Sound.

Always, then.

Then, as now.

Now, as he stands in his morning suit, as proud as the proudest of men, his heart thumping in his chest as he waits for his bride. Above him, the elm sways lazily in some breeze, conducting the slow lilting music of the band. *What'll I do when you are far away?*: he smiles at the irony, now, of that song, folds the tips of his fingers around the cuffs of his shirt. He thinks of the day – years ago – when the news of a body found dead on the tracks reached his ears, and knows it now as nothing but a dream. To him, in that moment, all sense is reversed, the life lived in dreams become the life lived in the world, and that life lived in the world become the real life of dreams. He closes his eyes, hears the squeak of new leather as he flexes his toes. '*Are we ready?*' says a voice – a whisper, solemn. He nods; his eyes open. All around him there are faces, smiling, each one a living testament to this day of all days. He turns, squints in the sun, searches the far trees for some sign of his bride.

'Robert?'

She is near – he can feel it – the satin hem of her dress gliding over the lawn, her hands like a child's hands, holding fast in her nervousness to a bouquet of fresh-cut summer flowers.

'Robert? Are you listening to me?'

He turns back, shivers as he feels the fingers of some other fake and distant world creep across his shoulders and circle slow about his neck. He frowns, turns again, but, again, the real world – that world in which all that *should* happen *does* happen and all that we deserve is weighed-up and sieved, leaving only all that is righteous and good – falters and shivers too like some distant mirage, and he closes his eyes, hanging onto its image, clenching his teeth in some great stoic effort, only to find that when he opens his eyes all effort was in vain, for he's back once again in the dread world of dreams, the world of wasted years and chances lost once and forever.

'There's news, Robert –'

'News?'

The face of Mr Zeitezmann is florid, as if he's been running, his chest, bound within his thick quilted smoking-jacket, heaving. He has a look in his eye that is something like madness – the madness, perhaps, of recycled hope. He steps forward, for a minute no longer employer and seller of arms – of guns and ammunition to any who will buy – but just a man – a father – whose son, thought lost, has again been given life, or the rumor of life.

Robert stares at Nathan Zeitezmann II – at the merchant of death as he retails the rumor as fact. He smiles and nods – for, aware in that moment of the old man's self-delusion, he feels pity for those trapped in such a fickle dream-world – but, then, more than that. More than pity. Unseen within his pockets, he clenches his fists, feeling as he does so such an anger rising inside him – anger that this dream-world that others call real has a hold on him still – and so, unheard except by the ear of his conscience, he wishes with all his heart and all his soul for that one death – that one sacrifice – that will finally and irrevocably release his own life from its limbo –

'Oh Lord,' says the old man, kneeling now, praying. The skin on the top of his head is stretched taut and pale. 'Amen,' he whispers then and begins arthritically to rise.

'Amen,' says Robert, as, far off in the distance – half an ocean away – the young man whose death he has so recently prayed for moves slow through a dark ship, the tips of his fingers touching cool, weeping metal, his ears tuned like a cat's to the sound of his own beating heart.

52

E ver since he'd been a boy, there'd been this thing within Nathan – a phrase, a mantra, if you like – that would rise up inside him during moments of fear, reminding him then of all that, cumulatively, existed within only him, and all that it was within his own power to lose. *You*, the voice would say – silently to all but him – *are the reason we all went before, the sum total of all of our lives.* Amongst other things, this phrase was a challenge to his notions of the individual sovereignty of man's actions – those notions learned in college deemed so dangerous by his father that simply to utter them was to jeopardize all that collectively had been achieved – notions which, once learned, could not, of course, be unlearned, and which, consequently, made of what had once been a certainty in Nathan's mind (that is, the collective advancement of man through generations) rather less than a certainty – made of that bliss which is ignorance rather less than bliss. Indeed, it had been that simple phrase (or rather, particularly, the cavernous divide between father and son that was illuminated by its substance) which had drawn him away from the family home – drawn him as far away, indeed, as Europe – and which, now, as he made his way slow – hands on the rails – down a dark iron stairway, spun around in his head, making him feel (along, to be fair, with the slow, gentle rolling of the ship) as unsteady as some drunk trying to walk that chalk line.

He paused, released one hand to wipe the sweat from his brow.

You are the reason we all went before, the sum total of all of our lives.

Squinting, the sweat bleeding like mercury into his weary eyes and stinging, he tried to pierce the darkness – tried to locate in the shadows and gloom the source of the screaming that, a deck or two earlier, had seemed so real, so pinpointable, but which now might as well have been a voice drifting in and then out on a radio-dial. He edged down another step. 'Staircase number five,' the captain had said, pointing to it on his blueprint. At the time, staring down at it, the great ship, in diagram, had seemed to Nathan to be made up of bones – the whole thing just a carcass awaiting breaking up by some great cook of the deep for broth. At the time, staring down, the faces around him lit yellow by the dull electricity, he'd thought of his mother lying sick in her bed, and how he'd longed for and dreaded the faint spider's touch of her fingers. *Remember, my darling, you're all that I have now.* Now, easing down onto the dark and unseeable deck, he thought again of how, as a child, she'd seemed so constant to him – so unbreakable, so undefeatable – and how, when the sickness that would kill her first drew across her body with the prescience of a shroud, he'd not wanted to touch her or to be touched by her, and how ashamed he'd been of his shallowness, and how, that first night, he'd lain in his bed knowing he should throw back the covers and go to her, comfort her, tell her he was here and always would be, but how he'd found his limbs too heavy suddenly to move and his will to do what was right – what was good – too weak before the willful urging of those voices in the night whose advice was to do only that which is necessary for personal survival – for, they said, we are all of us alone, all of us making our way through the darkness with only the dim light of conscience to guide us.

He paused at the far-off sound of voices. 'Hello?' he said. The voices drew nearer, echoing, drifted off. He lifted his lamp. The walls about him were sweating, the air thick with moisture. He turned, looked back. The staircase now was lost in the gloom. He turned back, moved on, aware with every step of the clipping, toe to heel, of his handmade leather shoes.

He was heading past the doors of the steerage dining-hall when the ship gave a lurch, sending him sideways. The doors swung inward at the touch of his shoulder, then swung back behind him, closing with a light flapping sound. Beneath him, the rolling ship settled. 'Hello?' he said. 'Is anyone there?' But then nothing – just the groaning of the ship and the thudding of his heart. He stepped forward. The end of a long wooden table loomed, then another. He swung the lamp; empty, upturned chairs appeared before his sweeping, then were lost again in the darkness. He turned at a sound, swinging the lamp, aware as he did so – aware with that part of him – that part that's in all of us – that only fear of the presence of death will wake in us – of the low, labored rasp of another's breathing and the gaze in the darkness of other eyes upon him.

James

53

If there was one thing more precious than his compass in the life of James Monkton Webb, well, he couldn't think of it. He'd tried many times – set his mind, time and again, to wandering over all that he owned – both those things he could touch and those he could not – but he always came back to that brass-backed glass-fronted handful of magic given to him by his father on the day of his father's second wedding. Which is not to say that he didn't value *other* things, for he did – he came to love his sabre for one thing, and for another, well, he could never have imagined being without the gift of humor – no, sir, it was just that that compass was special, carrying with it as it did not only the means of telling the way – but more than that. For James Monkton Webb, that compass, high-polished as he always kept it, carried with it also, by means of a series of words engraved on the inner case, a more profound – a more *spiritual* – direction – one, indeed, from which nothing could deflect him, not even the words (though silky they be and as smooth to the ear as the laughter of a loon at dusk-time) of a woman whose charms would surely deflect from grand purpose any other man but he.

'No, ma'am,' he said, smiling but resolute.

'What do you mean, *no*?' The woman, despite the day's breathless stillness, was having some difficulty maintaining her balance – a combination, James supposed, of her footwear and the effects, so early in the day, of strong liquor.

'By *no* I mean *no*, madam. And I would be grateful if you would remove your hand. As you will have observed, I have not stirred despite your best efforts, and will not, I assure you, do so.'

The woman swayed forward, hung her ghastly rouged face before his. 'Prefer fucking boys, do we?' she said, the words emerging from her now-mean but once-pretty mouth accompanied by a fine spray of spit. She gripped him harder between his legs; wincing, he tried to step away, but she held him fast. 'Can't manage a woman, love – is that it?'

With a wrench he pulled away. They were standing in a once-grand but now shabby salon in a mansion on the southside of Memphis, the pair of them striped by the room's deep velvet shadows despite the day's early hour. James straightened his clothing, felt with a fine kind of pleasure the weight of his sabre against his thigh. 'Madam,' he said, 'although it is scarcely your business, it gives me satisfaction to inform you that I am a family man –'

The woman scoffed. '*Family?*' she said, staggering a pace as she did so.

'– And *consequently* have no need of your services.' James paused (as if he were weighing something up, although, in truth, such weighing as was necessary – such looking, if you like, for direction – had already, of course, been done), then, with a much practiced smile both wry and childlike, he added, 'Except, madam, for one thing.'

The woman squinted, the sadness of self-loathing making counterfeit her smile. 'And what,' she said, '*sir*, would that be?'

Well, of course, in her stupor, she didn't see the blade coming, nor feel it in that moment as it penetrated her flesh. All she could feel – before she felt it all – all the agony – before she felt her life at long last releasing her and a numbness overcome her – was a coolness in her throat like the coolness long ago of her mother's lemonade. She blinked, then again, for a moment for the first time in years truly sober, then she saw herself falling – falling further than others had claimed she had already fallen – whilst in that same instant she was in spirit rising, released from the wretched embrace of the world and into the arms of a loving but incomplete God.

54

The city of Memphis in the state of Tennessee was, in that late spring of eighteen seventy-six, a city more in spirit than in size. Indeed, with permanent residents numbering fewer than four hundred thousand souls, there were, in fact, more horses within its muddy limits than people – a total increased but, barely, one morning by the passing unremarked of two blue-coated Yankees into the general throng. Here, if seen from the stars, or perhaps even from the top of MacCrindel's Corn Exchange (then the city's tallest and proudest building), they would have seemed indistinguishable – their progress through the streets in search of lodgings hard to follow – amongst all those others out for trade or for early pleasure that morning – indistinguishable except, perhaps, in one respect. And how so? Well, there was in the movement of one of them at least – the seeming leader of the two, in that it was he who strode a step ahead, while the other seemed content to shuffle a step behind – a definite and angular purpose in the manner in which he negotiated the streets, as if, though he were a stranger, he had a nose for the scent of what he wanted much as a dog in a certain season will know instinctively the whereabouts through her scent of a bitch. All of which would mean nothing, of course, if it weren't for what we know of the fate of that poor whore Claudine LeNoel, and how – at the very moment the men were striding (and shuffling, the reason for which becomes clear when we see all the boxes and the set of long metal legs this second man is carrying) along Fettermann Boulevard – she was watching their progress and thinking the first, taller, more elegant man good at least for a visit to the once grand but now decaying mansion beyond the gates behind her, and thence a dollar or two in exchange for what experience (bitter indeed) has taught her that all men would rather fight for – even kill for – or at least pay for, rather than get through soft words and the soft and gentle touch of a lover's hands.

So. From our perch (wherever it may be) we see the men coming (as she does), see her lean her body back against the black-painted but corroded metal railings, see and hear then (at least in our mind's ear) the brief exchange, the gentle haggling, as the taller man bows very slightly at the waist, and the other sets his boxes on the ground and looks away, as if from the scene of a crime.

And then? Well, we know what happens then. Then there is the sharp and forced laughter, then the pointing to the crumbling mansion, then the alley beside it and a door so discreet in the gloom that it could have been the door to some other secret world.

55

'Well, lieutenant, sir?'
    'What?'
    They were standing, the two of them, an hour or so later, in a windowless bar across the street from the mansion. The air in the bar was thick with the smell of horses and the river, the room quiet, the other drinkers as prone in their misery as angels cast with a great and public justice from heaven.

James lowered his glass, chinked it against Matthew's on the bar. 'Well, do you not think it worth celebrating, sir?

'Celebrating?'

'Indeed, sir. Is the reacquaintance of old comrades not worth even the smallest of cheers?'

Matthew looked up. The other man was smiling – had been, it seemed to him then, from the moment they'd met. He looked away, down at the whiskey in his glass. Celebrating was the last thing he felt like doing. Right now all he felt like doing was drinking and sleeping – or perhaps just drinking, as sleeping these days always led him into dreaming, and dreaming always led him straight back to the carnage of that ten-year-old war – and to Clare and her slow-rising belly, and then to the desolate landscape of his life. He lifted his glass, sank its contents, closing his eyes as the whiskey burned his throat.

'Or is it you still don't remember?'

He opened his eyes. The image of Clare – of her sitting in her room far away now at Miss Eliot's whorehouse – hung a moment before his eyes until the pale, smiling face of the other man replaced it.

'Or maybe that you just can't see no more – even if you want to?'

'Can't see?' said Matthew, 'What do you mean?'

James looked down, turned his glass in his fingers. He looked up – a sideways look, almost sly, his eyes narrowed like the eyes of some theatrical villain. 'Well,' he said, 'I was thinking –' He paused.

'Thinking what?'

'Well, I was thinking maybe it's working.'

'Working? *What's* working?'

He shrugged. 'This drinking. I was thinking maybe it's working after all.'

Matthew squinted back. He was weary from the journey and weary from the whorehouse – tired of the bartering for his pictures and his feelings always of disgust – but most of all he was weary from the shame he'd never thought he'd feel at abandoning Clare and the new life that was growing every day within her. 'Look,' he said. 'I don't know what you're talking about. In fact, I don't know what I'm doing here at all.' He pushed back, made to stand. A hand on his arm stopped him.

'Sure you do,' said James. For the first time in it seemed like forever, his smile dipped as his brows gathered in a mild sort of frown. 'You remember the penalty for murdering a state governor – *don't* you, lieutenant, sir? 'Cause if you don't, let me remind you. It's *hanging*, in case you're forgetting – from the *neck*, sir, until you are *dead* –' The hand gripped tighter, fingers bunching cloth and muscle. 'Lieutenant, sir, are you hearing me?'

Matthew turned. 'You're crazy,' he said, pulling his arm away. 'You should be fucking locked up–'

'Me, sir?' The frown bled away, was replaced once again by the most forgiving, the most benevolent of smiles. In the eyes, though, there remained a certain vulnerability, a certain tenderness like the tenderness of an old but still tender wound. 'No, sir,' said James. 'Not me, sir.' He turned back to the bar, gazed down again at his whiskey.

'I'm going,' said Matthew. He turned away, paused, turned back. 'And you know you *are* fucking crazy.'

James – former captain of cavalry – shook his head then, slow, left and right. 'No, sir,' he said. 'Like I said, I ain't crazy. At least not the way you mean.' He looked up. 'In fact, I'm the sanest person I know.'

Matthew closed his eyes as a sudden weight seemed to fall like wet cloth on his bones. 'Look,' he said, 'I don't know what the fuck you're talking about and, frankly, I don't care.'

'You don't, sir?'

He opened his eyes. 'No, I don't.' His eyes were sore and smarting from the smoke and from the days that had passed without sleeping. He reached up a hand, but rubbing his eyes only made them worse. He dropped his hand, squinting. 'And I'd be obliged if you'd quit calling me sir. The war, in case you hadn't noticed, is over.'

'No it ain't,' said James.

'What?' said Matthew.

'It ain't over. It ain't *ever* over. Leastways not for people like you and me. It's just different is all.'

'Jesus, you *are* crazy.'

James grinned, drained his glass. 'Whatever,' he said, shrugging. He wiped his mouth with the back of his hand. 'So tell me, sir,' he said. 'Where is it you's planning on heading?'

'Why?' said Matthew. 'What is it to you?'

Another shrug. 'Nothing, I guess.' James cocked his head, as if taking a new look at something old and familiar. 'It's just that I was thinking, well, what with us being brothers and all, we should maybe be looking out for each other, don't you think?'

'*Brothers?*' said Matthew. 'What the hell are you talking about? We ain't *brothers.*'

'Well, certainly we are, sir. You and me's as alike as any two brothers that ever lived. Why, you've only got to take a look at us to know that.' James nodded toward the mirror behind the bar, to their reflections side by side behind a row of cork-topped bottles. Matthew studied them hard. The two men in the picture were to him not in the slightest bit alike – his being shorter and fairer-haired, while the other man was taller and altogether darker.

'You see now?' said James.

Matthew shook his head. He looked at himself looking back, aware in that moment – really for the first time – that the image he'd seen most of himself, the one by which he knew himself, was all turned inside out and really not like him at all. He narrowed his eyes; his other self in the mirror did the same, as if mocking him. He looked away. The tall man beside him was studying him, still smiling.

'What is it?' said Matthew. 'What the hell are you looking at?'

'I'm looking at you, brother.'

'Jesus Christ. I told you I ain't your brother.'

'Whatever,' said James. 'Anyhow,' he said, 'it don't make no difference.'

'What do you mean? What don't make no difference?'

'What I *mean* is it don't make no difference what you say. A tree's still a tree whether you call it a tree or not.'

'A tree? What the fuck –'

'Same as a person with a price on his head. It don't make no difference what you *call* him, he's still a man looking to get hanged. He's still gonna swing from that tree just the same – don't matter if, he calls himself Jesus Christ himself. He's still gonna die 'less he gets him some help –'

'Look,' said Matthew. '*Asshole.* I ain't your brother and you ain't mine – alright? You got that?'

'I got that,' said James.

'Good.'

'It ain't true, but I got it.'

'Jesus Christ.' Matthew shook his head, turned, took a step.

'Say, where you going, lieutenant, sir?'

And then another.

'Sir?'

And then another, then another, walking foot after foot, until somehow he was standing again on the dirt street, a hand raised high against the blinding southern sun.

He closed his eyes, opened them at the sharp sound of cursing. Across the street, a man in a long dusty coat was shifting boxes – first one end, then the other – from off the back of a buck-board – piling them up, heaving and swearing at his maker as he did so, until he'd a pile of them stacked up on the boardwalk. Standing before them then, he raised his dusty hat and wiped the sweat from his brow with the back of his hand. As he moved, dust fell from the hem of his coat, fine in the light as a light summer rain. Matthew squinted harder, tried to make out the map of the man's features as he turned – tried to see him in that moment as he'd never seen himself (save perhaps in a photograph, although even a photograph, of course, captures only the skin trapped in dead time, and can show us neither the soul nor what time has bred in the bones) – but could not: like his long and narrow boxes, the man's face was just a shadow – just an island of darkness, backlit in an ocean of light.

Matthew turned, looked away down the street. The street in the noon-heat was near-empty, the city – seen from this corner of Bacon and Deloit – seeming smothered, still and breathless – a city caught, drowsy and prone, like a giant bloated bee trapped for sport in a schoolboy's airless bottle.

'Hey, mister, get help –'

The voice – distant, anguished – made Matthew raise his head, drew his gaze across the road to the alley.

'Hey, mister, did you hear me?'

The man was half in shadow, half in light, kneeling and waving like a man who'd found treasure. Matthew started toward him, but then something about the shape of the mound lying still before the man in the alley bid him stop. Instead, he stood and watched the man grappling with something – a bundle of bags filled with fruit, perhaps, or a woman caught short in the throes of giving birth – watching on, transfixed, until others arrived and the scene was obscured, and the moment was lost – at once, then, and forever – an exhibit left to wait its dusty turn on some shelf, in the desolate, echoing vault of the past.

56

'*It's a boy, my darling, I'm sure of it.*' Then silence, the tick of some clock. Then: '*Matthew – aren't you pleased? Aren't you happy, my darling?*'

Strange how the mind will trap a thought or an image – a sound or just a smell (or, indeed, something felt, something beyond description, that no single sense can adequately define) – hoarding it up then for years (for, sometimes, a lifetime) – for so long, anyway, that its presence becomes as familiar in the landscape of the memory and thus as unnoticed as some picture long-hung in a corridor, or the trees on some street whose lifespans are ten times or more that of man – only to produce them, unexpected one day, like coins from a pocket on some special occasion, or a look of distraction in a moment of love.

'*I thought we'd call him Matthew after you. I thought –*'

'*Thought what?*'

A minute passing then, like hours.

'*I thought –*'

'*You didn't think. You never think. You're a whore and whores don't think –*' Then footsteps rising slow on the stairs, passing then, then silence. Then: '*No child of mine will be born to a whore. Do you understand? Well, do you?*'

'*But you said –*'

Then a hand raised in anger, a strike, a falling, the breaking of glass, then crying, then silence, nothing. Just nothing.

'Lieutenant, sir?'

He closed his eyes. *No child of mine.*

'Sir? Lieutenant?'

'What do you want?'

'Want, sir? Well, nothing, sir. I heard the commotion is all.'

'Just go away.'

'Sir?'

'I said go away. Just leave me be, will you?'

He opened his eyes. Across the street, a body – the corpse of a woman – was being heaved roughly onto the back of a cart, arms and legs flailing. In a moment, then, the cart drew away, watched in silence by the slow-dispersing crowd.

'Sir?'

Matthew turned. 'Didn't you hear me?'

'Well, I was just wondering –'

The other man was standing beside and a little behind him. At his feet were stacked a camera box and a number of canvas bags. Matthew sighed. 'Wondering?' he said. 'Wondering *what*, for God's sake?'

'Well, was it a killing, sir?'

'A killing?'

'The commotion, sir. Would you say it was the consequence of murder?'

'What?'

The blow, sir, was grave but not fatal. I'm as certain as is possible that the child is alive.

'And would you say, sir, that the woman, sir – the *whore*, sir – will regret her liberation? Would you say that?'

Matthew shook his head.

'You wouldn't, sir?'

In the eye of his mind, he could see again the face of Mr Winter, veterinarian, who, in the absence of a doctor, had pronounced the child living.

'Nor I, sir.'

And the face, then, of Clare, and the birth, before his eyes – in that very moment – of the loss of faith, of hope, that would one day as guilt turn against her – but never against him.

'Sir?'

Matthew closed his eyes. Indeed, never once had his actions of that day been mentioned. Never once had she said *It was you*. Instead, her forgiveness itself had punished him – shaming him with its goodness, with its purity – reminding him of that morning, every day, every hour, every moment, of the life he had so nearly taken, and how that life had been a life undefended, and how he had to escape but could never escape – how all he could do was to run and keep running – how the best now he could ever hope for was the numbness of exhaustion and, finally, the silent and forgiving arms of death.

'Lieutenant, sir?'

He opened his eyes. *It was God that let it happen. It was God that raised your hand, my love. I know it. I know it.* The smiling man was suddenly before him on the street, his face a rich picture of concern.

'Are you well, sir?'

Matthew squinted, tried to focus.

'Should I fetch a surgeon?'

'A surgeon?' he said. 'What for?' *The child, as I told you, is breathing, sir.*

'What for? Why, to attend to your wounds, sir.'

'Wounds? What wounds? What the hell are you talking about?'

James smiled. How many times now had he seen such childlike denial? How often, on a battlefield such as this, had he witnessed such refusal to accept the demonstrably, the undeniably true? More times now, in truth, than he could possibly recall – so often, indeed, that its presence no longer surprised him; indeed, so familiar had its appearance become – such an image of home – that he'd come almost to welcome its arrival, its providing for him, as it did, a chance to practice his own surgeon's skills – an opportunity, if you like (and *he* liked – be certain sure of *that*), for his pale and skillful hands to remove from a body all that – though beating – was fake – to cut away, for once and forever, the badness in things – to lay bare and cauterize all that God in His pathetic goodness had let slip and flourish – all that His Holiness, on that day of creation, had let seep like some foul, stinking river into the earth, and thence – through the discursive reach of enduring life – into the breasts of women, and from there into the suckling mouths of babies, and on and on, its putrid decay spreading fast like some virus, until none of us is safe – until every one of us is lost in a half-world where the fake has become real and the real – once so precious – merely fake.

'I'm leaving now,' said Matthew.

'Leaving, sir?'

He took a step, paused. Then, without turning, without looking back, he said, 'And I ain't expecting company – understand?'

'Company, sir?'

He took a second step, a third, a fourth.

'Sir?'

A fifth, a sixth.

'Are you not forgetting something, sir?'

Seven, eight. *Don't stop now*, he thought, *not for anything*.

'Sir?'

And then – oh, miracle – he was walking hard, away, away, heading north or south or anywhere that would have him – anyplace that would let him just be – some place far away that would just let him breathe – let him sleep safe and sound beyond the dread reach of dreams.

57

B ut there is no such place – nowhere beyond dreams, for we carry
them in our hearts wherever we go.

'Sir?'

Fifty-six, said Matthew, his counting just a whisper, *fifty-seven, fifty-eight, fifty-nine* –

'You're forgetting all this –'

Sixty-three, sixty-four. 'I didn't forget. Now just go.' *Sixty-seven, sixty-eight, sixty-nine* –

The sound of breathing from behind, the banging of boxes. 'But how will you make a living, sir, without your, well . . . your *equipment*?'

Seventy-five, seventy-six. 'I want no living, therefore I need no equipment.' *Seventy-eight, seventy-nine* –

'But, sir, we all need a living –'

Eighty-one. He stopped. He turned. The pale man was paler than ever now and breathing hard, as if unused to such a pace, to such exercise. He was holding tight to the camera box and bags, the metal legs of the tripod trapped and shining beneath his arm.

'Sir?'

'Yes?'

'I believe you should reconsider.'

'Reconsider? Reconsider what?'

James Monkton Webb set down the box, the bags, the tripod. 'Well,' he said, his breathing steady now. He paused.

'Well what?' said Matthew.

'Well, haven't you forgotten something?'

'My equipment, yes. You said.'

'Aside from that.'

Matthew shrugged.

James smiled. Then he pushed out his tongue, gripped his throat and squeezed. His eyes bugged out, desperate and flaring like those of a man half-hanged.

'Jesus,' said Matthew.

James dropped his hand, smiling still. *Stop him*, he'd thought, *and I'll have him*, for he knew in the place where he should have had a heart that there is no man alive who can resist the vision of his own destruction.

58

'**Y**ou were *married*, sir? To that *whore*?'

The wedding (not *that* wedding – but another, and this one years ago) had been a spectacular affair – present, the best of Sonora society. Even the *Sonora Telegraph* (a paper scarcely given to exuberant reporting, save on the subject of the iniquitous Mr Lincoln and his slave-owning double-dealing) made much of its splendor, calling the nuptials 'A feast both for the eye and the palette', and referring in terms more than glowing (more glowing, some said, than the subject's past reputation deserved) to the qualities – both visible and assumed – of the new (of course, second) Mrs Ambrose M. Webb – formerly Miss Hannah McDell, only daughter of Mr and Mrs Balding McDell of Dudley, Mission County. Indeed, for all, it seemed, that mild September day had been, appropriately enough, a day not only of celebrating, but a day, also, of forgetting – forgetting, at least for the women and at least for a while, the war that everyone knew was coming and only the men seemed to want. Only the men, it seemed, had a love in those days for the language of conflict and the desire for the spurious nobility of some beautiful and 'worthwhile' death; only they – they and their sons (always their sons, of course, never their daughters) – had a seeming willingness to give up in some glorious misguided instant all that over so long and at such great cost had been achieved; only they – the men and the boys – had no time suddenly to waste on living, and time aplenty on their hands for dying.

'She's no whore.'

'A whore, sir, is a whore.'

And dying, of course, is what they would do – the fathers, the brothers, and eventually the sons. And, eventually, even those left alive – the survivors, or, should we say, those left breathing – would fall too – not down into the eternal, echoing silence of death, but into the whispering half-life of shadows from where only the cries of the slaughtered can be heard.

Matthew took another step – his eighty-second or eighty-third, some part of his mind calculated. He looked up, away, away, out toward the unseeable horizon. Ahead of him lay the toiling, anonymous city, and behind him too. He paused again: which way? The city, he knew, was a place to get lost in, a place in which to give up his secrets to those who don't care, and so rid them of their sting – but, with so much city, where to begin?

'Sir?'

He turned away from the face of a woman he knew but who didn't know him, cast his eyes down as she passed him and was gone. *I'm sorry, Clare, I'm sorry.* He felt the words growing on his tongue like flowers in some sudden and artificially fast-moving spring, and filling his mouth until he wanted to gag, *was* gagging, would choke for sure, was choking –

'Sir – allow me.'

Was bending double, the other man's arms encircling him from behind, jerking him hard, thrusting his chest up into his throat, until something rose in him – something sharp, something with *edges* that suddenly filled his mouth – then, with one final thrust, was expelled, bright and hard, spinning out in a great graceful arc, then down to the boardwalk where, like Jonah expelled unexpectedly from the whale, it lay, stunned and glistening in the afternoon sun.

James circled him, dropped down to his haunches. His fingers found the object, picked it up, turned it around. 'Well now,' he said, his voice toned with some kind of almost childlike wonderment, 'if I were a man of some religious conviction, I'd surely say this was some kind of sign –'

'Sign?' Matthew was blurry-eyed and heaving still.

'Indeed, sir,' said James, looking up as he did so toward his estimate of the whereabouts of heaven, in his eyes for a moment a son's look of fear, while in his heart there was nothing but the shadow's ancient longing for the light.

59

When the man was in his talking teeth he could talk (so it was said) from Thanksgiving to Christmas without need of a breath. Indeed, so voluble was Ambrose M. Webb liable to become, and so discursive his focus until he seemed to have no focus at all, that even his second wife, on the very evening, no less, of their wedding, is said to have become so profoundly enraged by his talking of God and of horses and of war and much besides, that she was moved to withdraw from her husband-of-a-day that which he had come to expect, with the consequence that the union was from the very start put in jeopardy (much as, as more than one wag would have it, the Union had been, it being, from the start, such an unnatural – and thus doomed – creation), with in turn the consequence that little Jimmy (who was not, in truth, so very little by then, his being – at least in height – nearly a man, although he was – in years – still only a boy) was forced to witness the kind of disharmony between a man and a woman that can only, in a child, lead that child to the belief – conviction indeed – that the sexes, while united by much are divided by more, and, consequently, that any union is doomed unless it is the union of the weak and the strong, which of course is no true union at all but merely a balance of, on the one hand, power, and, on the other, fear – a union, at any rate, both false and unstable, and really no example to offer a boy – especially a boy prone by his nature to excesses both of loneliness and arrogance – to one, indeed, who from his very beginning was in some way aware of his slow-creeping end, and who, consequently, came, through familiarity with its image, not to fear it, but to consider it a friend – and a friend, indeed, worth introducing around as a man will introduce around, to his friends and to all who will listen, the woman who has captured him and will one day be his wife.

'But I don't understand.'

'Understand, sir? What is there but the obvious to understand? You have rid yourself of this unpleasant object, and are surely the better for it.' James paused, slipped his tiny silver crucifix back into his pocket, looked up. 'Do you not feel, sir,' he said, 'better for its expulsion? Do you not sense about your person a new lease of life?'

But Matthew did not sense this: within him and around him there seemed nothing, now, but confusion – nothing but a sickening, sliding kaleidoscope of images – Clare, smiling, her belly rising with new life, then her falling, glass breaking, then, then –

'Sir?'

'Oh God,' came a voice, his own, from close at hand.

'No, sir,' said another, as the images kept coming – his brothers in that chapel, then their lining a trench somewhere down in Virginia, their bodies twisted and faces as empty as the land from which they had come and to which they were now returning, and on and on – General Custer, *the boy with yellow hair*, raising his sabre, then the silence of war's end and the wandering, always wandering, rootless, homeless; then, finally, the whorehouse and the pictures, the rancid stink of chemicals, and Clare, Clare, always Clare – oh God, how long would she haunt him? How long would he see her in his dreams and in the day? How far must he go to escape her forgiveness? How many miles and how many days would be enough for him to be out of her sight – beyond the embrace of all that he loved and loathed? He covered his head with his hands and tried to stop the pounding, but could not, and then, then, oh then other arms were encircling him, holding him tight, as tight as a lover is held, drawing him down and down to some place far away, the caress of secret breath close and warm on his skin and the words, '*Not God, sir, but me,*' crawling over his flesh and into his ear, there to twist and turn and burrow ever deeper, until they had him in their grasp – the essence of him – until that one place inside of him untouched still by a cynical and devouring world was overrun and the fight for faith lost, and all conflict suddenly was over, the front all quiet, the woods and the fields fallen silent at last.

Matthew opened his eyes, looked about him. The street, once so busy, was empty. *Not God, sir, but me.* He turned at the sound of a door. He squinted into the hard light, as a tall, thin man, pale-faced in a uniform of blue, approached. 'Sir?' said the man. He was smiling, his head cocked to one side like a bird's. Beneath one arm he was clutching a number of bags; in his hand, a box; beneath the other arm he had the legs of a tripod, gripped tight and glistening. 'Sir?' he said again. He stopped, maybe three feet away. 'Is there a problem, sir?'

'What?' said Matthew.

'Well, sir, you look a little troubled.'

His mouth was dry. He raised a hand to his head. His scalp was streaming sweat.

'Sir?'

'Where did you come from?'

'Come from? Why, the bar-room, sir.'

'But you were *here*.'

'Here, sir?'

Not God, sir, but me. 'I saw you.'

'Saw me, sir?'

'You were . . . well, *here* –'

Slowly, with the patient deliberation of a tolerant schoolmaster, James Monkton Webb set down his burdens. His hands, then, he held out before him, palms up as if confirming to a doubter their emptiness. 'Sir,' he said, with all the love of a father for a frightened, wayward son, 'I think we should leave this place.'

'Leave?' said Matthew.

'Continue north, sir. I hear General Custer is mustering forces for a new war. I hear, sir, that the Seventh is riding. I hear there's to be a great fight with the Indians, and that Crazy Horse himself has pledged a bullet for the general.'

Matthew looked up. 'Crazy Horse?'

'Indeed, sir,' said James, safe in the knowledge now of the completeness of his victory. 'Now, sir,' he said. 'Shall we ride, sir? Shall we stand once again with our brothers? Shall we head north, sir? Shall we?'

'North,' said Matthew.

'North, sir,' said James. Then, with a magician's sleight of hand, he dipped into his pocket and withdrew a small compass. This he held out before him on a flat, pale palm. The needle beneath the glass spun wildly, slowed, settled. 'There,' he said, looking up. 'We have our direction, sir, and we have our orders. Shall we follow them, sir, like soldiers? Shall we raise up our sabres? Shall we fight, sir? Shall we fight?'

Eddie

60

At six twenty-five on the evening of August ninth, nineteen seventy-four, a man on the very brink of his fortieth year, a man trim in aspect and fit (judging by his positive and straight-ahead striding), was making his way down a boulevard in the city of Memphis, in the grand old state of Tennessee, unseen by a soul except by those occasional drivers who obviously knew little of – and could scarcely care less for – the state of the nation in general, or the office of the Presidency in particular, when he paused for a moment at a line of wrought-iron railings behind which lay a neatly clipped lawn, a number of heavy-slung fruit trees and – beyond them – a grand southern residence (in truth, a little less than a mansion, though it was, at the same time, certainly more than a mere *house*), where, still unseen, he set down his bags, laid his foldaway tripod against the railings, and stared, wide-eyed as a child, at the residence's pillared portico and the long black limousine standing idle in the drive. It was a house – a residence – that, given who owned it now, was surprisingly modest, though more impressive for it.

And the name of that house – that residence?

Graceland, of course.

And the name of the man?

Well, the man was none other than Eddie Reno himself, only son of Eddie Reno, and the only photographer to have ever made President Eisenhower trip on a fireguard and tumble – balding head first – right into a grate full of month-old ash.

But that's another story.

For now, it's nineteen seventy-four, it's August ninth, it's a shade before six-thirty, and President Nixon is about to resign.

Eddie Reno stood a moment at those railings, peering in. It was a funny thing, but all the way down on the train from New York, he'd been trying to imagine what the great man's house would look like in person (as it were) – trying to picture it so as he'd not waste those precious all-important memory-storing moments just going WOW like some out-of-town idiot – but, however hard he'd tried (and he'd tried real hard – even taken a second glass of Jack Daniel's to assist him in the task), he'd been quite unable to come up with anything. All he'd got was just a blank – as if his mind was plain refusing to speculate, what with him being so close – just the train-tracks passing by, just the view from the window, just the face of his wife as she'd told him that morning (as she told him every morning) that *of course* she loved him, and how could he be so silly on this morning of all mornings?

'Yes?'

Standing before a pillar beside the gates, he leaned forward, dipped his head and pressed his lips up close to a grimy plastic grille.

'I have an appointment,' he said.

'You gotta name?'

This morning of all mornings. On the train he'd wondered about that too – wondered what on earth she'd meant – but, like his having tried unsuccessfully to picture the house, no words of explanation had come to him – just the lone nagging thought that he'd forgotten something, or something had happened – something important, something significant, something concerning him about which he knew nothing.

'I *said* you gotta name?'

Eddie cleared his throat. 'Reno,' he said. Silence. A crackling. In the background the burbling of a distant TV.

'*Reno*, you say?'

'Yes, sir.'

Another pause. A minute passed. *This morning of all mornings.* He reached up his finger, was about to press the buzzer again, when the gates clicked and began almost imperceptibly humming. Then slowly, at funereal pace, they opened inward, admitting him. He stepped forward, his feet finding gravel, aware as he did so of the slow-moving swivel of some electronic eye.

This morning, this morning. What on earth had she meant? Still he couldn't think. He frowned as he walked, his lips moving: *Put it out of my mind. Must put it out of my mind.*

The driveway swept left beneath the cool of some trees, then right and on, until it turned in an arc before the house. There were steps, three, then a heavy wooden door. Should he knock? Eddie looked for a bell, then stepped back, looked up. All the upstairs windows were draped against the sun – all but a corner room in to which the evening sun was allowed to stream. *Maybe it's the nursery,* he thought, then he thought *of course not,* as the daughter was – what? Fifteen? Sixteen? He stepped back, tried to see something – anything – through the downstairs windows, but could not: there was nothing to see – just the vague shapes of furniture, just a heavy, settled gloom like that which settles gradually on the features of a house during the first afternoon of a period of mourning.

And then it came to him – standing there – what she'd meant, and he closed his eyes, closed them just as the great wooden door opened inward, just as he saw in the eye of his mind her face again, smiling, heard her laughter in his ears, felt the sly, rhythmic beating of his own fickle heart.

61

B ut that was twenty-five years ago now, and those twenty-five
years that have since passed have passed, it seems to him now, in
less than the blink of an eye, as he finds himself standing again at
that great wooden door, this time in the company of one Swede, three
Americans, and fourteen Japanese. Bizarrely, thirteen of these fourteen
are dressed alike in white jumpsuits and heavy, clanking jewelry, their
oversized stick-on sideburns glistening in the sunshine, and the King-
curling of their little childlike lips sustained – despite the hour's wait and
the day's early heat – with that peculiarly oriental brand of stoicism that
some (they) see as honor, but which others – those mourning – know as
nothing but the engine of cold-hearted slaughter, and the way to some
stinking grave in some stinking far-off earth.

'Sir? Are you with us?'

Eddie turned his head, turning his gaze away from the still-elegant
sweep of the drive, away from the cool of those trees. 'Pardon me?' he
said. Before him, a coiffured, brittle-faced blue-suited woman was
smiling at him mirthlessly, her hands clutching tight to a clipboard.

'I was wondering,' she was saying, 'if you're with us.'

'With you?'

She sighed, letting slip with the sigh, then, a whisper of some
circumstance of her life – some disappointment, perhaps, perhaps in
love – that made, suddenly, of her brittleness – of the everyday effort of
disguise – something grand, something heroic even, and made Eddie, in
that moment, want to reach out and touch her and ask her her secret.
'On the *tour*,' she said. 'I was asking if you're planning on joining us on
the tour?'

'The tour?' Eddie glanced beyond the others to the green wooden
door. *I have an appointment*, came a voice from some long-distant past.

'Sir?'

And he thought once again of that day all those years ago, and how
he'd been so caught up in the details of his own life that he'd quite
overlooked the details of hers.

'Sir, we really should be going –'

'Of course,' he said. 'I'm sorry.'

Oh, how foolish he'd been – how hopelessly, how childishly caught up with the thought of actually meeting Elvis – actually standing there, *him*, in the presence of the King – that his own wife, his *wife*, for heaven's sake, had been sidelined and forgotten – but more than that. He'd forgotten, too, until that moment at this same door all those years ago, that that day had been the nineteenth anniversary of their wedding.

'Well then?'

The others were staring at him – the Japanese especially, their dark marble eyes inscrutable beneath the greased and frozen waves of their kiss-curls.

'Yes, I'm sorry,' he said.

'Okay then,' said the guide, as, one by one, the group made their way up the steps and in.

62

'He's watching the President on TV.'

Do not think I'm still hurting and *See how there's nothing that can touch me now*: this, above all else – way, way above the stillborn joy of a simple wedding anniversary – this was what she'd meant by her smiling. What she'd meant was that losing an only son in what sounded like such a casual way (sometimes, indeed – even to *her* – it felt like they'd just mislaid him, and that any moment now they'd discover him – smiling as he'd always seemed to be smiling – turn him up unexpectedly like you'd turn up a button or a long-given-up album of family photos) – that losing him in that way could no longer reach her – no longer cast her down, and that, from now on, it was all just some vague memory – just some story she'd heard one day on the radio or read about over breakfast in the *Post* or, more likely, the *News*.

Eddie shifted the weight on his shoulder of his camera bag. 'President Nixon's on TV?' he said. *Fourteen-year-old boy goes missing in movie-theater. 'I just turned around and he was gone,' said the father.*

'Uh-huh.'

The mother was hysterical and had to be sedated.

The man at the door was short and squat, a lightning bolt emblazoned on his grubby white T-shirt, the legend *Taking Care of Business* rising and falling over well-toned pecs. He smiled, revealing teeth as white as once had been his shirt. 'Elvis likes watching TV,' he said.

'He does?'

After three days and three nights, police are winding down their search.

'Yes, sir.' He drew a little closer. His smell was a combination of liniment and sweat – the sour, acrid smell of a locker-room. 'You know he's got seventeen?' he said.

'Seventeen?' said Eddie.

'Yup. Seventeen of the fuckers. Got them turned on day and night.' He shook his head, he was smiling still, the smile rich now with the casual ambivalence of a once-loyal but now corrupted courtier. 'Come see for yourself,' he said. He turned away, took a step, turned back. His eyes were narrowed suddenly, as if he were searching for something, some kind of reassurance perhaps. 'You ain't one of them Yankee faggots, are you? Elvis don't like no Yankee faggots.'

Eddie shook his head.

'Okay then,' said the man. He held his searching a moment longer, then turned. 'This way,' he said, and started walking.

Were it not for the light spewing forth from a bank of flickering television sets mounted in the far wall, the windowless room into which Eddie Reno was led that day would have been lost completely in darkness, the figure on the couch unseeable, his presence revealed only by the low and pitiful sound of his crying.

The T-shirt man withdrew, closing the door softly behind him. Eddie stood a moment, squinting, his eyes adjusting to the gloom. He looked at the TVs – fifteen of them maybe, maybe more – at the sweating, jowly face of the President at his desk away some place down in Washington – at the double-darkness of his chins, the glint of deception in his little button eyes, then back to the figure – a man, *the* man – on the couch. *Jesus*, he thought, in part disbelieving the stark evidence of his eyes, *it's him, it's really him*. The man was sitting slumped forward, his once-beautiful head in his hands, staring at the screens, eyes blinking through his tears, the rings on his fingers winking now and then in the light.

Eddie swallowed hard. *For God's sake, it's Elvis*. He cleared his throat. The man blinked but didn't turn. Minutes passed. Eddie tried not to stare, but couldn't stop himself. The man's face was deathly pale, the flesh heavy in the blue light, the dye from his famous black sideburns running down in lines across his cheeks. Eddie cleared his throat again. 'Sir?' he said. 'Are you alright?'

Elvis shook his head. 'Man, they did it,' he said, that rich southern drawl wracked with fear and distress.

'Did it?' said Eddie.

It's him, he thought, *it's really him. It's the King of rock'n'roll.*

'They screwed him, man. They screwed the President –'

Eddie shot a glance at the TVs, then back. 'They did?' he said. '*Who* did?'

'*They* did, man. *They* did.'

'Right,' said Eddie.

Elvis turned his head. His cheeks were wet, his face bathed blue in the light from the TVs. He leaned a little forward, flicked his eyes left then right, as if he feared being overheard. 'They're everywhere, man,' he said, 'everywhere,' his voice now just a whisper. 'Can't you feel them?'

'Well –' said Eddie.

Elvis frowned.

'Sir?'

He squinted hard at Eddie, something changing in his look. 'Who are *you*?' he said. He seemed suddenly sober – suddenly alert – as if he'd been drunk before, half-asleep.

Eddie felt his mouth go dry. 'Sir, my name's Reno. Eddie Reno. I'm a photographer with *Shining Star* magazine? I have an appointment –'

Elvis pushed himself up from the couch. Standing, barefoot, the man still was impressive, even in such gloom – still somewhere, way down, the man he'd once been – still glorious, but sad now – sad and slowly failing in his fight like some kind of cornered bear, his white karate robe drawn tight around his belly with a belt of blue or black. 'Are you lyin' to me?' he said. He stepped forward; Eddie stepped back. 'Are you packing some microphone someplace you ain't telling me about?'

'Microphone? No, sir.'

He loomed then in the low-light, raised up his jeweled hands, gripped Eddie's collar. He lowered his face, hung it in close, the lip curling now in uncertainty and fear as once it had curled in pure joy. 'Are you shitting me, man?' he said. He paused then, as if turning something over, as if he were trying to decide something important.

'Sir?' said Eddie. The breath on his face was sweet, peppermint-scented. 'Should I go fetch somebody? Is there somebody I can call?' He tried to push back, but found his legs jammed against a chair.

'Call? What do you mean, call?'

He shrugged. His heart was pounding so hard he felt certain any minute it would leap from his chest. 'Well, I don't know,' he said. He hesitated. 'I mean, isn't there somebody?'

Elvis paused a moment, moved away. Eddie watched him cross the room, stand before the TVs, up close, the light flickering on his face.

'Sir?' said Eddie.

Elvis shook his head, all the time staring at the screen – at the face of Richard Nixon as, tearful, he took his final leave of the nation. 'Jesus Lord,' he said. 'Will you look what they've done? Do you see what they've gone and done?'

Eddie looked at the screens, at a man amongst other men crossing a lawn, then turning and waving, then climbing some steps and disappearing, stooping, through the door of a waiting helicopter. However you looked at it, it was a sad scene – a picture of endings, a portrait of the final acceptance of a failure long denied.

'Sir?' said Eddie.

Elvis turned. 'No, sir,' he said, 'there ain't nobody.'

At which Eddie opened his mouth to speak, but found no words inside.

Instead he just stood there, looking at the King, thinking suddenly of his wife and his child – of a boy once so alive, so present, a boy with such a future – a boy whose voice now was silent and whose breath – once so warm – was as cool in its absence now as fall's first cooling breeze.

63

'Elvis, as you can see, was laid to rest beside his beloved mother.' Perhaps it was the silent and unseen breaking of some kind of link – some kind of father-son cord – that had turned his face away from the Roxette's silver screen that night – the finger's touch, perhaps, of some cool, other-worldly breeze that had shivered his flesh and turned his attention from the make-believe lives of Jay Gatsby and Daisy, and settled it on the presence of the huge and sudden absence that seemed to fill up the seat beside him. Or perhaps it was just that seeing Myrtle on the screen (and particularly that look of distress she could so easily manage – a look so beguiling to the more sensitive of men) made him suddenly feel a craving for more popcorn, and so turned him in his seat. Yes, perhaps it was nothing more sophisticated – nothing more elemental – than this. Perhaps it was nothing more than greed – a craving for salted popcorn. Or was it sugared? He could never remember. All he could remember – *was* remembering – as, twenty-five years after meeting him, after standing in his presence, he stood with the others in the Garden of Rest gazing down at the grave of Elvis Aaron Presley – was that sudden sickening lurch in his stomach, then a moment of cool (*this can't be happening*, he'd kept thinking, *this can't be happening*), then that panic in his blood, and the sudden searing knowledge that everything had changed in that moment of inattention – and that nothing would ever be the same again.

Eddie nodded, heard the whirring all around him of a dozen or more Japanese motordrives. He closed his eyes, felt the warmth of the sun on his face, felt the slipping then of years, felt a temporary relief from the deadening weight of accumulated time.

'Sir?'

And in a moment he was back once again in that theater, turning once again from that flickering screen, once again finding nothing – the boy gone.

'Sir, we should be moving on.'

He opened his eyes, looked around. Foreign faces were regarding him, some with a cocktail of pity and concern, most, though, with a look of annoyance at his willful, western disruption of a well-practiced routine.

'Sir?'

'Sorry,' he said. From somewhere he pulled up a smile. 'Miles away.'

'Mmm,' said the guide, unimpressed. Then she turned with her clipboard and marched off with some purpose, followed at once by all but two of her group.

64

O h of course they'd hunted and hunted (they'd raised quite a stink in the theater, causing, in the end, the movie to be abandoned, or at least postponed) but had discovered no trace, and soon their searching had ceased, foundering on that slow-creeping blindness that accompanies most enthusiastically a parent's desperation, and makes of their own heart's beating a curse – one from which in this life they may never be freed.

'What did you say?'

And then, and then –

'I said, you reckon he's in there?'

And then they were standing there on the sidewalk – just the two of them, suddenly silent, unspeaking, so completely bereft that not even the presence of each other could in any way slow the speed or ease the severity of that distant but oncoming pain.

'What?' said Eddie. He was squinting in the sun.

The stranger shrugged. 'Elvis,' he said. 'Do you think he's really down there?'

Standing in that shady Memphis garden, looking down upon that grave, Eddie Reno had thought himself alone – so much so, in fact, that he'd cried quite unashamed, and, quite unashamed, he'd felt the tears for his lost boy rolling cool down his cheeks, heard the thunder in his ears of the silence that night on the street, watched again in his mind's eye dusk's slow falling, felt again the rising in his heart of that tide of despair. But then a rustle in the trees and he'd turned.

'What do you mean?' he said. He blinked through his tears, wiped them away hastily with his sleeve.

'I mean that maybe he's not dead at all. I mean when people say they've seen him serving fries at McDonald's that maybe they really *have* seen him, or maybe he really *is* on a beach somewhere, just soaking up the rays with all the rest of them *so-called dead people*. Did you ever think of that, Mr Reno? Well, *did* you?'

Eddie raised a hand, shading his eyes. 'How do you know my name?' he said. He tried to find the stranger's face, but, with his back to the sun, the man's face, like the rest of him, was indecipherable – just an outline filled with different depths of shadow.

'You're tagged,' he said.

'What?' said Eddie.

The stranger pointed to his camera bag, from which hung a plastic-coated label. 'In case you get mislaid, I guess,' he said. There was the curl of a smile in his voice.

Eddie squinted harder. 'Who *are* you?' he said. 'What do you want?'

'Want?' said the stranger. The smile suddenly was gone. He stepped a little nearer, loomed a little larger. 'I want *you*,' he said softly.

'What?'

Then from nowhere – from the shadows – came the rustle of clothing, then the flash of a ring, then – *crunch* – a fist buried deep in Eddie's gut. He staggered forward, stumbling, as the stranger stepped back. He tried to raise his head, tried to focus, but the sudden, unexpected expulsion of wind had him crumpling, until – despite his best efforts – he was tumbling down and down, and then lying face-down on a gravestone, his body retching with the thud of every new blow to his side.

Josh

65

I t seems that, according to the bottle, these pills I've been taking 'make operating electrical machinery hazardous as they may cause drowsiness'. *Well, excuse me*, but isn't that the *point* of sleeping pills? I mean, for Christ's sake, what kind of sleeping pills would they be if they *didn't* make you drowsy? Oh, I suppose, to be fair (and we must be *fair* – mustn't we? – we being democratic Americans), they have to say these kinds of things – have to cover themselves – in case the person who's taking them is so spaced-out from lack of sleep that they get kind of mixed up (been *there* for sure, oh yeah) and instead of lying down and closing their eyes they get up behind the wheel of some forklift truck maybe, or maybe a school-bus full of other people's kids, and then the next thing they know they're lead story on the early-evening news and then there's people pointing and turning away from them in the street and soon they can't take the dreams any longer (oh, they're sleeping *now*, alright – now that there's bad dreams to dream) and so they find themselves standing in some hardware store someplace like Toledo maybe, having a conversation about the different qualities of rope and then standing like this on some cheap old piece of motel furniture just looking for the courage to push off and swing. And all because of a bunch of pills that were *supposed* to make things better.

Well Jesus.

You know, thinking about it now – thinking about all those circular, contradictory things that happen in a life – it occurs to me that to get through it in one piece you've either got to be pretty damn stupid (so as you don't even *see* the craziness of it all) or so smart that you can see it all, but you can *also* see that nothing really matters – that, in the end, it's all just about as important – as significant – as, say, watching a movie or eating a hamburger.

Or writing a book, for that matter.

On the subject of which, I should perhaps say that the circumstances in which you find me here are not exactly what they probably seem. Like most of my life, it's not real life – just research. You see, before I got distracted by those damn pills, I was thinking about THE STORY

(I don't know why, but I feel I should capitalize it) – thinking about Nathan and Libbie Custer and Robert the butler and poor, dead Care who may or may not be returning to life, and wondering quite how to work it all out. All I know is that not everyone can survive – and so someone must die. But who? And how? Okay, so perhaps if I'd figured it out before I started, then I wouldn't be in this mess now. But I didn't. So. Figure it out now is what I should do.

Okay then. Options. If it's Nathan (and there *is* that convenient bear, don't forget), then it's Robert that gets to smile as the lovely Clare returns to him, released (rather bizarrely, I'll agree) from the clutches of an early death. However, on the other hand (and there is always another hand), if that bear *doesn't* get him and he somehow survives, then it's goodnight, Clare, once and, finally, for all.

So you see my dilemma.

None of which, of course, goes any way to explaining this rickety table or, indeed, this rope.

Well, like I said, it's research. You see, if it's Clare for the old heave-ho, then how could Robert possibly cope? Well, the answer is he wouldn't. So what would he do? Hang himself is my guess – hence the situation you see before you.

Hence this research.

Anyway.

I guess I should take this thing off now and get down before Davie turns up for tonight's game. He already thinks I'm crazy enough (some irony that – Davie, that swears he's seen Elvis serving fries at McDonald's, thinking *I'm* crazy) – and there's no point in confirming it. Not, of course, that he'll necessarily come by at all. He didn't last night after all – nor, it occurs to me, the night before. Ah well. I guess if he comes or he doesn't come, it doesn't really make a whole lot of difference. Either way, it's just a different way of waiting. Either way, I'll still be here tomorrow, still be sitting here waiting for the time to pass, still be longing for and fearing the rasp of some engine getting nearer and nearer, and the sound of that voice in the parking-lot.

Nathan & Robert

66

'Hello?' He took another step forward. '*Hello?* Is there anyone there?'

Most times, for Nathan Zeitezmann III, the things he most longed for were also the things he most feared.

Like now, for example. How long had he dreamed of this chance of redemption (not for him, for another – but we'll get to that) – dreamed of this chance to face down his fear – to confront it and vanquish it, and so make of all that his name meant he carried suddenly nothing – remove, in one moment of selflessness, the stain that had been handed down to him as surely as a birthmark.

Another step in the gloom. He paused. He tried to listen out for something – a sign, anything (he'd heard breathing – he was sure of it), but all he could hear now was the thudding of his heart and the rushing of blood in his ears.

He lifted his flashlight, swept the walls. The walls were weeping, the air heavy with moisture. He drew a sleeve across his face, tried to blink the sweat away. He licked his dry lips, tasted the salt tang of blood.

Blood.

Always blood.

It was blood he'd been running from, blood that had sent him so far away to Europe, and blood, now, with his mother's slow dying, that was bringing him home. But most of all it was the curse of it – the stain of it – that for so long had marked him out – that for so long had covered his father's hands and so his . . .

For so long – but *how* long? Well, forever, had he known it – had he known as a child what had paid for that luxury, had he known, then, what (as they say) he knew now.

Which was?

Well, murder – nothing less. Nothing less, indeed, than butchery – and butchery on such a scale that it boggles the mind to consider it – so many bodies, in fact, that they could not – and never will – be counted.

And all in the name of progress.
And gold, of course.
All in the name, then, of progress and gold.

67

'**M**rs Zeitezmann?'

When, in the spring of eighteen sixty-seven, at the age of twenty-eight, General George Armstrong Custer (yes, it's that man again) was given his first command of cavalry on the great North American plains, he was like a man coming home. It was the challenge for which his whole life had prepared him. It was – would be – a challenge that would lead him in the end to Sitting Bull and to the Sioux's new shirt-wearer, Crazy Horse – that would lead to that desolate rise, then to that moment of peace amid the confusion, and to a life retold in the moments of death.

'Robert? Is that you?'

'Yes, ma'am.'

And it was that famous death (amid many, many others, both before and after) that had bought for Nathan Zeitezmann II this grand, empty house on Long Island – those guns, those bullets, those ghastly, bleached bodies stripped both of their uniforms and the dignity of the dead, that gave him that which – as a poor boy from Arkansas – he'd dreamed of at night and had been planning for with every passing moment of daylight.

'Is he home?'

Truly, it had been – was still – a life made from death – a future made flesh on the bleached and clean-picked bones of others.

'Home, ma'am?' Robert stepped lightly to the window, edged back the drape. The storm – so certainly predicted – was passing overhead and away now, moving slow like a shadow out to sea.

'Robert?'

He turned back to the bed. 'Ma'am,' he said. He hesitated.

Mrs Zeitezmann stirred. 'What is it, Robert?' Her voice – once so clear, so *musical* – was just a whisper now, just an echo of what it once had been.

'Well –'

The sound of rustling as she pushed herself up. Once the spirited belle of so many balls (*The lady shines like a sun*, it had been written of her more than once in various of the New York papers), she seemed nothing now but tiny – that spirit withered so, until all that remained of it was the little that was necessary to keep hope alive. 'Tell me,' she said.

Unheard, Robert drew a shallow breath. 'Well, ma'am –' He looked down at his shoes as if for strength, looked up. 'I fear, ma'am, the young master may be . . . lost.'

From the darkness of the bed a sharp gasp. '*Lost?*'

'Well, I fear, ma'am – no word having been received for some hours – that we must all, well, brace ourselves for the possibility of a tragedy –'

'*Tragedy?*'

'Yes, ma'am.'

Silence.

'Ma'am?'

'No, Robert.'

From far away came the distant rumble of thunder – from far away and growing further with every passing moment.

'But, ma'am –'

The turning *no* of a head on a pillow.

Robert stepped forward (only the sight of his tears, he knew, would convince her), and he would have stepped again had something invisible – some barrier – not stopped him. He sighed, for he knew what it was. For years he had known such denial – felt the strength of it – felt it in his bones and in the flow of his blood. For years the years and their passing had meant nothing. For years he'd been asleep.

'Robert?'

But now he was awake.

'It's true,' he said. 'You must believe me, Mrs Zeitezmann –'

'Believe you?'

'And believe how sorry we are.'

'We?'

'Mrs Jackson and I, ma'am. We really are both so terribly sorry.'

'*Mrs* Jackson? You're *married*, Robert?'

Robert couldn't in that moment stifle a smile. 'Yes, ma'am,' he said. 'This very morning. In the garden. Do you not remember?'

'Remember?'

'Certainly, ma'am. Do you not recall the flowers?'

'Flowers?'

'In your hair, ma'am.'

From deep in the gloom, a rustling of covers, the raising of a pale, bony hand. 'In my hair?' said a light and distant voice.

'And your dress, ma'am,' said Robert. 'All the other ladies were perfectly jealous –'

'They were?'

'Indeed, ma'am – what with you looking so radiant. Even Miss

Summerfield – that's Mrs Jackson now, of course – said so. She said she feared she would be outshone –'

From deep in the gloom, a low whisper.

'Mrs Zeitezmann?'

Robert padded up to the bedside, leaned forward, turned his head. 'Pardon me?' he said.

'I was well?'

'Indeed, ma'am. You were radiant. And dancing, ma'am, with such . . . *style* –'

'I was dancing?'

Robert nodded, a smile spreading across his face. In his mind's eye he could see her, turning in the arms of Mr Zeitezmann, the blue and gold of her dress shining, shimmering in the light cascading down from the French chandeliers.

'You were first on every dance card,' he said. 'Truly like a bride yourself –'

More rustling then, the straining of muscles for so long underused. Then, suddenly, a face looming out from the canopy's gloom. It was pale and drawn, skin over skull, stretched taut, eyes such a pale blue they seemed surely sightless, and, curling this way and that, wisps of hair so fine that it had to be the hair of some newborn baby, or come as a gift at the end of a life from some selfless, generous angel. The lips, so long ago red, but now faded like the scarlet fabric of an armchair left too long in the sunlight, opened slightly in an effort of speech, the price of which effort was reflected in a narrowing of the eyes.

Robert leaned a little closer, turned his ear toward the old lady's lips. Another whisper, too low to decipher.

'You'll have to speak up,' said Robert softly.

Again the parting of lips, again the faintest expulsion of breath. Robert narrowed his own eyes in concentration.

'Happy,' came the whisper.

'Happy, ma'am?' said Robert.

A pause, the low heaving of a chest, a rasping intake of breath. 'Was I . . . *happy?*'

Robert turned his head to face the old woman. Her eyes, so, so pale, were brimming with tears. She lifted her brows in a question, imploring.

Robert smiled. 'We were *all* happy,' he said. 'Every one of us. We were living the lives that had been meant for us. It was like . . . like we'd all woken up from some terrible dream –'

Mrs Zeitezmann eased back, laid her head on the pillow.

'Mrs Zeitezmann?' There were tears for sure rolling slow down the old woman's face. Robert eased forward; he was deep in the gloom now. He reached up a hand, laid it tender on her brow. She closed her eyes at his touch. 'Mrs Zeitezmann?' he said. Her flesh was so thin he could sense the cool hardness of the skull it so barely obscured. She stirred, half-turning her head. She opened her eyes. 'And Nathan?' she said, barely audible now. 'Was he grand in some fine suit? Was he the handsomest of all?'

Robert nodded. 'The handsomest,' he whispered, unashamed of the lie. Then he lifted his hand and closed the old lady's eyes as he'd seen people do, then sat for a moment before crossing the room to gently close the drapes.

68

'And in the midst of life we are in death. Amen.'

'Amen.'

Libbie opened her eyes as Captain Irvine closed his Bible. With all the dignity of his position, he motioned for all to sit – for the dinner in earnest to begin. The scraping of chairs then, and soon, again, there was chatter. To Libbie's left, the gentleman from Toledo resumed his (to *him* at least) most amusing tale concerning that city's last-but-one mayor, while, to her right, a man who called himself Barrington, but was quite obviously a Jew, tried to interest her *again* in the fortunes of his coke-smelting business. 'Can you believe such a thing?' he said, after a full quarter-hour's dissertation on the short-sighted faithlessness of the modern American investor. 'I mean, would you say that the general would have stood for such, such . . . feeble-mindedness?'

Libbie Custer looked up from her soup. Mr Coke-smelter notwithstanding, she couldn't help but feel the whole occasion both absurd and inappropriate. After all, what, really, had been achieved? The death of some poor wretched creature was what – a creature, indeed, greatly more sinned against than sinning, whose only crime had been to be born a bear and not a man.

'Mrs Custer?'

She raised her shoulders in the slightest of shrugs, turned her head disdainfully away. 'Sir,' she said coolly, 'I assure you I have never considered such a question.' She turned back, noticing as she did so – and with some satisfaction, her never having been able to abide the way a Jew will blame all but himself for some failure in business – how the face of the coke-smelter was suddenly a little paler than hitherto, his jaw a little slacker, as if he could scarcely comprehend the stark evidence of his ears. 'Now, sir,' she said. 'I wonder if *I* may ask *you* a question?'

'Me?'

'You, sir.'

Mr Coke-smelter nodded, uncertain. He straightened in his chair, as if in preparation for some minor but without doubt unpleasant assault.

Libbie looked down again at her soup. The soup was thick and a very pale green, all the time shifting this way and that with the motion of the ship, all the time ebbing and flowing with what seemed like a miniature tide of its own. 'Well,' she said. 'I was wondering –' She paused, held a beat, looked up.

'Wondering?'

She smiled. 'I was wondering, sir, if you quite realize the effect that a gentleman such as yourself can have on a mere feeble woman –'

The gentleman Jew swallowed hard, his face growing redder, as if warmed by the flames of some industrial furnace. 'Effect?' he said, his voice cracking on the word. 'Why, I'm sure, madam, I have no idea –'

'Or, more precisely, on *this* feeble woman. To wit, sir, an immediate and unshakable desire for the end of the world to announce itself – for the thunder to rage and the seas to rise, so that all this talk about coke-smelting might once and for all eternity cease, and I, sir, deceased though I may be, might be allowed a moment's peace.'

Another pause, then, as the coke-smelter and those adjacent to him looked aghast, open-mouthed, upon the scene of this sudden and unexpected ambush.

'I say,' said the captain, from away down the table, 'is there a problem? Is everyone quite at ease?'

'No, sir,' said Libbie, pushing her chair back without assistance and standing. 'I for one, sir, am far from at my ease –'

'You *are*, madam? But why –'

'*Why?*' She spread her arms wide, so encompassing all before her. '*This* is why, sir – this *celebration* –'

'But, madam –'

'It is a sham, sir –'

'A . . . *sham*, madam? What in the Lord's name can you mean? Are you quite well?' The captain rose from his chair, looked around for a steward, looked back to this strange, angry woman. 'Perhaps,' he said, lowering and sweetening the tone of his voice, 'perhaps you'll allow me to render you some assistance –'

'Assistance?' said Libbie.

'Maybe help you to your cabin –'

'My cabin? Why?'

'Well, it seems, madam, you are perhaps a little tired. The voyage, after all, has been, shall we say, on the eventful side –' Here he glanced around the table, a sudden broad smile drawing grateful reflection from the majority of his guests. Then he glanced to the steward, motioned him forward. 'Perhaps,' he said, 'a little rest is what the doctor might order –'

'The doctor?' said Libbie, brushing aside the steward's outstretched arm. 'No, sir. It is not *I* who is sick, sir. No, sir, on the contrary, it is you, sir – all of you, indeed – who is in need of attention –'

'Please, madam, be calm.'

'Calm?' said Libbie.

'You're hysterical –'

She shook her head. 'No, sir,' she said. 'I am quite calm.' She paused then, swept the room with her eyes. A full circuit, then she settled her gaze once again on the captain's reddening face. 'Captain,' she said. 'May I ask you something?'

'Ask me something?' He frowned. There was sweat, Libbie noticed, gathering in his beard and above the collar of his shirt. 'Well –'

'May I ask you,' she said, 'why it is, sir, you are so readily prepared to glory in slaughter? And so soon, indeed, after the death of your own son? Why, sir, you consider the cornering, outnumbering, and then *murder* of such a fine and noble creature a cause for such . . . *celebration*?' She paused, swept the faces, again, of the other startled diners. 'Well?' she said, addressing them all. 'Can nobody answer me? Is there no one amongst you who finds the events of this day in the slightest bit regrettable?' All eyes looked away; Libbie shook her head. She looked at the captain. 'And you, sir,' she said, 'are you proud of yourself now? Are you pleased with the success of this . . . *massacre*?'

The captain, sweating hard now, opened his mouth, intending to speak, but found himself unable. In the stead of words came the whisper of a long withheld sigh. He lowered his head, set his hands on the table. His eyes closed, as, unknown to those watching, he thought again of the tumblers he'd seen once as a child in a circus, and how the fear of their falling had stuck him fast to his seat.

'I thought so,' said Libbie, pushing back from the table and turning. She stood a moment, unsteady on her feet, then, slowly, with all the dignity her age and the ship's lazy rolling would permit, she crossed the silent room to the door, gripped the handle, turned it firmly, and stepped out into the corridor.

69

S he closed the door firmly behind her. She closed her eyes. She was breathing hard. She tried to gather herself in that yellow-lighted corridor, tried to think of nothing – but nothing – like everything – is beyond the capacity of the mind to imagine, and so she failed, and so, with regret, she opened her eyes. She stood, half-listening at the door for the sound of voices. None came. *You must take it easy, Mrs Custer. Be aware at all times of your age.* Unseen, she shook her head, as if disputing the words of Doctor Overstreet again, as if he were again in her presence. She stood a moment then, blinking hard. The overhead lights flared in her vision, settled. She found the pulse below her left hand with the thumb of her right and tried to count, but gave it up as a pointless waste of effort. She was alive, wasn't she? She dropped her hands, held her palms against the cool of her dress. In this way she stood quite still for a minute or so, then, moving into the gentle rolling pitch of the ship, she made her way down the corridor, the only sounds as she walked the light clip of her heels on the floor's high-polished wood and the whisper of her dress against the rail.

It took a while to find her cabin (there were so many turns – lefts and then rights – that seemed to have been set there just to confuse her) – such a time, indeed, that when finally she was turning her key – that when at last she was standing in her own precious space, the door locked and bolted behind her, she felt really quite light-headed, and, for the first time, really, in so long, the weight of every one of her sixty-eight years. She sat heavy at her dressing table. *Sixty-eight, sixty-eight.* Squinting, she studied her face in the light. Sometimes it was hard and sometimes it was easy to see all of her life in her eyes – in the lines that played about them and the shadows that cast their febrile darkness on her flesh.

Sometimes hard and sometimes easy.

Well, tonight it was easy.

She sighed, leaned a little forward. It was as easy, tonight, to chart all her years, as it had once, as a girl, been impossible to believe in their coming. Then, all ahead had been mystery; now, what was mystery was its so-swift passing. She touched her face with the tips of her fingers. Sometimes she felt – sometimes she could *see* – that she'd traveled so far and seen so much, only to lose it – the taste of it all, the smell of it, the feel of it – as soon as the moment had been lived and was past, and that, consequently, it felt as if she had really been no further – despite all the miles – than her father's house on Summerfield Avenue, and that – despite the evidence of so many years – she was still just a girl peeking out from her bedroom window at the young man in the street below with the long golden hair.

I'll stand here forever, Miss Bacon. Did you hear me? I'll stand here forever.

She smiled at herself smiling back in the looking-glass.

I'll stand here forever, until you are mine.

Oh, he'd had such life and such death in his eyes, and, that day – that greatest of days – such a shine to his sabre that it had trapped the spring sunshine and turned it upon her, until its glare had forced her head away – but only for a second – and, when she'd turned back, there he was still, just as he'd promised, leaning, so casual, against the oak tree, his boots so black, his uniform so blue, the smile on his face so filled with such joy.

A tap on her door.

'Mrs Custer?'

She frowned. 'Nathan?' she said, as that day of all days bled away.

'Ma'am?'

She rose hurriedly (too hurriedly, for such rising at such speed made her dizzy) and crossed to the door. Another tap as she fumbled with the lock, with the bolt. 'I'm coming,' she said. At last the bolt was back; she turned the handle and pulled. 'Oh, Nathan, I'm sorry –' she started, but the steward's pinched face cut her dead.

'Mrs Custer?' he said. 'Are you alright?' He had a thick woolen blanket folded over his arm. 'Would you like me to send for the doctor, ma'am?'

Libbie shook her head. Since early afternoon, since news had reached her of the death of the bear, she'd been waiting for – hoping for – Nathan's tap on her door, for the chance to see his smile again, for the chance to ask his forgiveness for whatever she'd said – whatever she'd done – that had driven him away.

The steward unfolded the blanket from his arm. 'A cool night ahead,' he said. 'Freezing fog, maybe ice. The bridge says we've to deliver these to the old . . . the more eld . . . I mean, well, to some of the passengers –' Flustered, he held the thing out.

'Thank you,' said Lilbie, still a little unsteady. She stood, waiting, until the steward turned away and, in a moment, was gone. She stepped back, once again closed the door. She stood then, swaying gently with the movement of the ship, as, far below her in the darkness, in the ship's iron belly, the engines drove on, driving them all, man and machine, slow through the dark, freezing waters, and on and on to their journey's end.

Josh

70

Everytime I see a car like mine coming the other way I always wonder where it is I'm going. Or if I see another man wearing shoes just like mine, I can't help but think that maybe my feet really are taking me someplace at last where I won't always feel this sense of dislocation – that maybe at last there's finally an end coming to this feeling I've had ever since I was a child that there's someone out there who's leading my life, and that this life *I've* been leading (with, it has to be said, some modest degree of success) is really someone else's, and should – at the earliest opportunity – be returned. All of which, of course, means nothing in particular – or would do, if it hadn't been for last night.

Last night? you say. (Or I *imagine* you saying – for which indulgence you'll have to excuse me, as it gets so damned lonely in this motel, even when Davie comes by, or, maybe, *especially* when Davie comes by . . .)

Anyway.

Last night.

Which went (as they say) something like this.

Well, I'd just got Libbie Custer on her feet at that dinner – just got her ranting at the captain – when I happened to look up and out at the parking-lot, where, to my (only partial) surprise, I saw myself looking back – looking (I see now) only partially surprised. Oh, of course it was only my reflection in the window – I know that now, and I suppose most of me knew it then.

Most, but not all.

You see (and this is the thing), there is, it seems, still that part of me – after all this time – that sees me (as I've said) driving other cars down other streets and wearing other shoes – that sees me, in short, living other lives.

But, you say (again my apologies), *we all feel like that*.

Which, *excuse me*, is bullshit. Okay, you *think* you do (oh sure, you might genuinely believe it) – but you don't. And how do I know? Well, I know because it's me that's sitting here waiting in this crummy motel – not you. Because it's me – not you – that's sitting here wondering what in the hell he's going to say (or do, for that matter) when the time comes around and he's off to that meeting, while all the time he's trying to keep himself together just long enough to finish this book that even now is so long overdue that his editor (bless you, Clare) has had time while she's been waiting to get married and divorced (not to mention have a baby) – not to mention send out a search party for me that even made the local news. And all because of a goddamn book. A book, for Christ's sake.

On the subject of which.

You know, it occurred to me earlier (while I was, again, waiting for Davie, which, I sometimes feel, is really all I'm doing here) that there's a couple of things in the story of Libbie and Nathan that I may not have made crystal clear – things which, if I deal with right now, might (at least for a while) put an end to this meandering and get me back on track.

So.

Number one is this business of Annie – the woman, that is, who left the Zeitezmanns' service having 'disgraced the house'. Well, is it clear that her 'offense' was getting herself pregnant? Or did I not say that at all? Sometimes it's so hard to keep track. Anyway, that (whether I said it or not – and, anyway, I'm saying it now) is the fact of the matter. *Why?* you say, by which I imagine you mean why the hell can't I leave any of these women alone? Why must they always be victims? And why, for heaven's sake, are almost all of them called Clare?

Well, I don't know, is one answer. (Not the right one, of course, as to tell *that* would be telling.)

Anyway, suffice it to say that the whole point of this exercise (as, indeed, was the whole point of *The Shadow Catcher*, my previous 'success') is, really, nothing more profound – nothing more *literary* – than a somewhat (I see now) pathetic attempt to persuade a certain person (no prizes now for guessing the name) that the mistake they made all those years ago was just *that* – a mistake – and that the man they looked at but never really saw really *was* worth seeing – a man so smart, indeed, that his name is on the cover, now, of a whole shelf of books, not to mention his picture sitting there in the pages of newspapers and magazines so numerous now so as to be beyond counting.

But I digress. It is, after all, the shortcomings (many, no doubt) and inaccuracies (who knows?) of my story that's supposed to be the real point of this rant, not my failure with the one person who's ever meant anything to me.

So.

Point number two, thus –

Do you remember I left Nathan down below, searching for the bear in that ship's darkest recesses? And do you also remember that I left him (quite callously, it seems now) aware of *'the labored rasp of another's breathing and the gaze in the darkness of other eyes upon him*'? Well, frankly, what the hell was all that about?

The bear, you say, *it was the bear*.

Well, maybe, maybe not. I mean, what if the bear had already been shot in some other part of the ship? Whose eyes, whose breathing, could it possibly have been then?

Search *me*. *I'm* only writing this shit down. You see, it doesn't come *from* me, but *through* me. You see, I don't know it until I write it, and even *then* –

But hey.

You're right.

Get a grip.

Okay then.

There.

So.

First, though, before I proceed – before I find out just what on earth's been going on with Nathan and that ship – a word or two about Davie, who, I feel, I may have been somewhat misrepresenting.

Okay, so he's crazy, what with his bent-barrel shotgun and his firm belief (you can't shake him – believe me, I've tried) that Elvis really *is* alive and cooking French fries someplace down in Oklahoma. Okay – but so what? To say that is not to say he's any crazier than the rest of us.

I mean, Jesus. Look at me.

Or, on second thoughts, maybe not. I, after all, am really not here at all, am I? I mean I, Eddie Reno Jnr, am really someplace else – am I not? Am I not on some freeway somewhere driving a car just like mine? Am I not someone else wearing shoes just like these? Am I not out there somewhere living my own real, intended life?

Nathan

71

J ust as, often, the mind will, in the quietest of moments, be deafened by the lightning and thunder of unsought and unedited thought, so will, often – in a moment of uproar – a silence descend – a silence so complete, so unearthly, that a man may look around and think himself quite mad, or, perhaps, think himself the only sane man in a world of the mad – which is, of course, in the end, the same thing.

Mad or sane, then – the face or the image of the face. We know them both – have studied them at bus depots, in mirrors, or on the streets of New York City – and we call them by different names. But they are the same – of course they are the same. It is only in the shifting, ever-changing means of their apprehension that we can draw that comforting line between them.

But they are the same.

And we carry them with us wherever we go: not *two* sides, but *one* whole.

Me.

And you.

And Nathan.

Stepping, now, an hour or so back in time, we find him – the now-motherless (although, of course, he doesn't know it yet) Nathan Zeitezmann III – standing, still, in the moist and seeping blackness of the ship's deepest cargo hold, listening, transfixed, to the distant, muted, pipe-borne sound of voices – then to a single booming voice (Captain Irvine's, he imagines, though he has, of course, no way of knowing) – then nothing, then the far-off sound of footsteps receding.

And *then*?

He holds his breath. He turns his head. It's maybe two hours – maybe more – since the shots (were they really shots? He's convinced now that they were), and still he cannot move. Still his limbs are heavy, immovable, still his thoughts frozen by the presence, somewhere – he knows it – of another living creature.

A sound.

He turns his head.

Those eyes, again, unseen.

He squints, harder.

Again that breathing.

'Hello?' he whispers, half-afraid of the giveaway sound of his own voice.

Nothing.

He closes his eyes. His mother lies before him then, as still as some corpse. He opens his eyes, dismissing the image. But the image, in that darkness, will not be dismissed. 'Oh Lord,' he says softly, aware suddenly of his heartbeat, and, consequently (for so are they linked), of the silence, now, of hers. He fumbles for his matches, strikes up the last, precious one. He stares aghast at the picture of his face on the water-bleeding wall.

You are the reason we all went before, the sum total of all of our lives.

The flame spits and burns out, burning his hand. The darkness envelops him.

You are the reason.

Alone.

For the first time, now, he is truly alone.

Just the two of him.

72

They would never be married, the two of them – not if that month (or any other month, for that matter) were suddenly to be formed from no other days but Sundays, or until at least one pig (unfortunate, that use of the P-word, given – as we shall see – the real reason behind this prohibition) had developed and exercised the means of natural flight. Cold days in hell came into it too, as did the threat (now, of course, redundant) of *what it would do to your mother*. In short, then, it was never going to happen – at least not with permission, with any kind of blessing. And without? Well, without meant, consequently, without money or a future – and what kind of future would that mean? No, the son struggled (or *appeared* to struggle), though in his heart, in truth (though he'd have thought about dying before admitting it) he'd been glad. *We're too young*, he'd told himself – her too. *Too young?* she'd said. *But we love each other, don't we? Yes*, he'd said, *but still* – and then she'd mentioned the baby. *I thought we'd call him Nathan*, she'd said, *after you* –

Nathan Zeitezmann IV, son of Nathan Zeitezmann III and Annie Campbell, for two months maid to Mrs Zeitezmann.

A *maid*, for heaven's sake.

And a Catholic.

A Jew and a Catholic?

Never going to happen, that.

And so, protesting (but not too hard, lest some miracle occur and his honor – his obvious wish to do the right thing – be rewarded), he went overseas. To London and Paris and Berlin and Rome he traveled, by ship, boat and train, equipped with his father's money (when faced with such an adventure, the word *bribe* – for that was what it was, and what he *knew* it was – soon lost its sting), and finally, then, to Florence – to rooms looking onto the Piazza del Giorno, and a bed so deep and so curiously concave that to sleep in it alone was to sleep, nevertheless, as if in the arms of a lover.

Not that he slept alone in it for long. He had money, after all, and looks – not to mention the smile, still undimmed, that had first enticed and then reassured Annie Campbell, and which, one evening, at the Pensione Garibaldi, over a dinner of spaghetti alla puttanesca, he laid before the eyes of a girl, maybe eighteen, maybe nineteen, who that evening returned to him, from her place beside the serving-table, a look quite the converse of his – a look both of curiosity and estrangement, like that which forms on the face of a child at a zoo as he stands before a cage in a light, unfelt drizzle, gazing in upon the face of some shallow, grinning monkey.

'Soup,' she said a while later, as she placed the bowl carefully before him.

He leaned forward (to take in the aroma, of course), brushing his arm against hers as he did so. Then he turned his head again, again that smile. '*Scuse*,' he said. She blushed, turned away, and in a moment was gone.

Another maid, then. History repeating itself? Indeed so – although this one would be more. She would be a mirror for that part of him that was not his father. She would be the curse of his conscience made flesh.

73

'Where are we going?'

Whether or not Botticelli's *Pallas and the Centaur* was a political or a moral allegory (or both, or, indeed, neither) was not a question that troubled Alessandra del Piero; nor did she care much for those whom it *did* trouble. To her – whose education had equipped her only for an appreciation of line and of color – an appreciation, indeed, of only those features that sit projected, upturned, on the cornea of an eye – such people were to be pitied for their willingness to forsake the immediate joy of natural sight for that blind disengagement of understanding, when, all the time, understanding – *real* understanding – the kind that you feel in your heart (and which from there, perhaps, may bleed into your soul) – comes not from the bridled restrictions of sense but from the senses unhitched and left free to roam.

'Ssh,' she whispered, half-turning. 'It's late now. People sleeping.'

'Yes – people like *me*,' said Nathan. He dropped his head back onto the pillow. Yawning, lying central (of course) in that strangely dipping bed, he spread his arms wide on the covers, like a man being crucified in great luxury. He stretched, let the fingers of one hand trace the ridges in the spine of the girl's naked back. She pushed up, stood; his hand fell away.

'It's time,' she said softly, turning. Her flesh – so palely tanned by the light of noon – was as gold now by candlelight as the day's rich golden sunset now nearly two hours past. She pulled her dress on over her head, let it fall. Nathan felt himself stirring at the thought of her nakedness newly covered. He stretched out his hand, but she stepped away.

'You tell me you want adventure,' she said. She bent at the waist to consider herself in the mirror. 'But you cannot leave your bed.' She turned to Nathan, the candlelight gleaming in her eyes. With a huff, she said, '*Americans*,' turning back then to the mirror.

Nathan sighed, lay a moment looking up at the gloomy stuccoed ceiling. 'Maybe I'd get out of bed if I knew what *for*,' he said.

'For *adventure*,' said Alessandra. She stood up; she was ready. She set her hands on her hips. 'You come?' she said.

Nathan turned his head on the pillow. 'It has to be now?' he said. 'In the middle of the night?'

She nodded. 'I wait downstairs,' she said. She turned, then crossed to the door, closing it gently behind her.

He closed his eyes, for a moment let himself drift. Outside, beyond and below the window, two cats were fighting, snarling and yelping. He opened his eyes, pushed himself up, looked around.

I thought we'd call him Nathan, after you.

He reached up a hand, rubbed his eyes. The candlelight flickered in some unseen draft, sending grotesque, bloated shadows arching over the bed, the floor, the half-open drawers of the simple wooden chest. He lay back another minute, then, with the self-righteous groan of a martyr, peeled back the covers, swung his feet around, set them on the floor. The floor – polished wood – was cool to the touch. He felt for his slippers (Robert always set them so neatly, just in the right place), but of course they – like so much on this trip, so many comforts – were absent. He cursed, silently. He pushed himself up, made his way around the bed to the washstand and the mirror.

I thought we'd call him Nathan.

He leaned forward, studied himself in the candle's yellow light. His face was sickly-looking, the color of parchment. He stuck out his tongue. *I can find nothing wrong with you*, Doctor Williams had said on the eve of his departure, *it's just nerves. A good dose of sea air will fix you.* Nathan winced at the memory of his sickness on the train and, again, at the lurch as the ship had left the quayside. He'd sat, then, in his cabin and wept like a baby – actually, shamefully, *cried* – only stopping when a kind of exhausted half-sleep had come mercifully to claim him. Then, in his half-dream (and here is the true worth of the mercy of such half-sleep), he'd stood by – a spectator – as a slow parade of faces had passed before him, each one the same but different – each one the face, of course, of Annie Campbell, each face a little further from that portrait of such joy her announcement had made of it, and a little nearer to that terrible, shaming look in the heaving, waving masses that had raised something in him and had made him turn away – but from which, of course, he could not turn away – a look of such mute acceptance, a look so other-worldly in its calm disengagement that it stayed with him that first night though he tried to dismiss it – though the ship with its ghastly pitching and rolling had him retching and wishing for death, while all the time there she was, staring upward from deep within the crowds, her eyes glazed, blind, her face pale, then growing smaller as the great ship eased away and out into the sun-dappled Sound.

74

'Alessandra?'

Without the continual and ever-changing ebb and flow of its people, the city of Florence at night had the empty, echoing feel of an ancient stone reservoir drained unexpectedly of water. There was that hollowness about it that makes the midnight walker so aware of the clipping of his footsteps – that makes him so self-conscious like a thief is self-conscious, lest the sound provide clues as to his whereabouts – clues that might lead to his arrest, and thence to his imprisonment and a life spent enclosed under lock and key.

'Alessandra? Are you there?' Nathan's eyes, despite the night's slow-rising coolness, were still blurry, his limbs still heavy from their sudden awakening. He stared off up the street, trying to make out the figure of the girl in the gloom. 'Oh, for God's sake,' he said low. He was squinting hard.

When at last his eyes found her, she was standing at the end of the street, waiting, leaning back against an old stone fountain formed in the shape of some vast exotic flower supported on the shoulders of four outward-facing lions. The fountain, at this hour, was as mute as the lions, the only sound, way off, the whispered breathing of the Arno moving sleek as a cat between its deep-ocher banks. She cupped her hands to her mouth. 'I learn all Americans are brave,' she called out, the seam of a smile running now through her words. 'All George Washington. All Mr Roosevelt.'

'Look, will you wait there?' said Nathan. He moved on, cursing, stumbling then on a raised and spiteful cobblestone.

Alessandra del Piero, maid, waitress, image of faithfulness, laughed. 'I learn all Americans can be presidents. I learn all Americans are pioneers. All rushing for gold.'

Nathan lifted his foot. 'Well, not this one.' He rubbed his instep, cursing harder, his curses spinning upwards, then dying, muffled, in the dark-shuttered street. He looked up. Suddenly, again, the girl was gone. He sighed; then, hobbling slightly, he moved on, listening all the time like some Indian scout for the sound of her footsteps, aware all the time (though he could not, yet, have so recognized it) of the lethal and corrupting stillness of night.

75

They would meet beneath the jetty – he and Annie – every evening the same, and every morning, at that slow-creeping hour, an hour or so before dawn, they would part – he to skirt the lawn with that thief's sly audacity, his shoes in his hand and his feet cool and glistening with the day's early dew, she to wait a while beneath the jetty's beams and slats with nothing to do but to watch the dawn rise and to plan, in those shadows, a wedding in the sun.

Oh, and what a wedding! Such dresses and flowers the like of which no one had ever seen – and the music, *What'll I do when you are far away and I am blue* . . . so lilting, and floating so on such a soft and silken breeze that it seemed to be coming not from the band at all, but from off of the surface of the silver-blue Sound, then spinning through the trees and cascading down and down so as to weave its gentle way among the dresses and the morning suits and all the wishes for a good life and the promises made and certain to be kept.

'Alessandra?'

And yet, and yet . . . something always dulled her sight on those evenings as the preacher sealed the bargain – and gradually then everything would fall blurry, and every night beneath those slats, the whole scene would fold up before her and move on like some traveling circus, and all she'd be left with in the end would be the creak of the jetty and the beating of her heart, and the certainty that, of course, there would *be* no wedding (never was going to be one) – that there would be no music, no dresses and morning suits, no flowers, and that that honeymoon had never been anything but a fantasy, and that, of course, being only a maid, she'd never see London or Paris or even New York – indeed she'd never see beyond that distant green light winking out across the Sound – that she was stuck fast to her narrow, ugly life – as permanent within it as the child growing slow in her belly and that sickness of mourning for all dreams lost that came to her every day and brought with it cravings for things, small things – fruit from the South Seas and other strange, exotic foods – that she'd never ever have – never even smell, and certainly never taste.

'Alessandra? Are you there?'

But then, every night – every rising morning – despite her knowing the futility of dreaming – she would creep once again beneath the slats of that jetty, opting, once again, for the fake world of blindness and that world of the deaf where all sights are wonders and all music sweet, that absurd and treacherous wonderland where all lives are lived in harmony – that place known only to the rich and the simple where no lives are lost – none sacrificed – before they have even had a chance to begin.

'Alessandra? Where are you?'

He turned a corner, stepped onto a cool, deserted square. Here he paused a moment, suddenly uneasy. Frowning, he laid a hand on his stomach. *I can find nothing wrong with you – it's just your nerves.* He touched his forehead. His forehead was cold, and yet he was sweating. He bent a little at the waist, then further, until, moments later, he was lying doubled-up on his side, his chin on his knees, his cheek on the cobbles, and a pounding in his head like the stamping of a soldier's heavy boots.

76

'**H**ey, *American* –'
When at last he came to, it was to a world changed entire – to a world of bright sunlight and the bustle of crowds, to the rising sound of voices and the wheeling of birds overhead, silhouette-black against a new azure sky – to all this – all this newness, all this life – where, before, there had only been darkness and stillness – where, before, there had been only that sickness in his stomach, now gone.

'Hey, you *hear* me, American?'

He sat himself up. 'What?' he said. He was squinting in the harsh morning light.

'I *said* you *hear* me, American?'

He shaded his eyes. The man was standing before him, his legs spread and rising from high-polished boots, rising to a belt and a gun, thence to gloved hands set arrogantly on hips – to a white shirt and a gleaming silver badge, to a dark, scowling face, then, and to a pair of pitiless, mocking eyes.

'Look,' said Nathan, 'I don't know –' He tried to stand, but the end of a nightstick pushed him back.

'You stay,' said the man. 'I say you stand you stand, okay?'

Nathan rubbed his eyes.

Another prod of the stick. 'I said okay, American?'

'Okay, okay.'

The man stepped back, hand on his holstered pistol. 'So stand,' he said. He was smiling.

Slowly, Nathan pushed himself up. He stood, swaying slightly as if as the consequence of some invisible, unfeelable breeze.

'Okay,' said the officer. He was turning the nightstick slow through his fingers, round and round like some out-of-work juggler who couldn't kick the habit. Suddenly, the twirling stopped.

'Look, I'm sorry,' said Nathan. 'I really don't know –'

'Ssh,' said the officer, the nightstick pressed lightly to his lips, then lowered. He leaned forward, still smiling. 'Your name,' he whispered, his breath sweet and warm. 'You have a name, American?'

'Zeitezmann.'

He frowned, shook his head slightly, like he was trying to remember something or to figure out some amusing conundrum. 'Zeitezmann,' he whispered, 'Zeitezmann, Zeitezmann, Zeitezmann.' He paused, as if, in that moment, the answer had come to him. 'A Jew?' he said. Slowly, the nightstick started turning again.

Nathan swallowed hard. He glanced beyond the officer, hoping, maybe, to catch someone's eye. But no one would meet his gaze – they all just moved quickly by, unable or unwilling to see him. He looked back to the officer just in time.

Or, rather, just too late.

The first blow struck him hard on the shoulder, spinning him around, the second – a thrust of the nightstick – doubled him up, pitching him forward, until the crown of his head caught the officer in the soft flesh above his belt, pushing him back, and then they were tumbling – the two of them – all boots and elbows, all hands and curses, until, suddenly, a crack like the crack of a skull on cobblestones, and all was still.

A moment's silence, then one man stirred. Slowly, he disentangled himself, rose. His cheek was bloody, his clothes hanging off of him like he'd come through a storm. He touched his face, he was swaying. He lowered his hand, wincing at the sight of his own blood, then, slowly – as if wary of what he might find – he raised his eyes to the crowd. The crowd – every man, woman and child – was standing silent, regarding him with a watchfulness both intense and benign – with a calmness quite remarkable, as if what was being watched was the waking amongst them of some strange toothless animal, or the rising, unexpected, from the cobblestones of some wild and exotic plant.

Nathan took a faltering step; the crowd braced itself as one. Another step, then another – where, in which direction, he neither knew nor cared. A fourth step, a fifth – every step drawing him closer to those silently watching. A sixth, a seventh; with a murmur, the crowd shuffled back, paused a moment, as if, in silence, it was weighing something up, then, with a beautiful precision, it split itself in two – its parting, in that moment, as graceful as the drawing of a pair of heavy velvet drapes, or the parting before some prophet of a very small sea.

77

L ooking back on it (as he would – and *how* – in the time he had remaining), Nathan Zeitezmann III would come to believe, and with some conviction, that his safe arrival that morning on the steps of the Uffizi Gallery was the result, if not of the wishes of God, then, certainly, as a consequence of the wishes of some other kind of force greater than he – some agent, perhaps, whose goal was his survival – an aim for which (he would come to believe) any and all methods had been sanctioned, and for which not only individuals but entire peoples would and should be inconvenienced, if, by so doing, that survival could be guaranteed.

But that was later – not now. Indeed, only later – much later – only when he was facing some beast in that ship as it pitched about in the middle of the ocean – only then would he think about these things – only then would he try (in vain, of course) to figure them out – only then ask himself *why me*? Only then – only later – not now. For now, at least, there was some kind of peace; for now, at least, as he laid his weary body down to rest on the gallery's broad stone steps, his thoughts were so jumbled, his mind so exhausted by his running, that all he could think of was the ghostly hollow sound of a skull cracking open and the blood oozing out like scarlet oil across the cobblestones – that, and the angel's face of Alessandra del Piero, of her smile, of the curve of her back, of her sly, teasing dance through the quiet midnight streets – one moment there, the next moment gone – and how he'd followed so willingly, so anxious had he been to possess again what he'd already conquered.

He raised his eyes from his boots at the sharp sound of voices from way off across the square. He screwed up his eyes in the light. Across the square, three girls and two boys were playing some kind of tag – darting, circling, about each other – their voices rising up through the heat. Nathan looked away. The noon sun was burning the back of his neck and the backs of his hands. He pulled up his collar and closed his eyes. He shouldn't sleep, he knew – but he couldn't raise the fight. And so he drifted, exhausted, then finally slipped away.

*   *   *

When he woke (perhaps ten minutes later, or maybe an hour, he couldn't say), it was to the soft touch of fingers on his sleeve. He sat up sharp; his head lurched. 'What the *hell* –'

'Oh, I'm sorry –' said a voice.

Startled, he pushed back, tried to focus. 'What is it? What's going on?'

'Well –' The voice was hesitant, American – from the north somewhere, maybe Chicago. 'It's just, I thought you might be unwell –'

He rubbed his eyes hard.

'I mean, should I fetch your companion?'

'My *what*?'

'Your companion . . . the young lady –'

Nathan shook his head, tried to shake out the sense in things. 'Look,' he said, 'I don't know who –' but the woman – she was elderly, maybe seventy and elegantly dressed – wasn't listening. Instead, she was scanning the crowds of sightseers, her eyes shielded from the sun by a pale, bony hand sheathed in a fine lace glove. She turned back; she was frowning. 'Well, that's strange,' she said, then the frown gave way to a smile – a beautiful, radiant, young girl's smile. 'I suppose she's stepped into the cool for a while –' She paused, considering Nathan with the gentlest of looks. 'Do you suppose,' she said, 'we might do the same? Do you suppose we might find ourselves some shelter from this tiresome heat?'

Nathan closed his eyes, opened them. 'Who *are* you?' he said.

The woman held out her hand. Nathan hesitated, but then something made him take it. It was tiny in his own hand, but strong, as if the bones had been fashioned from the oldest and sturdiest American oak. 'I am,' she said, 'an American citizen, here on a mission of enlightenment.' She paused. 'And you, sir? Who are *you*?'

Nathan felt, suddenly, an unsettling and unusual strength in the old woman's look. He glanced away. In the center of the piazza, a circus juggler on stilts was performing his tricks with a half-dozen brightly colored balls.

'Never mind, sir.'

He turned back. 'Pardon me?'

'Your name, sir. I said never mind. You're tired. Let us retire now, shall we?'

Nathan shrugged. For sure he was tired – so tired. He pushed himself up. Then the woman smiled – soft, indulgent. It was almost the smile – the look – an elderly mother might give to an unruly but favorite son.

Almost, but not quite – for there was more in it than that. There was something, also, that made Nathan feel like there was maybe a part of her that had never really aged – that there was something inside of her for which the process of aging had somehow been arrested – as if a part of her had been baked hard in some moment of joy or pain – a part that would forever remain unaffected by the passage of time.

78

'Is it one o'clock yet?'

'What?'

'I said, is it one o'clock yet?'

Nathan sighed. For sure he was glad to be out of the heat – but now all he wanted was to lay himself down in the darkness of his room, just close his eyes, maybe sleep if he could.

'Well, sir?'

'Look,' he said. He tried to raise a smile. 'I think I should go –'

'Go? But you've only just arrived.'

'Yes, but all the same –'

'Nonsense.' The old lady took his arm. She looked around, then raised a hand to an attendant by the cloakroom counter. The attendant – blue-suited, gold-braided – stepped over, a smile already forming on his face.

'*La prego di farmi sapere sepose esserle utile in qualunque modo gentile, signora Custer?*'

Libbie frowned. 'Pardon me?'

The attendant cleared his throat, as if he were preparing to sing. 'Signora Custer,' he said, pausing, then, to offer a slight, an almost imperceptible, bow. 'How may I helping such a lady?'

'Oh I see,' said Libbie, blushing, the rise in her color an echo, in its slightness, of the bow. 'Well, I was wondering if you were aware of the time?'

'The time, signora?'

'Hey, wait a minute,' said Nathan. Libbie and the attendant turned as one. 'Did he say *Custer*?'

'He did,' said Libbie.

'As in *General* Custer?'

She nodded. 'As in, sir, as in.'

'Then you're –'

'Signora?' said the attendant.

Libbie turned, leaving Nathan for the moment quite speechless. She studied the attendant's suit-coat, spied the loop of a fine silver chain half-hidden beneath on his waistcoat. At this she pointed; the attendant looked down, frowning, as if expecting to find there some unpleasant, some unforgivable stain. 'The time, sir,' she said. 'Do you, perhaps, have a knowledge of the time?'

A moment passed as the attendant – *Snr P. Maldini* by his name-badge – divined, at last, her request. Hurriedly, then – as if the time remaining for telling the time were itself running out – he pulled out a high-polished, silver-backed watch. He turned it around, hung it steady before the old lady's face like a trainee hypnotist who'd yet to learn the importance of his instrument's swinging.

Libbie squinted at the dial. 'Splendid,' she said, thanking and dismissing the attendant with a nod. She turned back to Nathan. 'Sir,' she said brightly, 'we've precisely two minutes.' She lifted her arm. 'Would you be kind enough to lend an old lady your support?' She cocked her head. 'Sir?'

'Pardon?' said Nathan.

'Shall we proceed, sir –'

'Proceed?'

'Botticelli, sir, awaits.' Taking his hand, she settled his arm on hers. 'There now,' she said. 'Are we ready, sir? Are we ready?'

79

'**D**o you see, sir, how the light falls just so?'

Nathan looked at the picture; mirroring his ignorance of all art (and therefore most of life), the picture seemed to look back at him, calm and insolent in its willful, mocking blindness.

'Well, Mr Zeitezmann? Do you not feel the power? Do you not sense the artist's . . . *strength*? His Christianity, perhaps?'

So tired, now, he knew he was too tired to sleep, he let his eyes trace the figures – Pallas with her halberd, her shield, her crown of leaves, the centaur with his bow, his pose of subjugation – let them pause on the canvas, then move on, let them wander like distant newcomers on some vast and sandy beach, let them loiter in the sunlight that had spun down upon the painting at the very moment of their arrival.

'Mr Zeitezmann?'

He shrugged. In truth, to him, it meant nothing. To him, it was just canvas and paint – just make-believe, just fakery, having nothing to say but dull, dull, dull. 'I'm sorry,' he said.

'Sorry?' said Libbie.

'I guess I'm just tired.'

She reached up, lightly touched the bruise on his temple with the tips of her fingers; he winced, pulled away. 'What happened?' she said.

'Nothing,' said Nathan.

'I see.'

Minutes passed – so slow in the still air you'd swear you could almost see them passing by like the carriages of a train, almost feel the tiny fingers of a draft as it slow-marched by. Despite the coolness of the room, the slowness was stifling; still staring at the painting (he didn't dare to look away for fear of the looks he might see), he drew a long, shallow intake of breath. Beside him (he could see from the corner of his eye), the old lady was peeling off her gloves. These she folded and tucked up her sleeve. She stood, then, awhile, as silent as he; then she said, 'My husband was very fond of Botticelli.'

Nathan felt himself frowning.

'Although, being a *patriot*, American painting would always be his choice. Mr Gilchrist of Ohio, especially. Do you know of Mr Gilchrist of Ohio, Mr Zeitezmann?'

Nathan said nothing. *My husband, my husband.* It seemed so absurd, so unlikely, finding the wife of such a notorious figure so far away from home.

'That's a shame,' said Libbie. 'He's no Botticelli, of course, but I think you might appreciate his work. Like you, it is all so . . . so determined.'

He sighed. It was so unlikely, indeed – so absurd finding *her* right *here* – that it had to be a lie.

'Mr Zeitezmann?'

Slowly, he let his head turn. Quite clearly she was no more the wife of General Custer than he was the son of some Indian chief. 'Look –' he said. The old lady was smiling. The smile – so kind, so gentle – made him pause. He sighed. 'Alright,' he said. 'So what's so funny?'

'Ah, nothing,' said Libbie.

'Then why are you smiling?'

She frowned. '*Smiling*, Mr Zeitezmann? Heavens, no. As you know, sir, I am a widow, and widows – as you should also know – never smile. It's not permitted.'

Nathan shook his head. He'd read about people like her in Doctor Summerfield's magazines – women and men who flee overseas to escape some scandal – exiles who then spend so long denying their own identity that eventually it atrophies and then ceases to exist at all, leaving them, in the end, with nothing left to cling to but the lives and identities of others. He sighed. Either way, right now he didn't care. Right now all he wanted was his room, his bed, maybe a minute with Alessandra – to maybe ask her what the hell was going on – what, in God's name, she was playing at. 'Look,' he said again, and he was going to go on – going to make his excuses and leave – but Mrs Custer (or whoever she *really* was) stifled his words with the touch of her hand – the lightest of touches, like the touch of a child or an angel – on his chest.

'Mr *Zeitez*mann,' she said. The hand drew away, but left its image, unseen, upon him like a shadow. 'I am aware, sir, of what you are thinking –'

'You are?'

She lowered her hand, fixing him, then, with a look of such defiance that it made his eyes scuttle away, made them seek camouflage in the depths of the painting.

'Oh indeed I am, sir,' she said. She paused. 'Mr Zeitezmann?'

His eyes rested a moment on the pale face of Pallas. *Virtue restraining vice*, a passing tour guide had solemnly informed his group, *an allegorical denunciation of the brutality of man.* He moved his gaze to the face of the man-beast. His flowing hair was raised, pulled tight by the hand of virtue, his bow and his arrows no longer any protection against the cruel strength of goodness.

'Mr Zeitezmann –'

He looked away, back to the old lady's face.

'You asked me,' she said, 'if I knew what you were thinking.'

'I did?' said Nathan.

'You did, sir. And the answer is you were thinking, am I telling you the truth? You were thinking – as so many people have thought before you – is she *really* the widow of General George Armstrong Custer? And you were thinking – as they all think – if she *is* who she *says* she is, then why can't she just stay quiet, just live out her sad life where no one can see her, and where we won't be reminded of what we did – how we sent such a man to do our bidding – to fight for us – knowing that we were sending him to his death, and knowing that when he needed us we would not help him – that we would abandon him and then attempt to forget him. Well, let me tell you, Mr Zeitezmann, that my husband will *not* be forgotten – that I will *not* permit it – that as long as I have breath enough to speak I *shall* speak, and that when I am made invisible to all by the short-sighted cowardice of some in my own country I shall travel overseas and so make myself so sharp once again in their sight that, however much they try to stay blind, they will see me still and know in their every waking moment and in their dreams what I know – that though the hands on the rifle that killed my husband were a red man's hands, the bullet that stopped his dear, loving heart was an *American* bullet, and that the rifle from which it was fired was an *American* rifle, and that the trade of arms to our nation's enemies while our nation is at war that provides some men and their sons with their fortunes provides others, Mr Zeitezmann, with the fortune only of death. *Death*, Mr Zeitezmann – did you know that? Do you know how many heroes' widows must be made before even the most modest of grand houses can be built? Well, do you, Mr Zeitezmann? Mr Zeitezmann? Are you dumb now, Mr Zeitezmann? Has the cat got your tongue?'

Somehow, drawing strength from way, way down someplace, Nathan managed to shake his head. His heart was thumping, despite his weariness, his mouth dry. He stepped back. 'I'm sorry,' he said, 'I don't know what –' and he would have gone on (to say *what*? he would wonder later – much later – for what was there to say, except *It was not me, but mine*?) – gone on to say *something* more at least, some form of excusing words – had it not been for the look in the old lady's eyes. It was a look, then, of such pain that it made him shiver – a look of such anguish stored over so many years that it made him just want to turn away, lest such pain – such anguish – bleed somehow into him, and so accelerate the process that he'd long known had already begun – that passing down from a father to a son all that has been so carefully, so

painstakingly gathered – that handing on, from generation to generation, of good and bad and all in between, that slow-merging that makes
as nothing the barricades of time and space erected between those
generations – all that makes us only, in the end, as good or as guilty as
those who went before us, and, of course, as good or as guilty as those
who have yet to come.

But he didn't say this – or, indeed, anything more. Instead he just
turned, started walking, aware with every step of the weight of his soles
on the high-polished floor; no, instead he just walked and kept on
walking until the gallery and the glare of its windows was behind him in
the gloom, and he was moving on, unseen and unseeing, walking hard,
as if with some urgent purpose, through the shadows and the sun.

80

I t was waiting for him when at last he returned to his room – slipped under his door like a note from some secret lover. So weary, he stooped, picked it up, crossed to the bed and sat down. *Some men and their sons.* He closed his eyes a moment, tried to clear his mind, but his mind would not clear. *Do you know how many widows.* Unseen in the gloom, he frowned. Then he opened his eyes, looked down, turned the envelope over in his hands.

How long he'd been walking he couldn't have said, but for sure he'd been walking for hours, turning this way and that with no thought for direction – no thought for anything, in fact, but how he had to keep walking lest something catch up with him – exactly what, he didn't know. In the end, somehow, he'd found himself standing outside the hotel, his feet aching from the walking, his mind numb from the effort of trying to explain the inexplicable. He'd looked down at his hands, then, and found them to be shaking. With monumental effort he'd pulled on the bell. He'd nodded blindly at the night-man and watched, as if from a distance, his hand – palm upward – take his key.

He drew a long, shallow breath, fed his finger beneath the flap of the envelope. Slowly, clumsily – as if his fingers were now beyond his control – he pulled out the envelope's contents. He stared down, squinting hard. The words, blurred, shifted before his eyes, then slowly reassembled, sharpened:

Mrs Zeitezmann nearing end. Return NY at once. Robert.

He sat a moment quite still, then folded the note, slipped it back into the envelope. *Some men and their sons.* He reached forward, set the envelope with care on the nightstand. He lay back on the bed, closed his eyes.

It was a strange thing, but, all the way back to the hotel – all the way through the empty, echoing streets – he'd had the strongest sense of his having been followed – so much so that he'd turned every now and then, but, of course, had found nothing, no one, only the emptiness of the city

– nothing, and yet he'd kept on pausing, kept on looking, kept on *expecting*. But expecting *what*? That night, walking hard, he couldn't have said, except to say that, whatever it was, for sure it was gaining on him, and that soon – any moment now – it would suddenly appear in his path, slipping out from the shadows to stand before him, barring his way –

He woke abruptly, sat up. He was sweating. He blinked, again, hard, tried to focus, seeing only then the painting in its frame.

The brutality of man.

He swept his face with his palm. His mouth was dry, his eyes smarting.

Some men and their sons.

He lay back down, turned his head on the pillow. He reached for the envelope on the nightstand, touched its smoothness with his fingers, then let it be. He laid an arm across his eyes, tried to picture the face of his mother, but could not. He lowered his arm and let his eyes close. He would never, he knew then, see his mother again.

It was nearing dawn when he woke. He rose at once, quietly. He packed his things, crossing the room to and fro with a savage economy of movement. Then, without looking back, he stepped onto the landing and closed the door. He descended the stairs as quiet as a thief.

The night-man was snoozing at the desk, his head hidden beneath a newspaper blanket. He woke at the touch of a hand. Words were exchanged, a signature produced. Nathan turned and crossed the lobby. He paused at the door, looked back.

'Signor?' said the night-man.

Nathan thought of Alessandra, but then shook his head. 'No matter,' he said, and he turned away. He pushed on the door. He was gone.

Eddie

81

I t had become, for Eddie Reno, custom that, every morning before he rose, he would consult the old blue-backed journal – and so decide, with its silent and so persuasive aid, just exactly where that day might take him. Indeed, so much a part of each morning's routine had it become (and so vital, consequently, to what he believed was left of his sanity, his being, as he was, a man to whom routine was the bones to the ever-expanding, ever-graying flesh of his life) that to suddenly be without it was to suddenly be that flesh without those bones: in short, to be a man pitched suddenly and without mercy into chaos – a chaos from which – on this particular morning – he felt certain he would never emerge.

He peered over the bedclothes and uttered, unheard, a barely audible whimper. He ducked back under. *Oh Jesus*, he thought, *what happened? Where am I?* He frowned, tried to think.

And think.

And think.

And then, in the womb-like warmth and gloom of the bedclothes, he remembered. He closed his eyes, flexing his toes (this, an attempt at reassurance: it didn't work) in a way he'd not done since his youth.

Oh Lord.

Again he peered over the bedclothes. He squinted in the morning light, flicked his eyes around the room. A lamp on a writing table, a chair, another table, more chairs, blinds, drapes glowing cheerfully golden, another bed (empty, thank God), his clothes, patchy-red, his shoes, one sock, another –

He paused, flicked his eyes back.

Patchy-red.

He swallowed hard.

Oh Jesus – *blood*? And if it was – whose blood was it? He pushed himself up, then, gingerly, peeled back the covers. He gasped, closed his eyes, counted to ten (*be calm*, he told himself, *be calm*), opened them.

The bruises on his body from his beating at Graceland were so numerous that he gave up trying to count them at fifteen; indeed, so many of them were there – and so neighborly were they, one to the next – that his whole body, now, seemed to be covered in just about one big bruise, with only his feet having been spared such a hurtful and grotesque fate.

A knock on the door.

He froze.

'Hello? Edward? Are you Dolly-decent?' The voice – a woman's, perhaps elderly, perhaps crazy – was muffled.

'Who is it? he said, wincing at the effort even of speech.

'It's Dolly Two.'

He frowned. 'Dolly who?'

'Dolly Two. Dolly One sent me, *Mr Grumpy-chops*. Said to tell you it's D-minus-forty –'

'It's what?'

A slight huff from beyond the door. 'Whatever *that* means. Honestly, why she can't just say "*The Dollybirds are leaving in forty minutes*" or "*It's forty minutes till the Dollybus sets off*", I don't know. If you ask me, being Dolly number one has gone straight to her head. If you ask *me*, I think it's the burden of leadership – it's got to her, just like it got to Georgie Patton. Did you know he had a dog called William the Conker?' Another huff. 'Seems like a real strange name for a dog to me.' This time a sigh. 'Anyways, I'd best get scooting. Wouldn't want madam to choke on her sausage now –' A pause. Another tap. 'Edward?'

'What now?'

'So shall I tell her you're coming?'

Unseen, Eddie Reno shook his head. He'd heard about these weirdos who hang around motels – sad, empty people whose own lives are so dull, so going-nowhere, that, though to start with they're content to just watch other people, soon they're up to breaking in to others' conversations – or tapping on doors in the hopes of finding some other poor loser whose own life is also hanging from the finest and longest of threads.

'Edward? Can you hear me?'

'Go away,' he said.

'Oh, Edward,' said the voice, the tone descending like that of a disappointed schoolmistress. 'Now that's not *nice*. A person who talks like that to a friend surely don't deserve any breakfast –'

Eddie gritted his teeth. 'I *said* go away, will you?'

'– *Nor* to sit next to Mr Tefertiller on the Dollybus – *that's* for sure –' Another rap of knuckles on the door. 'Edward? Did you hear me?' Another pause. 'Did I mention there was sausage?'

Eddie sighed; his ribs smarted.

'And chicken-steaks? Did I say there was chicken-steaks?'

He pushed himself up, pushing through the pain. He drew a long, shallow breath. 'Look,' he said, trying to stay calm, 'I don't know who the hell you are. Nor do I know what you *want*. Nor, *frankly*, do I care. And so I would be grateful if you'd just take your sausage and your chicken-steaks and stick them in your Dollybus or whatever the hell you said AND JUST LEAVE ME ALONE –'

From beyond the door, then, a silence. Then, low, but purposefully audible, the unmistakable sound of sniveling.

Oh Jesus.

With monumental effort, Eddie swung his legs out from under the covers and stood. The room swirled for a second, then settled. Slowly, painfully with the leg-by-leg gait of an arthritic gunfighter, he crossed the room to the door, gripped the handle, turned it, and pulled.

Nothing.

No one.

He squinted in the light. 'What the hell –' he started, but a tapping on his kneecap stopped him dead. He looked down, felt the raging in his neck. He gasped. 'Jesus H Christ,' he said before he could stop himself. In all of his life, truly, he'd never seen such a sight. He felt himself weaken then, and, in that moment – swaying slightly with the effort of standing – he felt certain sure he would fall.

82

B ut he didn't fall; somehow he stayed standing. Somehow, despite
being bruised from near head to foot, and despite being faced so
early in the morning with the upturned and smiling face of (what
would turn out to be) one of twenty-two sequined, big-wig-wearing,
make-up-plastered (not to mention surgically enhanced) midget Dolly
Parton lookalikes – despite all that – despite such provocation – he did
not fall; indeed, he did not even blink (so stunned was he) when Dolly
Two (such was the title on her name-badge) withdrew from her cleavage
a small square of paper, which, with some care, she proceeded to
unfold. This, when the unfolding was complete, she offered up. 'Here,'
she said, smiling bravely through her tears, 'read this, will you,
Edward?'

'What is it?' said Eddie. His voice sounded somehow not his own.

'Just read it for me, will you?'

Then he watched, as if from some distance, as a hand reached out,
took the paper, turned it around. He glanced at the paper, then down to
the face smiling up at him. Despite the efforts of the make-up to make
her seem as youthful as her idol, all it really achieved was to underline
her years. To Eddie it seemed she could maybe be fifty – perhaps older.
Her eyes, behind her tears, were that pale, watery blue more common in
the elderly.

'I can't read it,' she said.

Eddie frowned. 'What?'

'It's my eyes. I'm stigmatic.'

'You are?' he said, despite himself. 'Couldn't you get them . . . *fixed*
or something? Maybe some kind of operation?'

Dolly Two (real name Florence Hannah Winterplatt, for heaven's
sake) shook her head sadly. 'No,' she said. 'Not now.' She seemed
suddenly ashamed. 'You see, I don't have the money.' Then she looked
up, for a second brighter. 'I mean, I *did* have the money –' The
brightness faltered, was replaced in a second by gloom. 'But then I
spent it.'

'You spent it?'

'On the operation.'

Eddie sighed. 'But I thought you said –'

Sheepish, Dolly Two flicked her eyes down to her chest, then up.

'Oh, I see,' said Eddie. He swept his face with the palm of his hand. *This is crazy,* he thought. *Here I am – an old man – standing naked in the doorway of some godforsaken motel in God-knows-where, discussing the surgical options or otherwise available to a stigmatic or at any rate half-blind Dolly Parton lookalike dwarf.* 'Look,' he said. 'I'm sorry for your troubles, I really am, but, well, hell I got my own –' He held out the piece of paper, tried to give it back.

Dolly Two shook her head. 'You keep it,' she said. 'It never was any use to me.' Then, sighing, she turned away, moved slowly, round-shouldered, down the path. She paused at the point where the path disappeared from view. Looking over her shoulder, her eyes sparkling still, she said, 'See you for breakfast, maybe?'

In the doorway, Eddie Reno felt his shoulders give a shrug. 'Maybe,' he said (he couldn't believe he was saying it), then he heard himself withdrawing, heard the soles of his bare feet sucking hard on linoleum, then he saw himself shaking his head, disbelieving, then quietly closing the door.

83

With what can only be considered an unnecessary, indeed a gratuitous, perhaps even an *unconstitutional* cruelty, room thirty-two (head down the side of Block A, turn right at the burnt-out seventy-eight Chrysler Fairmile, keep going to the yucca-stump and you're there) of the Bison Moror Inn, five miles or so shy of Bowling Green, Missouri, had been so designed that should an old man of, say, sixty or more – an old man, moreover, who had come to hate the very shape, the very *existence*, of even his shadow – should such a man choose to set his meager backside on the end of the left-hand of the two narrow beds and gaze, eyes front, in some stupor toward the wall, then he will, with just the tiniest effort of focusing, be faced with the squinting, naked vision of a man – perhaps sixty, perhaps seventy (though he'll probably seem closer in his ghastly decrepitude to eighty, maybe even ninety, or, at any rate, some age beyond counting except in hours, maybe minutes, in its certain proximity to a lingering death) – a man, at any rate, not unlike himself – a man, in this case, not unlike Eddie Reno – a man, in this case, not unlike a man who'd fled his job for no good reason (or, at least, no good reason he could *remember*), only to find himself, then, driving and driving, and all just to get himself to a place where he could be beaten to within a hair's breadth of his life – and on the gravestone of (for heaven's sake) Elvis Presley, and then, and then –

What then?

He squinted at the old man in the mirror squinting back. What the hell had happened *then*? How on earth had he wound up *here*? – *now*? And where was his car?

Oh Lord.

His weary heart sank.

The car.

The trunk.

The *diary*.

Oh Jesus.

He swallowed hard, watched the old-man's Adam's apple rise and fall in the mirror.

The diary, the diary.

He stood up – maybe it was here someplace, maybe he'd thought ahead for once (yeah, *right*) and taken it out of the trunk for safekeeping – anyway, he stood up, feeling, as he did so, something flutter from his lap to the floor. He looked down. A piece of paper, half-folded, lying still between his pale and vein-ribbed, bony feet.

I can't read it.

His heart sank again, a little further.

It's my eyes. I'm stigmatic.

Slowly, moving as slow, as careful, as a corpse might move if that corpse had been given one more fleeting moment of life, he reached down, gripped the thing between forefinger and thumb. He slumped back down onto the bed. The diary. Gone. He turned the piece of paper around in his hands until it was up the right way. He couldn't believe it: how could he have been so *careless*? He sighed, then, and with an effort of will he'd have guessed well beyond him, he forced the blurry shapes on the paper into sharpness.

You never know what you've got until it's gone. How trite. How true. And you never *really* know what it is that is *really* sustaining you – really keeping you going – until you leave it, like some senile old fool, in the trunk of a beaten-up seventy-eight Toyota Supreme, then you go and decide to leave that beaten-up seventy-eight Toyota Supreme in some godforsaken place, the location of which you can no longer, of course, in your excruciating vacant-mindedness, remember.

Well, brilliant.

Just brilliant.

He shook his useless head, tried to think.

But he couldn't think.

All he could think was how empty, suddenly, how naked he felt (*truly* naked, that is, not just *unclothed* naked, but the kind of naked a man feels when he's standing on a highwire a mile above a waterfall and he sees, way, way down below, the first breath of wind shift the tops of distant pines) – all he could think was how terribly vulnerable he felt without the book, now, to protect him.

Without the book.

A hundred-year-old journal.

To *protect* him.

Right.

Okay, maybe it *was* crazy, but, whatever – crazy or not – the truth of the matter was that diary had come, somehow, to mean something to him that he never could have predicted (not that he ever had been much good at predicting stuff – just look at how he'd thought that that whole Watergate break-in malarkey would blow over) – something, in fact, the importance of which, even now, sitting on that bed and staring down at Dolly Two's folded and unfolded (many times) *Itinerary of the Dollybirds Tour*, he would scarcely have dared to articulate, as to do so would have been to admit, finally, that he couldn't get by on his own anymore, that he could no longer trust himself – that he was no longer captain even of such an old creaking vessel – that he was prepared, instead, to give up the helm to something – a voice – whose words he knew but whose purpose he couldn't understand, and that he was happy like an idiot is happy to allow his route to be determined by nothing less than a mystery.

But, as every man knows, there is something safe in a mystery, some kind of relief to be had in giving up, in submitting, in laying down that which a man is never supposed to lay down lest he cease, in that laying down, to be really a man.

Really a man.

Eddie looked hard at himself in the mirror.

Really a man.

Had he not given up the title so long ago now that to even dream of getting it back (whatever was, or ever had been) was really, now, just some absurd and embarrassing fantasy?

He looked away, lay back.

And to have given himself up – his direction – to a book. *A book.* Nothing could be quite so ridiculous. He closed his eyes. *I am ridiculous*, he thought, and he thought, again, of the journal, now lost. He pictured its pale, weathered covers, and how at first, and for a long time, he'd strained his eyes so in trying to make out the words within. Then he smiled, recalling the moment when, as if a light had been switched on overhead, he'd suddenly found himself reading – really *reading*, really *understanding* the words before his eyes – and how, then, he'd known, just by the tone of them, that they had somehow been written exclusively for him.

He opened his eyes.

For him.

But by whom?

Another mystery. (Mysteries within mysteries.)

He turned on the bed, lay, then, like a child, curled up on his side. Who would write such a thing just for him? How could it even be possible? He frowned. The diary was a diary, and older than the century. No, it had to be just his imagination.

Another frown, harder.

Didn't it?

He closed his eyes – so weary, suddenly, of the fight to make sense of things. He curled a little tighter, made himself a little smaller. Then he let go his grip, heaved a shallow sigh, and just let his ship drift.

84

'Edward?'
He drifted into dream, into memory. Faces appeared, grima-
cing, then passed by – his father in his spangly stage-suit, *Queue
here for* The Last Stand*! See Custer get his chips!*; his mother, un-
consolable in her tears; then Clare – darling Clare – her joy at her
announcement – *I thought we'd call him Edward, after you* – then
silence, then the splash as her body hit the water, so bloated now with
new life; then, further back in time, his wife – ironically another Clare,
The Great Gatsby and that cinema in the dark, then the starkness of the
street, and the emptiness, then, of a son gone for good – of a boy so
loved that no words or actions could begin to express it (and so never
did – oh Lord, the pain, now, of that failure, the guilt so thick around
him sometimes that it seemed to want to choke him, to squeeze from
him what little remained of his life) – a boy so absent so suddenly that
the mind will not accept it, until a Tuesday rolls around, and then
another and another, and there's no joy anymore (never will be) in ball-
games, and no point in eating – no point, in fact, in anything but
sleeping, or trying to sleep, trying to let go –
'Edward?'
A light tapping on the door; he stirred but didn't wake.
'Edward? Can you hear me?'
The voice was querulous, anxious, its anxiety, though – its querulous-
ness – lost to the ears of Eddie Reno who, in the half-world of half-sleep,
could hear nothing, see nothing in the half-light, but the howling – his own
– that had woken him some nights, that had left him, some mornings, with
a throat raw from howling, and a heart so empty that nothing but an act of
God's mercy could ever possibly fill it – an act, though, he'd always
known would never be, so dismissing, so arrogant had he been toward
that God – so sure in his youth, and in the happiness of that youth, that we
– all of us – are truly all we need, and that anything more is just weakness,
just sloth, just the endless, unheard crying of some child left abandoned in
some shadowed, empty mall at the moment of the day's death and the
start of the slow-rolling incoming night.

A tapping, harder now, bled into his dreams.

'Edward? Please answer if you're there.' More tapping. 'It's an *emergency*!'

He opened his eyes; his dream-figures loitered a moment, as if reluctant to leave, then, one by one, they crept away, slinking back into the darkness from which, released with the aid of fevered sleep, they'd emerged.

He wiped his brow, rubbed his eyes, circling, with the flesh of his palms. Slowly, he sat up.

'*Edward! Please! Edward!*'

He set his hands on his knees, fixed his eyes on the floor, again tried to think.

'*It's Mr Tefertiller! He's run off!*'

But all he could think was how they'd given up so easily – how, because they were tired (*tired*, for God's sake), one day they'd just stopped looking – and how, from that day forward, they'd not been able to look at each other for shame, and how, in time, that shame had turned to blame and the blame to hate, and the hate to fighting – to bruises hidden from neighbors and friends, and then to his arrest – to his walking like Charlie Chaplin, his ankles bound together by a short length of chain, and strangers in a gallery, then the *clunk* of a key at dusk, and then, finally, at last, silence.

'*Edward! Answer me!*'

He looked up. 'What do you want?'

A sound – light thudding – against the door, like someone crumpling.

'Oh, thank the Lord!'

'I *said* what do you want?'

More knocking on the door. 'Won't you let me in? We need to *talk* –'

'Talk? Why? I don't even know you –'

'Yes you do!'

'No I don't!'

'But it's me!'

Oh Jesus. Eddie sighed. He pushed himself up, again crossed the room, again reached the door, pulled it open. '*Look*,' he said, knowing this time to look down, 'whatever bad thing has happened, or whatever bad thing you *say* has happened –'

'But it has, *really* –'

'– Whatever bad thing you *say* has happened is really of no interest to me – *okay?* – and I'd be grateful –'

'But he's gone to Toledo!'

'– *Grateful* if you'd just stop coming by, just stop banging on my door, just stop . . . well . . . oh, I don't know . . . *JUST STOP, OKAY?*'

'But, *Edward* –'

'*NO!*'

'But we need you!'

'*What?*'

Suddenly, silence.

Oh Jesus.

Then, again, the faint sound of tears. He covered his eyes. 'No,' he said.

'*No?*' said Dolly Two. '*But –*'

'I said *no*. Absolutely not.'

'*But –*'

'NO!'

'BUT WE CAN'T REACH THE PEDALS!'

At which, Eddie Reno shook his head, stepped back and closed the door. There was definitely, categorically, *absolutely no way* he was ever going to find himself in this life sitting up and smiling at the wheel of the Dollybus filled with Dollybirds on tour. Not *him*. No chance. No way. No, *sir*.

85

'**M**r Reno?'
No chance, huh?
Not him?
Yeah, *right*.

He flicked his eyes sharply to the mirror, then back to the road. 'Can't you read?' he said.

'*Read*, sir?'

Only ten minutes or so out of Bowling Green, and already he hated that road – hated how horribly straight it was – how smooth – hated how casually, almost *arrogantly* competent it was at the business of *being* a road. And he hated that mirror, too – how it forced him to look at such a sad man looking back. In fact, he hated everything about that wretched Dollybus – what with its frills and that endless, endless music.

'Sir? Mr *Reno*?'

Jolene, Jolene, endless bloody *Jolene*.

He stabbed at a notice – NO TALKING TO THE DRIVER WHILE THE BUS IS IN MOTION. He hated how the notice was stuck crooked on the dash.

Dolly Two squinted, all the time swaying with the movement of the bus.

'Well?' he said. 'Can't you see what it says?'

'Well –' said Dolly Two, hesitating.

And then he remembered – '*It's my eyes. I'm stigmatic*' – and he hated himself too, now, for forgetting. He sighed – tried to indicate by that sighing that he was sorry. He cleared his throat, ground the gears down to third as the bus hit an incline in the road. 'So what was it?' he said.

'Nothing.'

He twisted round in his seat, tried to smile. 'Come on now,' he said. 'It was something. I *know* it was something –'

Dolly shrugged. 'We were just wondering,' she said. She paused.

'Wondering? Wondering what?'

'Well, if maybe we could stop awhile –'

'Stop?' Eddie turned to the road at the sound of a horn, yanked the wheel, correcting a swerve, looked back. 'But we only just got going –'

'It won't take long.'

He shrugged. 'Okay,' he said. 'It's your bus, I guess. But if you want to get to Iowa tonight –'

Dolly glanced back down the bus. All heads were watching – all the Dollys with their hairdos and their smiles – all, that is, but the head of Dolly One, which, at that moment, was the head of one very sick Dolly, suspended and vomiting, as it was, above the lavatory in the cubicle in back, the consequence of too much chicken-fried steak at breakfast. Dolly two looked back to Eddie; she also was smiling. 'We want to buy you a present,' she said.

'What?'

'A present. We want to buy you a present –'

'Jesus,' said Eddie (he tried to think of the last time someone had used that form of words to him, but could not). 'What for?'

'Well, for driving, for one thing –' She gave a glance down the bus, then edged up a little closer, dropped her voice to a whisper. 'And, well, *you* know –'

Eddie turned away from the road. 'Er . . . what do you mean?' he said.

For sure, Dolly Two, beneath her make-up, was blushing. 'Aw, Eddie,' she said.

And she winked.

Oh Jesus, thought Eddie, and he thought again of that whole bunch of hours that was, for him, still a mystery – still empty and unaccounted for.

'Well –' he said, uncertain how best to proceed. For the moment he settled on just raising a half-smile (the kind of smile, he hoped, that could mean just about anything) – just smiling and staring out at the road – just smiling and staring and hoping that that lost time, any minute now, would return.

Or that maybe it would not.

86

L ost time. O lost time!
    There was this joke Eddie Senior used to tell about a man who, having lost his memory, found himself standing on the ledge of a very tall building. 'My God,' the man thought, trying not to look down, 'what on earth am I doing here?' Well, he tried to remember what terrible thing had happened to him – what could possibly have been so bad that it had gotten him to that ledge in that city on that day, but, try as he might, he just couldn't think. Had his wife, perhaps, run off with another man? Or maybe he wasn't married – maybe that was it? Maybe it was some painful, unrequited love that had led him to that ledge? Or maybe he'd lost all his money in some foolhardy venture? He racked his brains, but he just couldn't remember. He turned out his pockets. Nothing. No clues. Anyway, an hour went by, then two, three. Soon it was dusk, and his spirits had gotten so low from thinking about all the terrible things that might have happened to him that, with a sudden, monumental effort of will, he jumped and within seconds lay dead on the sidewalk below.

'*Edward?*'

Well, some people gathered, just to gawp at the body, and then more and more stopped to look, until there was quite a crowd.

'*Edward? Can you hear me?*'

'Who is it?' they all asked, and, 'Why did he do it?' Well, in a while, a woman appeared and pushed her way through. She stood beside the corpse, looking down. 'Do you know him?' said a voice from the crowd. The woman nodded. There were tears in her eyes.

'*This is the one, Edward – our exit –*'

'Then why –' said the voice, suddenly stopping, silenced by the woman's holding up a brown paper bag. 'It's my husband,' she said, her voice shaking with emotion. 'Your husband?' said the voice. 'Yes,' said the woman. She looked down at the bag. 'He forgot his sand-wiches.'

Eddie blinked, focusing hard, wrenching the wheel at the very last minute, sending the Dollybus squealing like a stuck pig down the off-ramp toward a K-Mart, and the Dollybirds within leaping as if for joy from their seats and tumbling, pint-size, like drunks in the aisles, until (with a sudden, quite startling, self-possession) he slammed his size twelves hard together on the brakes and the bus and its contents came (with some grace, to be sure) to a slow-spinning stop, then sat resting – silent but for a barely audible ticking, in a cloud of pale Missouri dust.

For a moment, a curious, limbo-like calm, then: 'Jesus Christ!'

Dolly One was lying upside down and crumpled in the footwell by the door. She struggled to right herself, all kneecaps and elbows, then set her hands on the step, her face scowling, her hair now a bleached and lacquered bird's nest. 'What the *fuck* –' she said, pausing, then, to spit out a mouthful of dirt, 'what the *fuck* do you think you're *doing*, asshole?'

Slowly, like a man rising up from the deepest of sleeps, Eddie lifted his head from the wheel. He narrowed his eyes; everything was blurry. 'What?' he said. He raised up a hand, touched his forehead, squinted at his fingers.

Blood.

Oh Lord.

Not *again*.

He twisted slow, took a look through the pain down the bus. 'You okay?' he said. His voice was hoarse, as if he'd been shouting.

'Okay? *Okay?*'

Wincing, turning back to the footwell (Dolly One was on her feet now, tiny hands on tiny hips – and, boy, did she look *mad*), his eye caught something moving in the slow-twirling dust – shapes coalescing into, well, *what* exactly he couldn't see. He leaned forward, frowning, peering hard through the windshield.

'Well?' said Dolly One. There was fire in her eyes. 'Ain't you got *nothin'* to say?'

'What?' said Eddie.

'Jesus fuckin' Christ, Reno. You damn near kill the lot of us and all you can say is *what?*'

'I'm sorry,' he said.

'Sorry? You're *sorry?*'

His heart, suddenly, was pounding in his throat, as the shapes in the dust – so blurry at first, but getting ever sharper – drew nearer and nearer, all the time, slowly, arranging and rearranging themselves like the pieces of some crazy, swirling jigsaw, until gradually, finally, a figure emerged – a *man*, surely – a man with scowling eyes, a man who – *wait a minute* – wasn't he, like, *familiar*? Eddie squinted hard. *Jesus Christ*. Wasn't there something *recognizable* about him – something about that ghastly, leering countenance – something about those eyes narrowed so with such ill-concealed contempt?

'*Hey, Reno, are you listening to me, asshole?*'

And then it came to him.

Those eyes.

That grin.

Oh Jesus.

He swallowed hard, heard the click in his throat. He closed his eyes, held a beat, two, opened them.

Oh Lord.

Surely no.

He shook his head, tried to dismiss the figure from his sight, but the figure would not be dismissed. Instead he drew ever nearer, pressed his nose against the windshield, his face white with dust, his flesh pale and bloodless, like the flesh of some desperate, unspeakable ghoul.

87

I f ever, in the life of Eddie Reno, there was a case of good news and bad news, then this, surely, was it. Not that, in that moment, the good news was exactly evident to him; no, sir, on the contrary, in that moment, the news, for Eddie Reno, was all bad, bad, bad.

'Mr *Frampton*?' he said. His voice sounded distant, lame – a voice come surely from a dream.

'Who the *fuck* is Mr Frampton?' said Dolly One. She was standing by his side now, her head level with his, her hands on her hips still, her eyes squinting out at the dust.

He's the man I killed. He's the man I hit over the head with a wastebin.

'You did *what*?'

He turned away from the windshield, uncaring in that moment, that his thoughts had been words. This was all surely just a dream – or a nightmare, maybe. 'What?' he said.

Dolly One shook her head. 'Jesus Christ, Reno. You're one sick dude, you know that?'

Eddie closed his eyes. When he opened them, for sure he'd find he'd just been snoozing – he'd find himself for sure back home at last, easing back for the evening in his Rest-A-Matic armchair, his feet in his slippers and his belly full of beer.

He counted, slow, to ten.

Then he opened his eyes – just slits at first, then open wide.

'Hey, Reno – are you *listening* to me?'

His heart sank, as his eyes, looking around, took in all the details of the bus. Slowly, bracing himself, he eased them back to the windshield.

'Edward?'

Nothing. No Mr Frampton.

'Are you alright, Edward? Are you *hurt*?'

Just glass, now, and dust – just the concrete of the off-ramp and a K-Mart in the distance, squatting long and low in the center of a parking-lot.

'*Alright?*' said Dolly One. 'Jesus H Christ – of course he's not *alright*! He's a goddamn *fruitcake, that's* what he is!'

Ignoring this, Dolly Two reached out a hand, set it lightly on Eddie's shoulder.

'Edward?'

A hand squeezed – little fingers bunching flesh. He winced, turning. Dolly Two was smiling, her smile so tender it made him feel like a little boy again. 'I thought I . . . saw something,' he said. Her smile made him feel close to tears, like they were welling up inside of him and searching for a way out. He closed his eyes in an effort to stem them.

'Hey now,' she whispered, and she touched the back of his neck, stroking him gently with the tips of her fingers, just as – so many years ago now – his mother had done when he'd cut himself on a stone playing ball in the park, or come home from school with his knees grazed and bloody.

'But . . . I *did* . . . I'm *sure* I did –'

'There, there,' she said, taking his head to her ample bosom, and stroking his ear with soft, stubby fingers. 'Whatever it was, it's gone now, Edward. It was all just a dream –'

'Hah!' said Dolly One, shaking her head. 'A dream? A *dream*? Was it a *dream* that Mr Loonsville here nearly totalled the Dollybus?' She turned to the rest of the bus – to an audience of disheveled but recovering Dolly Partons. 'I don't *think* so – do *you*?' She paused, again shook her head, this time with the forced, weary smile of someone burdened with others' cares. 'No, fellow Dollys, it was not. It was certainly no dream that you – the Dollybirds – whom, I remind you, *I* created, thus giving you sad bunch of freaks your dignity, not to mention an income – nearly lost your lives – nearly went, prematurely, to greet your loving maker – and *why? Because of . . .*'

'*. . . because of . . .*'

She spun around, stabbing a blunt, pointing finger at the small one beside her.

'*. . . because of HER – THAT's why!*'

Gasps from the audience, twenty sets of eyebrows raised.

'What?' said Dolly Two.

Dolly One turned to face her. 'You heard me,' she said. Eye-to-eye, she stepped closer – as close, indeed, as four bosoms would allow. 'I know what you've been up to,' she hissed, leering, exposing as she did so her multi-capped, pearly-white, all-in-a-line Dolly-teeth. 'I know you've been scheming – don't think I don't, missy. Don't think I ain't heard you – you and that little-girly voice of yours – telling everybody how it's *you* should be Dolly One, not *me*. And don't think I don't see you creeping about with that butter-wouldn't-melt smile, being everybody's *friend*, telling everybody how if you *was* Dolly One, then the

Dollybirds would be playing Sioux City or someplace by now, and not just these two-bit goddamn county fairs –' Warming to her theme, then, she drew closer still – so close, now, that Dolly Two could feel the kiss of warm breath on her cheek. She dropped her voice to a menacing whisper. 'And don't you think, neither, that I'm just gonna sit back and take it, okay? *'Cause, believe me, I ain't –'*

'Look,' said Dolly Two, in some evident confusion, 'I don't know what –'

But Dolly One raised a hand, stopping her dead. Then, pulling herself up to her full four-foot-one, she turned to the bus, stilled the murmuring of her Dollybirds with a withering – no, a threatening – look.

'Ladies,' she said gravely. She paused, scanning the faces before her. Scarcely one of them could meet her glance without turning away. Buoyed, then, by this victory, she continued. 'A question,' she said. Another pause. This time she sighed, feeling, now, with some pleasure, the presence of a much-practiced tear in her eye. This she expelled, feeling it roll with great drama down her cheek. 'The question,' she said, 'is a simple one. The question, sisters, is are we stronger together than we would be apart?' Another scan of the bus, another victory. 'Well, sisters? Would you rather we quit now, after all that we've achieved? Would you rather we do as Dolly Two here would have us do – rather we break up this whole lovin' enterprise – and *now*, of all times, when we're just on the verge of that breakthrough I've been promising you?' Here she paused, glancing pointedly at Dolly Two, who was standing, amazed, her mouth open, fillings gleaming. 'Well, sisters,' she said, *'would* you? Would you rather I tell Jerry that the show's a no-go after all?'

'Jerry?' said a small, timid voice from the bus. 'You mean –'

She nodded. 'Indeed,' she said. Then she sighed. 'Would you rather I disappoint the American people? Is that what they *deserve*? And would you rather I drag the good name of the Dollybirds through the dirt by breaking a contract? Well, would you?'

'There's a *contract*?' said the voice from the bus, and, in that moment, Dolly One knew she had them. She knew, in that moment, that her victory was complete, and that Florence Hannah Winterplatt was history as a Dollybird, and that the grip she'd felt failing was now re-established – and she knew in her heart that glorious righteousness that comes only to those to whom history gives the chance to face down the red menace – knew that heady scent of victory given only to those who stand their ground, unflinching – those to whom justice and democracy are sacred – those to whom America is not just a nation – not just the people and the land in which they live – but the rich gift of hope handed down to us by God – an ideal beating, still, despite all – despite the efforts of insurgents – in the brave hearts of men.

88

'Do you think she really meant it?'

'Meant what?'

'About having a contract.'

Eddie shrugged. They were standing, the two of them – an old man and a midget – in the dirt beside the off-ramp, squinting through the dust at the Dollybus as, way off now, it headed west down the highway (Dolly One at the wheel, Dolly Three at her feet, her hands on the pedals and grit in her eyes) – all the time growing smaller as it wove its way erratically up to the top of a rise, then dipped over and was gone.

'I mean maybe she *did* mean it. Maybe there *is* a contract.'

Eddie said nothing. His whole body was hurting too much to talk – and, besides, what the hell was there to talk about? They were stranded, and that was it.

'Edward?'

'What?'

'Well, do you think?'

He turned sharply. 'Look –' he said, and he was about to go on – about to tell her, and with as much aggression as he could muster, how it was *her* fault they were stranded right there in the middle of nowhere (or, at least, in the middle of Iowa, which, for God's sake – at least to Eddie – was just about the same thing), and how he wished – more than he'd ever wished for anything before – that he'd never clapped eyes on the Dollybus and the Dollybirds, and especially not on *her* – when something in the look of Florence Hannah Winterplatt stopped the words dead in his throat.

'Edward? Are you alright?'

He turned away. There was something about her now that chilled him – something that made her seem not so much the strange kind of child he'd come to think of her as, but someone older – someone much, much older (perhaps someone older, even, in some way, than he) – someone, at any rate, small and lost in a large and lost world.

'Oh, I'm sorry,' he said.

'Sorry? What for?'

He shrugged. *For everything*, he wanted to say. *For everything I've ever done*. Instead, though, he turned, tried to raise up a smile, tried to summon up the will to go on.

Florence sighed. 'Edward?' she said.

'What?'

'I'm sorry.'

'It's okay,' he said. Then, with a monumental effort of will, he raised up his hand, so shielding his eyes, and started scanning the horizon and scowling like he'd seen John Wayne do in *They Died With Their Boots On*. '*So, pardner*,' he said, attempting a Wayne-drawl, '*this is Iowa, huh? Ya doan say –*' He flicked his eyes toward Florence, who, already, was smiling – even now. '*If you'd care to take a look, sergeant-major, I think you'll find that there's Injuns beyond them hills and they ain't come to wish us a Merry Christmas –*'

Florence Hannah Winterplatt squinted hard at the horizon. 'Injuns?' she said. 'Oh, my Lord! Do you think they've come for us?'

'*Well, sergeant-major, let me put it this way. If you're looking to retire any time soon from this man's army, well you might just be getting the chance –*'

'You *mean* –' she said.

Eddie lowered his hand. '*I mean, sergeant-major, that old Mister Crazy Horse sure ain't come lookin' for recruits. Specially no yellow-belly horse-thievin' sons-of-bitches –*'

Eddie stopped as a finger poked his ribcage. He looked down. '*What is it, sergeant-major?*'

Florence was scowling hard. 'I got news for you,' she said, jabbing again with her finger. 'I don't care what they say back east. I ain't no yellow-belly, horse-thievin, son-of-a-whatever –'

'*No, sir?*'

'No, sir! And you know what? I ain't a sergeant-major! Hell, I ain't even in this man's army! And you wanna know why?'

'*Well, I guess you're gonna tell me, sergeant-major.*'

'Well, it's because . . . because . . . I'm too short – that's why!'

'*Too short?*'

'And I can't see straight!'

'*You can't?*'

'No, sir – but that ain't all –'

'*It ain't?*'

'No, sir, it ain't. The real reason I ain't in this man's army is . . . is . . . THIS MAN AIN'T A MAN!'

Eddie Reno felt another jolt in his ribcage, then something like some kind of sickness rising up through his chest. He frowned harder, trying to keep it at bay. 'You mean, sergeant-major,' he said, 'that you're a . . . a . . . WOMAN?'

Then Florence was laughing and he was laughing too – for what he'd thought to be sickness was not sickness at all, but laughter, and soon he was down, a grateful pilgrim, on his knees, his chest heaving, his eyes streaming, for the first time in so long his spirit released, if only for a while, from the tight-fitting suit of his own hopes and fears.

89

Well, they laughed and laughed – oh, how they laughed! – and when at last they were through laughing they just lay on their backs in the dust of that incline and let the heat from the sun dry the tears on their faces.

John Wayne.

Duke.

Eddie covered his eyes with his forearm, felt the cool of his cuff-button on his cheek. He'd not thought of him, not old Duke Wayne, in so long – not pictured him, for years maybe, riding his horse in some echoing canyon, or standing tall in the middle of a threatening saloon, his hands on his six-guns and his Stetson tipped back – not since, maybe, that night after the Roxette when he'd stood so drunk and raving in the street – swearing to himself (and to anyone else who would listen) that it was the *movies* that had somehow gone and stolen his son – and how all those sons-of-bitches implicated in their making (for some reason known only to him then, he'd singled out Louis B. Meyer and John Wayne as the most culpable) should be locked up or worse, and all theaters closed down and bulldozed into rubble.

'Edward?'

He lowered his arm.

'I was thinking –'

And then – *Good Lord* – he'd found himself, that night, walking slowly – plodding, really – through a light, steady rain for mile after mile, peering (some, later, at the station-house on 32nd Street, would say *leering*) at the faces of everyone he'd passed, hoping – half-expecting – to find there (surely in *one* of them) those beautiful features he'd come to know and to love – to so *cherish* – so much better than his own . . .

'Thinking?' he said.

'About what we should *do* –'

'Do?'

He closed his eyes.

'Like maybe we could hitch a ride?'

But of course, that night, he'd discovered no such features – only those that made the faces of those found, not those lost, and in the end he'd given up and just sat on a bench in some park, staring blindly at the rain as it darkened his shoes.

'Well, do you?'

He opened his eyes.

'Excuse me?' he said. He was staring up now – now, a century later (or so it seemed) – his eyes unshaded – his sight unprotected – his muscles flaring at the brightness of the pale, unforgiving, western Iowa sky.

Florence huffed. 'Oh, *Edward* –'

'What?'

'Oh, never mind.'

He sat up. 'No, what?'

She was standing, looking down at the K-Mart.

'Florence?'

She shrugged. Dust rose and fell from her shoulders. 'Well, I was thinking,' she said. She paused.

'Yes?' said Eddie.

Another shrug. 'Well, maybe if we *do* hitch a ride, then maybe we could all, well, go in the same direction –'

Eddie frowned. 'What do you mean, *the same direction*? The same direction as what?' Then Florence half-turned, and he knew. 'You mean you want to go *back* to them? After all that's happened?' It was the look he'd seen earlier – the just-controlled panic of that child in that mall at the gradual, creeping onset of that night.

'Do you think?' she said softly, her voice, now, the voice of that child.

'I don't know,' said Eddie. 'It's up to you.'

'Then you'll come?'

'*Me?*'

Suddenly, she brightened. 'Oh, *Edward*, I'm sure she won't mind – not if we both say we're sorry –' Then, as swiftly as it had arrived, her brightness faded. 'Edward? What is it?'

'Look,' he said. 'You go, okay?'

'But what about –'

'I'll be fine. Besides, I've got things to do.' He tried to laugh, but it came out fake: all his laughing for the day (and for how many more days?) was through. 'Anyway,' he said, 'I'm going *north*, and you're – they're – going south –'

'But why?' said Florence.

'Why?'

'Why are you going north? Why can't you go south?'

'Well –'

'Is there – somebody there?'

'Somebody?'

'Somebody *special* –'

'Special?' He shook his head. 'Oh, no – nobody.' He paused. 'At least –' In his mind's eye, suddenly, came the most absurd of images.

Florence frowned. 'Don't you know?'

It was Angelia. Her face, dipped in shadow, moved away.

'Edward?'

Squinting, he tried hard to retrieve it.

'Edward?'

But it would not be retrieved. No, like so many other things in his life, once it was gone it was gone for good.

'*Ed*ward –'

'What?'

'Hey, are you alright? You look like you've just seen a ghost –'

'A ghost?' He blinked.

'You look so pale –'

'Pale?' Alone, the blood and bone of him pulled up a smile. What was left felt it spread like a flannel on his face. 'No, I'm fine,' he said.

'Well, you don't *look* fine.'

'I *said* I'm fine – okay?'

Florence huffed. '*Jesus*, Edward, I was only *saying* –'

'Okay, okay, I'm sorry. It's just, well . . . oh *I* don't know –'

A hand touched his thigh. 'Edward? Is there something wrong?'

'Wrong?' Eddie sighed, for a moment so tempted, there and then, to say it all, to tell everything – how he'd been such a fool – but worse than that – how, with his own father's expertise, he'd somehow made his son disappear, as surely as if it had been some new trick he'd learned, and then how – as surely as if he'd pushed her – he'd sent Clare and a new child off the side of that Florida bridge and into that water, so killing them both (and how he'd tried to shut it out, but could not) – and how, now, with such cruelty that it could only, surely, come from God, he'd been spared and given time to remember – time enough to hear their screams and to feel every morning and in the dark of every night the shaming ease of his own silent breathing, and to hear, then, the silence of a heart that – though beating – was surely and forevermore dying . . .

'Edward?'

Dying, maybe dead.

'Should we get something to drink maybe? Would you like that?'

But he didn't say anything. All he said was, 'Okay,' and he let himself be led, then, like an old man down the incline and over the burning tar road.

90

'I s Coke alright?'
    'Coke's fine.'
    'It was Coke or iced tea.'
'This is fine. Really.'

Florence pushed in her straw, puncturing the cup's plastic top. She drew in a mouthful of the dark, sickly-sweet liquid, her eyes, all the time, fixed on Eddie, who was scanning the mall. Beyond the chairs and tables set out for the customers of the TexMex Tacos Bar (five, he counted, including the two of them), there were maybe a hundred others, and then, beyond them, a fountain in the shape of a sheaf of ripe Iowa corn.

'Well, do you?'

Beside the fountain (from which sprung a single jet of water, maybe six foot into the air), a young man in a Pittsburg Stealers sweatshirt was touching himself and rocking to and fro, his eyes closed tight in concentration. Eddie pulled his eyes away. 'Sorry?' he said.

'*Jesus*, Edward, haven't you been listening to me?'

'I'm sorry. What did you say?'

'I was saying, do you want to get something to eat?'

He shrugged.

'Well, do you mind if I do?'

He shook his head, tried to smile, as Florence eased herself out of her (for her) high chair. He watched her move between the tables, saw the heads turn to gawp. He turned away, looked for the young man by the fountain. The fountain was switched off, the water and the young man gone.

They were drifting through the mall – it was mid-afternoon, now, and Eddie was tiring, every one of his limbs desperate for rest – when Florence pulled up outside JC Penneys. She pressed her nose against the window.

'Hey, look –' she said.

Eddie sighed. For an hour now he'd been trying to figure out how best to say that if they were going to split up (and they *were* – make no mistake about that – as he certainly had no intention of going back the way he'd come, as that way lay, well, *nothing*, he'd had to gloomily conclude), then it really should be soon – or, at any rate, sometime before the afternoon drifted into dusk and rides became scarce – scarcer, that is, than they already were, for an old man alone who was starting to look like some really hopeless kind of bum; so far, though, despite all his efforts, he'd come up with nothing.

He moved up beside her, placed both hands square on the glass and leaned into them. 'What is it?' he said. The window was full of children's clothes on sale – the centerpiece a cowgirl's outfit, complete with Stetson, tassels, boots (white, of course) and a gun. He glanced to Florence; Florence was transfixed.

'Oh,' she said, sighing like a girl, 'it's so beautiful – isn't it?'

'Yeah, it's pretty,' said Eddie. And then a thought struck him. 'You want it?' he said.

Florence turned.

'Call it a going-away present.'

'Really?' she said. Her eyes, suddenly, were full of tears, making her look more and more like the little girl Eddie had thought her, once, to resemble.

'Come on,' he said. He held out his hand.

Florence held up hers in response, but then withdrew it. 'One condition,' she said.

'Condition?' said Eddie.

'You'll see,' she said. Then, hand in hand, together they moved through the doors, for all the world like a father and daughter out on a spree.

91

'You look splendid.'

Eddie shook his head. His Stetson wobbled. 'I *look* daft. *You* look splendid.'

Florence considered herself in the window of McDonald's. '*I* look like some weird kind of Barbie doll.' She clicked the heels of her boots together; *ker-chink*, *ker-chink* went her spurs. 'You hear that?' she said.

'I hear it,' said Eddie. Smiling, then (oh, he couldn't *stop* himself now, so bizarre did the whole scene – his whole *life*, in that moment – seem), he matched it with a click and *ker-chink* of his own. He raised a hand and raised his hat, and Florence curtsied, smiling too, then she took his hand in hers and together they danced to the sound of a jaunty cotillion – turning, this oddest of couples, this way and that, she with her tasseled dress and he in his chaps, and all with a slow grace and suppleness that made as nothing (at least for a moment) those misfortunes of life handed down to them by God or by fate or whomever –

'Florence?'

Or they would have done – they would have danced, and would be dancing still – had the world in that moment been at Florence's command.

'Yes, Edward?'

But of course it wasn't – never had been – except, of course, in her mind. In her mind, at least, she was liberated (had been many times) – in her mind, in that moment, she was desirable, and no longer, at least in that moment, just the object of pity or scorn or of eyes turned away and made blind.

But only in her mind.

For in the mall, alas, there was just an awkward silence between two battered people – one very short, the other very old – each aware of the cost of each other's wounds, but each so tired that they'd rather look away than acknowledge the existence of those wounds, and so, by acknowledging them, take on a portion of their burden themselves.

'Well –' said Eddie. He glanced down at his boots; they were bull-hide and expensive – Tony Lama's, built in Texas – strong and made for riding. He looked up. 'I guess this is it.'

Florence shrugged. 'I guess so,' she said.

And that, indeed, was that.

They said goodbye in the parking-lot (there were no kisses and no handshakes – just the briefest of nods, at once distant and intimate, like those of two spies passing by on some far-off, neutral bridge), then Eddie withdrew to the shade of the K-Mart entrance and watched Florence make her slow, labored way between the standing cars and onto the off-ramp. Here she paused, turned, raised a hand in a wave. He waved back, watching as she turned away, then moved slow up the off-ramp, over a rise onto the highway, and was gone.

'Hey, cowboy – you want a ride?'

The car swept to a halt in a cloud of dust. Eddie pulled his eyes down from the ramp, bent at the waist, peered in. It was dark inside the car, the driver deep in shadow.

'Excuse me?' he said.

'I said do you want a ride –'

'A ride?' He hesitated, a voice in his head saying *no*. 'Well –' But then the voice faded, was replaced by another. 'Are you going north?' he said.

'North?' said the driver. 'Sure. Get in.'

Eddie gripped the handle, pulled open the door and eased himself in. He was just turning, then, aiming to maybe explain his costume, when his eye caught a familiar-looking No Smoking sticker on the dash. He reached forward, was about to touch it when something hard, something metal, found his ribs. 'Hey,' he said, 'what the –' but he got no further, as, in that moment, the driver leaned forward, revealing a pale, sweating face.

Oh Jesus.

He swallowed hard.

'*Mr Frampton?*'

The driver smiled.

'I . . . I thought you were –'

It was a smile Eddie knew from a thousand K-Mart mornings. '*Dead*, Mr Reno?' he said. 'Is *that* what you were thinking?'

Eddie opened his mouth but could say no more. He looked down to the pistol, gleaming so in the gloom, as a strange kind of peace came over him. *At last*, he thought, and he closed his eyes, closing his heart, once and for all, to the chance of escape that he'd once, fleetingly, as a younger man, thought possible, but which now – now at the end of things – he knew to be nothing more than the cruellest of hopes raised and then dashed by the cruellest and most spiteful of worlds.

92

'**S**o, punk, you feeling lucky?'

Just as, as the saying goes, there can be no show without
Punch, so could there never, it seemed, in the life of Eddie Reno,
be an end to that life without a finger of the past coming back to jab him
in the belly, and so remind him that what we once were we are still, and
that today can never – however swift – outpace toward the future that
most fleet-of-foot adversary, the past.

A finger.

Or, in this case, a pistol. In this case, the solid-steel barrel of a forty-
four Magnum, the most powerful handgun in the world.

'Lucky?' said Eddie. He opened his eyes, half-expecting to find himself
already in the Kingdom to come. Again, he swallowed hard. Could it be,
he thought (oh, for sure this was crazy thinking, but what else could you
expect?), that the next world was in fact just the same as this one – the
point being that you cannot ever escape, not even through death?

The pistol pressed harder, finding the soft flesh beneath the lowest of
his ribs.

'Well, Mr Reno? *Do* you?'

He shook his head. In truth, he felt many things right then, but lucky
was not one of them. Mostly – despite the wildness, now, of everything
– he just felt exhausted, so tired way down in his bones – too tired, now,
to feel anything but that strange kind of calmness that comes (or so he'd
read) to those on the brink of execution. He sighed. 'Go on, then,' he
said, his voice down to a croak.

'What?'

'I said go on, if you're going to. Get it over with.'

'*Get it over with?*'

The pressure of the pistol lessened. 'Jesus, what kind of crazy old
fucker are you?' Then the pressure resumed, increasing until the lowest
of Eddie's ribs was really hurting. 'Don't you know I *mean* it, old man?
Don't you know you could lose whatever brains you've got in a second,
right here, right now? Get them pasted all over this goddamn useless
car?'

Eddie shrugged, something in his head discounting the pain.

Another prod of the pistol. 'Is that what you want, old man?'

So much so that he felt suddenly light-headed, as if he'd not eaten for a month, or was breathing air so oxygen-rich as to make a man faint.

Another prod, harder.

'Well, *is* it?'

He let his eyes close, tried to think of other things – anything but this crazy fantasy he seemed to be living now. Things like cars – this car. He opened his eyes, glanced about him.

'Say – you listening to me, old man?'

The car, it occurred to him, was mighty familiar. For one thing, there were the scratches on the dash from a ex-neighbor's dog, and, for another, that dent in the door where he'd bashed it – years ago – with the end of a heavy metal curtain-rod. He frowned, tried to think of that ex-neighbor's name – or the name, at least, of the dog.

The pistol returned, digging in, chasing the dog and the neighbor from his mind. 'Hey, I *said* are you listening to me, *Mister* Reno?'

He blinked, rested his eyes, then, on the face of Mr Frampton. Mr Frampton was scowling, his pallor touched now with the pink of frustration. His jaw, Eddie noted, was darkening – a day or two shy of a razor. Still in his dream-world, Eddie had the strongest desire just to reach out and touch it.

Mr Frampton pulled back. 'What the *fuck* are you doing?'

Beneath the tips of his fingers, the stubble was unexpectedly soft – soft like the soft, downy growth on the chin of a boy. Eddie dropped his hand. 'I'm sorry,' he said. 'It's just –' He paused, tried to think what it was he was meaning to say, but could not.

'Just *what*?'

Instead, he just shrugged.

'Look, old man, you pull another stunt like that and I'll blow your fucking brains out all over your precious car – okay?'

Your precious car.

That was it.

Eddie reached forward, touched the dash. 'Good gracious –' he said. He looked at Mr Frampton. Mr Frampton, now, was smiling.

'You really don't get it – do you?' he said.

'Get what?' said Eddie.

'Why I tracked you.'

'You tracked me?'

'Sure I did.' Mr Frampton raised the barrel of the pistol to his lips, blew on it, then, like a gunfighter. 'You want to know why?'

Eddie just stared, for something else had occurred to him. It had occurred to him that if the man had the car (he must have stolen the keys from his pocket after hitting him over the head at Graceland), then maybe – was it possible? – he *also* had the book –

'Well,' said Mr Frampton, 'to start with, I'll admit it was just plain revenge – you hit me, I hit you, that kind of thing. Childish, really, I suppose. Anyhow, that – plain and simple – was what it was until I started reading.'

'Reading?' said Eddie. His heart, suddenly, was thumping.

'That's right – reading. And you know what I was reading?'

Eddie shook his head; his mouth was dry.

Mr Frampton tut-tutted. 'Come now,' Mr Reno,' he said. 'I'd be obliged if you'd at least do me the courtesy of not treating me like a fool. It is I, after all, who am in possession, now, of – shall we say – all the relevant information. It is I – is it not? – who is holding – shall we say – the whip hand –'

Eddie shook his head. 'I don't know what you're talking about.'

But Mr Frampton just sighed. 'Oh dear,' he said wearily, 'oh dear, oh dear, oh dear. Just as I feared. You've really not the brains to have figured it out – have you?'

Eddie frowned. 'Figure what out?'

'The value, ironically, of a single photograph.'

'A *what*?'

'A photograph, Mr Reno. You know, those things you used to make a living out of producing.' Another sigh. 'Don't tell me you don't remember?'

Eddie opened his mouth, but no words came forth.

'Oh *dear*, Mr Reno. How *sad*. However, whether or not you remember your former career, it is to your great advantage – indeed it is your salvation, no less – that *I* remember. For it is this former skill of yours – skill that, I have no doubt, you will – with perhaps a little prompting from yours truly – recover – that has kept you alive thus far. In short, Mr Reno – although it pains me greatly to say this – I need you.'

'You do?'

'Sadly, yes. For the time being, at least. So, you see, you *could* say (and I'll admit there's a certain pleasing symmetry about this) that who you *are* – what you've so regrettably *become* – has been – for the time being, at least – saved by who – by what – you *were*.' Mr Frampton raised a finger, then, as if drawing his own attention to the shortness of time. 'However, all that is, now, just so much eyewash. What *really* concerns me – and what, believe me, will really concern *you* – is the condition, once found, of that photograph, and how best to preserve it, and, so, prepare it for sale.' Here Mr Frampton paused, smiling benignly, like a schoolmaster waiting for an answer. 'Well?' he said, when no word was forthcoming.

Eddie Reno said nothing. There was nothing to say. He knew nothing of any photograph, nor the sense to be found in making any plans. All he knew was what he'd always known. All he knew, sitting there in that parking-lot, beneath the gaze and the gun of his former employer, was that the life that he'd thought, once, was at least his to extinguish, never had been and never would be, and that God or whatever – whomever – was in charge meant to play with him yet a while longer – meant to twist him some more as a punishment for his sins, meant to turn him in the wind like some fool living still at the end of a rope, until he called out for mercy, and, in so calling, called down upon himself all the wrath of the faithful – the faithful and the good, with their blessings sharp as knives and their ghastly loving hearts.

Matthew & James

93

'And so, gentlemen and ladies, in conclusion –'

'Thank God,' said a voice from the crowd.

Standing high on his soapbox in the center of the town's dusty main street, the Reverend Theodore Randolph, first (and, in truth, only) minister of the Church of our Savior's Salvation, Galesburg, Illinois, let only the faintest trace of annoyance color his features (he was used, indeed, to such barracking – and worse – from audiences of such obviously unrepenting sinners) as he raised his eyes to the heavens and then dropped them, scanning the faces before him. 'In *conclusion,*' he repeated, 'let me just say this –'

'You just said that,' said the voice from the crowd, to the accompaniment of much laughter.

'Let me, *gentlemen and ladies*, just leave you with the words of our esteemed President, General Ulysses S. Grant –' Here, the Reverend Randolph paused, observing as he did so (and with some satisfaction) the sudden stilling of that laughter, and its replacing with a quiet, almost religious, reverence. He cleared his throat, preparing, as he did so, his grave and sonorous (and much-practiced) quoting voice. 'If,' he said, raising his finger and pointing it skyward, 'if it is, as I believe, true that it is the manifest destiny of our nation to expand, lest, by our sloth, it stagnate and wither, then it is also true that all real Americans must aid in that expansion, as the territorial restraint of one American is surely the territorial restraint of *all* Americans.' Another pause, then, another scan of the upturned faces before him. There was amongst them, now, a touch of confusion, his words not at all being those expected of a minister. Thus encouraged, the reverend slowly lowered his finger, pointed it, then, at the now-silent and so-attentive crowd. He leaned forward, dropped his voice to a hissing, conspiratorial whisper. 'People,' he said. 'Sons and daughters of our great state of Illinois –' Here, again, a pause, a slight shake of the head, a slow-raising of his voice to a booming, chest-beating holler: 'Children of this Union! O, children of a Union so battered and bruised, but still standing, will you, now – now, in the hour of our nation's greatest challenge – dismiss our President's call? Will you shirk the sacred duty that stands before us now? Well, will you?' Breathing hard now, his mortal chest fairly heaving with righteousness, he thrust out his hands, palms upward, imploring – neither seeing nor hearing as he did so, the dropping of a camera-shutter from way off beyond the crowd – in fact, from the shadows of the Galesburg Saloon. 'Well, will you?' he repeated, searching the faces before him, settling, at last, on the face of young Jamie Brown, whose father, ten years back now, had been shot in the head at Gettysburg and left to die slowly at that ghastly Bloody Angle.

Jamie Brown looked about him, his face flushing. He looked back to the reverend. 'Me, sir?' he said.

'You, sir!' said the reverend.

He swallowed hard. For a month now, while pushing on his broom in Ronnie Raye's Supreme Barber's, he'd listened hard to all the talk of General Custer and those terrifying Indian devils – how for sure the Seventh Cavalry was just about the one outfit that could whup them, and how, once that whupping was done – once the general had cut himself the fresh and bleeding scalps of those bloodthirsty, white-woman-violating savages Crazy Horse and Sitting Bull – how, for sure, then, those old boys in Washington would just *have* to make him President – maybe even (and this was the rumor most frequently circulated not only in the barber's, but all over the town, and – although they didn't know it – pretty much all over the country) make him President for life, and Mrs Custer the First Lady for life.

'Well, sir?'

He opened his mouth, hesitating.

'Have you nothing to say on this most important – most *pressing* – of subjects? Have you nothing to say on the future of our nation?'

'Well –' he said at last. He paused, fearful of speaking – fearful of the fool it invariably made of him.

'Well?' boomed the reverend. 'Speak up, sir! Speak up!'

He licked his lips. They were dry and cracked. He cleared his throat. 'Well,' he said, 'I . . . I surely don't know nothin' 'bout no terrible restraint –' Another pause, another look around – at the eyes fixed upon him, at the attention the like of which he'd never before experienced. He straightened his back, looked back to the man dressed in black and standing tall on his soapbox in the center of Main Street. 'But, well, sir, I reckon –'

'Yes, son?'

He drew a deep breath, pushed out his shallow chest. 'Well, I reckon General Custer's gonna whup them Injuns good!'

'Hear, hear!' called a voice from the crowd. 'Yes, sir!' called another.

'– And I reckon, well, well I reckon when he does, I'm gonna be there!'

'You are, sir?' said the reverend.

'I am, sir!' said little Jamie Brown, who, indeed, would be there, and whose seventeen years would be ended, there, in terror, as he, the last man alive on that Montana rise, would see death approaching, feel its twisting in his gut, hear in that future, as yet unrecorded, his own ghastly howling –

'Hallelujah!' cried the reverend.

Then witness, in the heat and the blood, the vision of some cool, eastern parlor, hear the ticking, then, of a clock, and see the falling, in his mind's eye, of his mother's wretched tears.

But not yet.

Not now.

Now – then – on that main street in Galesburg, Illinois, he just beamed, brave and foolhardy, as others of the young men took his lead and so carelessly, so willingly, so stupidly gave up their lives, and his hand was taken and pumped hard with gratitude, and all around him were so joyous, so filled already with their inevitable victory over the savages, that none saw the sun dipping slow in the sky, nor the captain of cavalry (for such rank did his uniform denote) as he made his stealthy way forward amongst them, or the glint, then, of the sharp and steel persuasion he offered Reverend Randolph in exchange not just for his soapbox – but in exchange, indeed, too, for his pious, bloodless life.

94

Horses aside (and that, heaven knows, is a big exclusion), the one thing that James Monkton Webb just couldn't abide – the one thing that raised within him that which he was pleased to call his 'devils' – was that notion of honor, of courage, of devotion, best expressed by the willingness of young men to suffer gravely and to die for what was really nothing more than a bunch of colored cloth and that inattentive loser called God.

God.

Standing on that soapbox, in the center of that crowded main street, with all eyes upon him (especially those of the young men, who, he noted, with a hangman's delight, couldn't wrest their rapt attention from the silver of his buttons and the blue of his tunic), he shook his head gravely, then slowly tipped it back, until his eyes were considering the pale, cloudless sky, and whatever lay beyond.

'Who are *you*?' said a voice, in a while – a woman's – from the crowd.

James held a beat (oh, the sky was so beautiful, and so, so blue), then lowered his gaze, fixed it hard and steady.

God, he thought.

The woman tried to fight him, but the battle soon was lost. She dropped her eyes, defeated.

God.

'I, madam,' he said softly, 'am Captain of Cavalry James Monkton Webb – a Webb of the Webbs of Sonora, California.' Here he paused, as if such information were sufficient to explain his sudden presence.

'Hey, mister – do you know General Custer?' came another voice – a grown man's, this time – from the crowd.

He closed his eyes, let go a little sigh. The dispute, in his view, as far as God was concerned, was not whether He existed at all (for he'd sure and certain knowledge that He did), but, given that He *does* exist, then why, in heaven's name, is He such a spiteful – such a negligent – God? He opened his eyes. 'Hmmm,' he said, 'Custer.' Then he said it again, then again, as if he were turning the word over and over on his tongue so as to isolate exactly its taste.

'Well, mister? Do you or don't you?'

He lifted his right hand, palm upward, and settled his gaze on the lines thereon. In *his* view, the answer was this: that, simply put, God – He in whom so much hope is placed by so many – though He *is* a God (indeed, *the* God), well He's just not very good at it – at the business of *being* a God; no, in the view of James Monkton Webb, of the once-numerous Monkton Webbs of Sonora, California, God is a hopeless God, eternally compromised by vanity and ignorance – and, thus, of course, is man so compromised, his having been made in the image of that God. All of which, standing up that day on the reverend's soapbox, looking out across the crowd, made him feel once again that sudden surge of strength – of *possibilities* – that comes to a man who discovers that those chains he'd once thought made of iron are, in fact, only links blown of black-painted glass.

Another voice, then, from the crowd: 'Get your tongue, did he – Georgie-boy? Catch you sweet-talking that Libbie when you should have been whupping them southern boys, huh?' The voice was full of sneering – full of the courage of the over-age, flat-footed, one-eyed volunteer. He turned to those gathered at his shoulder, pleased with the rich, manly tone of his voice – at the way it vibrated in his throat. 'See?' he said, the sneer growing into a thin weasel smile. 'See how our friend here – our captain of cavalry, Mister James Monkey Webb – has lost his tongue to Miss Hannah's old cat?'

On the soapbox, the reverend's successor raised his hands, at which the burbling of the crowd (and the laughing of Gilbert Creek, father of three sons, all slain by that drunken murderer Grant in his stumbling, blood-letting wilderness) was stilled, and a silence descended, thick and heavy, in its stead. He lowered his hands, set his eyes on the face of old Gilbert. He smiled, then, a smile of his own – the calm, forgiving smile of a Botticelli saint – then flicked out his tongue, withdrew it. He said something softly, his voice just a whisper.

'What?' said old Gilbert, looking about him. 'What did he say?'

'He said *meow*,' said the man at his shoulder.

'Meow?' said old Gilbert.

'Meow,' said James again, and in that moment he knew he had them. *Make them laugh*, a bright fellow had once told him, *and their tears will forever be yours*. Slowly, he withdrew his sabre, turned it, gleaming, in the sun. 'Your nation,' he said, directing the sabre at the face, first, of one young man, then another, 'needs you. For,' he said gravely, 'there is blood to be spilled.' He stilled his sword, then, as it rested, pointing, at the face of a sallow, consumptive youth. The young man, fearing such attention, swallowed hard. The sabre twisted, blinding, in the sun. 'Sir,' said James. Then he spread across his face a troubled, quizzical look. 'Would you know,' he said, frowning, 'what day it is?'

The youth shook his head.

'No, sir?' said James.

Again.

'Well, sir.' And then he was smiling, leaning forward. Mesmerized, indeed as if hypnotized, the crowd, too, leaned forward, as James, unseen, bit his lip, tasted, then, the salt tang of blood on his tongue. '*Hoka hey*,' he said softly, then he said it again, then a third, then a fourth time – in fact again and again, until, driven by something within them that both terrified and aroused them, the crowd was chanting too – disturbing even, in time, the ears of Miss Hannah's mangy cat as it dozed out of sight in the cool of an old empty barrel.

95

I n years to come, the photograph, erroneously (and, perhaps, ironically) entitled *The Boys Marching Home*, would rest under glass, an exhibit of a bygone – of a long-dead – age, in a cabinet in some scarcely visited museum, its presence remarkable only for the location of its original discovery (it had been found, bizarrely enough, in the upholstery of a reproduction French-style love-seat, following that article's restoration), and not, in general, for the picture itself, nor, in particular, for the long-gone individuals represented therein. Indeed, those individuals – those raggedy, ill-kempt but smiling soldier-boys – would remain unnamed – their identities known only to the grave and to God. Even the fellow leading that fifteen- or twenty-strong Galesburg procession – he with his uniform, his horse and his sabre – even *he* is a mystery, appearing, as he does, in no military record, nor in any letters written home by subordinates in the field or in camp.

But how so such a mystery?

Surely *somebody* knows.

Well, maybe. But to *know* is one thing; to *care* is another. And what is clear, here, is that nobody cares. Nobody cares who they were or where they were headed (you can be sure from the lightness of their looks that they were *not* headed home, as their smiles mean for sure that the carnage is still before them, and so is, as yet, unknown) – for who cares for the dead, except the dead themselves?

No, sir.

All is gone, all is past. The dead are only so much dust, so much fading paper.

And yet, and yet –

Visit Galesburg, Illinois, and stand, today, on the very spot from which the photograph was taken.

There.

Can't you feel it? Can't you feel Matthew's breath still warm now on your neck? Can't you hear the soft click of the shutter as it drops?

I can.

So will you.

Just listen.

Yes, the past lives. It's behind us, nudging us, all the time pushing us on, the tips of its fingers grasping at shirt-tails, or at those laces left so carelessly untied, or reaching, in the evening, for the hand that reaches out for the hand of a lover in the onrushing, uncertain, unbreathing night.

96

' **A**re you sure you know what you're doing?'

They marched for all that remained of the day and into the evening. At dusk, halted by the raising of a white-gloved, imperious hand, the two-abreast column stopped as one, each man gratefully lowering his bundle of hastily gathered possessions and stretching his aching limbs, or, in rather more cases, just dropping to the ground – right there on that dusty country road – and resting, some reaching for bottles (some of which were filled with whiskey, whilst others – those belonging to the more thoughtful amongst them – contained what remained of the now-warm, but always brackish local water); some even closed their eyes, their heads cradled in their arms or on rough, knapsack pillows that were, after such exertion, no hindrance now to sleep and to dreams.

'No, sir.'

'You don't?'

'No, sir. And therein lies the wonder.'

And some just lay back, looking up at the stars, their hearts already lonesome for their lives left behind – though their blood, being man's blood, was still running hot for fighting and for the glory – oh, the glory! – of dying for the flag.

Matthew studied the other man's face, searching for the trace of an ironic, knowing smile. Finding none, he shook his head. 'Jesus,' he said. 'You're serious, ain't you?'

They were standing, the two of them, a way off from the rest, James smoking a cigarette and leaning casual against a tree.

'*Serious?* Why, sir, of *course* I'm serious.' He exhaled a thin stream of smoke, smiling then and watching the smoke rise, curling, until it disappeared overhead in the darkness. 'I never know what I'm doing. Not *seriously*. Do you? Does anybody?' He shook his head, smiling still. 'No, sir, I just take what comes along – slip, shall we say, into whatever shoes are provided.'

'You're crazy,' said Matthew.

'Maybe, sir. Maybe.' Another lazy drag on the cigarette, its tip glowing red in the gathering dark. His eyes, then, flicked to Matthew. 'But, sir,' he said, 'consider this. If, indeed, as you say, I am crazy, then are our friends in that field there not more so?'

Matthew glanced to the road. From the field beyond, there drifted the sound now of muffled talk, and, above that, one voice raised in lonely, plaintive song. He turned back. 'What do you mean?' he said.

'Well, what I *mean* is, anyone that's crazy enough to follow a crazy man – well, he's gotta be *real* crazy, wouldn't you say?'

Matthew shrugged.

'I mean *really*, sir, would *you* do such a thing? Would *you* follow a man who's promised you nothing but wandering and fighting – maybe even dying?' He paused, long enough to take another, final drag. 'Well, *would* you, sir? Would *you* be that crazy?'

'But I ain't following you,' said Matthew, the words in the moment of saying ringing hollow in his ears.

'No, sir?' said James. 'You mean if I hadn't come along when I did you wouldn't still be living and dying in that whorehouse – or maybe hanging by now on the end of that rope?'

Matthew looked away. The fields now were dark, the talk and the voice raised in song silent now.

'Well, sir? Did I not save you?'

He turned back sharp. '*Save* me? What do you mean, *save* me?'

'Well, did I not rescue you from a long life of underserved bliss? Did I not spare you the dreadful comfort of companionship? Did I not relieve you of the terrible burden of fatherhood?'

Matthew squinted hard. *I'm dreaming*, he thought. He closed his eyes.

'Well, sir, did I not?'

Any minute I'll wake and be sweating in my bed. Any minute there'll be hands cool and tender on my brow. Any minute, any minute –

'Why, I do believe you're sweating, sir.'

The hand, warm and smooth, withdrew from his cheek. 'Clare?' he said. He opened his eyes, his flesh smarting from the absence of her flesh.

'Clare?' said James. 'Was that her name?' Another smile, then – this time concerned, a fatherly smile. 'That whore, sir, is gone –'

'Gone? What do you mean, gone?'

'I mean she is dead, sir.'

Matthew swallowed hard. '*Dead?*'

'Quite dead, sir, I assure you. She and that whore-child –'

'*She's dead?*'

James nodded.

The terrible burden of fatherhood.

'You mean she . . .'

'Aye, sir.'

'You . . .'

'It was the act of a friend, sir.'

Matthew felt a sickness rising. In his mind's eye he saw her, then – really for the first time her rising, bloated belly – felt there, for the first time, the presence – and now absence – of life and hope –

A hand touched his arm. He flinched.

'Perhaps you should rest now.'

'You killed her.'

'She was in misery, sir. It was my duty –'

Again he squinted. Again, that sickness – as if there were, suddenly, something alien inside him – something he'd been nourishing unknowingly for years – something that was now, suddenly, in that moment, full-grown and busting to break loose and so destroy him.

'After all, sir, you've had quite a day.'

He felt his legs weaken.

She and that whore-child.

He put out his hands, felt his palms touch the rough bark of a tree.

Oh Jesus.

'No, sir,' said a voice from far off. 'James is the name.' Then the voice drew nearer, was suddenly up close. 'Sir?' it said, hot breath on his ear. 'Are you sure you're quite well? Would you like me to send for the surgeon?'

97

He was, she'd said, the only one she'd let kiss her. Kissing, she'd said, was for lovers; kissing, she'd said, was too intimate for strangers; it was, she'd said, the gift of the breath of life.

The breath of life.

He shivered, felt a chill in his bones.

You're the only one, she'd said, her whispers like kisses in the darkness, then she'd kissed him, her kisses soft as whispers.

He turned, unseen, felt something cool – something damp – on his cheek.

You're the one.

You're the one.

She'd covered him, then, in the darkness, sheltered him for free from the unspeakable dangers of the unwelcome night. She'd traced the pattern of his face with the tips of her fingers, her touch as light as the touch of an angel.

'Hey, mister – whatchoodoin'?'

The toe of a boot in his ribcage; he peeled his eyes open.

'What?' he said, bleary, as the angel and her fingers slipped away and were gone.

'I said whatchoodoin', mister?'

He tried to sit up, but sank back. His cheek touched the damp Missouri earth.

'You sick or somethin'?'

The sky overhead was pale – early morning maybe. He squinted, slid his eyes to the boots planted firmly on the ground.

Would you like me to send for the surgeon?

He let slip a moan, as that from which sleep or sickness had rescued him returned, and he saw, once again, the man's uniform and sabre, then the face and swelling form of his one last chance at life anew, now gone.

'My daddy gonna whup you good he finds you here. My daddy don't like no Yankees. 'Specially no Yankees he find livin' in his field.'

She and that whore-child.

'Oh Lord,' he said, as the past, once again, overran him, and he let his eyes close, let his body surrender, let his spirit just drift.

He woke to the sound and sensation of dragging – of *being* dragged, of his shoulders and the back of his head rising and falling – bumping – over hard, stony ground, and his feet raised before him, and, beyond them, the blurring back and narrow shoulders of a skinny man or some tall, lanky boy.

'Hey,' he said roughly, unheard.

Another bump – this time over sharp stone; he winced, tried to brace himself for more.

But then suddenly there was no more, and he was lying – calm and level – on something soft.

He lifted a hand; his fingers found the back of his head. Wetness. Blood.

'Hey, mister.'

A face loomed, blocking the light.

'You thirsty?'

Thirsty.

He tried to nod his head, tried not to cry out as arms encircled him, sat him up. He rubbed his eyes, tried to focus. Something cold – maybe water – touched his lips, wound smooth as silver through his chest to his belly. He wiped his mouth. The faces before him coalesced into one.

'Who are you?' he said, his voice just a croak.

The face was that of a pale, thin boy – a face too young for shaving, but way too old, surely, for the innocence of youth.

'Name's Danny,' he said. 'But you can call me Dan-Dan. Everybody calls me Dan-Dan. Say, what's your name?'

Matthew told the boy his name. The boy frowned. 'Can I call you Matt-Matt?' he said.

Matthew shrugged.

The boy smiled.

'You want some pie?'

From his pocket, then, he pulled out a small paper bundle. This he unfolded, offered up its contents. 'Go on,' he said. 'It ain't gonna bite.'

It was only when he started eating that Matthew realized quite how hungry he was. He ate and drank as if he'd done neither for days or maybe weeks; when he was through, when his belly was full, he wiped his mouth with his sleeve and looked about him. They were sitting, the two of them, in a barn – amongst bales of what smelled like rotting hay, some empty grain sacks, a stack of old farming tools that must have been saved, once, for some purpose, but which, now, were plainly rusted and useless. 'Where is this place?' he said.

The boy shrugged.

'Don't you know?'

Another shrug; he looked down.

'Jesus,' said Matthew.

A moment passed, then the boy looked up. 'I saw them, you know,' he said, his face brightening.

'Saw who?'

'Them Yankee soldiers.'

Something twisted, then, in Matthew's heart – some kind of yearning for what had been, maybe – or maybe for what was to come. 'Where'd they go?' he said. The boy pointed at once to one wall of the barn and beyond. Matthew turned his head to look, as if he were expecting to see them. 'Is that north?' he said.

The boy looked blank.

'Alright.' Matthew sighed. 'Do you at least know *when*?'

'When?'

'How many hours.'

'Hours?'

'Since they left.'

The boy shrugged, then held up his hands, fingers extended.

'Ten hours?' said Matthew.

The fingers flicked.

'*More* than ten?'

Another flick.

'Twenty?'

Another.

Matthew pushed himself up. 'You mean it's been *days*? I've been lying here for *days*?'

The boy nodded.

'Jesus Christ.' Struggling, Matthew somehow got to his feet. The boy rose too, suddenly wary.

'Where you goin'?' he said.

'You got a horse?'

'A horse?' The boy shook his head. 'Only Hannah, but –'

'Where is she?'

'Why?'

'I have to take her.'

The boy smiled. 'You can't *take* her. She's my *horse*.'

'I have to.'

'But she don't like nobody but me.'

Matthew pulled out the contents of his pockets: some old biscuit, a few coins, a brass button roughly embossed with the words *United States Army*. He looked up. 'How much?'

The boy's smile disappeared, a look of some confusion replacing it. 'You mean money?' he said.

'I mean money,' said Matthew.

The confusion turned swiftly to suspicion. 'You mean *real* money? Of my *own*?'

Matthew selected two coins, held them out. 'Twenty cents,' he said.

The boy's face flushed pink. '*Twenty cents?*' He stared at the notes, bit his lip a second, thinking, then shook his head.

Matthew sighed. 'Alright. Forty.'

Another shake.

'Fifty, and that's it.'

'I want that,' said the boy. He was staring at Matthew's palm, his face glowing suddenly bright.

'What?' Matthew looked down.

'That,' said the boy. 'I want that.'

Matthew picked up the once-gleaming but now-dull brass button. With it – as ever – came the image of Custer. He turned it over. *I said charge those southern bastards, lieutenant, or I'll goddamn shoot you myself.* He looked up. 'You want this for the horse?'

'Uh-huh,' said the boy. He held out his hand. 'I ain't never had no gold button before,' he said. Matthew shrugged. 'Okay,' he said, then he placed the thing in the center of the boy's roughened palm, watching with a mixture of pity and envy as the boy closed up his fingers and turned it around, as if what he held so tight now in his hand were not just a brass button made a decade ago to decorate some war, but, truly, some tiny, personal, life-giving sun.

98

S omehow he'd always known it – known it without being told.
Somehow he'd felt it someplace deep down – someplace so deep
that when he turned his head this way or that, or closed his eyes
real tight, then all trace – all sound of it, all sight – was, like a miracle,
gone, and his life then and its comforting misery could, for that moment
at least, remain undisturbed.

Then – but not now.

Now – now that she was dead – now that the child of his dreams and
his nightmares was dead – now were they, cruelly, ironically, for the
first time really alive.

Alive.

But dead.

Oh Jesus.

He pulled hard on the reins, drew the old nag to a stop. Unseen then
by a soul on that dusty country road, his head dropped. 'Oh Lord,' he
whispered – knowing in that moment that he couldn't go on.

He slumped forward, let his cheek touch the horse's matted mane. He
listened, barely breathing now, to the horse's beating heart.

In the beginning he'd been flattered and amazed by her attention –
aroused, even (this for the first time in years, and with such sudden force
that he'd felt like a schoolboy again) – so much so, indeed, that he'd
started to imagine that all the time that had passed hadn't really passed
at all, and that, really, he was just like those men who every day
knocked so furtive on Miss Eliot's crimson door, then climbed the back
stairs to give and to take whatever it was that they needed, only to
emerge, then, light as sinners, newly, freshly anointed by the cleansing
hands of some all-seeing, some all-forgiving mother confessor.

In the beginning, yes.

But even then – even in the beginning – even in the joy of revisited
youth – had he felt, again (this so distant to start with, but always,
always getting closer), the warm breath on his cheek of that whole other
self – that self so wracked with disgust and self-loathing – until, in the
face of it, that new self had fled, leaving just the old – leaving him fearful

of the future and looking for escape – leaving him, well, slumped over on the back of some mangy old horse, eyes staring, heart thudding, one hand hanging down, the other gripping tight around a pistol, the barrel of which was pressing cool against his temple.

He let his eyes close, sought courage in the darkness. But courage, though, like driftwood to a drowning man, could be grasped but not held. He opened his eyes, stared down at the dust.

She and that whore-child.

'Oh Jesus,' he whispered.

A minute of silence, then.

Then he pulled the trigger.

Nathan & Robert

99

'**M**rs Custer?'

She knew at once that he'd come to apologize by the way First Officer Philip Parr tapped so lightly on the door, and by the way he spoke so softly – whispering, almost, as if he were in the presence of a king or a pope, or, indeed, that of a bear's owner whose bear had been quite callously and unnecessarily murdered.

'Yes?' she said.

'Well, ma'am, we were wondering –'

'Wondering?'

'Well, madam, as you were, well, friends –'

'Pardon?'

A drawing of breath beyond the door. 'It's just that, well, we were wondering if he'd made any last requests – or perhaps there was some final message to offer to the, well . . . *parents?*'

Libbie frowned. It wasn't enough, obviously, that they'd seen fit to throw a party (a *party*, for heaven's sake) to celebrate their slaughter of the bear (of *her* bear, indeed); no, they had to compound the offense by indulging in such tasteless and regrettable attempts at humor.

'Ma'am?'

She gripped the handle, swung the door inward. Philip Parr stepped back, as if forced to retreat by the elderly lady's sheer strength of will.

'*Well*, sir,' she said, stepping forward, defiant. 'It was *you*, sir – was it? – that was chosen as the conduit of such ridicule?' Another step; Philip Parr, his face touched now with panic, stepped back. 'Or did you volunteer, sir? Did you seek such a . . . such a . . . *dishonorable* role? Did you consider such an errand a ready boon to your career, perhaps?'

'*Ma'am?*'

She shook her head slowly – a diminishing look of such utter contempt that it made the pink face of the ship's first officer turn quite as pale as the napkins neatly folded every morning in the first-class dining-room.

'Well, sir – have you nothing to say? Have you no script to follow?

No witty remarks to utter, so withering that they're to be preserved for the nation in some great embossed book of such remarks?'

'Well, no, ma'am. It was just, well, we thought . . . well, that is, the captain thought –'

'The captain?' said Libbie. Another utterly damning shake of the head. 'I see,' she said. She nodded. 'All, now, is clear. It is, I see, the general – a man so obviously despised by the captain – as is ever the case when a great man is considered by a scoundrel – who really is the target of this . . . this . . . *performance* –'

'The *general*?' said Philip.

'The general,' said Libbie, investing that word with her customary grave elegance. 'A man, now, no longer able to defend himself.' She lifted a gloved hand, one finger extended. 'A *man*,' she said, poking Philip's chest, 'who *perished* on that *hillside* for *you*, sir – for *you*!'

'For me?' said Philip Parr, bewildered even more now by the mention of a hillside. He closed his eyes tight, tried to clear his head – tried to remember exactly the errand he'd been sent here to perform – but his head would not be cleared; indeed, in that moment, so crowded did it suddenly become with so many howling Redskins (each one a refugee from the Roxette on Maple Street) that he felt certain sure (as certain as he'd been on those long-ago Saturdays) that any minute he would fall beneath their sharp rain of arrows, and his scalp would be lifted and his heart cut – still beating – from his chest.

'Well?'

He opened his eyes; like a miracle, the savages retreated. 'Oh Lord,' he said, breathless.

'What's that?' said Libbie.

He frowned hard at the woman, trying to place her; he looked down in alarm at the gold rings on his sleeve. *Good heavens*, he thought, *I'm a sailor!*, and then – as if cued by those very words – the present came crashing in, so banishing the past, and he remembered the seriousness of his errand. He cleared his throat and pushed back his shoulders. 'Madam,' he said. He felt the sweat streak his back. 'Then there was nothing?'

'Nothing?' said Libbie, suspicious. 'What do you mean, nothing?'

Philip Parr drew a long shallow breath. 'Very well, madam,' he said, 'I shall have that passed on to the father by wire.'

'The father?'

'Indeed, madam. Mr Zeitezmann was most anxious to know if there'd been any message.'

Libbie felt her heart stop. 'Mr Zeitezmann? You mean *Nathan* Zeitezmann's father?'

'Well . . . of course, madam. Madam? Are you alright?'

She stepped back, suddenly unsteady. In her mind's eye she saw the boy as last she'd seen him – full of the courage and duty expected of a man, but still, despite that, just a boy. Her hands found the arm of a chair; she sat. In her mind's eye, then, she was back for a moment on those far dusty plains, her fingers stilled suddenly within the folds of a quilt, and her ears tuned again to the distant sound of horses.

Josh

100

S o he's dead then, poor Nathan.
What killed him?
The bear, you say.
WRONG!
How so?, you say.

Well, the bear, if you recall – if you've been paying attention (or even if you haven't) – was already dead – slaughtered for revenge in quite a different part of the ship.

All of which means, of course, that if it wasn't the bear that killed him, then what the hell was it?

Well, search me. Right now I've no idea (I suppose it'll come to me) – no idea, because, right now, there's this other thing that's been exercising what remains of my mind – this other thing that's had me sitting here all morning, just staring out of the window – the thing for which, bizarrely enough, I have to thank Davie.

Which is?

Well.

I shall have to backtrack.

Okay.

You see, it was when we were drinking beer last night and watching the Channel Nine news – some report on the famine or drought or whatever in Egypt or Ethiopia (or some such place) – that Davie turned to me with that kind of sneering look that settles on his face whenever there's something he doesn't understand (which means, of course, that it settles on his face more often than not), and then said, quite out of the blue, 'Look, Eddie, if *we're* in the *first* world, right, and *they're* –' here he stabbed his can of Coors in the general direction of the TV '– *They're* in the *third*, well, where in the *heck* is the *second*, huh? Can anybody tell me that? Does anybody know where that puppy's hiding?'

Well, good question, I thought – and I'll admit I was stumped. At first I thought maybe it's like a whole bunch of them gray kind of countries – countries where they drive them tiny cars and everything's always in black-and-white – countries like Poland, Romania, Albania maybe, that kind of thing – but then Davie took to nodding like he was agreeing with me, and so I knew that that just couldn't be right. Anyways, that was the question that took to bugging me then, and it's still bugging me now – despite my just having had a thought.

Maybe a solution. (Which, frankly, I doubt, but anyways . . .)

Anyways, what I was thinking just now was this: if nobody's *seen* this place – this second world – and nobody knows where it *is*, then maybe – just *maybe*, mind – *it doesn't exist*. Maybe there *is* no in-the-middle kind of world – maybe it's just some kind of a bridge – or maybe (and here I know I'm starting to sound just a little *strange*) something to pass through – on the way from the third to the first.

Or from the first to the third.

Which brings me to the other thing I was thinking. I was thinking that maybe we've got this whole thing turned on its head: maybe, in terms of worlds, we should be counting *up* instead of *down*; in other words, maybe the third world is really, like, the *best* world, and the first world is really just some wretched kind of place for people to climb out of if they can.

Sure, you say – so who's got all the Chevys – them or us? And who gets to scoot down to Florida in the winter, or gets to get their teeth straightened, polished and capped?

Well, we do, of course.

But that's not what I'm getting at.

What I'm getting at is you look at them real piss-poor people in India or Pakistan or wherever and they look so goddamn *accepting* of things – like they know things are shit, but, hey, they also know the shit could be worse, and, besides, maybe they *deserve* that shit in the first place, due to something they did in some other life, and maybe that's something to work on in this one. Leastways, that's what they look like to me. Miserable, sure, but somehow peaceful too.

Or maybe I'm crazy. Maybe being piss-poor in Pittsburg still beats being piss-poor in Ho Chi Minh City – I don't know. But I doubt it.

So, it seems, does Mr Daryl J. Sportsfield of Wallistown, Georgia, the 'much revered' author of this here book, *Buddhism in a Nutshell*, which, as luck (or otherwise) would have it, I discovered along with my personal copy of the Bible, right here in the left-hand top drawer of this charming pine-veneer desk.

All of which, now – to return to where I started – leads me to thinking that maybe it was some kind of skewed bad karma or something that somehow killed poor Nathan – some kind of sins-of-the-father type of thing that got him onto that particular ship in the first place, and then down to the cold and damp place where he died.

Maybe.

Maybe not.

Anyways, whatever, I need to get it done – need to get it written – before Jerry Springer at noon – as, today, apparently (and how's this for irony?), he's discussing the heartbreak of runaway kids.

So then.

Select a sheet of paper from the slow-decreasing pile (no creases, no marks), then feed it with care (keeping it straight now) into the workings of this infernal machine, thus.

And then?

And then, well, this.

Nathan & Robert

IOI

'**B**ut I don't understand.'
    'Don't try, madam, and you will.'
    'I will?'
'Indeed you will, madam. Indeed you will.'

Had it not been for the work of Mr Daryl J. Sportsfield of Wallis-town, Georgia – had it not been for his quite singular and (at the time, to say the least) *unusual* approach to all things pertaining to life and to death – then the passing away of Nathan Zeitezmann III, that fall, aboard the SS *Liberation*, would have remained, surely, just another sad tragedy in a long list of tragedies – just another example (as if, for heaven's sake, another example were needed) of the casual and see-mingly quite random justice handed down to His Chosen People by our Lord Jesus Christ. Indeed, had it not been for the outrageous co-incidence of not only that particular (and, some would say, peculiar) gentleman's general presence on that ship, but also, specifically, his arrival, first, at the scene of the death, then the inexplicable would have somehow been explained (for few men and no women like a mystery that cannot be vanquished by logic and reason), and, thus, the real meaning of that mystery would have been forever lost – buried like some still-breathing corpse beneath the heavy, clogging sod of falsely manifest truth.

'I do believe, sir, you are quite mad.'
'Mad, madam? Maybe so, maybe so.'

Libbie shook her head, then turned her face with much purpose from the mostly-empty Roseberry Room, toward the window and the ocean, and the lights, far off, of what she guessed to be the small towns and grand houses that dotted the Long Island shore. She let her eyes close. The voyage home, now, seemed to have lasted an eternity. She sighed. Weak, still, from the news of Nathan's death, all this talk about Buddha and karma and the Circle of Life was making her head spin – not to mention, on top of that, there was the most unwelcome way the wretched man had of touching the back of her bare hand with the tips of his fingers, as if she and he were letter-writing relatives come together for support in a time of family crisis. She drew a shallow breath. 'Indeed, sir,' she said, at the same time withdrawing her hand, 'I would be most grateful if you would leave me to my thoughts and my view of the ocean.'

'Yes, of course,' said Mr Sportsfield. He paused. In the mirror of the window, Libbie watched him shift his not-inconsiderable weight from one squeaking shoe to the other then back. He cleared his throat, raising a white-gloved hand to his mouth just too late. 'There's just one further thing I'd like to say – if I may –'

Again Libbie sighed. For all his 'society' look of Mr Whistler's portrait of Theodore Duret (he'd even the same sloping ski-slope of a chest and that solemnness – even sadness – of eye), he was clearly, beneath his clothes, a man quite out of his class – a person with a fortune sufficient in size to buy his place at the table, but a fortune not old enough to buy him, there, his ease. 'Very well,' she said. 'What is it?'

Mr Sportsfield, traveler, author, refiner – in his younger days – of sugar from the, then, untapped resources of the African continent, nodded slowly, solemnly, as if agreeing the wisdom of words not yet uttered.

'Well?' said Libbie. Way off, in the far-distant distance, there was a tiny, glowing light, emerald-green and set in the darkness like some precious jewel suspended, winking on and off, on and off, on and off. It had the look, to Libbie, of a message being tapped out in some secret code – a message, perhaps, uniting two forbidden lovers, or a call sent in hopeless hope – a call from someone lonely and lost in this world to someone settled and secure in the next.

'– Which may, perhaps, be some comfort at this time.'

She turned away from the light. 'Pardon me?' she said.

'I was saying,' said Mr Sportsfield, no trace in his voice of annoyance at having to repeat himself, 'that though the poor gentleman has indeed departed from us in body, in spirit, madam, he is very much amongst us.'

'Oh *really*,' said Libbie, unable to disguise, then, a wearisome feeling of déjà vu.

'Indeed, madam. Indeed. And not just in spirit – oh no!'

She sighed. How many times since the death of the general had she heard that not only had his *spirit* returned, but his *body*, too? Indeed, he'd been seen all over the country, from Bangor, Maine (where he'd been spotted, in full uniform, selling candied apples from a cart), to Portland, Oregon (whose Jesuit newspaper, *The View from the Pew*, had, apparently, been making use of his writing abilities as its deputy editor and sports correspondent) – but, of course, in every case, such reports, following the most rudimentary of investigations, had proved quite false. And how many times had her need – her bottomless desperation – led her like a fool into dark and shrouded parlors, there to sit face-to-face with some charlatan mystic who claimed to hear voices – one voice in particular – a voice whose message was always of love and always of that love's endurance? Well, too long – that's how long. She set her jaw firm. No longer would she wait for what never would come. No longer would she search for what never could be found.

'Madam?'

No, from now on she'd just wait – wait for death and for the life that follows death.

'*Madam?*'

Fingers found her hand; her hand half-withdrew, then rested. She raised her weary eyes to those of Mr Sportsfield. Mr Sportsfield was smiling, his eyes richly creased with the kindness of care. 'Please,' she said softly. 'The general is gone.'

'The general?'

'General Custer, sir, of the Seventh. He is gone from this life, but awaits us in the next.'

Mr Sportsfield nodded solemnly. He opened his mouth, then, in preparation for speech (it crossed his mind to say something of the boy – of the way he'd been found, his limbs set in such a curious position), but he thought better of it, and he let his mouth close. Instead, he lowered his head in an attitude of prayer and considered the polish on his shoes. There was a time, he knew, for talk, and scarcely ever time enough for silence. So, this thought in his mind, he closed his eyes, felt a change in his water as the SS *Liberation* started turning in an arc, in preparation for docking, looking up, then, just in time to see the towers of New York rising up through the dense morning mist, slow and elegant, like the slim, godless spires of some lost silver city.

102

' **S** ir?'
⠀⠀⠀Here seen from there; there seen from here. What a difference a
body of water can make.

'You've a call, sir – a gentleman from St Paul.'

Nathan Zeitezmann II turned away from the Sound, away from the
winking green light. For an hour now – maybe two – he'd been watching
the great ship heading into New York, thinking all the time of its now
silent cargo, and remembering the midnights and the threes-in-the-
morning when such a silence had seemed itself a distant memory –
something impossibly rare – something even, at times (and, oh Lord,
now how he regretted it) – in the heart of those nights – to be longed for –
to be prayed for even – a silence that, now – with his family taken nearly as
one – Nathan Zeitezmann II would have time enough to enjoy – time
enough, indeed, to go mad with it, and to fill it in time with his own
wretched cries of remorse, then hours, like these, spent gazing at the sea
stretching out from California – all the way (this he'd come to believe with
all the stupid, willful blindness of those who believe, still, that our world is
not circular, but flat), all the way to some watery paradise on earth.

He nodded.

Robert turned, paused a minute, turned back. 'Sir?'

Mr Zeitezmann sighed. 'Yes, Robert?'

'Well –'

'Speak up, Robert, speak up.'

Robert glanced down at his newly polished shoes, as if seeking there
the strength or, perhaps, the permission to go on.

'Robert? What is it?'

He looked up, emboldened by the depth of their shine. 'Well, sir,' he
said, 'we were wondering, Mrs Jackson and I, if we might be allowed to
attend the, well, ceremony.'

For a moment, Mr Zeitezmann – both son and father of other, now
gone, Mr Zeitezmanns – looked blank; it was the lost look, momentarily, of a newly abandoned child, or of a dog, perhaps, who's run off too
far and cannot find his way home.

'Sir?' said Robert. He took a step forward. 'Are you . . . alright?'

'Alright?' said Mr Zeitezmann, frowning suddenly, as if the word were new to him. Then the frown dissipated as he drew a hand across his features, seeming to bring to them in its path some semblance of life, of attention. 'The funerals, you mean?' he said. The frown reappeared momentarily then he turned away, turning back to the Sound and that distant green light.

Robert waited. He opened his mouth to speak, but there was something in the set of the older man's shoulders that seemed to make inappropriate any words he might say. He stood a while longer, then turned away. Three silent steps, four, then a voice turned him back. 'Sir?' he said.

Mr Zeitezmann was smiling, though there were tears streaming clear down his face. 'Of course you must come,' he said. 'Nathan loved you. Of course you must come.'

'Thank you, sir,' said Robert, and then, turning again, he made his way slow across the lawn to the house, remembering only as he reached the French doors about a ringing in the parlor and a certain gentleman on the line from St Paul.

Matthew

103

C lick.
    Again, *click*.
    Again, *click*.
Jesus Lord.
Click, click.

Fate, in this case, an empty chamber. A life saved through the absence of the means to end it.

He lets his hand drop, lets the pistol fall from his fingers.

A horse stirs.

Reluctant, like some sleeper disturbed, he opens his eyes. A horse's matted mane; dusty ground; eyes straining to focus.

Silence.

A breath of wind in distant trees.

Slowly, he sits up, feels the blood running swiftly from his head. His blurred vision shifts, shifts again. '*Jesus Lord*,' he whispers, unheard by a soul. He blinks, harder. Again the horse stirs, stirring his memory. *She and that whore-child.* He groans, unheard – groans like an old man weary of an old man's existence. But he is a young man, still not yet twenty-five. He has all of life ahead of him – so many years, so many months, so many days. More days than he could ever count during which to remember. He raises his hands, shields his eyes from the truth – from what he's done and what he's let happen. *Do you love me, Matthew Princeton? Shall we live – the three of us – in our own special world?* But the truth won't be shielded: it bleeds in through the gaps between his fingers; it reaches deep down inside of him, then slips, palm and fingers, a cool satin glove around his heart.

Revenge, it whispers.

He breathes long and slow.

An eye for an eye, a life for a life.

With a child's deliberation, he picks up the reins, holds them tight in his hands. A moment of silence, then he's squinting at the sunlit dusty road, then the heels of his boots find the horse's scrawny flanks, and he's riding, slow at first, but then faster – as fast as the old nag will take him – his ears filled with the wind and with voices, his eyes with the stinging prairie dust.

He rode and rode, punishing himself, grateful for the punishment – grateful for the pain and for the first payments it made on the larger, incalculable debt that would only be cleared, he knew – only made void – by the spilling of blood – of two lives given for the two lives taken. Indeed, so grateful was he that, had there been a soul there to watch him, that soul would have seen him grinning, his lips pulled back and baring his teeth in a ghastly smile not seen on his face since he'd stood, barely more than a boy, in the slow-running waters of Antietam Creek, his bayonet twisting and turning in the belly of a stranger, and his eyes looking into the desperate, slow-dying stranger's eyes and wondering, appalled, at his gurgling, blood-frothing words – words that sounded like *please*, words that sounded like *help me*, words that sounded in the chaos of dying like a prayer, like *Dear Holy Father*, words that sounded like the words of a tiny, frightened child left abandoned in the night.

The horse stumbled, jarring Matthew's bones. He lifted his head. *Help me.* The road was rising, twisting this way and that, winding its way toward some undisclosed summit. *Help me, help me.* He reached down, touched the horse's sweating neck. 'Come on now,' he whispered, surprised by the disengaged distance in his voice. He dug in his heels. The animal, breathing hard now in the ever-thinning air, moved on.

104

*H*elp me.

    On and on they went, horse and rider, climbing higher and higher, until it seemed, any minute, that the tops of the trees would soon be scraping the sky – until the air was so thin that both man and beast were gasping for breath.

    Help me, help me.

    Matthew let his eyes close, turned his face to the sun, tried to think of other things – tried to recover some moments of joy – but none would come. He opened his eyes. Before him, now, the scrawny, dusty, skeleton trees, and the road (now really only a track), ever turning, ever rising. He pushed out his tongue. His tongue was swollen, his lips dry and cracked.

    Help me, please help me.

    Like a blindman, he touched his face with the tips of his fingers, felt the harsh, rising stubble of his beard.

    Dear Holy Father, help me.

    For one year entire he'd searched for the parents of that dead southern boy, carrying his photograph from Charleston to Phoenix, from Little Rock way down to the Florida Keys. Jesus, how many times had he taken out that old battered photograph – how often been faced with that frown and that slowly shaking head? And how many times had he heard himself listening to that *No, son, I'm sorry*? Too many times. Too often he'd walked away empty-handed, and too often, then, he'd found himself doubting the very sanity of his search, the very value of atonement – doubting the use of such pointless contrition: what use, after all, were mere words in the face of such loss – in the face of such ruin? And so, often, he'd give it up – swear on a bottle that he'd look no further – but then he'd find himself nights in some flea-pit hotel or wrapped in his blankets on the hard frozen ground, his belly full of whiskey and the eyes of his mind looking down at the boy lying dead in that creek, the ruin of his guts spilling out of his tunic and the creek running red with his innocent blood. And then? Then, again, he'd be down on his knees in the water, uncaring of the chaos and the dying around him – caring only that the boy he'd so mangled should live –

But of course the boy was dead.

And then so was he, as the fragments of a shell drove like glass through his hand, then a darkness like the curtain in a theater descended, and he felt himself falling, felt the cool of the water and the warmth of the sun, heard the singing, then, of voices – his brothers' voices – in a chapel, then the howling of the wind as it rips through winter trees, then the silence of snow, then darkness, then nothing.

Another stumble; the horse buckled, nearly falling, jolting Matthew from his memories of that day, so long ago now. He let go the reins, felt them slip from his hands. He sat a moment, just listening to the animal's labored breathing; then, with an effort that seemed almost beyond him, he gripped his right leg and heaved it over the saddle. He dropped hard to the ground. He paused a minute then, trying to settle himself. Then, as slow as an old man with aged, brittle bones, he made his way over the track to a tree. Here, with gritted teeth, and to the sound of the weariest of sighs, he lay the burden of his body down to rest.

105

When he'd come to, that far-off summer's day, nearly ten years ago now, he found himself lying in the sun, his limbs cradled in the dips and hollows of what seemed to be some vast, foul-smelling mattress. He gazed up at the sky. The sky was so pale – almost white. He let his eyes close. *I am dead*, he thought, quite calmly, but then something in the foulness of that smell told him no. He turned his head, strained to focus. Shapes, blurring, circling. He blinked hard, tried to raise up his hand, but his arm would not heed his command. He tried the other: nothing. He squinted harder; slowly, the shapes coalesced, their edges growing sharper, more defined.

An arm, then.

A bloody hand.

A face, up close and staring, blue lips puckered as if for a kiss.

He frowned, stared hard at the eyes staring back. He blinked, again; the eyes of the boy from the river did not. Was he asleep? No. There was something in his look – in the grayness of his flesh – that seemed to say that neither sleep nor wakefulness would visit there again. *Death*, it seemed to say, *is all that resides here, and all, now, that ever will.*

A moment, then, of silence.

And then?

Then a screaming and a struggling, but the harder he pushed and the harder he struggled, well the deeper, *oh Jesus*, he seemed to be sinking down into that foul-smelling quicksand of blood and corpses and shit and piss – sinking and drowning, *oh Jesus, oh Jesus*, drowning and sinking his head going under down and down until he couldn't breathe couldn't struggle anymore . . .

But that was then and this is now. The crack of a rifle-shot and he woke, his heart suddenly racing. He tried to get to his feet, but his legs were so stiff from his sleeping that they buckled beneath him and he fell back, as heavy as a corpse, jarring his shoulder against the tree.

'Morning, lieutenant – or should I say afternoon?'

He raised his busted hand against the sun, squinted hard. 'Jesus Christ, what the hell's going on?' he said. 'Who the fuck are you?'

'Me, sir?' said James.

'You,' said Matthew.

'Indeed, sir?'

He tried to push up again; this time his legs held firm. He looked blearily about him. 'What the fuck are you doing here? Where's the rest of them?'

James shook his head then, a look of sadness dropping over his pale face like a shadow. He cast his eyes down, as if to consider the dust on his boots. 'Oh, a tragedy, sir,' he said softly.

'A what?'

He looked up. 'And all such fine young fellows.'

'You mean . . . you mean they're *dead*? *All* of them?'

'All but one, sir, yes.'

'Jesus Christ,' said Matthew. His eyes caught the rifle hanging down at the other man's side.

'Sir?' said James. He glanced, too, at the rifle, then looked up, his face broadening in a smile. 'Oh no, it wasn't *I*, sir, but the savages. They fell upon us like a plague, sir, taking every scalp but one.'

'Two,' said Matthew.

'Two, sir?'

'They didn't take yours.'

James shrugged. 'No, I was fortunate in my escape,' he said. 'Besides – ' He took off his hat, leaned forward. 'As you can see, I have, you could say, very little to take.'

Jesus Christ. Matthew felt his heart thumping, saw again, in his mind's eye, Clare's slow-rising belly, felt again its distant beating against the palm of his hand.

James raised his head, frowning, cocked it head to one side. 'What is it?' he said. 'Do you imply something with your silence?'

'Imply something?' *She and that whore-child*. 'No, *sir*. I'm *saying* something.'

'And what would that be?'

Matthew took a step forward, stopped at the raising of the rifle.

'Would you be saying you believe I *murdered* those boys? Is that what you're saying? Because if that's what you're saying – if that's what you believe – then your duty as a man and as a soldier is clear.' James tossed the rifle forward. It skidded, circling, in the dust, stopping finally at Matthew's feet. Matthew stared down at it.

She and that whore-child

'Well?' said James. He spread his arms wide, threw his head back, exposing his throat. 'Come on, then!' he called out. 'Come on – take a shot!'

Matthew picked up the rifle, raised the sight to his eye. He swallowed hard; he was shaking. His finger found the trigger. He closed his eyes, opened them. *She and that whore-child.* Slowly, then, he lowered his aim, aiming for the man's vacant heart.

106

He found the horse while he was searching for the stones with which he planned to cover the body. The horse was dead, lying on its side, its limbs already stiff, its skull in part blown away, its brains splattered wet but drying now on the hard dusty rocks bleached white by the sun. What was left of its head, now, was a moving mask of flies; Matthew picked up a stone and threw it hard. The flies rose angrily, disturbed for a moment in their feasting, but then settled again. Matthew threw another stone; again they rose, then again they settled. Matthew sighed. Their patience was limitless. He turned away. He continued his search for stones.

How many times he'd pulled the trigger he didn't know. All he knew was the first slug had caught the man dead in his chest, sending him backward, stumbling, the second in his temple, entering and exiting his head as cleanly as if it had been nothing more than an empty skull. And after that? After that, he didn't know. All he knew was that he'd just gone on firing and firing until all the cartridges were spent, and then he'd moved in close, turned the rifle around and used the butt as a club, heaving it up and then bringing it down with all the weight he could muster – until there could scarcely have been a single bone in the man's body left unbroken – until what had once been his face was, now, just a gleaming mess of blood, brains and bone, and quite unrecognizable – until there was nothing further to ruin and degrade, and all that remained was some limp kind of mannequin covered in a uniform that had once been so blue, but which was now dark as tar, seeping and stiffening in the afternoon heat.

Working slowly, he covered the corpse with a layer of stones, then another and another, until he'd made a long, shallow pyramid, about as long and as wide as a man. When this was done, he stood solemnly over it, his head lowered in a gesture of prayer. He knew he should say something – but what? He knew he should pray to God for peace or forgiveness or something, and he searched within himself for the words. 'Dear Holy Father,' he began, but then the words dried up like Jackson's Creek in the summertime. He closed his eyes, but still nothing came. He stood a while longer, his mind quite blank; then, his bladder being full, he unbuttoned his fly and started pissing on the stones.

At dusk he lay down beneath the spread of a tree, and here he remained whilst the full dark came on and the vast western sky became gradually littered with stars. These he studied – just as he'd studied them as a boy – his eyes moving from one to the next and on, until his eyelids grew heavy and sleep and dreaming came at last to claim him.

At first he dreamed he was back in that chapel, his brothers beside him, the sound of their voices filling his ears, the smoothness beneath his fingers of the polished wooden pews. And then, moving backward in time (for such is the perverse way of dreams), there he was – just, really, a boy – standing still in Jackson's Creek, waist-deep in the cool, clear water, the first breath of fall playing tag in the trees, bringing with it, then (though he could scarcely have known it), the first whispers of war across the land.

And then?

Then he is standing in a field of rotting corn, stiff and sweating in the thickness of his uniform, squinting hard through summer's searing heat, his eyes following Reverend Watt as, far off – so far, indeed, that even the grinding of cartwheels on the road is stifled before it reaches him by the still, breathless air – the reverend leads a thin black line of mourners slow along the dirt road, his head gravely bowed, step by silent step, until he pauses for a moment beside the low wooden gate that gives onto the family plot. Then, at this – in his dream, now, just as he did, all those years ago, in his life – Matthew turns away and *OhLord-OhLordOhLord* starts walking, pacing his steps to his whispered incantation, because *JesusOhJesus* no longer can he bear to see those two-flag-draped coffins, nor picture in his mind's eye the crawling, seeping darkness of those holes, newly dug in the rich Arkansas earth – earth from which so many had sprung and into which all in the end will return. And so he walks and he keeps on walking, striding on and on through that brittle rotting corn, until his feet are so sore and bleeding in his too-stiff new boots – walking until the night rises up all around him and he finds himself in time no longer marching like a soldier, but shuffling like some fearful old man – like some weary old man who's lost in the darkness with nothing but the stars in the heavens to guide him.

Nothing but the stars.

Matthew stirred in his sleep, but didn't wake. In his dreams, again, he was studying those stars, growing ever more angry at their silence – at their mute refusal to guide him as they should – all the time unaware, in the silence of his dreaming, of another's eyes watching him – of dark eyes squinting hard, taking aim along the barrel of a US Army carbine.

Danny

107

W hen my great-grandfather discovered the Bluecoat asleep on Lakota land, he knew at once that it meant the end for his people. Not that day, nor the next – but soon. In time, he knew, there would be others – so many of them that, no matter how many were killed, they would just keep on coming – hundreds and thousands of them – consuming everything in their path like locusts, and so destroying all that they claimed to need so badly. And soon, he knew, the buffalo would be gone, and so, in time, would his people, to whom the buffalo meant not only food but clothing also, and a thousand other things, all of which, cumulatively, were essential to the life of the Sioux.

My great-grandfather's Indian name was Looks-To-The-Stars. My great-grandfather – your great-great grandfather – was a dreamer – but a warrior also. He fought beside Crazy Horse on the Powder River, and in raiding parties against the soldiers along the Bozeman Trail. He was struck once, in his left shoulder. He took many scalps, and, although their characters were very different (my great-grandfather was a talker, while Crazy Horse hardly ever said a word), the two men became friends. Indeed, when Crazy Horse became shirt-wearer, and even when he stole Black Buffalo Woman from No Water in the spring of eighteen sixty-seven, it was Looks-To-The-Stars who was first to stand by his side. And even though by then their paths through life had diverged (Crazy Horse saw no future in making peace with the white man, while Looks-To-The-Stars saw no future but death in continuing the fight) – even despite that, even when Crazy Horse, having finally surrendered, his people dying from the white-man's gifts of disease and starvation, only then to be caged like a bear, was murdered by the soldiers at Camp Robinson, my great-grandfather helped the family carry the body back to the Spotted Tail Agency, and from there to, well, nobody knows.

Anyway, as I said, it was this old photograph that I wanted to talk to you about. Here, take a look. As you can see, it's very, very old, and very precious. So be careful.

Who is it?

I don't know. Nobody knows. All I do know is that he's just about your age – eighteen, maybe nineteen – and that – although he's still so young – he's already a soldier. He was a southerner, fighting in the Civil War, and, judging by the hand-me-down look of his uniform, the picture was probably taken in sixty-three or sixty-four, when the south was so poor that they hardly *had* uniforms anymore.

Anyway, you're probably wondering why I got you out of bed so early today of all days just to show you some old photograph. Well, it's because this old beat-up picture – this actual piece of crumpled paper – represents a man's life.

Why?

Well, okay. But to answer that I have to go back to that day I mentioned before – to that sleeping soldier and to your great-great-grandfather, and how the very fact that the soldier *was* sleeping, combined with what Looks-To-The-Stars had seen in his dreams of the future – how the white man was already victorious, even though he was losing so many men that you'd think he'd have given in to defeat – how together those two things served to save the soldier's life. You see, it was taught that no man should kill another man while that other man was sleeping, as to do so was thought to be bad medicine. It was taught that when a man is sleeping, his spirit is elsewhere, and so to kill him would be to kill just the body and leave his spirit alive – alive, so that one day it may return and take its revenge. And then there was the fact that, to your great-great-grandfather, once defeat is a certainty, then further killing can only be killing for vengeance and could never, therefore, be right. All of which, I know, does not explain that photograph. But please bear with me. You've time, haven't you? When does your bus leave?

Okay, then.

Right.

The photograph.

This is where it maybe gets a little complicated.

Okay.

You see, despite what I just told you about revenge being wrong and about killing a man when he's sleeping being really not killing at all, well, my great-grandfather was still a Lakota and he had his loyalties – he had a family, after all, that needed his protection – and he knew that he had to do *something*.

What did he do?

Well, he killed him – but not with his stolen army rifle. No, sir. He killed that soldier in a way that, though his body would still be living, his soul would be gone – stolen from him whilst he was sleeping.

That's right.

This. He took *this*. He went through the man's pockets, searching for something – he didn't know what. Except when he found it, he knew. You see, like Crazy Horse, he believed that should a man let his image be taken – be captured, if you like – then with it will go that man's shadow and, with that, his soul. He believed, you see, that the soul of a man resides in his shadow, and if that shadow is stilled – captured – then that shadow – and so that soul – will have been stolen from the sun's command – the sun from which all souls spring, and to which every soul must return if the sacred circle of life is not to be broken.

What's that?

Oh, I know, I know.

The soldier was a Bluecoat, while the boy in the photograph is clearly dressed in gray.

That's right.

They were not the same man. You see, you have to remember that all white men looked alike to the Sioux – just as, today, I guess a Chinaman finds it tough to tell two Americans apart.

Anyway. He took the picture and he carried it with him – carried it all the way to the Rosebud and the Custer fight and beyond – all the way, in fact, to this very spot, to this very house – indeed, to this very porch, where, in nineteen thirty-six, at the age of eighty-one, he died.

There.

So that's the story of this picture. I guess you could say there's some kind of moral in it somewhere – but I don't know. It doesn't matter. All that matters is knowing that a person's soul is something that is easily lost – easily captured – but, once lost, can never be retrieved.

Which, I guess, is maybe the moral.

Anyhow.

This picture. It's yours now. Take it and keep it safe, and when you get to Parris Island, and when they send you to Vietnam, keep it close to you, and if ever you're scared you just think of old Looks-To-The-Stars and remember your value – just how much you are worth – and how thousands of years of the Sioux nation will be judged on your conduct alone. Be worthy. Earn your past, or the weight of it will crush you.

Now go. Go embrace your mother and tell her not to wait for your return. Tell her to expect you only when she sees the dust rising from your boots.

Now go, go, we've both got things to do, and a son should never see his father cry.

Matthew & James

108

It was a feeling – a sense of something – that woke Matthew from his dreaming – a presence, or, rather, the sudden absence of a presence. He sat up. It was the padding of footsteps receding, perhaps, or maybe the breaking of twigs underfoot. Bleary still, he looked about him. Or maybe it was just the last dregs of his dreams to disappear before the onset of wakefulness – his dreams of searching for that southern boy's mother, of that photograph, of standing, then, before her grave in Alabama, all hope of forgiveness – of redemption – gone. He closed his eyes a second, drew a slow calming breath. Once again he felt that hard southern rain beating down on his face, saw again, in his mind's eye, the rich unkempt grass and the mud seeping in through the holes in his boots.

He opened his eyes.

Taken by the Lord in her fifty-third year.

For a moment, then, he was numb – numb while his senses awakened.

Beloved mother of a son, believed killed.

Instinctively, as it did every morning and every night before sleep, his hand reached up, slipped inside his tunic.

The photograph.

Gone.

Frantic suddenly, his fingers searched one pocket, then the next, the next.

Oh Jesus.

He stood up, his head swirling, thrust his hands into the pockets of his pants.

Nothing.

He frowned hard, tried to think – but no thought would come. Only this: a feeling – a sense, a fear – that more than the picture was gone.

But what?

Be calm, be calm.

He breathed a long calming breath: in, hold it, then out, slower, the breath squeezed like a stream of water through pursed lips.

At first he didn't see it (he was for the moment too caught up with the act of seeing – caught up with the very workings in his head of his eyes – to be able to see what it *was* he was seeing), and it took a deal of staring at before he really saw the stones – before he registered the fact that his neatly piled stones were no longer neatly piled, but dispersed now, and the body within them gone.

Gone.

No – surely not.

Not possible.

He dropped to his knees, digging frantic in the hard ground, until his fingers were bleeding – until something in the breeze bid him cease, and he sat back on his haunches, his face streaming sweat, his eyes blurring.

He wiped his eyes with the back of his hand. *Mad*, he thought, the thought finding life through a whisper in his throat, *I am mad, I am mad, I am mad* –

But was he?

No.

At least no more than you or I, for the body *was* gone – risen, you could say – and there was nothing left behind it, now, but the stones themselves and the edge of something metal – brass, maybe – set within them, something small and gleaming yellow in the sun.

He scrabbled at the stones, fed his fingers beneath and around the metal object. He lifted it up, holding it, then, squinting, clear up to the light.

At first he couldn't make out the inscription, but then slowly the lines, twirls and dots coalesced into words. *Heavens above*, he read, his lips moving in silent articulation, *Heavens above, and don't you forget it.* The words were etched with fine and delicate craftsmanship into the compass's polished back plate.

Heavens above.

He turned the thing over, laid it level on his rough and bloodied palm.

Heavens above, and don't you forget it.

Essentially the compass was undamaged (sure, the brass itself was a little scratched, and the glass thick with dust) – its sharp silver needle still suspended, still so nervous, so tentative before it settled, within its fine crystal prison. He frowned, looked again for explanation to the stones. But the stones were saying nothing – they were as mute now in their knowledge of a secret as ever they'd been in their ignorance. He looked back to the instrument on his palm.

We have our direction and we have our orders.

The remembered words came to him as, slowly – still studying the thing closely as if he feared it might any moment disappear – he struggled to his feet. *We have our direction.* In his mind's eye, then, he saw again the face of the man he'd killed – saw it, once again, mashed to a pulp, and his body broken and bloodied.

A dream, he thought.

He looked again at the stones, at the compass in his palm. Oh Lord, sometimes it was so tough to tell dreams from what was supposed to be real. He closed his eyes, clenching his fist, felt the cool of the brass on his flesh. Sometimes these days there seemed nothing left to anchor him – nothing heavy or substantial enough to keep him from floating right up into the sky and then on to the heavens beyond.

109

That journey, those ten years ago now – that search for the mother of the southern boy he'd murdered, the boy from whose corpse he'd pilfered the photograph – had been a journey (as, surely, is true of all journeys) that was both a traveling to and a traveling from – or, perhaps, more accurately, in the case of Matthew Robert Princeton, Lieutenant, United States Cavalry, less a traveling *to* than a headlong and increasingly desperate search *for*, and less a *traveling* from than a *flight* from – fleeing, as he was – due to his having refused an order (a *direct* order, mind) from no less a personage than General Custer himself – the sure and certain death of a coward – his body, that is, strapped tight to a post thence to have all life terminated by six friendly bullets in his chest, whereupon his corpse, then, would be laid to unrest – indeed to ferment in torment – in some foreign, neglected, some unconsecrated ground.

Which absurdity, of course (at least to the victims) – which waste of human liberty, the preserving of which was the stated, noble aim of this, such a *civilized* war – is and was the logic of war, and especially *that* war, where to murder your own brother was the very point of the game, and to go *on* murdering until, when the last has gone, you've the freedom finally to mourn your brother's passing – the liberty, indeed, to proclaim his blood sacred – to declare it a necessary sacrifice in the divine struggle whose goal was to reunite that house that had once been so divided.

All of which is fine talk indeed, but somewhat in back of the point – the point being that journey, the point being Matthew Princeton at that one year's anniversary standing weary beyond telling in that Alabama graveyard, the rain streaking his face and dissolving his tears – the point being that what can a man do but keep moving – keep running – keep searching (even when the object of that searching is gone), even, in the end, to the point of exhaustion and collapse – even death – when he knows that to stop and stand still would just be to stand and to wait like a martyr for that death? To be caught, if not by the nation's soldiers, then by those nightmares and visions that no kind of running can in the end outrun?

So he was damned if he ran, then, and damned if he didn't.

And so?

And so he ran. (Always better, he figured, to be master of nothing, than to be nothing's slave.)

And ran.

And ran.

Okay – but where to?

Well, *anywhere* is where – to Texas and Oregon, to Maine and Macon, Georgia, and in the end, of course, to New Orleans, where his pausing for weariness on an empty street corner would change everything and nothing – as we shall see, when what happened has happened, and he's hunched, again, across his desk like some invalid, his pen in his good hand, the first words of his diary, *A Personal Account of Travels to the Dakota Territories*, wet but drying quickly on the page.

But first.

That New Orleans street corner, a few yards from Miss Eliot's whorehouse – a street corner only empty to those who count whores as less than nothing.

'Hey, mister, you looking for something?'

Which Matthew did not – himself being less than nothing, and whores, what with their uses, being worth more – that is, just about nothing flat.

He turned his head away, kept walking, kept shuffling in that old-man's way he'd developed since the soles of his shoes had given out someplace north.

'Ain't you got you fifty cents, mister?'

Fifty cents.

He dropped his head lower, felt it hanging like a cow's head from the bones of his shoulders. He had fifty cents – fifty cents exactly – knew exactly where it was – swore he could hear it chinking in his pocket.

Fingers touched his shoulder, hot and sharp like the Devil's tongue.

'Hey, mister – you a faggot or something?'

Fifty cents, fifty cents. He watched his feet slow down, stop. Without lifting his head, he said, 'No, ma'am, I ain't no faggot,' but the words sank and drowned in the grease and the wire of his beard.

'*What's* that?' said the girl.

He looked up, felt the water in his old-man's eyes, felt it stinging like tears as it came to blur his vision. He drew a rasping breath. 'I said I ain't no faggot, ma'am.'

'Ma'am?' The girl laughed, threw her head and her hair back, exposing a white china throat.

Matthew turned away, shuffled on.

'Hey, mister.'

That hand again; again he flinched as if the bones and that flesh carried with then some sharp stinging poison. He shrugged hard, like a man getting rid of some bug. 'Leave me be,' he said, looking down again now.

'You know I like you, mister.'

It was with some surprise that he saw his feet were still.

'And *I* don't like *nobody* –'

'I ain't got it,' he said, still studying his shoes, their strange set on the sidewalk.

'You mean fifty cents?'

He said nothing.

'I tell you what,' said the girl.

'What?' he said. It was for sure queer, this not moving.

'You got a penny?'

It was like suddenly quitting spinning round: it kind of made you feel dizzy. 'I ain't got no penny,' he heard a voice saying.

'Jeez, mister – ain't you got nothing?'

It sounded real far-off, that voice, like it was somebody shouting to him from way out across some misty morning field. It was true: despite his life and five dollars, for sure he had nothing.

The girl shook her head. 'Jesus,' she said. 'You sure are one sad individual, ain't you?'

Matthew shrugged, felt again that vivid sting as a hand found his cheek. This time, though, he didn't move; he no longer had the will. He closed his eyes as the hand slipped down, found his. She stepped away; hand in hand, he followed, his eyes opening. 'Where are we going?' he said. 'Where are you taking me?'

'Sssh now,' said the girl, as she led him into shadows, and then he was falling, letting go of all he'd known – just letting himself be carried away, swept along like an old piece of driftwood on some sweet and tender tide.

110

Clare Summerfield, Clare Summerfield: the sound of her name then and now. Now, as he dragged his weary bones up the last of that rise, it was nothing but a distant incantation – the suffocating reproach of dreams willfully shattered –

Nothing, now, yes – but then – ah, *then* –

He lowered his head, so as to avoid the dipping branches of a pine. *Then.*

So long ago now.

He stumbled, nearly fell, paused a moment, breathing hard. '*Where are we going?*' came the echo of an echo. A snake slithered past him, then doubled back, sliding over his boots. Matthew moved on, lifted his head as the track between the trees grew narrower and ever steeper. Soon, he knew, he'd be down on his knees, crawling like some baby whose legs have yet to grant him the good grace of walking. He raised his hands to his eyes – tried to rid his eyes of the dust, but could not. He lowered his hands as his knees began to buckle. Soon, he'd thought, but not *this* soon, and he tried to stay upright, tried a little longer to resemble the figure of a fully-grown man – but it was no good. He was going – his muscles losing their struggle – going, going, then gone, as his palms found the dust and sharp stone of the track – his knees too, and for a moment he let his head hang down heavy, let his thoughts rise and burn with the heat of a fever, his eyes flaring wide like the eyes of a blindman whose blindness is a new thing and still a torture. He moved his fingers in the dust, felt, then, the blade of a stone as it slit his tender palm, then another at his knee as, slowly, with an effort both tiny and yet monumental, he started on his crawling, his mind crowded with faces, his ears spinning with their words.

I I I

'*D*o you love me, Matthew Princeton? Shall we live – the three of us – in our own special world?*'

His crawling was inch by inch – his progress so slow, indeed, that sometimes he was certain he wasn't moving at all – certain that one day, years hence, they'd find him – just a skeleton – right there – right *here* – no closer to his quarry for the hours that had passed than he would have been had he just rolled over and let the sun and her satellites, the buzzards, take him.

'*Well, shall we?*'

'*I suppose, I suppose –*'

A prairie dog scuttled, zig-zagging, across the track; Matthew turned his head, squinting.

'*And shall we call the boy Matthew, after you?*'

He frowned.

'*The boy? What boy?*'

Then harder, as, in the eye and the ear of his mind, they were once again standing in his small airless room, the stink of his chemicals thick around them like some invisible fog – she with that smile on her face that meant surprises and her hand on the flat, still, of her belly, he with that slow-rising panic in his throat and the rattling sound – distant, still, but coming for sure – of those sweetest of chains and the faraway turning of keys in prison doors.

'*Well, our boy, my darling. Our son – yours and mine –*'

He let his eyes close, saw again her lovely face, knew again in his heart that briefest moment of joy, but knew again, also, in the moment of that joy's perception, that tight-fitting grip, again, of a dead man's shoes (this quite literally, quite truly), and the breathlessness and sourness and clutter of that room now – how old Stotter's tripods and polished boxes (these so dark and deeply waxed, with handles of gleaming brass that made you think they were the handles of tiny, children's coffins) – all that and musty lengths of thick velvet cloth that had seemed to grab at Matthew in that moment with their fingers like freshly abandoned children. He knew all that, and also how, when the room by possession had become his, there'd been the silence of some absence for sure – but the feeling, too, of the remnants of a presence – and not just in the evidence of so many neatly annotated pictures (oh Lord, there'd been box after box of them, all carefully stacked up in the wardrobe) – nor in the existence of photographs so numerous as to be beyond counting, so intimate of subject that that very intimacy – that very closeness, that very *detail* – made of those subjects – of those living, breathing women and boys – just anonymous creatures, so stark was their nakedness and so mournful their smiles, so counterfeit their pleasure – no, it was more, then, than that: it was the strongest sense – the smell, perhaps – of a life corrupted not by sin but by the *knowledge* of sin – not by what has been done but what has been *seen* to be done – by a looking-on from afar, and a mistrust of action – by, finally, a watching and waiting, until what it is that's being watched and what it is that's being waited for is the only thing left when all else has withered – when there is nothing to cherish but the end of cherishing – when death is all there is, and to live is not an option but a ludicrous fantasy found only in dreams.

A stone bit his palm; he winced.

In dreams.

He lifted his hand; his palm was red-streaked with blood. He thought maybe he should lick it, but then thought, *no* – for what use is there in cleanliness when the whole world is filthy?

Filthy, filthy, the whole world is filthy.

And so he crawled on, disregarding the pain, thinking only of Clare's sweet lilting voice, of the rising, in time, of her belly, and of the child – his boy – who had never made it out of the womb – of his son whose life was never more than the adjunct of another's, and who – thanks to him – would never live to see him crawl, never know – *thank God* – from what worthlessness he had sprung, never live to regret that first breath of life –

He paused for a moment, breathing heavy, but smiling, thankful – for a moment at least – for James and the bullet that had saved the boy so much distress, and for the presence of a God so wise that He'd allowed such a mercy to occur. 'Oh, thank you,' he whispered to none but the prairie dogs (whose rapt attention seemed to him some kind of benediction), 'thank you, Lord, thank you' – and he made his way crawling up and up to the rise, stopping only when the rise itself stopped.

Frowning hard, he reached forward with his hand. Nothing – just air. He reached out a little further – still nothing. He stared at the ground between his hands, tried to figure what the hell now was happening. Where, suddenly, was the earth? Was this the end of it? He shook his head: couldn't be. Columbus proved the impossibility of things just ending – didn't he?

Slowly, agonizingly, Matthew pushed himself up. Swaying, he nearly fell, but just caught himself, leveled out. He lifted his hands, rubbed his eyes, lowered them, blinking, staring hard through the pain.

At first he saw nothing – just the vast sweep of sky; then, down below, way, way below – so far below him that it had to be miles – his eyes made out figures, black and tiny as ants, and then the slow-curling rise of smoke from a fire. And then? What then? Well, nothing, of course, nothing and everything – just the great North American plains stretching out, on and on, flat and ever-rolling, vast and endless, a land rich with the dozing, pious arrogance of some ancient and brand-new American eternity. 'Jesus,' he said, looking out across the vastness, just as Jesus in His heaven was looking down upon His brother, as His brother warmed his palms against a fire.

Eddie

112

'Are you *crazy*?'

In his sleep, once, Eddie Reno had dreamed he'd been kidnapped by Castro, then taken to Havana where he'd had his head set on fire, then his feet and ankles sucked on by the Big Man like he was nothing but some big old cigar. Another time, he'd dreamed he'd been riding in a limo with Jack Kennedy, just cruising in the sunshine through the broad streets of Dallas, when from somewhere far off a shot had rung out and then someone had screamed, 'Look! The President's so hot!' whereupon, turning, as one, in his bed and in his dream, he'd watched quite dumbstruck as JFK – quite the nation's favorite and for certain the coolest of men – had gone up like a firework, all sparks and leaping flames, leaving, in moments then, nothing behind him on the cow-hide bench-seat of the governor's limo but a small pile of presidential ash and – bizarrely enough – a copy, untouched, of that week's *Weird But True Magazine*.

'Jesus Christ! What the *fuck* do you think you're doing?'

Without pausing in his struggle with the old Supreme's never-really-did-fit sunshine roof, Eddie called out, 'I can't *breathe*!'; his words, however, were snaffled by the wind and sent flying back to nowhere behind him.

Mr Frampton jammed on the brakes, swung the thing over to the side of the highway, ripped on the hand-brake and got out. Before him, then, was the singular sight of Eddie Reno, aged sixty-two but looking more like a thousand and one, half in and half out of the Toyota's dusty yellow roof, his hair looking for sure just like Albert Einstein's would have looked had anyone thought to stand the great man upright in a wind-tunnel and just let that wind blow – not to mention his face (Eddie's face, that is, not Albert Einstein's) all burned red by the wind and the heat.

He slammed the door hard, set his hands on his hips. He shook his head slow. He was going for disdain. 'Oh, for God's sake,' he said (his breathing, though, was coming real hard now, and just made him kind of gasp), 'will you tell me what the *fuck* you think you're doing, old man? I mean, are you trying to get us both *fucking killed*?'

For a moment, Eddie gave up his struggle for freedom. 'I was trying to get some air,' he said lamely, aware at once just how weak he must sound, and how obvious his attempt at escape must seem.

'*Air?*' said Mr Frampton. 'What do you mean, you were trying to get some air? You want some air, you wind down the fucking window!'

Eddie shook his head. 'Window's bust,' he said. 'Can't shift it. I always meant to get it fixed.' He felt himself glowing, then, at the sound of such a foolish – such an easily discoverable – lie. 'You know how it is,' he added, trying to smile.

'You reckon?'

But Eddie couldn't smile – not a real smile anyways. No, sir, the best he could come up with was some sick-looking kind of leer. And Jesus – who could blame him? There he was, after all, jammed tight in the sun-roof opening of what used to be his car – jammed in by a pair of fake plastic six-guns, no less (not to mention a gun-belt that read *I'm a straight-shooter* on its fake plastic buckle), when all the time (and, for God's sake, surely not unreasonably), all he'd been trying to do was to somehow get away from his former employer (who was, of course, nothing less than a former – at least he *assumed* former – assistant manager of some wretched K-Mart) – a man who, quite obviously, had had no trouble in covering the distance from nuts to bananas, and who, even more obviously, had given himself up to a particular strain of bananadom that had as its final consequence nothing short of bloody murder.

'*What?*' said Mr Frampton.

Eddie tried to raise his spirits, though his spirits were sinking. 'Pardon me?' he said.

'What the fuck you say that for?'

He frowned. 'Say what?'

'All that stuff about my mama, asshole –'

'*Your mama?*' The man, quite clearly, was neither nuts nor bananas, but quite seriously deranged. 'I didn't say nothing about your mama.'

Mr Frampton raised a finger. 'You *did*,' he said, stabbing at the air. 'I *heard* you.'

'*What?*'

He stepped forward, leaned up against the car, withdrawing as he did so his own gleaming pistol. This he thrust forward across the Supreme's dusty roof until the point of its barrel nuzzled cool in Eddie's side. He flicked a look left, then right, as if he feared being overheard, then spoke in such a low voice – so conspiratorially – that Eddie couldn't hear a thing and had to plead age and a consequent deafness.

'I said,' hissed Mr Frampton, 'as if you didn't know, that *she* heard it too.'

'She *did*? *Who* did?' said Eddie. 'Heard *what*?'

Mr Frampton shook his head, a yellow-toothed grin splitting the ghastly pallor of his face. 'Oh, come now,' he said, 'Mr Reno, *please*. Do not think that I do not know your game.' A click, then – the click of a thumb pulling back on a pistol's hammer. Eddie swallowed hard, felt whatever nerve he'd managed to salvage draining away. 'No, sir,' said Mr Frampton. 'Do not think that I am not aware of your pathetic old-fool's attempts to divert me from my task by insulting the memory of my dear departed mama – oh no, sir! Don't think that for a minute!'

'But I wasn't – I didn't –' said Eddie.

At which Mr Frampton drew the pistol to his lips. 'Sssh,' he hissed, darting his eyes upward – upward toward the sky and the heavens beyond. Then, still studying the blueness overhead, he turned his head, cocking an ear. He screwed up his eyes, an aid to concentration. 'Did you hear that?' he whispered.

Eddie said nothing; all he could hear was a thumping in his chest and that tell-tale feel of tightness in his bladder.

Mr Frampton opened his mean eyes, fixed them sharp as tacks on Eddie's face. 'Well, did you?' he said.

'Did I what?' said Eddie.

Again Mr Frampton shook his head, disbelieving, again spread his lips across his teeth in a leer. 'Don't give me that bullshit, old man. You heard.'

'Heard *what*?' said Eddie.

But Mr Frampton said nothing. He just narrowed his eyes and uncocked the pistol. Then he nodded a slow, knowing nod, acknowledging with it the wisdom of one special one who was always looking down on him from above. 'Thank you, mama,' he said, and he smiled a little boy's loving smile. She was right, of course – he knew it. But then, of course, to her son, mama Frampton was always right – always had been, even when, in the judgement of the great state of Florida, she'd been oh so terribly wrong.

113

S haring the name but not the talent (nor, of course, the fortune) of a famous rock guitarist – a man, indeed, responsible, in 'Baby, I Love Your Way', for perhaps the greatest of all love-songs – was just one of the many examples of ill-judgement or ill-luck that, since the very day of his birth, had dogged the thirty-eight years of life of Peter Kevin Frampton. Indeed, looking back, that very day itself – the twenty-eighth of September nineteen sixty – had seemed to set some kind of trend, being, as it was, the day on which – as luck or otherwise would have it – a confused flock of native Cuban brown-backed pelicans had decided (for reasons still unknown) on the urgent need for an emergency landing on the roof of the Seminole County Hospital, but which, misjudging the swirling of the winds between buildings, had crashed at some speed through the south-facing windows of the hospital's maternity ward, so causing, in the following terrible confusion, a child – guess who? – to be born three weeks prematurely, and his mother, as a consequence of such a trauma, to be rendered, in that moment, due to some ghastly gynecological repercussions, quite unable to provide her new son, at any time in the future, with either a brother or a sister.

But so what? you say – and you'd be right. You'd be right to say that such examples – though undeniably unfortunate – would not *on their own* provide reason enough why a shit *becomes* a shit (given, of course, one accepts that nobody is *born* a shit); however, in the case of Peter Kevin Frampton there were so *many* examples in the years that followed that some excuse really *has* to be found in them, as there's surely not a man alive who could have suffered so much often bizarre misfortune without being understandably adversely affected. For example, who would *not* be affected – and adversely so – by the discovery at the tender age of nine that the man you'd thought was your father wasn't, in fact, your father at all – nor, indeed, was he even a *man*, but a woman (and a woman, damn it, from *Mexico*) – and not even, then, a *regular* woman, but a woman who'd served a sentence in Chiahulpa State (or some such godless place) for the attempted strangling of a foot doctor from Baltimore who'd displayed a great (and, as it turned out, unwise)

318

interest in a certain woman's (or man's) husband (or wife), and whose assailant, following her (or, by now, definitely *his*) release, had sought asylum from discrimination of a sexual nature in the United States and had somehow, despite her/his conviction, been quite unexpectedly granted it.

All of which is bad – but bad enough?

Yes, indeed.

But, hey, there was more – *much* more.

There was, for another example, the case of the infected chili-dogs served up to the boy on his thirteenth birthday that had made him hallucinate and see the face of Willie Nelson on the end of his penis and the face of a smiling Tammy Wynette in the palm of his right hand.

But that's another story.

One of many. One of so many, indeed, that there's not a soul alive, surely, who could reasonably expect such a boy to turn out anything but a little unbalanced – not to mention downright screwy – an expectation that Peter Kevin Frampton was not, in later life, to disappoint.

For example, in that car, on the side of that highway, somewhere in Nebraska, on the edge of those great northern plains – as, in that car on those plains, muttering like some crazy man to his now long-dead mama, all he could think was how he'd been again deceived, and how everything – his great plan – was already faltering, and how his life, as usual, was turning to shit.

'What's the matter?' said Eddie. He could see the man's talk with his mama was going badly, and he feared, consequently, even worse now for his safety. 'Is there a . . . *problem*?' he said softly, trying not to antagonize.

Mr Frampton lowered his eyes from their heavenly contemplation. He frowned. 'What?' he said.

Eddie cleared his throat. 'Well, I was wondering – is everything *alright*?'

'Alright?'

With as much tenderness as he could muster, he pointed his index-finger up toward the sky. 'I mean . . . *upstairs*,' he said.

'Upstairs?'

'I mean –' here he cast his eyes upward, fixed them a moment at a point in the sky, then cast them back down '– is everything *okay* up there? Is she, like . . . *well*?'

'*She*?' said Mr Frampton. 'Who *exactly* do you mean?'

Eddie hesitated. *Oh lawdy*, he thought. 'Well,' he said, 'your mama –'

Mr Frampton frowned harder then, a touch of color returning to his cheeks. He thrust his head forward menacingly. 'Mama's dead,' he said sharply. 'Didn't I tell you that?'

'Dead?' said Eddie – his heart was back to thumping. He pointed gingerly to the sky. 'Well, I guess I sort of figured –'

Mr Frampton bared his teeth. 'Well if you *figured* she was *dead*, then how could she *possibly* be *okay*? How the *fuck* could she possibly be *well*?'

'Well –'

And then his frown like the tension in a theater suddenly broke, and he shook his head and smiled his demon's smile. 'Oh, *I* get it now,' he said.

'You do?' said Eddie.

That smile, Eddie knew, wasn't really a smile at all, but a grin like the grin that was all fangs and blood on the face of a werewolf after dark.

'Indeed I do,' said Mr Frampton. Then he threw his arms wide, as if to encompass the vast plains around them. 'This is all a distraction – isn't it?'

'A distraction?'

Then the smile, as quickly as it had come, was gone – replaced in an instant by the screwed-up snarling face of a bullying child. 'Don't you think,' said Mr Frampton, hissing, 'that you will *ever* distract me from my purpose. Don't think *for one second* that I'll *ever* forget why we're out here – okay?'

Eddie swallowed hard.

'I said, okay?'

'Okay,' he said, certain sure in that moment that the man was clearly mad, and that, consequently, his own chances of survival that had once been real slim were now even slimmer – so slim, in fact, that if you turned them around and took a look at them sideways, you'd probably see nothing at all.

114

'I gotta go.'

It was just about midnight when they crossed the Mississippi at Winona and cruised, headlights off, down the main street of town. The town was in darkness, the main street deserted. The only lights visible were the lights of a gas station up ahead and those stars in the night sky (as witnessed through a sun-roof now jammed permanently open) which, seen together, and with the aid of some imagination, had seemed to Eddie to make up the shape of a suitcase with a handle – or a bucket, perhaps, or an upside-down hat with a chinstrap.

'What do you mean, *go?*'

'I *mean*, I gotta go –'

At the wheel, Mr Frampton shook his head.

'But I *gotta*,' said Eddie.

'You don't gotta.'

'But I do!'

Without turning his head, Mr Frampton flicked his eyes from the road. 'Jesus,' he said, 'ain't you got no bladder control?'

'What do you mean, bladder control? When you gotta *go* you gotta *go* –'

Mr Frampton paused a minute, obviously turning something over in his mind; then, the question resolved, he said, 'But *I* ain't gotta go –'

'Well, *you* ain't sixty-two.'

Another moment's pause, then, as – this fact being for sure beyond dispute – he just stared out ahead, frowning somewhat – his lean hands, as ever, gripping tight to the wheel.

'*Well?*' said Eddie.

'Well, *what?*'

'What do you mean, *what?*' The strain of holding on was forcing him into recklessness. 'I *said*, I gotta *go*, and I gotta *go* –'

'Well –'

'NOW!'

Another frown at the wheel, a suspicious sideways flash of the eyes, then back. 'So you're not kidding me – right?'

'OH, FOR GOD'S SAKE,' said Eddie. 'JUST STOP THE CAR, ALRIGHT?'

'Well, okay,' said Mr Frampton, easing off the gas, 'but don't you try anything foolish – you hear me?' Touching the brake, he turned the wheel. 'I *said*, you hear me?'

'Oh, I hear you,' said Eddie, and then, with the car still rolling, he was out of there and struggling with his gun-belt and wrestling with his chaps, just trying to get the damn things to shift either one way or the other or at least somehow so as he might get his pants down in time and not piss himself again like he'd done down in Florida but *oh, for God's sake* the damn things wouldn't shift and then he had them and he ripped them away and then down went his pants and *oh Jesus oh Jesus* at last he was letting go –

'Hey, you done yet?'

– letting everything go – all the tension of retension – until *hallelujah* he was slowly but surely getting to feel like himself again and all he could think in the joy of his relief was *I don't care what happens now* and all he wanted was just to be left alone – alone to savor his survival – to be left just to stand there at the side of that trail, his pants around his ankles, and to just thank the sweet Lord all the rest of his days for the release of even an outlaw as desperate as he from such terrible, terrible torment –

'Are you *listening* to me?'

He opened his eyes. 'What?'

'I *said*, are you *done* yet –'

He frowned. All before him was dark – the night as dark and impenetrable as the darkest and deepest of nights on the range. He looked down. *An outlaw as desperate as he.* Sure enough – just as he'd been dreaming they were – his pants – for some reason that now was beyond him – were bunched around his ankles, the pointed toes of his pale snake-skin boots peaking out from beneath them like they knew something bad was going to happen but they couldn't figure what –

The click, then, of a pistol.

Oh Jesus.

Slowly, he raised up his hands, not daring to turn, lest, in the turning, the lawman who for sure had him cold put a plug in his back (he'd only be doing his job after all) – plugged him and left his corpse just lying there on the trail for the wild dogs or Indians to mutilate, then the buzzards to pick clean. He cleared his throat. 'Hey, sheriff,' he said. He had to think fast –

'*What?*' said the man.

– and it had to be real fast, or for sure – if the man didn't kill him right there – then the hangman in Dodge would have work real soon for his rope. 'Well, sheriff,' he said, trying to sound calm – calm like a six-gun at his back didn't bother him one bit, 'I was thinking –'

'*Thinking?*' said the man. 'What the *hell* is this? *And who the hell are you calling sheriff?*'

Eddie swallowed hard. 'You mean,' he said, his mind suddenly racing, 'you *ain't* the Dodge sheriff?' He turned slowly, twisting at the waist, lowering his hands as if to shield his eyes against some sudden bright lights. 'You mean you *ain't* Wyatt Earp?'

Mr Frampton, glaring hard, took a step back, away from the car. 'Get in,' he said. He flicked the barrel of the pistol toward the passenger side.

'But –'

'Just get in the car and don't say a word – not one more word, okay?'

Eddie Reno stood a moment, disbelieving his floundering senses. 'But I thought – I was sure –'

Mr Frampton raised a second hand to the pistol, so as to steady the first. 'Get in the fucking car,' he hissed, 'or, God help me, I'll shoot.'

Eddie stared at Mr Frampton, moved his eyes to the Toyota – to its beat-up fender and bright, blaring headlights – then back. *Mr Frampton?* Oh lawdy. What the hell was he thinking? What on earth was going on? He closed his eyes a minute, tried to think. But he couldn't think – he was, suddenly, just so awful tired.

'*Hey!*'

He opened his eyes.

'I *said* get in the car –'

'I gotta sleep,' he said, his voice echoing in his ears, 'I just gotta sleep –'

'You gotta sleep?' said Mr Frampton. 'You gotta *sleep?*' He shook his head, curled back his lips with monumental disdain. '*First* you gotta *go* – *now* you gotta *sleep.*' He waggled the pistol. 'Tell me,' he said. 'Is there anything *else* you gotta do while we're here? I mean, maybe you gotta write *Mr Wyatt Earp* a letter? Or maybe a postcard or two, huh? I mean, *wish you were here* – that kind of thing, huh?' Another waggle of the gun. 'Ah, but then I'm forgetting – he *is* here, *isn't* he? Huh? *Isn't* he?'

Eddie felt his knees weaken, then something like a gyroscope shifting in his head. He stepped forward, laid a pale, trembling hand on the car's dipping roof.

'Well, *isn't* he?' said Mr Frampton. 'Isn't *that* what you *said?*'

Eddie rubbed his eyes with his free hand, tried to focus. He squinted hard, but he couldn't make things sharpen: everything was blurry and shifting before him – the lights, the car, Mr Frampton (all three of him now – now four), the road and the stars in the sky – all was pitching and rolling –

'Hey, old man, you want this or not?'

– rolling and pitching, until all he could see – getting nearer every second – was a great hollow blackness dotted sharp with tiny lights, and all he could hear was the beating of a heart, then the sound of running water, and all, in that moment, he could smell was the scent in his nostrils of rich summer pine.

115

'I said you want this or not?'
     He blinked.
     'It'll help. Believe me. But you have to help me.'
Still blurry – everything was still blurry. 'What's happening?' he said.
'Sssh.'
He tried to sit up.
'You'll wake up your friend.'
But he couldn't seem to move – couldn't lift his arms. His head was
heavy like it was made of stone. 'Jesus Christ,' he said. He blinked
again, harder. 'Am I dead?' he said. 'Is this heaven?'
     'Heaven?' Laughing from somewhere far off. The shapes began to
slow in their swirling. 'No, it's only Winona, I'm afraid. It's maybe the
closest you'll get to heaven around here, though. But then I guess I'm
biased.'
     Everything seemed to flicker a moment, as if caught between two
competing worlds, then was still.
     'Mr Reno? Can you hear me?'
     He screwed up his eyes. The light was intense.
     'I just need to dress your wound. You had quite a fall. Lost some
blood.'
     Slowly, daring himself, he opened his eyes. He was lying on his back
in what looked to him to be some kind of bedroom (there were two beds
as far as he could see – his and one other), a figure – a man – standing
over him – leaning over him real close – so close, in fact, that he could
feel the man's breath on his forehead. The man's breath smelled of pine.
     'Edward?'
     He was thirty-five, maybe forty years old, and darkish-skinned –
Indian maybe. Eddie stared at him hard, tried to picture him somewhere
in what he could remember of the recent past.
     'Edward? Can you hear me?'
     He shook his head: he couldn't place him.
     'You can't?'
     'I can hear you,' he said.

'Ah, good.' The man smiled. Against the dark of his skin, his teeth were a brilliant, even white – white like the teeth in some toothpaste commercial. He raised a hand, trying to show something to Eddie. 'Now this just might sting a little,' he said.

Eddie frowned. Despite trying real hard, he just couldn't think who the hell the man was. He tried to place him in some context – in a bar, maybe, or maybe in the auto-shop with a wrench in his hand – but it was no good. He closed his eyes – but that didn't do it either. So he opened them again.

'Okay, now?' said the man. 'Are you ready for this? Like I said, it's gonna sting –'

Maybe he was crazy but – eyes open or closed – all he could see was the dark-skinned man in that TV commercial for Colgate or Supawhite or whatever the hell it was, and how, in the commercial, the man kept banging on about Korea or something (something military, anyway) and how especially important it was *in this day and age* for a veteran to have white teeth.

'Okay – you better brace yourself –'

In this day and age.

'Edward?'

It had always seemed such a strange thing to say – as if the problems of being a veteran (whatever they were these days) were going to be made a whole lot better if you had a good-looking set of teeth on you.

'Here we go –'

Which of course was crazy – 'JESUSFUCKINGCHRIST WHAT-THEHELLWASTHAT?'

'There now – all done.'

'WHAT THE HELL DID YOU DO THAT FOR?'

'It's just a little antiseptic –'

'ANTI*WHAT*? JESUS CHRIST!' He squinted at the dark face before him.

'Like I say, you fixed yourself quite a cut when you fell.'

He touched the top of his head with the tips of his fingers. It was tender as hell.

'You should get some rest.'

And wet. 'What?' Had to be blood.

'I said you should rest. Call it doctor's orders.'

There was that face again. *In this day and age.* 'So you're a doctor?' he said.

The man smiled. 'Not exactly.'

'You're not? Then what the hell *are* you?'

He shrugged.

'You don't *know*?'

Again. 'Well, I own this *motel* –'

'Motel?' Eddie turned his head, left and right.

'Which I guess makes me a motel-owner.'

Of course: the beds, the cheap furniture, the TV fixed to a stand high up on the wall. He looked back to the man. 'Where is this?' he said. 'Where am I?'

'Like I said, this is Winona, gateway to the west –'

'What?'

'A joke, Edward, a joke.'

Again, Eddie looked about him. On the nightstand, a chipped and tasseled lamp, an ashtray with some kind of model car stuck on top, a match-book. He squinted hard, tried to make out the name.

'Edward?'

He turned back.

'I was saying is there anything else you want –'

'Want?'

'Like something to eat? Some soup, maybe?'

'What the hell happened?' he said.

'You mean how did you get here?'

He felt suddenly so exhausted, his eyes now growing heavy. He let his eyes close.

'Well, I don't really know. You just showed up. You and your friend here. Your friend was saying something about some accident –'

'Accident?' The word sounded distant – muffled like a word heard through a wall.

'But I don't know. I mean, I couldn't find no accident. And your vehicle seems okay. Except for the blood, of course –'

'Blood?' He could feel his limbs light now, his body drifting to and fro like he was floating on some thick, salty sea. *I should fight this*, he thought, but he had neither the will nor the strength, so he just went on drifting, heading further out to sea, until he slipped like a drowning man beneath the surface of sleep . . .

'Hey, *asshole* –'

. . . letting everything go, until he was gone and the darkness wrapped itself around his body like a shroud, and only the faraway beating of a heart remained.

'I *said* wake up –'

He stirred, but didn't wake. Standing over him, Peter Frampton was scowling, his hair sticking up every which way, his clothes all disheveled. Behind him, the bed was a mess – sheets and blankets in tangled disarray. Bending at the waist, he leaned over, his lips up tight to Eddie's ear. 'Hey, old man,' he whispered, hissing, 'don't you give me any trouble – you hear?' He nudged the barrel of his pistol into Eddie's ribs. 'You feel this?' he said. 'Well, don't think I won't use it. Just one word to

Tonto and I'm squeezing this trigger, okay?' Another nudge – harder. Again, Eddie stirred. This time, his eyes flickered.

A tapping on the door. 'Hey – you guys awake in there?'

Shit. Peter Frampton slipped the pistol inside his bathrobe.

Another tap.

'Okay, okay,' he said. He stood up; the gun slipped down to the floor with a clunk.

A key in the door.

He kicked the thing under the bed.

The door opened. 'I've got that soup here.'

'Great,' said Peter Frampton. 'That's great.' He watched as the owner of the Looks To The Stars Motel crossed the room with a tray, set it down on the desk. The man turned. 'I was thinking. You want I should call the police?'

'The police?' he said. For a moment the blood stood still in his veins.

'I mean about the accident? You want to report it?'

'*Accident?*'

The man frowned, half-smiling. 'Yeah,' he said. '*Accident*. You mean you don't remember?'

Peter Frampton tried to smile. 'Oh, it was nothing. Really.'

'Nothing? But your friend here –'

The smile, he knew, came out a sickly leer. 'Him?' he said. 'Oh, he's okay. He just needs to rest. You said it yourself.'

The man stood a moment, half-frowning as if he were weighing something up. But then he shrugged. 'Okay,' he said, and he turned to go. He paused at the door, though, turned back. 'Look,' he said. 'I was wondering –'

'Wondering?'

'If you fancied a beer, maybe? While your friend's getting that rest?'

'A beer?'

The man smiled, exposing those white teeth. 'It sure would be the friendly thing to do,' he said. 'You know it sure would make my day.'

116

'**S**o what's going on?'

In the twenty or so years that had passed since what had once been his kneecap had been shattered into a thousand pieces by (ironically enough) an American bullet fired in all the panic and confusion of those last desperate days by an American marine from an American M-16 rifle, Danny Sundance, medic, Third Battalion, Seventh Armored Cavalry, had seen some strange cases pass through his motel, and heard stories so bizarre and so rich with unlikely coincidence that for sure they'd had to be works of nothing more than pure fiction, that this story now of an accident that quite clearly had never happened would not, ordinarily, have raised within him the slightest flicker of interest; indeed, had it not been for the journal he'd discovered on the floor behind the driver's seat during his search of the vehicle for clues, he'd have let the thing go – just filed it away under Man, Small and Sad – and not let it bug him as it had been bugging him ever since he'd turned the last of those pages and closed up that book and just let his thoughts drift, then as the evening now gone had fled before the light and rising heat of morning.

'I don't know what you mean.'

Peter Kevin Frampton (the Kevin had been his mother's idea, after the one boy she'd kissed without consequence in high school) was perched, so ill at ease, on the edge of a beat-up old couch in the room behind the office that was, for Danny Sundance, one-third living-room, one-third pool-room and one-third shrine to the memory of a young woman from south-east Asia for whom emigration to America – there to become a bride – had been a process so fraught with delay and as long-drawn-out as her death, once there, had been swift.

'Sure you do. Coors okay?'

'What?'

'No?' Danny Sundance eased down to haunches before the fridge, squinting in. 'Well, I've maybe got some Bud in here someplace.' He turned, he was smiling. '*That* okay for you?'

Sensing trouble and a threat to his plan, Peter Frampton stood up, raising himself to his full five foot six. 'Look,' he said, smiling too – he was going for amiable, plus a little confused – 'I *really* have *no* idea what you mean by *going on –*'

'Uh-huh,' said Danny Sundance. The smile didn't waver as he, also, raised himself up. Closing the fridge door, then, with the toe of his boot, he flicked the top off a bottle of Bud, held it out. Reluctant, but trying not to show it, Peter Frampton stepped forward, took the bottle, stepped back. 'Thanks,' he said. 'But, like I say, I haven't got a clue, *really –*'

'No? Well, maybe it's the accident.'

'What?'

'Maybe it affected your memory –'

'My memory?' Peter Frampton felt the sweat streak like missiles down his sides.

'Couldn't that be it?'

He shrugged, tried to smile a sort of joshing man-to-man sort of smile. 'I mean a bump on the head can do all kinds of stuff –'

But the truth was, the two of them, just then, didn't seem to him man-to-man at all; no, right then, it seemed more like very-big-man-to-very-small-boy, with himself as the very small boy. 'Look –' he said again, not knowing what he planned to say next.

'Except there was no accident – was there?'

'Yes there *was*. It was like I told you, we were driving along and then all of a sudden –'

But the big man shook his head. 'No, sir,' he said. 'No accident. Unless of course you call kidnapping an accident –'

'Kidnapping?' Peter Frampton felt the contents of his stomach drop with speed to his boots. 'What . . . what do you mean?'

'I mean that I know what you're up to. I know about the book, and I know about the picture –'

'The picture?' He was suddenly unable to stop himself gulping for air. '*What* picture?'

'The picture in the book, Mr Frampton. The photograph of Crazy Horse this Matthew character claims to have taken. The picture that doesn't exist.'

Peter Frampton froze. 'What do you *mean*, it doesn't exist? Of course it exists.'

'So you *do* know what I'm talking about then.'

Shit.

'And I am *right* about your . . . *situation*. Right?'

He scowled, tried to figure a way out, but could not. All he could figure was that suddenly – in one single wretched minute – things had all gone to hell – just as in his heart he'd always known they would. Just as they always did. He let his shoulders droop. He just felt like crying.

'Well, *am* I – or not?'

He'd barely the spirit now to speak. He sighed a great sigh. It was over – he knew it.

'Mr Frampton?'

But then – quite out of the blue – he remembered.

'Is this what you're looking for?'

The gun, you idiot, the gun.

And his heart started pounding as he tried to trace back – tried to think what he'd done with it – where the hell he'd gone and put it.

Danny Sundance, manager and owner of the Looks To The Stars Motel, raised up his thumb, pulled the gun's hammer back with a click. 'Mr Frampton,' he said. 'I don't believe you're listening to me.' Then, closing one eye, he sighted the thing, crossing phantom M-16 wires on the other man's forehead.

'Oh fuck,' said Peter Frampton.

'Indeed,' said Danny Sundance. Then, as Uncle Sam had taught him, he squeezed on the trigger like he was squeezing a baby's finger – picturing, as he did so, in the eye of his mind, the sweating, grinning face of some piece of white trash at the wheel of an eighty-six Chevrolet, then the dark-skinned body, like the body of some delicate dark-skinned child, lying still on the highway, dying.

117

'*Okay, okay. You win –*'

Slowly, Danny Sundance lowered the pistol. He cocked his head like some quizzical bird. 'Win what exactly?' he said. '*What?*' said Peter Frampton.

'You said I win. Well, win what?'

He sighed. *Oh Jesus.* This was all he needed – a gun-toting Indian with a literal mind. 'Look,' he said. 'I'll make you a deal, alright?'

'A deal?'

'That's right.'

The deal is that gook bitch takes her fuckin' commie ass back to fuckin' Hanoi or I'll blow it fuckin' further – okay?

'But first you have to put down the gun.'

In his mind's eye, even after all these years, Danny Sundance could still see that Chevy coming on at such speed, and still feel himself squinting in the glare of those headlights – still hear, then, that ghastly hollow thud, then a whooping and hollering like kids going fishing, then the silence of death on the cold hard highway.

'Hello?' said Peter Frampton.

And still – even now – he could feel himself kneeling, his hand hovering above her belly, so fearful in the cold air – suspended there, for a moment not daring to move for fear of what he knew he'd find; and then, still, he could feel himself working, hear again the flatness, years back, of the lieutenant's Boston vowels – *Well, you sure are one calm SOB, Captain Sundance* – working, as they'd told him way back at Parris Island, with God's careful speed but without the Devil's haste – working on and on until all but the tiniest, most hopeless hope was gone, and there was nothing more he could do but carry her tiny, sparrow's body to the side of the road, there to wait for the Hueys and that long ride home.

'Hello? Are you listening to me?'

His turn to sigh now as he lowered the pistol. He turned away. 'Just get the fuck out of here,' he said. He slumped down on the couch, hung the gun between his knees.

For a moment, Peter Frampton didn't move. He studied the face of the Indian on the couch – fearing, certain, indeed, it was some kind of trick. 'Look,' he said softly, just testing (no point in riling the man), but the man didn't move. He just sat there, staring at the turned-off TV like he was watching some real engrossing show. Slowly, still mindful of deceit, Peter Frampton backed away, stepping with care, one foot behind the other, until his back found the door. He snaked his hand behind him and twisted the handle.

When he reached the room, the old man was still sleeping, curled up within the covers like a child in the womb. Impatient (God knows, there was no time to lose), Peter Frampton poked him in the back with his finger, then again. The old man stirred. 'Hey, wake up,' he hissed; another poke, another. Then the old man coughed and woke, sitting up then, bleary-eyed, just as – at that very minute, though some distance north – Libbie Custer turned again in her bed in Miles City, unable to sleep for the movement of the child (as yet still unknown to her) that was stirring deep within her – stirring as if he or she were already impatient for that first breath of life.

Clare

118

S he knows not the reason for her wakefulness – nor, in consequence, as she stands before her mirror, does she know how her
life has already been transformed.

She turns her head away, looks back.

Every morning, all summer long, this has been her task: to be Clare,
but not Clare; to be Libbie – to Elizabeth Bacon Custer, wife of the
General – to dress as she dressed, to stand as she stood, to look out of
that window as *she* looked out, and finally – every day at a little after
three (no show on Sundays) – to mourn as she mourned – with, that is,
dignity and grace.

Ladies and gentlemen –

She unbuttons his shirt, lets it fall to the carpet.

Welcome to the general's winter parlor.

In the mirror she sees herself smiling – smiling as she feels again the
touch of his lips on her breasts. *Jesus, Libbie, has it been raining down
there?* She closes her eyes, as her hand – as if by some power of its own –
moves like some water-skimming bird across the flat of her stomach,
then down –

Oh, baby, I love your way –

Unheard by a soul, she starts humming the tune (it won someone fifty
bucks yesterday on KZMC), pretending, as she does so, that the hand is
not hers at all, but his, and that the summer's longest day isn't long past
at all now, and that fall isn't waiting, watching, impatient now for the
gaudy show of summer to end.

'Honey – you'd better get going.'

She opens her eyes at a tapping on the door.

'Coming,' she says, and then, as if sharing a secret embarrassment
with a friend, she laughs – laughs right out loud.

'Clare, darling, if he doesn't leave soon your daddy's going to be
late –'

She flicks on the radio.

David Cassidy.

Urgh.

She scoots round the dial, finds Kool and the Gang, is happy. She pulls on her jeans, her T-shirt. She leans forward, shakes her head, loosening, throws back her rich auburn hair.

119

'So today's the day is it, honey?'

Seen from on high, twenty years ago now, a Chevy moving straight along the Bozeman–Bismark Highway.

She shakes her head; her father turns. 'Honey?' he says. 'Is everything okay?'

Summer in the Territories is hard, and the ground so dry as to be quite inhospitable to both fork and spade.

'It's tomorrow, Daddy,' she says, sensing his attention. She is studying the land, the vast ocher sweep of it, trying to picture how it must have looked then. She frowns. *The same*, she thinks.

'Tomorrow?'

I cannot believe that even the hardiest of God's creatures could flourish in such a place. 'The twenty-fifth of June. Today's the twenty-fourth.'

'Right. Of course.'

Vince Summerfield turns back to the highway, drops down the visor. Unseen, he opens his mouth to speak, but then thinks better of it. These days, whatever he says seems to come out sounding wrong – muddled somehow. *It'll change*, he keeps telling himself, though not with any great conviction. He reaches out, flicks the aircon to High. 'Jesus, this heat,' he says.

'It *is* summer, Daddy,' says Clare.

He nods, tries to smile. 'Right,' he says. He touches the gas. He thinks without joy of the morning ahead.

A sense of disengagement: this is the problem. It's been coming on slowly – in fact, for years now – creeping over him like a shadow and leaving him, often, with the strongest feeling that he's somehow slipped outside of himself – that, somehow, when he wasn't looking, he'd got to be no longer living, but *watching* himself living – that he'd become fixed in some weird kind of cruise control that no pumping the gas or touching the brake can unlock.

'Hey, Daddy –'

He lifts his foot off the gas.

'Yes, honey?'

And not only that: somedays, too, it's like he's driving with the steering lock stuck on, and no amount of turning the wheel will fix it, and all he can do is just sit there, hanging on, just waiting for the carnage that for sure is on its way to wrap its arms around him, squeezing, suffocating –

'Aren't you going to ask me then?'

'Ask you what, honey?'

'You know you want to.'

Another look: this time she is looking straight at him, the lenses of her sunglasses obscuring any softening of tone in her eyes.

The vehicle, we understand, was involved in an accident. A young woman was killed.

'I'm sorry, love,' he says. 'I'm not with you.'

She snorts, turns away, stares once again at the featureless land. *Fucking plains*, she thinks, and she wonders, for the hundredth (or maybe thousandth) time, how a woman like Libbie could ever have stood it – ever lived for so long with the endless nothingness, the heat, the flies.

'Honey? Are you alright?'

Not to mention her idiot husband.

'Look, is there something bothering you?'

How she ever put up with *him* was the real mystery. Except of course she loved him. *My own dear Autie*. The way she'd write about him sometimes – *My life is your life, and yours mine* – had to make you wonder: what was it about him that made so many follow him – some, even, in the end, to their deaths?

'Honey?'

A hand touches her shoulder; she turns.

'What?' she says.

My life is yours.

'Well, I was thinking –'

And yours mine.

'Thinking what?'

Her father frowns: there is something on his mind. 'Well,' he says, flicking his eyes from the road, then back, as if he's looking for something – some sign maybe. 'Well, I was thinking we could maybe have some dinner tonight. Like go out, I mean. What do you think?'

'Go out?' she says.

'The three of us maybe.'

Your life is mine, and mine yours.

'Sorry,' she says. 'I'm busy.'

'Busy?'

In fact I'll always be busy from now on. In fact after today you won't see me again.

'But I thought –'

'I'm going out with Josh, Daddy.'

'Oh –'

And I'm never coming home.

'I thought he quit college.'

Seen from on high, a Chevy indicates, slows, turns off the highway.

'He did. *So?*'

'Nothing, honey. It is just I thought he went to New York. Wasn't he going to be an actor?'

'He *is* an actor, Daddy. What do you think he's doing here?'

'Well, yeah, I didn't mean –'

'And, yes, he *is* going to New York. Just as soon as we're finished up here.'

'Oh, okay.'

She pauses. *Say it now*, she tells herself, *say it now*. 'Daddy,' she says.

'Yes, honey?'

When he goes to New York, I'm going too.

The car slows, pulls onto gravel, stops beneath a sign: *This Way to the Little Bighorn Battlefield Site.*

'Honey?' says Vince Summerfield.

Say it now, say it now –

'Ah, nothing,' says his daughter, as she turns away, pulls on the handle. The door opens. He watches her step out. *Disengagement*, he thinks, with a terrible sadness. He watches her crossing the parking-lot that once was just a field. He watches her until she is gone from his sight. He starts the engine, sits awhile. He thinks of a beach with a family sat upon it. He pushes the gear-stick to Drive. *Welcome to the Keys*, says a voice from the past.

120

Despite the fact that it was most likely just coincidence (or perhaps not even that: maybe he *needed* a point for it all to have begun, and maybe this was just there – just convenient), he couldn't get it out of his head that this feeling of estrangement from things – this feeling that things were as they always had been, but at the same time, in some way, quite different – was all, in the end, in some way that he didn't understand, down to the car – down to its having been stolen one night (when? – oh, this was *years* ago now) – or, perhaps more accurately, its having been found by the Miles City PD abandoned just two days later on the side of some old dirt road, and then returned to him, its tires all scuffed and its fender stove in, and (of course) its radio ripped out with such lack of care that the dash had been buckled and was buckled still.

He straightened his arms, gripping the wheel tight, trying not to think of those days – just trying to think for distraction of the morning ahead and a summer-school class of earnest moon-faced students, each one of whom was desperate to learn enough American history to satisfy the local immigration board, and so qualify, in time, for that prestigious title that would, they believed (and in this belief they were not discouraged), guarantee them a place in the great racial melting-pot that they still (thanks largely to him) believed America to be.

America.

He flicked on the radio.

Land of the free. One nation under God.

Oh, how weary it made him these days – this smiling and fakery that seemed to him – more and more with every day that passed – to be really little more than lies – and how he'd come to hate himself for this creeping lack of faith, this day-on-day, month-on-month erosion of all that only a few years ago he'd held to be certain – all that, it seemed to him now, had finally slipped away, once and for all, when he'd answered his door one bright spring morning to find a state trooper standing there on the porch, his thumbs tucked into his gun-belt and his eyes quite disguised behind the darkest of glasses.

'Hey, Vince –'

He looked up. *We've recovered your vehicle, sir. It's down at the compound.* The sun was streaming in through the windshield.

'You okay, Vince?'

He raised a hand against the harsh light. 'Marsh?' He looked around, squinting, his eyes slowly taking in the half-empty parking-lot, then, beyond that, the university's low ocher humanities wing.

'Say, you look real tired. That wife of yours kick you out last night?' Marshall Grimshaw was grinning. 'Or maybe she *should* have, eh?'

'What?' said Vince Summerfield. He rubbed his eyes, took another look around. He just couldn't understand how one minute he'd been sitting by the side of the highway, then the next he was *here* . . .

'Jesus, Vince, you are in a bad way. You sure you're going to be okay?'

He nodded, tried to smile as Marshall Grimshaw walked away. *Must've driven*, he thought, though he couldn't recall a single moment of the journey.

Unfortunately, the vehicle was involved in an accident. A woman was fatally injured –

He let his eyes close, resting his hands on his thighs, just trying to remember something – anything – of the trip (for God's sake it was twenty miles at least – maybe *more*) – but nothing came. All that came was what so often came to him these days, and always unbidden (though not entirely unwelcome, so certain, so unchanging, were they now in his changing, shifting world) – memories, that is, of the day – long gone now – when he'd slipped like some murderer into the back of that state trooper's squad car and headed off to the compound to identify his vehicle – memories so strong, still, that he didn't hear the squealing of tires across the parking-lot, nor see, as a consequence, the expulsion through a sun-roof of an elderly cowboy, nor witness that cowboy's inelegant flight, nor his landing, upside down, in the arms of a large and spiky bush.

Well Jesus.

Of course he didn't see it. How could he? That, for Christ's sake, was the seventies –

'What the hell d'you do that for?'

– while this – God help us – is the late nineteen nineties.

Eddie

121

'I *said*, what the hell d'you do that for?'

'You said stop –'

The Toyota Supreme stood ticking, tires smoking, suddenly at rest now just inside the parking-lot's far-off, furthest exit.

'I *said* pull over.'

Peter Frampton gave a shrug. 'So? I pulled over. What's the big deal?'

From the gloom of the back seat, Danny Sundance loomed forward. He raised his silver pistol, leveled it steady at the back of the driver's head. 'The big *deal*,' he said, 'is Mr Ed out there. The big *deal* is what the hell were you trying to do?'

Peter Frampton felt the gun's muzzle pressing cool against his flesh. He gripped the wheel tighter in an effort to steady himself.

'Well?'

Oh Jesus, he thought, cursing himself for having made such a dumb, such an all-star stupid move. 'I didn't think,' he said.

'You didn't think, huh?'

But that was a lie. Oh, for sure he'd been thinking about it, and for miles; in fact, ever since they'd pulled out of the Looks To The Stars Motel and onto the highway heading north, he'd been thinking about nothing else. He'd been thinking about how he had to do something and *fast*, and how if he chose his moment right and slammed on the brakes real hard (yes, this was his big idea), then maybe everything would somehow get tossed in the air and when it came down then maybe he'd find the game changed, with himself (yeah, *right*) in control. That, at least, was the plan, and just maybe it would have worked, if it hadn't have been for Mr-I-gotta-get-out-of-here Eddie bloody Reno. I mean, Jesus – how the hell was he to know that, at the exact same moment he was standing on the brakes, the old fool would – clear out of the blue – decide to make another break for it through the sun-roof?

'Well, think about this –'

The truth is he could *not* have known, of course – although, the way things had been going lately, he might have guessed it. 'What?' he said lamely.

From the back seat, Danny Sundance edged a little closer – close enough, in fact, for the sweating man at the wheel to feel his breath. '*Hierarchy*,' he whispered. He nudged the gun harder, felt the man stiffen. 'It occurs to me that you don't seem to understand the *hierarchy* of this situation. You know, like who's in charge of who – that sort of thing.' He paused. Another nudge. 'And in particular, it seems, you don't seem to follow that really very special hierarchy – that chain of command, if you like – that exists between, well, what shall we call ourselves? *Kidnappers?*' Another nudge. 'Is that the correct term, eh? Well, is it?'

Peter Frampton opened his mouth (he knew, from having watched so much TV as a boy, the importance of dialogue to a madman), but, search as he did, he could find no words within. Instead, he just sort of whimpered, half-wishing – if it was going to – for the bullet with his name on it to fly.

'Well, whatever, I think it'll do – don't you? You *do*? Terrific. Now, putting that aside for the moment, what I mean by the problem of hierarchy, in this case, is the following. Okay. Now, Person A comes along and kidnaps Person B, because Person B has something that Person A wants – in this case, a supposed knowledge of photography, right? Right. Now this is where it gets complicated. You see, a little time goes by, and Persons A and B are just driving along, just minding their own business, when – hey presto! – Person C comes along and – my God! – he goes and kidnaps Person A and Person B! Well! Imagine the confusion! Imagine how Person B feels when he discovers that not only has he been kidnapped, but that the person who *kidnapped* him has been kidnapped, so making him a sort of two-time kidnapping loser – all of which leads me back to Person C, who, you could say, is a two-time kidnapping winner – right?' Danny Sundance cocked the pistol. 'Right?' he said.

'Right?' said Peter Frampton.

'In other words, you could say Person C – a sort of kidnappers' kidnapper, if you like – is kind of the man in charge, right? Yes, that's right. All of which means that Person A better do what he's told from now on – hadn't he? – or he just might live to regret it. Or, of course, he might not.' Another pause. 'So then, do we understand each other now, would you say?'

Peter Frampton couldn't move: the blood in his veins felt frozen, his limbs stiff.

'Well, do we?'

Somehow – from somewhere – he managed a nod.

'Good,' said Danny Sundance, withdrawing the pistol. He sat back. 'Now then,' he said. 'Don't you think you should go help our friend in the bushes?'

Vince

122

One thing he'd never forget about her was her eyes – how they'd had about them such a steadiness, such an unwavering desire to see only the truth – so much so that when he'd lied and told her that he had no wife, no child – in fact, no family to speak of – he'd felt so ashamed and so obvious in his shame that he'd let go her hand as if her hand had meant death to him, not life, and he'd watched her, then, in her confusion – studied her, then, as he'd driven away, as she'd been growing ever smaller in his rear-view mirror, all the time not knowing where he'd go, except knowing for certain that he couldn't go home, as he had no home – not to mention no wife, no child, and no family to speak of.

Thirty years on, he raised his weary eyes to the mirror: scrubby trees, mesh-fencing, the highway, far off. He looked at the clock on the dash, noted again, for perhaps the thousandth time, how the buckling of the dash had offset it slightly, shifting eleven o'clock to where twelve o'clock should be and so on, until it never looked right and you had to look twice if you wanted to be sure you were seeing the right time.

He reached out a hand, touched the dash.

Yes, it's driveable, sir, although there's no guarantees –

Because of the blood he'd discovered in the compound, caked hard on what remained of the fender, he'd figured for sure he'd be selling it; he'd even gone so far as to put an ad in the paper – *Beat-up sixty-eight Chevy, for repair or salvage* – and a man from upstate had even offered him what he'd been asking, before something inside of him had told him no, and he'd said *sorry for bothering you* and then turned the man away. After that he'd just kept the thing locked in the garage for a while, but then gradually he'd taken to using it again – just small trips at first, until, after a month or two, he'd gone as far as the university.

That it had been her blood – Vietnamese blood – on the fender had come to him in class one day, striking him with the force of a punch and quite winding him as, handing out assignments for the Labor Day holidays, he'd passed by what had once been her desk, and, in that moment, all that he'd closed his eyes to for so long stood suddenly before him, demanding his attention: those eyes, her tiny hand falling away, *I have no wife, no child, no family to speak of*, then her face caught bloodless, in those headlights, then the sound of hollering so close it was deafening, then the thumping of his heart and the terrible welcome that night of the family he'd denied, the sickening embrace of the life he'd so nearly thrown away.

He pulled the door's handle, stepped out. The sun was rich on his face, soothing, its warmth softening the sharp edges of his guilt. *Look forward*, he told himself, for he knew he had no choice. To look back, after all, is giving up, surrender. He opened the rear door, drew his briefcase from the back seat, slammed it shut. *Land of the free*, he heard himself saying, *one nation under God*. Then, not stopping to lock it (the locks had got busted somehow in the smash), he stepped away from the car, heading with purpose for the bitter sanctuary of his classroom – as careless of the sounds coming faint across the parking-lot as he was of the beating of his own stifled heart.

Eddie

123

'Hey, Reno – you okay?'

If a father were able to leave his son with only one ability – if he were allowed one bequest that might ease that boy's inevitable troubles – then he could perhaps do worse than teach him, like a soldier or an acrobat is taught, how to fall – how to land, that is, without doing himself serious injury, so enabling himself to rise up without harm as if from the dead – to come back, if you like – to return fit and well, in order to fight (or at the very least, to stand) another day.

Such, happily – given the circumstances extant in that parking-lot – was just about the one practical gift handed down to Eddie Reno III from his father, Eddie Reno II. 'Go floppy,' had been the old man's advice. 'Act like a sponge.' Stiffness, he'd said, was anathema to survival: be flexible and you'll weather life's storms.

'Hey – can you hear me?'

Eddie opened his eyes. Whilst in flight he'd been expecting – on his inevitable landing – the swift following of a quick death by whatever lay beyond; so, now, his first vision in that place being the upside – down face of a frowning Mr Frampton, he was at once disappointed and surprised. Not to say alarmed. 'Oh, Jesus,' he sighed. He could scarcely believe it. Had he gone through all this – all this *living* – just to be back where he'd left things when eventually he died?

'What did you say?' said the upside-down man.

'Ah, nothing,' said Eddie.

'Did you break anything?'

'Break anything?' Another sigh. At that moment, such concern for things earthly seemed to Eddie, in the circumstances, bizarre.

'Well, can you move your arms and legs?'

And then it came to him: *of course*, suspended as he was, he had to be hanging in some kind of limbo, probably awaiting a decision on whether his particular eternity would be benign or simply firy. He closed his eyes, attempting some sort of impromptu prayer.

'Can you feel *anything*, then? Like your toes maybe?'

Then opened them. 'My toes?' The man was surely mocking him. He tried to break free from his hanging, but a spike jabbed his backside, bringing tears to his eyes. 'Look,' he said, 'how long have I been here?'

Mr Frampton shrugged. 'I don't know. Five minutes, maybe. Why?'

'*Why?*'

He edged a little closer, bending at the waist. He glanced over his shoulder, furtive, like a robber expecting pursuit. 'Which, between you and me,' he said, his voice down to a whisper, 'is just about five minutes longer than I reckoned – '

'What do you mean?'

Another glance, this one accompanied by a shifty sort of smile and an upside-down wave. 'Well,' he said. 'You must have noticed. Don't tell me you haven't noticed.'

'Noticed *what*?' said Eddie.

Mr Frampton bugged-out his eyes, let his tongue hang loose, rolled it lolling like a cow's between his lips. 'Crazy,' he said, the performance ending as quickly as it had begun. 'Surely you noticed that the big man's a nutcase?'

Eddie frowned. He could hardly believe his own ears. 'Nutcase?' he said. 'The big man? You mean . . . *God*?'

At this, Peter Frampton screwed up his pale face, stepping back with all the speed of the Devil unmasked. 'Jesus,' he said, shaking his head. 'Are you *crazy*? He's big, for sure, but he ain't *that* big –' Another glance, then, another wave, another bending at the waist, his voice once again dropping down to a whisper. 'In fact,' he said, 'he ain't so big that you and me can't take him. I mean, he may be a Sioux or some goddamn thing, but, Jesus, he's still only *human* –'

'*Human?*'

'And besides, if we don't do something, then he gets his hands on the picture – *our* picture – then, well, it's thank you and goodnight, Mr Crazy Horse –'

Again, Eddie Reno closed his eyes. For sure this was all wrong: *he* was all wrong – had to be. *Must think*, he thought, *must think* –

'– And all because of some stupid superstition. I mean, *Jesus*. All that shit about capturing souls – baloney! And then expecting us to believe that a photograph – a *photograph*, for Christ's sake! – is in actual fact some kind of goddamn prison for the spirit . . . I mean, what kind of primitive bullshit crap is that?'

And then, like the sun dipping out from behind a cloud, it came to him.

'I mean, this is the goddamn twentieth fucking century!'

'You mean,' he said, trying to twist his head to level in the bush, 'this isn't, well . . . *limbo*?'

'What?' said Peter Frampton.

'And I'm not, well, *dead* or nothing?'

He screwed up his eyes. '*Limbo?*' he said. 'What the hell's *limbo*, for Christ's sake? Jesus Lord, this ain't no goddamn *limbo* – this is *goddamn South Dakota*!' He shook his head, sighing heavy. 'Jesus Christ, you must have hit your head real bad. I mean, I knew you was as old as the fucking hills, but I didn't reckon you was crazy too.'

'I'm not crazy,' said Eddie.

'Yeah, *right* –'

'No, really. It's just, well, I thought –' But then the wisdom of discretion overtook him, and, instead, he said nothing.

'Anyway,' said Peter Frampton, leaning forward again, again – and this time with some weariness – dropping his voice to a whisper. 'You and me have to stick together – right? I mean, being as we are on the same team. And what with Tonto back there having the gun and all –'

'A gun?' said Eddie. 'He's got a gun?'

'Jesus,' said Peter Frampton. He could feel what remained of his patience drain away. He leaned in closer still. 'Look, you goddamn stupid old fucker,' he said, his voice just a hiss now, 'if we don't get going and soon – which means you getting out of that goddamn fucking bush – then if *he* don't shoot you, *I* will – right?'

'But –'

'I said *right?*'

'Right,' said Eddie Reno, the tumbling of his life (although of course he didn't know it) very nearly complete. Very nearly but not quite. First, before finally he could rest, he had one more turn in the road to negotiate, one more demand to meet, the arrival of one more figure from the past to endure.

Josh

124

You know, I don't care if it is an old story and you've heard it all
before. I don't care because it's the truth – and it's the truth –
isn't it? – that's supposed to set you free – which, sitting here
feeling trapped as I am right now waiting for Davie in this hopeless
motel, is something I could use. Anyhow, we shall see. As far as I'm
concerned, whoever it was that said that (was it Lincoln?) sure was one
hopeful son-of-a-bitch.

But already I'm off track.

So.

Like I say, it's an old story, this love-at-first-sight thing, but one that
in my case is absolutely true. The moment I saw her – the moment I
walked up those steps for the first time and there she was – well, Jesus, I
fell. And I mean fell. It was like tumbling from some highwire, with
nothing but space below. And to think, that morning, dressing, I'd
thought for sure nothing could ever be stronger than how stupid I was
feeling getting myself up like General Custer (I even had a stick-on
mustache, for God's sake, that just plain refused to stay stuck on) – but,
I tell you, that feeling just disappeared when I saw Clare and started
feeling what I felt then and still feel today even though she's been dead
so many years now.

But I'm jumping ahead, and God knows I don't want to. If I could I'd
never go forward from that day. If I could, I'd still be standing at the top
of those steps in front of the Custer house on one side of the Fort Lincoln
parade ground, just staring at her still as I stared at her then – just
knowing that nothing was ever going to change.

But it did change. Things do. In fact, so much has changed in these
last twenty years that it's amazing I can still remember those days with
such clarity. But then some things, I guess, you just never forget. For
example, I'll never forget how tiny and serene she looked in that long
calico dress, and how she had her hair all done up like Libbie's, and
how, when she spoke, she shook my hand – *this* hand – and how she
smiled when she said *Good afternoon, general*. And then how, when we
got talking and she told me she was at Black Hills too, I just couldn't

believe I'd never seen her before. I mean, by then – by the start of the second semester – I thought I'd seen everyone. But I guess I was wrong. Of course it came to be less strange when she said she lived off campus – but even so. A face like that you don't miss, and you certainly don't forget. It was some kind of family trouble, she said, that kept her living at home – her mama was sick, I think – and I suppose her daddy being on the college staff and, consequently, seeing so much of the place maybe had something to do with it. Whatever. The point is, when I saw her that day of that summer's first re-enactment rehearsal – I knew she was for me. And I knew in that minute (I don't know *how* I knew, but I knew) that she and I would have a baby, and that that baby's name would be Grace. Of course what I didn't know then was how they'd burn one night in her daddy's old Chevy, and how something as small as a broken piece of fender getting lodged between the discs could cause so much damage.

Well, I know that now. I've learned that lesson. I know how from little acorns do big oaks grow. The secret is to dig them up before they get a chance. With a man and his memories, it's kill or be killed. And how do you kill them? The same way you kill secrets – by telling them, by speaking out – by publishing all and being damned. On the subject of which – publishing, that is – I really should get back to the real point of my being here, which – aside from waiting for the man who was once my father to arrive – is to finish my story of Nathan and Libbie. It would be something if I could at least wrap that up. Well, maybe tonight. Maybe tonight I'll be able to write down those sweet words 'The End'. Maybe tonight I'll find the courage from somewhere to turn this damn thing off and just breathe.

125

Yes, of course I know what I should do now – now that Davie's gone and taken his shotgun with him (he won four hands of poker tonight – surprise, surprise); what I *should* do is get back to my story – get back to poor Nathan, Robert and Libbie – get back to it before I completely forget what I've already had happen – or before (and this, I fear, is more likely) I finally lose interest in this, just as I've lost interest in everything else I've ever written, all of which, now, just seems like so much preposterous lying.

So then.

Before *that* happens, here goes –

Except.

Except *what*? I hear you say.

Except there are a couple of things that have been bugging me – things that I feel I haven't made clear – things that, for the record at least, I feel I should set down here and now.

Such as?

Such as, for starters, my name. On the covers of my books, my name is Josh. Josh Parlor.

My name is Josh and I'm an alcoholic.

Of course I'm also a writer, but increasingly less so these days – a circumstance, as the years go by, I feel more and more justified in pinning on my father. And not just because of the beatings he gave me with those sharp-edged cameras of his – no, sir. Oh, it was *that* alright – but not *just* that. Oh no. Eddie Reno – the man who'd once photographed just about everybody from Nixon to Elvis, not to mention being down there in Key West when Hemingway had *first* tried to copy *his* father by shooting himself – Eddie Reno, son of a magician – the great man who – as a kid – had even snapped a picture of President Eisenhower, no less – no, he has much more cause to feel guilty than just that. For example, by drinking like he did – by gracing my life with such a wonderful example – he made me what I am today. That of course it nearly destroyed him too – made him fall from the height of his celebrity shutter to slicing meat at some counter in a deli down in Florida – was always some consolation, though never, of course, enough. What I wanted for him – ever since that night I slipped out of the cinema during *The Great Gatsby* – was to feel that emptiness – that sometimes overwhelming sense of disengagement – that comes to a person who's escaped and survived, only to see what he'd escaped from come to visit him in his own life – only to see himself come to be that very person from whom he'd thought he'd escaped.

But hey.

I know what you're thinking, and you're right. I beat her because he beat me is no excuse. It's a reason, but it's no excuse. Even if you have to receive, you don't have to give. Just like I didn't have to threaten Clare with New York (oh, why couldn't I just have said, *Hey, baby – let's go*) and then beat her in the end when she wouldn't just come – just like I didn't have to make her want to escape me one winter's night by taking our baby and her daddy's car and driving so fast like there was some kind of monster behind her – so fast that when the fender broke loose and she couldn't steer no more that all she could do was take Grace in her arms and just watch that gully and those trees coming on and pray to God to deliver them at last into his merciful loving arms.

But you don't need to know this. This is *my* life, so fuck off – okay? Jesus. All you deserve of me is what I show you, and what I show you is what I write.

So.

Here, at last, it is: *The Nathan and Libbie Show*, co-starring a man called Robert. None of whom, of course, is me – or even a part of me. None of whom, of course, is anything but a lie.

Part Three

THE SOUND

126

'**D**early beloved –'

Being, as it were, a double ceremony – that is, the simultaneous burial of both a mother and a son – the scene that afternoon at the Oyster Bay cemetery overlooking Long Island Sound was one quite littered with duplicates. Indeed, there were, in so many cases, two of things – two horse-drawn hearses, for example, two teams of grave-diggers, two holes, of course, of equal size in the earth, and so on – that a person looking on, were that person's sight not anyway the soundest, could be forgiven for thinking the condition of his eyes to have become suddenly much worse, and, consequently, another visit to Mr Eckleburg, the famed oculist, to be urgent, if not already long overdue.

'We are gathered here on this sad day, in the loving sight of God –'

– All of which, of course, is not to imply that there was anything particularly *odd* about the occasion (Americans, after all, had been dying in pairs quite regularly by then for considerably more than a century) – just that, perhaps, were that poor-sighted onlooker searching the scene not for doubles so much as evidence of the Lord's loving care, he might find such evidence not exactly in abundance –

'– To say farewell to our sister Evangeline and our brother, her son, Nathan –'

– As who, in their right mind – what kind of a God – would end the lives simultaneously of both a mother and her son, leaving, then, a husband and father so bereft?

'– And her *son*, Nathan –'

A jealous God, or a careless, incompetent one, is who. Or one with, at least, a belief in the literal value of His word – in the value of revenge, of payback –

'*Excuse* me –'

A God –

'Will you please be quiet? I'm trying to hold a *service* here –'

Who, *me*?

'Yes, you. You with the . . . the *bottle* in your hand –'

Okay, okay.

'In fact, perhaps you'd like to leave us –'

Leave you? Don't be ridiculous. You can't say that. You're *mine* – I *created* you. For Christ's sake, you wouldn't be here at all – none of you – if it wasn't for me –

'In fact – in the name of these poor mourning people – I demand that you leave –'

You *demand*? Well, that's rich.

'– And right away, if you please, otherwise I shall be forced to have you removed –'

You will? I'd like to see you try. Don't forget I could write you out of this scene anytime I wanted.

'No you couldn't.'

Yes I could.

'Couldn't.'

Could.

'Oh, Lord –'

Well, shame on you, father. And you a religious man.

'Alright, then. You leave me no choice. Officers? Remove this man.'

Now, wait a minute –

'At once, if you please –'

Hey, get your hands off me. Whoa – you can't do this –

'I think we can, sir –'

Hey, hold on, who are you guys? I didn't write you –

'No, sir, we wrote ourselves –'

You did *what*?

'We can do what we like now –'

But this is crazy –

'Please just come quietly, sir. There's no point in causing anymore trouble – is there now?'

Let go of me!

'Come along –'

I said, let go!

'Or we'll be forced to take measures –'

Measures? You can't take *measures* unless I say you can. I made you!

'Oh, I think we can –'

You're *mine* – all of you. Oh God, what am I saying? You're not real – any of you –

'Oh, we are now –'

No you're not!

'Yes we are –'

No, no, no. You're crazy –

'*We're* crazy?'

358

I mean *him*, for example – he's not a *real* priest at all – and you – you're not real policemen –

'So how come I got this gun?'

And him – that guy – Robert – will you look at his hair? He had white hair – don't you remember? Well, look at it now! It's *black*, now, for God's sake! Oh, don't you see? I *made* it go black – with joy! It's *me* – all of this! It's my fantasy! You're all in *my* fantasy!

127

When I woke up this morning, it was to the sound of voices in the parking-lot. The voices are still there. Even though it's now past ten. I sneaked a look earlier, but somebody saw me. Bizarrely, the fellow who saw me was dressed in the blue and gold of the United States Cavalry – as were maybe twenty or twenty-five of the others. *Are*, I should say, as – as I said – they're still out there. As far as the rest are concerned, from what I saw they seem to be dressed up as Indians – the men in leggings and braided jackets, the women mostly in dirt-colored dresses. And there are horses, too. And everyone's sort of milling about, as if they're waiting for something – or someone.

It's Autie, of course, they're waiting for. It's just come to me. This being the twenty-fifth of June, of course, they're waiting here (where else but here – here at the Last Stand Motel?) – waiting here for Crazy Horse and the general to show up (or, strictly speaking, the boys who, this year, are playing the parts) – Crazy Horse, newly elected shirt-wearer of the Lakota Sioux, and General George Armstrong Custer, Commander-in-Chief, of course, of the glorious Seventh Cavalry.

Glorious?

Hmmm.

Well, maybe not.

Anyway, you know, sitting here now, looking over the nothing I wrote last night (did I really get arrested and thrown out of my own story? Jesus, I *must* be going crazy) – looking over these scribbles, it amazes me that I didn't think of it before – that the arrival of those two oh-so-important impostors is what they're all waiting for. I mean, what with my history – what with my once having been the mad bastard myself. Or maybe I *did* think of it and it just didn't register. Maybe I just forgot I thought of it. I'm forgetting a lot these days – things like, er, er, er – oh Lord, I forgot now (ha-ha) – but I'm also remembering a whole lot of things, which, at least in part, is the problem. I mean, if only a person could choose what it is they'll remember – choose to remember doing something (or not) *while they're actually doing it* – wouldn't that be great? Wouldn't it be great to be able to short-cut your conscience *in advance*? Oh, what freedom!

But yes.

You're right.

Enough.

Time to get back to the funeral, as promised.

So. Where was I?

The Sound. Ah yes. They were all within sight of the Sound – all the pairs, the two of everything. And the priest was saying his piece. He was – as I recall – originally meant to be a tall, thin man, although now, it seems, he's rather short, rather portly. And his voice that was going to be low and sonorous has turned out to be rather light and reedy – so much so that when he speaks – *spoke* – those listening (especially Libbie Custer) had to strain hard to hear. Not that she really cared to listen to the words, as – God knows – she'd heard them all so many times before. No, indeed, after a while, she abandoned the strain on her ears in favor of her eyes, which – though also strained (she was, after all, by now an elderly lady, with the beginning of never-to-be-diagnosed cataracts) – she employed to look about her, with the aim, perhaps, of finding out something more about the boy from the appearance of those now who were mourning him – something that might bring to her (and to us all) at last some clues as to the truth about exactly what had happened on that ship.

So.

She let her eyes fall on the father. He seemed a shrunken man now, though obviously a man who – judging by the ill-fitting size of his mourning suit – had once been powerfully built. He had a look about his features of some disengagement – as if, perhaps, like some half-ghost, he were not entirely present – a look almost, even, of boredom, like the look you'd likely see on the face of some ne'er-do-well school-boy as he sits on his hands during end-of-term speeches.

'Excuse me – Mrs Custer?'

She blinked, turned her head sharp – too sharp.

'I'm sorry. Did I startle you?'

For a moment she felt herself unsteady and as if she might fall.

'Here, take my arm. Please.'

She peered up at the face before her. It was a face she'd seen before – someone, she thought, from the ship maybe. Perhaps she'd seen him at dinner one night – or maybe walking on deck. At any rate, he was somehow familiar, so she smiled as he smiled.

'You don't remember me, do you, ma'am?' he said.

'Remember you? Well, of course –'

He stepped back, gave a sharp bow. 'My name, ma'am, is Parr. Philip Parr. I was first officer on board the *Liberation*. I believe I had the pleasure of conversing with you on a number of occasions – about the general, ma'am –'

Libbie nodded. 'Yes, of course –'

'– Though of course you wouldn't likely remember. And even if you did, I fear you might recall how much I must have bored you –'

'Bored me?' Libbie shook her head, though in truth, as yet, she had only the faintest recollection of their talks. 'On the contrary, sir, I believe I found our talks most . . . stimulating.'

Philip Parr looked down, attempting unsuccessfully to disguise a sudden blushing.

'Indeed, sir, our subject being the general, I do not believe boredom was even a possibility.'

A sudden cool breeze off the Sound swept the cemetery, easing the sudden warmth in his cheeks. He looked up. 'I was wondering, ma'am,' he said, 'if you'd do me the honor of letting me accompany you back to the house –' He frowned. 'Unless, of course, you have already made arrangements –'

Libbie's turn, then, to frown. 'The house?' she said. It was strange, but, every time she'd thought of the funeral, during the four days or so they'd been home, she'd not once thought beyond it. It had not once occurred to her that there would be anything beyond the priest's hollow words and the blackness of the dresses and the somber look of faces in ill-disguised distress – nothing, in fact, beyond the grotesque finality of the grave.

'The procession will be leaving soon, ma'am –'

'Leaving?' she said. 'But what about the service?' She turned back to where the priest had stood.

'The service is over, ma'am.'

'Over?'

It was true: the graves, now, were nothing but unattended channels in the earth. Indeed, not even the grave-diggers standing casual in the trees had yet stirred themselves. She turned back. 'Goodness,' she said.

'Shall we?' said Philip Parr. He held out a crooked arm. 'Ma'am?'

'Very well,' said Libbie Custer. Then, with a final look back to the dark, disturbed earth, she took hold of the young man's arm, and together they made their way slow to the cars.

128

'This way, ma'am.'

Despite having, in all her (so far) sixty-three years of life, witnessed death close at hand only twice, Elizabeth Bacon Custer had seen enough of it to know – or, perhaps, more accurately, to believe (for no one but the dead can be certain of these things, and they, of course – being dead – are too distant to be consulted) – that life is not ended when the heart falls silent, but merely altered – its carriage transformed with a deft sleight of hand worthy of the greatest, the most accomplished of magicians.

'Ma'am?'

However, as to where it goes – this spirit, this essence – when it flees the mortal body to find its new home – well, that was anybody's guess. All she knew was that it goes somewhere, and that in some cases it seems to hang around as if it has something to say or some advice, perhaps, to give – while in others it's gone to its new world straightaway, leaving those behind in this one still breathing, bereft.

'Thank you.'

'Will there be anything else?'

She looked to Philip Parr who shook his head at the butler. The butler nodded, the hall chandelier's light flaring bright as he bowed from the brilliantined black of his hair.

'Mrs Custer? Shall we?'

Libbie Custer watched the butler move away. There was something about him that struck her as strange, although she couldn't say what.

'Mrs Custer?'

Still puzzled, she turned to her companion, who, for the second time that day, offered her his arm.

'That man,' she said, nodding toward the understair passage into the darkness of which the butler had disappeared. 'Who is he?'

'Man?' said Philip Parr. His eyes were already wandering amongst the grandeur of the vast light-filled parlor. He turned his head away a second, followed Libbie's gaze. 'Which man was that, ma'am?'

The man with secrets and the shiny black hair.

'Ma'am?'

But then she turned away, too (she was just being foolish, she told herself), looked up at her companion, smiled a pale, troubled smile. 'Oh, no one,' she said; then, for the second time that day, she laid her hand on his deep-blue and gold-braided arm and let herself be guided across the hall, toward the somber, milling throng.

129

I n all his years in service, Robert Jackson had never once felt a single moment of jealousy toward those whose station in life afforded them the means of his employment. Indeed, on the contrary, had he, as a young man fresh to the game, taken to counting the times he'd felt pity for these anxious, fretting people (the sort of pity, he'd often thought, that a bird on a wire on a cold autumn day must feel for his cousin, so safe and warm in his rich, gilded cage), then by now the total would surely be in thousands – enough pity, he'd once idly calculated, to fill up the better part of a lifetime. All of which is not to say, of course, that – even since the return of his once-lost love – he'd ever thought his own life to be a life free of troubles – no, sir, again on the contrary, he'd been well aware of their existence – but aware, also, that – most troubles being, as they are, nurtured by geography and circumstance – he could at any moment retire to his room, fill his bags with all that he owned, and move on quite unnoticed – just ease the back door and slip away with the morning, and keep going, then, until he was gone. He was, in short – had for so long been – free of the debts to fortune so eagerly amassed by his betters. He was, in shorter still – had been for so long – free to come and go as he pleased.

'Love? Are you there?'

He clicked open the door of the downstairs parlor, looked around. Unseen by a soul, he frowned. Hadn't he mentioned he'd be straight down? He crossed the thin carpet, clipped his way down the short hall and into the scullery. 'Hello?' he said. The big copper kettle was cooling on the range, the teapot on the table, still empty. He sighed, stood a minute, as if trying to remember something or figure something out, then, turning swiftly, he left the room.

He tried the staff bedrooms (only one of which – his – was occupied these days, since the house had been – discreetly – up for sale), but all were empty, the still air within them untroubled by breathing. Neither was she sitting as she sometimes did in his study, turning the pages of *The Last of the Mohicans* or some other wild adventure, nor engaged in her toilet (he listened, barely breathing, at the door), nor standing in the vegetable garden with that solemn look of distance on her face that only spread across her features when she thought herself alone.

A bird hit the window; he started. Settling himself, then (thankfully, the glass was unbroken), he stood a moment, trying to think (surely she'd not have left the house without permission, nor – heaven forbid – made her way upstairs in such an unkempt state?), and was still doing so when a bell started ringing for attention in the hall. He stood a moment longer (had he not told her – and firmly – that she really mustn't stray?), then, moving swiftly through the kitchen, he made his way down the hall (he had no need to look up at the bells, for he knew each one by its sound), then up the shallow steps his duty once again to perform.

'We were wondering – could you settle a small wager, ma'am?'

'A wager?'

Moments later, he was standing in the drawing-room, attending an elderly lady and two rather loud and drunken gentlemen. The gentlemen had their collars unstudded and quite a sweat on their brows, whilst the lady (who, he understood, was the widow of General Custer, and an acquaintance of young Nathan's from the ship) seemed most ill-at-ease.

'Hold it up, man!'

He lifted his palms, raising the cushion that sat upon them a little higher.

'That's better. Now –'

The first gentleman, who was taller than his colleague (though his colleague was redder in the face), set a caviar canapé in the center of the cushion, pressing it in, then, to secure it. A second he set on the cushion's furthest slope, then a third alongside it, perhaps six or seven inches away. 'There,' he said, withdrawing his hand. He looked to his companions with exaggerated pride. 'Do you see, now?' he said.

'See what?' said the other man. By now a small group had gathered around them, each member of which was craning his head to get a better look.

'Well,' said the tall man (a Mr Watt of Rochester, New York), raising a hand and extending a finger, 'this,' he said, stabbing unsteadily at the central canapé, 'this . . . this is the general –' He looked up, smiling blearily at the lady before him. 'Your esteemee . . . esteemated . . . esteemenated . . . *bloody fine husband*, ma'am!' Nodding his head, then, he clicked his heels, stepped back unsteadily into the hurried support of those gentlemen behind him. 'Bravo!' said one of their number; 'Hear! Hear!' called another. Gathering himself, then, he stepped forward, a sudden look of great sourness on his face. 'And here,' he said gravely, stabbing hard at the further canapé, 'is that coward Benteen, and here –' another stab '– here is that drunken swine Reno –'

Still supporting the cushion (though, in truth, his arms, by now were raging against such cruel and unusual treatment), Robert cast a gaze at the old lady. She was staring, unblinking, at the cushion, her face a deal paler than hitherto it had been.

'Now,' said Mr Watt, raising his hand and stabbing at the air, 'what we need you to settle, ma'am, is simply this.' Again he nodded, looked about him, obviously well-pleased with the strength of his oratory. He settled his gaze on the wife of the general, a furrow creeping into his brows. 'Well, ma'am,' he said. 'Have you no opinion? Will you not put Mr Cheesman here out of his mystery . . . I mean misery?'

'What mystery?' said Mr Cheesman. He frowned at his colleague. 'As I *told* you, sir, the question is settled to the satisfaction of historians –'

'Oh, it *is*, is it?'

'Indeed, sir!'

At which, Mr Cheesman turned his heavy head in a barely controlled arc. 'Mrs Custer,' he said, squinting hard now, 'is it not a . . . not a . . . undisputed . . . er . . .'

'Fact?' came a voice from those watching.

'Fact, yes,' he said sharply, trying to ignore the sudden laughter. He drew himself up, just as firm and straight-backed as he was able. 'Is it, ma'am, not an *undisputed fact* that it was that ghastly savage Crazy Horse himself who slayed your dear husband?'

A gasp from all about the room.

'Indeed, was it not that very fiend who took out his bloody knife, then cut out our noble hero's still-beating heart and ate it?'

More gasps, then silence.

He looked about him. 'What?' he said. 'Wasamatterwithevery-one?' All eyes around him were studying Mrs Custer; he turned his to join them.

'Madam?' said Robert. 'Are you alright? Would you like to –' He watched her sway a moment like a sailor on a ship; then, dropping the cushion and the three canapés, he just managed to catch her as she fell.

130

She had come to the house a girl, and as a girl she had left it. What, then, had happened in between? What, then, was the difference between the girl who, one fine spring morning, had set her bag so nervously down on the hall's polished marble and looked about her with all the fear and curiosity of the last soul but one left alone on the planet, and the girl who – barely twelve months later – had walked the four or so miles to the tracks outside of town where she'd laid her swollen body down and waited, longing, for the end?

Nobody, of course, but the girl herself knows – she and, perhaps, one other, although even *he* would never know how she was those last hours – whether she whistled a tune in the warm air as she walked so as to keep her spirits up, or whether her steps met with silence, her last thoughts being of family, perhaps, or of dim and faded dreams; or maybe her last thoughts as she touched those silver rails were of *him* – of his shoulders or the dip at the small of his back – or even, perhaps, his thick shiny hair, so black it looked blue sometimes when lit on the pillow by the pale yellow moon –

Old Mr Zeitezmann drew his coat about him. The day was cool now – these last evenings of summer a whisper of the cold to come. He drew on his cigarette, squinted through the smoke.

'Clare?' The voice was close by.

Unseen, he frowned.

'*Love? Are you there?*'

Lowering his cigarette, Mr Zeitezmann stepped soundlessly back, disappearing into the shadows that bordered the western sweep of the lawn.

'*Clare? Is that you?*'

He let his eyes close, suspended his breathing, as the squeaking footfall of leather approached; a rustling of leaves, then a pause – breathing, close at hand – then the shoes and their occupant squeaked away and were gone.

Silence – just the drifting of a breeze, the shivering of leaves overhead.

And then? Nothing. He just stood a while – breathing now, but lightly –
his weary eyes closed to the mournful sights of dusk.

Clare.

Clare.

Oh Lord.

He lifted his cigarette, flared it orange in the dark. As if in response, a
light in the distance, green and coquettish, winked out, a sly beckoning,
across the waters of the Sound.

131

'**M**adam?'
The first one to lie to her (that is, to actually say the words, and not just shuffle his feet and look away) had been the commander-in-chief of the army himself, William Tecumseh Sherman. Of course, following his illustrious example, others, then – so emboldened – had found the courage to look up from their boots, or away from whatever it was that, suddenly, upon the unfortunate revival of this question, had so taken their attention, and together and separately they'd nodded and muttered *Quite so, quite so* – whilst all the time knowing that lying, in the end, helps nobody, and that the truth – in all cases – is the only sure path to the freedom of peace.

'There's someone to see you, madam –'

She turned her head on the pillow, drew a face from the blurs.

'He's been waiting all night –'

'All night?' she said. She turned her head again, looked about her. A window, somber paintings, the dark polished wood of a four-poster bed.

She tried to sit up.

'He says he won't leave without seeing you.'

But she could not – a pain in her side forbade it. Instead, she squinted at the face of the man beside her bed. 'Who are you?' she said. 'Where am I?'

Robert leaned forward, the better for soft, soothing words to be heard. 'Madam,' he whispered (just as, previously – too many times, indeed, for counting – he had whispered to the late Mrs Zeitezmann – the bed's only other occupant), 'madam, you are safe –'

'Safe?' said Libbie. 'What do you mean, *safe*?'

'You fainted, madam –'

'*Fainted?*'

'But be calm, madam. The doctor believes you have broken no bones.'

She frowned. *The doctor believes*. Beneath the heavy covers, her hand found the cloth of an unfamiliar nightdress. She looked up. 'Who brought me here?' she said. 'Who –'

Robert smiled, easing back until he was standing straight. 'It was my own dear wife that . . . *prepared* you, madam. Thankfully, Mrs Zeitezmann's . . . *belongings* had not yet been packed away.' Still smiling, he turned away, then, stepped back to the table by the door. On his return to the bedside, he was carrying a tray, upon which sat a shallow china bowl whose contents was a gray-looking soup. This he set down on the bed. 'She also made you this,' he said. 'Soup, she says, is just the thing.' He nodded, as if hearing his beloved utter, right then, those very words. 'She really is a marvel,' he said.

'I'm not hungry,' said Libbie.

Robert frowned. 'You must eat, madam.'

'I said I'm not hungry.'

He sighed. 'Very well, madam.' He stood a minute, like he was totting up the chances of persuasion, but then lifted the tray, made his way toward the door. Here he paused, turned back. 'And your visitor, madam?' he said. 'What shall I say?'

Libbie lay back, closed her eyes. 'Oh, send him away,' she said.

'But, madam –'

She sighed. 'I said send him away, didn't I?' She turned her head, then, opened her eyes, watched as the butler, the tray on one palm, twisted the handle of the door with the other. She let her eyes close again as he clicked the door shut behind him. *He was perfectly untouched. The general's body was recovered entire.* She drew in a breath, held it a moment, then let it out in an oh-so-weary sigh.

'*He was buried in the field, ma'am, his brothers beside him –*

She listened idly for the sound of distant footsteps in the hall.

The manner of his death, ma'am, was a credit to the nation –

Then she let herself drift, let her arms fall away, let the warmth of the bed come to claim her.

She'd been standing that day, all those years ago now, in the parlor of some grand house in Washington, just chatting to the wife of one of her husband's former comrades (the poor man – Lieutenant Chellis by name – had fallen from his horse and broken his leg on the morning of the fateful expedition), when General Sherman appeared at the door, accompanied as ever he seemed to be in those days by General Sheridan. One tall, the other short, they had struck her then as an odd pair – more like a gentleman out with his best hunting dog than two generals of the United States Army. Anyway, she acknowledged their arrival with the briefest of nods, then turned back to her companion and continued their talk. In time, having paid their respects to their host and a dozen others, the two generals found themselves (quite by chance of course) standing before her.

A moment's silence, then, from the room; then the talk resumed.

'Generals,' she said.

They bowed; she nodded.

'Madam,' said General Sherman. 'May I say what an honor it is to reacquaint myself with the beloved wife of such a fine and greatly mourned American.'

'Widow,' said Libbie.

The two generals exchanged glances. General Sherman cleared his throat. 'Indeed, ma'am,' he said, again bowing.

'Indeed,' said General Sheridan, bowing also.

'And pauper,' said Libbie, to gasps from the room.

'Madam?' said General Sherman.

'Widow and pauper.'

Another brisk exchange of glances. General Sherman tried a smile: it failed, getting lost somewhere on his pockmarked face. 'Madam,' he said, 'I feel this is neither the place nor the time to discuss matters . . . *financial –*'

'You don't, sir?' said Libbie.

'No, ma'am. I don't. We are here, as you know, to celebrate the President's re-election. Should you have any other concerns, then I suggest you come to see me at another time. Good evening, ma'am.' Then he bowed (General Sheridan bowed, too), and was just turning away when the tip of his sword caught the hem of Libbie's dress. 'Excuse me,' he said, trying to withdraw it – though unsuccessfully, caught as it was in the dress's thick satin folds.

Libbie set her hands on her hips, as all around stopped to watch the nation's highest soldier try gracefully to extricate his sword from a lady's ballgown. 'Really,' she said, as he tried a gentle tug, 'you should be more careful, general. That sword of yours could have someone's eye out.'

The general again tried a smile; again it failed. 'Madam,' he said. 'Only the eyes of barbarians need have anything to fear from my sword.'

Libbie leaned forward, until her lips were a scandal's-length away from the general's sunburnt ear. 'And rivals,' she whispered. 'Don't forget rivals. Don't forget what a use it can be as an instrument of sacrifice.' She leaned back, just as Mrs Chellis sank to her knees amid an ocean's swell of skirts and unhooked the offending sabre.

The general stepped back. He was red-faced, clearly outraged. 'Madam,' he said, 'were you not a mere weak woman, but a gentleman, I would seek satisfaction for those scurrilous remarks. However –' he drew his head back, raised it in the manner of a wronged but forgiving Caesar '– *however*, I am reminded that I must make allowance for the ravages of grief, and so shall turn a deaf ear to your words.' He turned away, then paused, turned back. 'Oh, and by the way, madam, since you've seen fit to raise the subject at this time, may I say, on behalf of the President and, indeed, a grateful nation, that your . . . *allowance* . . . has, from this moment, been raised as requested, and that it is our dearest wish that, henceforth, you may be able to live out the remainder of your life in the comfort to which we all sincerely believe you are entitled.' Here, the great general finally turned away, crossing the room to the sound, first, of General Sheridan's lone clapping, then – the crowd thus encouraged – to a general and spirited applause.

'Mrs Custer?'

'What do you want?'

'It's me, Mrs Custer. Philip Parr.'

'I know.'

A shadow crossed the darkened room. Libbie sighed. 'What are you doing?' she said. She had no energy – no strength at all in her limbs.

'I need to talk to you.'

'Need?'

The tinkle of something glass tipped over, a curse. A fumbling, then, a failed striking of a match, a second.

'What are you doing?' said Libbie.

Another strike. 'I'm trying –' A fourth. 'I'm trying to –' Then, finally, the match flared, lighting Philip Parr's face a ghastly waxen yellow. He looked about him for a lamp. He crossed to Mrs Zeitezmann's French writing desk. 'May I?' he said.

Libbie said nothing.

He clicked on the light.

The room, these days – these hollow days, after the visit of death – was the same as it had been, but different also. Whilst there was, of course, the same paper on the walls and the same grand stuccoed ceiling, the same four-poster bed, the same desk, the same ornate lamp – whilst there was, still, all this (though not, in truth, for long, as all movable items had been valued and cataloged, ready for the auction), there were, now, no personal items on display – no photographs in frames, no clothes in the closets, hanging limp and still as corpses, no evidence of fine combs cut from ivory and brushes on the high-polished dressing table – nothing but their shapes cast like shadows in the slow-gathering dust.

Philip Parr approached the bed. He was dressed, now, not in his uniform, but in a slightly over-large dinner suit, the arms of which revealed nothing of his cuffs. His face seemed flushed in the sudden strong light, as if he'd been running or – more probably – drinking. 'Look, I'm sorry,' he said.

'Sorry?' said Libbie. How quickly, she thought, and how without warning or ceremony, had she shed all embarrassment – all that her mother, so long ago now, had once called *A lady's best protector*. She looked up at the face of Philip Parr – she was suddenly so, so weary now – caring nothing now for lips unrouged or hair so unkempt. 'Mr Parr,' she said, but then she paused, unable to think of a single thing to say, except to ask of the young man why it is that life must be so cruel – why memory can't die with the death of those remembered, and why, consequently, the living must be tortured so. But she didn't say this, of course – for what good is to be had from asking questions that only God Himself could answer – and, only then, were He the kind of God in whom so many crave belief, but for whose existence there is so little evidence? No. She said nothing. She just lay still, her body wrapped in borrowed sheets like some still, shrouded corpse.

'To disturb you like this,' said Philip Parr.

'What?' she said.

'I mean, you must need your rest. It's just, well, I just had to talk to you.'

'I know. You said.'

'Yes, quite so.' He slipped his hands nervously into the pockets of his jacket, then withdrew them.

'Well?' said Libbie.

Then, again pausing, he looked about him, like he was looking for some kind of assistance. Finally, having found sufficient resolve from somewhere, he turned back. He swallowed hard, set his face in what passes in the young for the face of bitter fate. 'It's Mr Zeitezmann,' he said. He drew another breath.

'What about him?' said Libbie.

'Well, he asked me to stay for dinner and, though I was real surprised, well, I *did* of course, and, well, we got to talking –' Another pause, then, as if resolve were wavering. Suddenly, he shook his head. 'Oh, I don't know,' he said. 'I guess maybe he was just . . . well, maybe he was just upset.' He nodded. 'Yes, that's it. He was just upset. He didn't know what he was saying –' He nodded again – like something was settled in his mind. He sighed, smiling with relief. 'Oh goodness,' he said. He blew out his cheeks. 'Really, I should go.' He turned away, took a step toward the door. But then he stopped.

'What is it?' said Libbie.

Nothing. Then he shrugged. His shoulders were stiff.

'Did he say something?' She could hear him breathing hard, see his hands clenched in fists.

Another shrug.

'Philip?'

'Like I said, it's nothing.'

With some effort, she pushed herself up, rested back against the pillows. 'Then there's no harm in telling, is there?' she said. 'If it's nothing.'

Another sigh; he turned. The sweat on his brow sparkled bright in the lamplight. Libbie held out her hand. She patted the covers.

'Okay,' he said. 'But I'd rather stand.'

Libbie shrugged. 'Very well.'

He nodded.

Silence.

'Well?' she said.

He raised a hand, swept it across his brow. 'Well, like I say, he was, well, obviously upset, what with it being both funerals –' Looking down, he slipped his hands into his pockets again, then, again, withdrew them. He cleared his throat. 'Which, I guess, is understandable –'

'Of course,' said Libbie.

'And, well, when he started talking about Mrs Zeitezmann and his son, I guess I reckoned it was kind of, well, *natural* – you know?'

Libbie nodded.

'Anyway. After a while he started saying things that sounded real strange –'

'Like what?' she said.

'Well –' He sighed. 'Well, he was saying things like how he knew he should be sorry for what he'd done, but how he just couldn't feel it – sorry, I mean. He kept saying how he just felt like he was already dead and how he couldn't feel anything anymore. And then –' Again, Philip paused. He looked up from his hands. 'And then, well, he started talking about, well, about the *general*, ma'am – about how he could have been President – how he *should* have been President, and how for sure he *would* have been, if he hadn't have, well, if he hadn't –'

'Died,' said Libbie.

'Yes, ma'am. If he hadn't have died.'

She nodded. 'It's true.' Unexpectedly, then, she smiled. 'And he would have been a *fine* President – don't you think?'

'I *guess*,' said Philip. He shrugged. 'Though I don't know much about politics, ma'am.' He looked down again at his boots, then up. 'Ma'am?'

It's ours, my darling, the presidency's ours.

She blinked and the face from so long ago started slipping.

'Ma'am? Are you listening to me?'

Just let me whup those Indians by the second of July.

'I'm listening,' she said.

And by the fourth there'll be no one that can stop us –

'Alright, then. 'Cause there's more.'

'More?'

Once again Philip's hands found his pockets; once again, as before, he withdrew them. 'Yes, ma'am. It was after he said about the presidency –'

about how he and some others were going to make it a certainty – that he got real kind of low – saying all those things again, about how sorry he was and how it was all his fault, and how he shouldn't ever have sold the guns when he did or to the people he sold them to, knowing where for sure they'd end up –'

'Go on,' said Libbie.

Philip shrugged. 'Well, that was all, really. Except –'

'Except what?'

'Well, nothing, really. It's just, well, you know how I said I was real surprised when he invited me to stay for dinner – just me of all people – well, I think I sort of figured it out.'

'You did?'

'Well, maybe this is stupid, but I think he wanted to tell me things, so that I'd, well, tell you –'

'Tell *me*?' said Libbie. 'Why?'

Another shrug. 'I don't know. It just seemed like that to me.'

Libbie nodded. She paused, then said, 'Where is he now?'

'Now? I don't know. I guess –' Philip hesitated when he saw Libbie Custer shaking her head. 'What is it?' he said.

'Nothing,' she said, then she laid her head back and closed her eyes, aware, at last – after so many years – of the pleasure to be had in the arrival of long-delayed justice, and of the ease to be found in the balance of all living things.

'Clare? Is that you?'

There was one place, finally, he hadn't looked – one place so obvious that when he saw her in the distance, as he crossed the midnight lawn to the sound of the now-receding tide – when he saw her all bunched up in their own special place below the jetty, he cursed himself for not having thought of it before. 'Oh, my darling,' he whispered, as he slid down the low shingle bank and dipped down below the jetty's seeping boards. 'Oh, my darling, you shouldn't be here. What were you thinking of? You should be inside –'

But then something stopped him – something in her absolute stillness. 'Clare?' he whispered, though he knew in his heart there would never, now, be an answer. He stood a moment, then, barely able to breathe. Then, slowly, he reached out a hand, his hand shaking as if he were reaching through bars into the mouth of a tiger. He flinched, unseen, as his fingers found wet cloth, then a cheek, unshaven. 'Oh Jesus,' he said, 'oh Jesus, oh Jesus,' as the world, having turned and turned again, turned once more.

Part Four

LOCKED
AND LOADED

Josh & Clare

132

That summer, that day, that moment, twenty years ago now, I remember, still, as clearly, as warmly, as *physically* as I remember the hour or so that has just passed since I packed up my things, placed them neatly in the trunk, then walked across the courtyard, aiming to drop in my key, maybe have a final chat with Davie. Not that I had anything in particular to say to him – it's just I have this thing about leaving a place without saying goodbye – in the same way that, these days, I have a thing about neatness. Precision, if you like. I'm not happy these days unless everything's in its right place. Locked and loaded, is how I think of it. Locked and loaded.

But anyway.

Back to old Davie.

Well, he wasn't there, of course – which, of course, I guess I knew already. I guess I knew without really having to think of it that he'd already be watching TV in the backroom (*I Love Lucy* is his favorite show these days – that and *Bonanza*, God help him), and that, consequently, what with the re-enactment people having moved out early (no way you could restart the battle not on time: certainly – God forbid – not *late*) – consequently there'd be no one about – no one minding the store. All there was was the sound of the TV, and the humming (and sometimes rattling) of that old ice-box behind the desk. Not to mention, of course, his daddy's old bent-barrel shotgun, lying right there under the counter – right where he always left it. And a packet of shells, of course. Old Davie always had plenty of shells.

But hey now. Don't go getting that look. It's just a gun, just shells. And, after all, isn't it every American's right to bear arms? I believe, sir, it is. And besides, haven't you ever heard the saying 'It's not guns that kill people, but people that kill people'?

Well, of course you have.

Which just goes to show how you and I have so much in common. It just goes to show that we're practically brothers. Yes indeed. We're just about blood, you and I.

133

'Good morning, general.'
    'Good morning, Mrs Custer.'
    That summer, that day, twenty years ago now – June twenty-fifth, nineteen seventy-eight.

'How's your daddy today?'

Clare shrugged.

'He didn't look too sweet.'

'You saw him?'

Josh Parlor pulled down the strap of his helmet, eased the thing off. He threw back his head, tossing his blond Custer curls. 'Sure,' he said, smiling, raising a make-believe rifle. He squinted, sighting. 'Had him in my sights. You think I should have shot him?'

'Jesus, Josh.'

He dropped his arms. 'What?'

Clare looked about her. Although it was early, there were already people moving about on the parade ground – men dressed in cavalry blue stacking rifles, pitching army-issue tents, their voices rising up now and then through the warm, clear air off the plains, rising and rising, then, until they were lost overhead, drowned in the vast, blue Montana sky. 'Nothing,' she said. 'It's just –'

'Just what?' Josh unzipped his leather suit, pulled it off of his shoulders. He paused, the thing hanging round his waist. 'Oh, don't tell me,' he said.

'What?'

Shaking his head, he reached down, unzipped his boots, kicked them off. 'Well, let me guess. You were wrong. He's not so bad after all – right? He doesn't deserve it – right?' He sighed. 'Jesus, Clare. When the hell are you going to make up your mind *and then stick to it?*'

'I have. I am. It's just –'

He pulled his suit down all the way, stepped out of it. 'Look,' he said, crossing the old Custer porch, his leathers slung over his shoulders. He stopped in front of Clare. 'Let me put it like this. There's a spare helmet on the bike – right? Well, it doesn't *have* to be used.' He gripped her by the shoulders. 'Do you hear what I'm saying?'

She half-tried to pull away, but the hands held her firm.

'Well, *do* you?'

'I hear you,' she said.

'Good.'

The hands released her; she moved away, stood at the top of the porch's wooden steps, looked out across the parade ground to the vast, open prairie beyond. 'Do you *want* me to go with you?' she said. Her heart was thumping hard. She turned. Josh was standing in the doorway, leaning against the frame, his hands thrust deep into the pockets of his jeans, his head back, eyes closed. 'Josh? Did you hear me?'

'I heard you,' he said.

'Well?'

'Well what?'

'*Do* you?'

Silence. Then: 'Are you saying you have a choice?'

'What do you mean?'

He opened his eyes, pushed away from the frame. 'I *mean*, are you saying you have a choice?'

'I don't understand.'

'Sure you do. You know you can't stay here any more than I can. We're bigger than this place. *You* know that.'

She heard him move toward her then, heard the padding of his bare feet on the boards. She sensed his breathing, felt his arms encircle her.

'Least *I* am,' he said. He pushed himself against her. 'Don't you think so?' He pushed again, harder. 'Don't you know I'm so big I'm most likely too big for some little girl like you?' She could tell he was smiling – and so, in a moment, was she. She turned to face him.

'You reckon?' she said.

His lips found her ear. 'You want evidence, Mrs Custer?' he whispered.

She narrowed her eyes, fetched up a frown. 'No, sir,' she said.

'You don't, ma'am?'

'No, sir.' She let her hand drift down to his crotch. She squeezed. 'I don't want *evidence*, general, sir. I want me some *proof*.'

They made love, as ever, upstairs in the general's tiny bed; then, when they were quiet, they lay together, listening to the sound of the day's preparations.

'Did you hear that?' said Clare. They'd been still for maybe an hour. She turned her head. 'Josh?' she whispered. His eyes were closed, his features so calm in sleep. She sat herself up. Slowly, she withdrew her arm from beneath the covers, touched his lips with the tips of her fingers. He stirred, but didn't wake. *I've a friend in New York who'll find us work.* She smiled, though only with her eyes. *He's an actor. He's doing real good.* She sighed, lay back. There was no friend, no actor in New York: this she'd known from the start.

'Josh?' she whispered again. Still nothing. She closed her eyes.

At first, she'd thought he'd only said it – only lied – so as to make the gamble of leaving seem not quite so scary – and for her sake, not his. But now she knew better. She knew now (quite how she knew she couldn't have said – but she knew alright) that the lie, really, was for him – but more than that. She knew now, also, that lies were the same things as dreams to him – that he couldn't see the difference – and that only when he wrote (he'd a novel, *The Shadow Catcher*, as yet unpublished) – only then, when he was squinting at the paper through the smoke from his cigarette, did he really believe that the world could be a good place, that deed and consequence were inextricably linked, and not just a pair of loose buttons going round in a dryer.

'Hey, what are you thinking?'

She shrugged.

'You know what I was thinking?'

'You were asleep.'

'Well, dreaming then.'

'What?'

'Don't you want to know?'

'Sure I want to know. It's just we have to get up. They're already downstairs.'

'Ah, fuck 'em.'

'Right. Good attitude.'

'What's the matter with you?'

'Nothing.'

'Sure.'

'We have to get up.'

'Go on then.'

She pushed up, swung her legs from beneath the heavy covers. The floorboards were cold to the touch. 'Josh?' she said. She turned.

'What now?'

'Well, I was wondering –'

'Oh shit.'

'No, seriously. I was wondering what they were really like.'

'Who?'

'Custer and Libbie. I mean, do you think they really loved each other? I mean, really –'

Josh sighed. 'Jesus. I don't know. Why?'

'I don't know.'

'I guess she must have done.'

She turned. 'Why?'

'Well, she followed him, didn't she? All the way out to this shithole? Talk about *proof* –'

'Yeah, maybe.'

'You don't think so?'

'I said maybe.'

'But?'

'Well, I don't know, maybe she just didn't want to get left behind. Maybe she just didn't want to be where she was.'

Josh sat up. 'So what are you saying?'

'Nothing.'

'Yeah, *right*.'

Voices, then, from the parlor below. Clare stood. 'Come on,' she said. 'Time to get dressed.'

134

'Pepsi okay? We ain't got Coke.'

If you're asking me what happened then – why exactly we didn't go – well, I'd have to consult my diary. It's just a shame I don't have one. I guess when everyone else was getting diaries for Christmas, I just wasn't on the list. Maybe they reckoned I'd never keep it up anyway. Which is true. Diaries are for people who want to remember. I just want to forget. Which, incidentally, is easier than you'd think. All you have to do is whistle. You know how to whistle, don't you?

'You want some pie with that?'

You just put your lips together and blow.

'What kind of pie?'

'What?'

'I said what kind of pie, sir. We have blueberry today on special.'

Just put your lips together.

'Sir?'

'Yeah, right. Blueberry's good.'

'You okay, sir?'

'Me? I'm fine. You?'

'Me?'

'Are *you* okay?'

'I guess.'

'You guess? Don't you know?'

'No, I don't. Does anybody?'

'*I* do. *I* know.'

'No you don't.'

'You don't think so?'

'Listen, if you were okay, would you be sitting here now with your elbow in a plate of blueberry pie?'

'Oh shit.'

'That's four twenty-five.'

'What?'

'For the pie. And the Pepsi. You want a serviette for that?'

'I'm okay.'

'Sure you're okay. You sure you don't want no serviette?'

She's right, of course. Or was. Right when she looked at me so disbelieving when I said I was okay. For sure I've been kidding myself. I mean, sitting in that motel, just trying to write – trying to *make stuff up* – about Matthew and James (was James dead or alive when I left him? Jesus – I can't even remember *that*) is hardly the thing for a grown man to do at the best of times – and this ain't the best of times. Nor is it the worst of times. No, sir. The worst of times was the times I've been trying to forget (so I lied when I said it was easy) – times that I can't seem to help but remember.

So.

You want to know, I'll tell you.

First, though, a word of warning. As you know, I'm a writer, and writers are liars. The best you could say for us is that – at our best – writers are liars in search of the truth – and how reliable is that?

But onward.

Why, you wonder (do you?), didn't we go that day as planned? Why didn't we just finish up that day and get on that old bike of mine and just go? Well, the short answer is her daddy chose that very day to get worse. Or claim he was worse. Or whatever. I don't know. All I know is we were just for the last time getting rid of our costumes (Jesus, how I'd come to hate all that cavalry stuff – all that saluting and not being able to cut my damned hair) – just gearing ourselves up to really do it, when Clare got a call from the hospital in Bozeman. Apparently, he'd all of a sudden just kind of lost it – he'd got home okay from the university, but that was it. He couldn't get any further. Anyway, Clare's mama had found him just sitting there in the driveway, his hands gripping so tight to the wheel of that old fucking car that she just couldn't prize them off. It was like they were stuck with glue or something. And he wouldn't talk, neither – except to say how he couldn't go on because he didn't have enough shirts – and where, for God's sake, were his pants? He just kept going on about shirts and pants and not having enough, and was still going on (he especially wanted pants made of corduroy – God knows why) when the paramedics arrived and tried to talk him out. Which of course they did in the end – but not before he'd said a whole bunch of stuff that nobody could understand. It wasn't that he wasn't making sense – it wasn't that you couldn't understand the *words* – it was just he was talking about things from his life that not even Clare's mama – his wife – recognized. I guess he was just rambling – either that or he really was some killer like he claimed. Which sincerely I doubt. I mean that man didn't have the guts he was born with. He couldn't get up the nerve to swat some bug even if that bug was some weird kind of suicide bug and was just lying on its back and begging to be killed. No, sir. A shortfall of nerve that man had for the killing thing. Which meant, of course, he was just crazy. Although not so crazy that he didn't know what his being crazy was gonna do to Clare. Oh sure, he knew. Believe me. He knew there was no way, what with him in that hospital tapping his feet to some tune in his head and going on and on about his goddamn fucking shirts – no way that she was gonna leave with me. No, sir. Way too loyal to her daddy she was, and he knew it. Oh yeah, he knew what he was doing – and you know what? He knew I knew it too. Oh for sure. It was like sometimes, later on, we'd be sitting there – the three of us – in his room, and he'd, like, catch my eye? Well, let me tell you, he could talk for sure then without speaking. The bastard. It was like he was laughing at me. So don't tell me he didn't know – okay? I know he knew.

But hey.

Whatever.

I guess the point of all this is that we didn't go as planned. At least she didn't. In the end I went on my own (that spare helmet didn't get used after all). But even then I only got as far as Minneapolis. Which is where I met Nicola. But that's another story. I guess the main story is how I managed to leave Clare so beaten that even her mama didn't recognize her in the hospital (mind you, her mama never *was* real smart), and still got to spend the time I did in Minneapolis without getting arrested or nothing. I mean, every day I was kind of expecting it, until one day I figured well it hasn't happened yet and so maybe it never will. Which is when of course Nicola and me broke up. And I went back. By then Clare was just about okay. To start with I used to drive by her parents' house (her daddy was out by then and just used to sit in his den watching TV), and sometimes I'd catch her going in or coming out, and I'd duck down so she couldn't see me watching. In the end, of course, she did see me, and when she didn't scream – when she just looked at me and *smiled*, well I knew then I was okay. I knew then that nothing was ever gonna get me. *Fucking Superman* – that's what I thought. And that (as you may or may not know) is what I called my second book.

Fucking Superman.

Some joke to find it here. At a gas station, for God's sake. And such a new, spine-intact copy too.

Look at it. Never once been opened. Never once been read.

'That's twenty-six dollars dead. With the gas.'

A bargain.

The story of my life (or at least a part of it) – twenty-six dollars, with gas.

A bargain indeed.

And no word of it a lie.

Honest.

Eddie

135

'Stop, for Christ's sake!'

For Eddie Reno, the long journey north had (in his mind at least – and, Lord, *there* was a place) long since taken leave of any sense he'd once had of it – the sense, that is, of it being a journey *to* something, a quest *in pursuit of* something. No, since around about Memphis, he'd come more and more to think of it as flight – as some ham-fisted, pigeon-brained farce of an escape – although an escape from what he couldn't have said. All he knew (or, more accurately, all he *felt*), and more and more these days – in fact, just about the only thing left he felt *certain* of – was that something was following him – something mean and spiteful that, try as he might (and God knows he'd tried), he just couldn't shake off.

And this was?

'He said stop, granddad! Jesus, you old fool! Didn't you hear our native friend here give that particular instruction?'

Well, that was just it – he didn't know, couldn't figure it out. I mean, he couldn't see it, feel it, smell it or hear it. And yet he knew it was there – was certain of it. All of which made doing something about it just about impossible. In fact, in the end he'd figured all he could do was keep moving – keep driving – in the hopes that he might outrun it, although *so* far . . .

'Hey! Granddad! Ain't you hearing me? Ain't you got no fuckin' ears?'

'Okay, okay –' Easing his foot off the gas, he steered the old Toyota to the side of the road. The car stopped. Weary, he pulled on the hand-brake.

'*Jesus*,' said Peter Frampton, leaning across, hanging his face – a ghastly gargoyle – about an inch or so away from Eddie's cheek. 'Look,' he said, 'when the bossman says you ain't going the right way, then you ain't going the right way, right?'

'You mean we ain't – I mean we're *not* – going the right way?'

Peter Frampton edged himself even closer – so close, in fact, that the rancid tang of his foul-smelling breath made Eddie nearly gag. 'No,' he said, scowling, 'this *ain't* the right way – unless –' He paused, narrowed his eyes. 'Unless, of course, the *right* way's the *wrong* way, right?'

'What?' said Eddie.

The former K-Mart assistant manager sat back, a self-satisfied sort of leer easing over his face. 'Oh, don't think I don't get it,' he said. He nodded. 'Don't think I don't get your little game –'

'My what?' said Eddie.

He twisted round in his seat. 'Hey, bossman,' he said, 'you get his little game too?' He frowned. 'Bossman?' Then, in an instant, the leer disappeared, was replaced by a narrow-eyed twinkling of opportunity. He twisted back. 'Hey, granddad,' he hissed.

'What now?'

'*Ssssh* –'

'Eh?'

Holding his breath, he reached out a hand, his fingers already curling, aiming for the sleeping man's gun, oh and *Jesus* he was just within an inch of it – just a hair's breadth away from his freedom – when the Indian, his eyes still closed, raised up the pistol, cocking the thing with his thumb at the same time and touching the barrel's end to Peter Frampton's sloping forehead – all in one smooth, practiced move. 'Now what do we have here?' he said, his eyes still shut tight. 'Hmmm. Let me guess.' He frowned. 'Could it be a rebellion? Could it be there's dissension in the SAK?'

'The what?' said Peter Frampton. He was sweating hard.

At the wheel, Eddie Reno gave a sigh. 'The Society,' he said, 'of American Kidnappers.'

'Correct,' said Danny Sundance. He opened his eyes. 'Now,' he said. 'Mr Reno. I'd be obliged indeed if you'd be so kind as to turn this vehicle around.'

'Alright,' said Eddie.

'Good. Oh, and one other thing –'

'What?'

'Not you – *you*.'

'Me?' Peter Frampton blinked hard, the barrel pressed tight, still, above the bridge of his nose.

'Yes, *you*. Will you do something for me?'

'Do something? Yes, yes – anything!'

'Splendid.' Danny Sundance paused, watching as Eddie Reno three-pointed the car, then shifted to Drive. 'Okay,' he said. 'While Eddie here's driving, and I'm resting up, your job's, well, to entertain us –'

'*Entertain?* But how –'

'You will sing, Mr Frampton.'

'*Sing?*'

'Yes, sir. You will stand up like the fine, upstanding fellow you are and give us the benefit of your "Unchained Melody".'

'My what?'

'You heard me.'

'Oh my Lord,' said Peter Frampton.

'No,' said Danny Sundance, his face beating off a smile. 'The first line, I think you'll find, is "Oh my *love*".' He waggled the pistol. 'Well?' he said. '*Well?* What are you waiting for? Get singing, Mr Frampton! Get singing!'

136

'Jesus, what was *that*?'

And so it was that on the morning of June twenty-fifth – the day indeed of the one hundred and twenty-first anniversary of the Battle of the Little Bighorn – a car later described to police as *some kind of a beat-up and real dusty foreign-type sedan* crossed the state line at Fargo heading west toward Bismark, containing *one dark man, one old man and one man standing up through the vehicle's sun-roof singing songs from the shows at the top of his voice*. That this description only reached the ears of the highway patrol out of Bismark, North Dakota several days later (and, consequently, too late for it to be of any real use – the car, by then, not to mention one of its inmates, being somewhere up in Canada heading way, way north) was thanks in large part (and here was an irony) to the – then – ongoing hostage situation at the Culpepper farm that bordered the highway – a situation, incidentally, resolved to the great satisfaction of the combined forces of the FBI, the ATF, and state and local police, the only death (this time) being that of Mr Lincoln, the Culpeppers' dachshund, who, so excited did he become with all the noise, chose to dash like the Devil from the Culpepper house, up a bank and onto the highway, where, unlucky as ever (this was a dog whose head had lost most of the sense it had ever contained when it was struck one day in the middle of nowhere by a stray bolt from *Apollo Thirteen*), he was hit and killed instantly by a dusty and beat-up Toyota Supreme containing a dark man, an old man and a rapidly tiring man who was standing, his head, shoulders and weedy chest pushed out through the sun-roof, singing songs he could barely remember at the top of his unlovely voice.

Danny Sundance sat forward. 'What was what?'

'That noise,' said Eddie. Without taking his eyes off the road, he sort of poked Peter Frampton in the shin.

'Hey, I'm singing! I'm singing!' came a cry from above. 'Jesus – can't you *hear* me? *Night fever, night feveeer, you know how to do it –*'

'Hey you, that's enough,' said Danny Sundance.

'*Night fever, night feveeer –*'

'I SAID THAT'S ENOUGH!' He grabbed the poor singer by his belt and pulled him down. 'I *said* that'll do – okay?'

Eddie Reno pulled his eyes from the road, risked a look. 'Say, you alright?' Peter Frampton was all windblown and disheveled, his hair standing wild like a scarecrow's.

'*Me?*' he said bitterly. 'Oh *yeah*. *I'm* just *fine*.' He twisted in his seat. His face was nearly black. 'You any idea how many bugs there are in this goddamn fuckin' state?'

'Not,' said Danny Sundance, 'as many as there were.'

'Yeah well – fuck you.' Peter Frampton turned away, defiant – then at once turned back. There were tears now in his eyes. 'And you know I don't *care* no more if you *have* got the gun, you're still a . . . still a –'

'Native?' said Danny Sundance.

Peter Frampton screwed up his face, his brain working overtime. 'Still a . . . still a REDSKIN!' he said finally, investing the word with all the nastiness – all the bile – he could muster, then turning away for the last time, triumphant, the manifest destiny of the white race having once again been asserted – triumphant, that is, until his overworked brain worked a little harder and conjured up in his mind's eye the scene, in sound and vision, of its having been plastered all over the dash, and his corpse, thereafter, being tossed like the corpse of some mangy old dog from a fast-moving, beaten-up, dusty old car and into some gloomy old worm-squirming ditch.

'Oh dear,' said Danny Sundance, 'me heap big upset.'

Peter Frampton closed his eyes. Then, uttering in silence a feverish, pleading prayer, he shrank himself as low down in the seat as he was able – so low, indeed, that he hoped he might just disappear.

Josh

137

O h, how strange it is to see her again – and how strange to see
myself. How strange to watch them – *us* – from this vantage-
point; how strange to watch them parade as, twenty years ago
now, *we* once paraded along that same wooden verandah – to see them
wearing (who knows?) the same costumes we wore and into which we
changed on that faraway day. And how strange to be standing here at
the foot of these steps and to be talking –

'Hi, how are you?'

– to a new Mrs Custer and a new (no doubt improved) general – to
watch them through the window playing cards as we once did, and to
watch them laughing, the touch of their hands.

'I'm fine,' she says.

'Good day for it,' I say. Then she looks at me like she knows – like
maybe she's seeing the ghost of a ghost, but then she looks away. Has to
go, she says.

Me too.

I must straighten up and be ready. I must return to the ranks of my
fellow re-enactors – to the bankers and farmers and department-store
assistants all out for a day in the sunshine. Not that they don't take it
seriously – it's just that their seriousness is the wasted, inconsequential
seriousness of children in a schoolyard. They hold their rifles and
shotguns (it costs too much to be too accurate) as if their rifles and
shotguns are toys – which, in a sense, I suppose they are, none of them
being loaded.

It's the rules.

None of them, of course, but one.

Sitting here on this bus, heading for Custer Hill, it occurs to me that
perhaps this obsession with reliving things (I mean, is there really
anything else on TV these days but re-enactments of true crimes and
disasters?) speaks somehow to the American character. It may of course
be nothing more than the fact of this nation having the comfort of so
little history that what history we *do* have has to be endlessly recycled –

everything played over and over and always to the same conclusion. It's like some constant need we have for reassurance – like a man who wins some huge lottery but, even when he's surrounded then by all the riches of the world, still cannot believe his good fortune and, consequently, never sleeps for fear that he'll wake one day to find it all gone. Sometimes I think America is that rich, sleepless man. Who said it I can't remember, but somebody said (was it Washington?) that the price of freedom is constant vigilance – which is true enough I'm sure. But what about the price of constant vigilance? Is it not exhaustion? Is this not just the cycle of rising and falling? Of the more you have simply meaning that the more you have to protect, and that, in so protecting, you stretch yourself too thin and make yourself vulnerable?

Oh shit, I don't know. Maybe I'm just rambling. Maybe the springs in this bus are addling what's left of my brain.

Here's a funny thing: the 'colonel' of our 'regiment' stands up at the front of the bus to issue instructions (how the 'honor' of the so-and-so regiment rests on our shoulders, blahblahblah), when – just at the same moment – his pants fall down. And what's he wearing underneath? Boxers stamped over and over with the phrase EAT MY SHORTS. Jesus Christ. Things are worse than I thought. I'm being led into battle by Homer fucking Simpson.

Some people, it seems, take this whole thing way too seriously. The whole convoy (there's maybe fifteen to twenty buses in total) stops at a gas station off the highway, right, and everyone piles into the restaurant. Well, I'm just about to sit down at a table of 'Indians' when a guy from my 'company' (I think he's a 'sergeant' or some such piece of crap) yells out, 'Hey, soldier – you can't sit with *them*!' 'Why not?' I say, playing dumb – which really pisses him off. 'Because,' he says, 'you sit with them you're one of them.' 'Well, fuck you,' I say, and I sit down.

I don't think I've made myself very popular.

Jesus, but some things sure have changed. Twenty years ago, people would make the trip from Fort Lincoln to the battlefield in whatever they had. There'd be pick-ups and all kinds of farm-trucks and tractors and so on. One time I remember seeing this guy called Tony in his daddy's sixty-two Mustang lose his sump on a rock and then just stand there beside the damn thing, pissing on it for spite like it was just the most normal thing in the world to do. Jesus Christ! A sixty-two Mustang! I nearly pissed my pants too, seeing that.

So we're here. There it is. Just like before. Just like I remembered. Down there the plains, brown and yellow in the sun, then the river, obscured now by trees. And here, on this rise, the same heat, the same flies, this dirt.

She said to me once that she dreamed of New York. She said it was her kind of America. I said it was mine too.

But I was wrong. My kind of America is an illusion more powerful than anything dreamed of by my grandfather. My kind of America is an unimaginable place where the past is the past – dead and gone. My kind of America is not this bloodied earth – it is elsewhere. But my eyes have been closed like a boxer's, and my hands tied. I am deaf, and mute, too; my search, it seems, is hopeless.

I think of my child and I cannot stop the tears.

138

G race was born seven months after my return from Minneapolis. That the birth was 'straightforward' and the baby born without any visible defects I took to be a sign that my actions of the previous fall had been without consequence. It was, I assumed, a sign from God (or from providence, or fate, or whomever – I didn't care) that what I'd done had somehow been forgiven – and I managed to convince myself that, as long as a lesson had been learnt, then, really, in a sense the whole thing had been for the best. After all, the only lessons that really count are the lessons that hurt. Of course, the fact that the hurt in this case had been to somebody else, I managed conveniently to sidestep, by telling myself that – as she and I were one, locked together obviously by destiny or whatever – anything that hurt her hurt me blahblahblah. All of which I know now of course to be just so much self-serving crap. At the time, though, I really believe I really believed it. I wanted to, of course, and maybe I had to. At this distance it's hard to remember.

Anyway.

The baby.

Grace.

Oh Jesus, she was beautiful – always smiling, right from the start, like she'd heard some real funny joke in the womb that she just couldn't get out of her head. I used to spend hours just watching her smiling, wondering what the joke was. One day, I thought, she'll tell me. One day, I thought, she'll sit right up and say, *Hey, Daddy, there were these three guys in a bar, and the first one said* . . . But of course she never did. Never will now.

But hey. All of that's past. I'm glad that I no longer think of how old she'd be today (twenty, twenty-one maybe) or what she'd be doing, or how, if my hands hadn't raised themselves that one last time, then she and her mother would not have burned in her daddy's beat-up car, and perhaps the three of us might have made some kind of family . . .

Perhaps.

Perhaps not.

Maybe I'm still deceiving myself. Maybe you cannot escape the patterns laid down for you. Or maybe you can, and I didn't. I don't know which is worse. All I do know is that things are handed down to you that are real hard to break, and that sometimes you just cannot help doing things you swore you'd never do. It's like you're driving in your car, just going your own way, when suddenly there's some kind of tracks in the road and you feel your wheels locking and you can no longer steer – you can't do anything, in fact, but look straight ahead and just wait for what was always going to happen to happen.

'When you're ready, soldier –'

'Ready?'

'We attack in an hour. That's assuming the general shows up.'

'He's not here?'

All of which, I know, is maybe crap. I just don't know anymore. Maybe we *are* in control – maybe there *is* nothing else, nobody else – maybe we *can* decide what we choose to hand on. Like I say, I don't know. I *have* thought sometimes that all the bad stuff is maybe just, like, something so hot that you either hang onto it and burn, or you pass it on to the next person, and then *they* either burn or pass it on, and so on. In which case, maybe my daddy was just passing on what was too hot for him, and what was too hot for him was too hot for me, and what was too hot for me wound up burning in that wreck – the wreck, incidentally, from which nothing was recovered but this.

Sure. Go ahead. Turn it over.

Apparently they found it under the burnt-out front seat. Of course the chain's gone now, but if you look close you can still make out the name – *Sundance D.*, see? – and some parts of the number. How it got there of course nobody knows.

Nobody, that is, now, except me. Clare knew because she'd caught her daddy one night, making out in that front seat with one of his students. A Vietnamese girl, she was – married a GI – our friend Mr Sundance. Seems she must have been wearing it as some kind of keepsake and then dropped it – and there it stayed until it was found in that wreck. To this day I still can't figure why Clare told me about it. Although maybe she was just handing something on. Maybe that was too hot for her to handle.

Anyway, I don't guess any of this stuff matters much anymore. All I guess that matters now is they somehow find the general and get this show on the road. Already there must be a thousand people here. You can see them from here, scattered down on the plains behind those ribbon kind of things the police use. Some of them are having picnics, and some of them are just sleeping in the sun, enjoying the day. All of them, of course, have come for one thing. They've come – every one of them – to see every one of us die.

139

Well, he's turned up, apparently, in the Jack Daniel's marquee – apparently somewhat the worse for wear. Some people are saying, of course, that he was just getting into the part – sort of acquainting himself with all the prevailing factors at the time, so as to give his forthcom-ing performance a greater ring of authenticity. Well, this would, of course, be all well and good were it not for the little (but significant) fact that Lieutenant-Colonel (brevet General) George Armstrong Custer was, ever since his second meeting with Elizabeth Bacon (as was), teetotal. Having promised abstinence from that day forward, he stuck to it, never once letting alcohol pass his lips again. Of course, were the part to be played today that of Custer's ultimate commander, former General, but now President Ulysses S. Grant, then drinking (and drinking to excess) would have been more than appropriate – and not just Grant, but pretty much any other soldier connected at the time in any way with this, the wild frontier.

But I digress.

The point is he's been found, and should soon be amongst us to lead us screaming down the hill, then back up again, where – on that rise over there (the one, yes, with the ghastly great memorial stone) – we shall all do our best to fight valiantly but in vain, until, of course, there is no one left standing but the general himself (another historical anomaly, but who cares?) – that is, if the general himself isn't, on this occasion, still too full of Jack Daniel's to stand.

In the meantime, though, we wait.

An exchange overheard amongst my fellow 'soldiers':

'You reckon we'll be through by dinnertime this year?'

'I don't know. Maybe. Depends what time they get our scalps.'

'Well, Jesus, they could have mine now. It's pork tonight. I ain't missing no pork.'

Well, now they've gone and lost him again. They had him, but he somehow got away. My guess is – this being his first time and all – he's taken a look at the size of this crowd (which must be close to fifteen hundred by now), not to mention the hordes of afternoon Indians with their cell-phones and tomahawks, and just done what Custer himself should have done – in other words, got the hell out of there and fast. Either that, or he's doing himself some personal scouting, which – though laudable in a way – would be just about as inappropriate as the drinking, given the fact that Long Hair that day was so confident (arrogant) that he claimed it didn't matter what any scouts he sent out might find as – one brave or one thousand – he seriously believed that his underfed, undertrained, mutinous Seventh Cavalry could whup them all like they were nothing but a bunch of silly schoolgirls on a trip.

None of which, of course, matters here today. Today is a day for fantasy: a day of warm, reassuring history – the history people want played out for them quite shamelessly in exchange for their dollars and cents. It's not real – but it's real entertaining. And after all, who on earth wants the truth when the fantasy's so sexy?

Speaking of fantasy, I have to admit that I cannot help but feel a certain pride in the manner of my revenge. How appropriate is it that a man – my father – who did nothing but lie to me should in the end – after all these years – be drawn to his death by such a clever little fantasy? Well, very is the answer. Which fantasy in particular?

Jesus. You mean you haven't guessed it?

Matthew

140

I f all evidence supports the notion that a man, once dead, has risen from the grave, then such evidence must also support one of two further assertions: firstly, that that man, though having given all outward indication that he was indeed dead, in fact was not; or, secondly, that that man was not a man at all, but some ghost or ghoul or fantasy bred of a sick and delirious mind.

Matthew kicked at the fire's dust, revealing the last of its still-glowing embers. He straightened at a sound, looked about him. High in the height of the hard blue sky, a vulture was wheeling and cawing. It had already feasted on more than one corpse, having plundered from several the eyes and tongues and other of the juiciest organs, and so was easily shifted by a stone thrown high. 'Yeah! Git!' Matthew called out as the bird, ever widening its circle, drifted, finally, away and was gone. He wiped the sweat from his forehead on his sleeve, dropped down to his haunches. He kneaded his crippled right hand with his left.

He'd known them to be corpses from way off – from way before he'd been sure they were soldiers. They'd had about them a stillness quite foreign to those merely sleeping. And besides, what man would not respond in such desolate emptiness to the call of another? No, they'd been dead alright, and he'd walked toward them with the quietness that most save for when approaching those who can no longer hear. The strange thing was that, the closer he'd got to them, the blacker they'd seemed to become, until, on clapping his hands (and Lord how that clapping had echoed), a great mask of flies had risen from each man, revealing, beneath, faces so distorted by the twisting of pain, so ruined by the great winged scavengers, that scarcely would a mother have recognized a son, or a wife a husband, such was their ghastly trans-formation. And of the twenty or so bodies, all had been mutilated – work having been performed on their flesh with such a careful ferocity that it could only have been the work of another man: no four-legged creature would see the sense in inflicting such pain so gratuitously, when a life can so swiftly be dispatched. No, this was man's work alright. Thighs had been slashed, revealing the white, bloodied bone within;

fingers had been severed and penises too – these last thrust, in most cases, into other men's mouths; ears had been punctured, their workings within ruptured by fine-pointed sticks; and, of course, scalps had been lifted, the flesh parted from bone with a surgeon's deft touch. All in all, what had until only recently been a circle of safety (the fire's embers were still warm) had become like a scene from some barely imaginable hell. There was nothing, now, of humanity here; there was only its absence, only the presence of merciful death.

He screwed up his eyes, trying to unsee what had already been seen. But it was no good. A sight seen once is a sight seen forever. He opened his eyes, let his head hang heavy between his knees. *All of them is slain, sir – all but one.* Sometimes these days he felt just so weary that he could scarcely raise the energy to breathe. *All of them is slain, sir.* He gathered up his knees, hugged them to him. *All of them is slain.* Sometimes these days all he wanted to do was to just close his eyes and lie back in the sun –

'Hey there –'

– and to lie there long enough for the dust of the earth to reclaim him for its own.

'Hey –'

Something sharp, then, in his side and he opened his eyes.

'So you *is* alive –'

'What?' In a scramble he tried to sit up (he was lying on his back now, the sky above him so bright he had to turn his head away), but the sole of a large dusty boot on his chest pushed him back. He struggled, squirming, but the boot held him firm – that, and the unmistakable priming of a new repeating rifle. 'Who are *you*?' he said. 'What do you want?'

'*Want?*' A spit and a laugh, then, from the silhouette above him. 'You think if you had something I wanted you'd still be alive?' The boot's pressure eased. Another spit. 'Listen, boy, you's just lucky I's a business-man – not some fuckin' bastard Indian –'

Matthew pushed up as the boot withdrew. His head and his heart were thumping hard, his side still smarting from the kick. He lifted his busted hand, sheltering his eyes.

The man was shorter than he'd first appeared – perhaps a shade above five foot – but broad, his thick neck supporting a closely shaved head, the flesh of his face so sun-dark and dirty that his age was impossible to guess. His clothes were disheveled and layer upon layer, the top one of which was a stained and dusty uniform of army blue and gold.

'Where'd you get that?' said Matthew.

The rifle still leveled, one-handed, at Matthew's head, the man, his chin pressed to his chest, considered himself. 'You mean this old thing?'

he said. He looked up. He was smiling, his smile half-concealed in a frown. 'Well, let me see now.' He raised his free hand, so as to cradle his chin. 'Hmm,' he said, then he brightened. 'Yes now, *I* remember. I was riding along one day, just minding my own business, when I comes across a whole group of you brave soldier-boys, and I says to them, real friendly-like, you boys have a need for something I could maybe supply? Well, silence is what I get for my trouble – ain't none of them even bother to look at me – like I was so ugly it was catchin' or something. Anyhow, I's about to ride away, when I sees that one of them boys ain't got no eyes and his dick's where his tongue shoulda been, and then, well Jesus, I sees ain't none of them got throats that ain't been cut, and *between them* they ain't got enough fingers to play no piano – and so you know what? Well, I figures them brave soldier-boys is, well, dead, and, consequently, will be having no further use for their shiny new uniforms, and so I borrows one – borrows it, mind, until such a time as the good Lord Himself sends me up to heaven to join them boys, whereupon I shall return of course what is rightfully theirs. In the meantime, though, waste not, as they say, want not.'

'Well, *I* ain't dead,' said Matthew, his heart still racing hard. He squinted at the tip of the rifle's shiny barrel.

'No, sir,' said the man. 'You's alive alright.' Smiling, he lowered the rifle and, with his free hand, reached inside his clothes and pulled out a silver cigarette case. This he opened, one-handed, and withdrew from it a fine eastern cigarette which he placed with some care between his lips. Exchanging, then, the case for a match, he lit the thing with a flick of his thumb. He took a drag, sighing as he breathed out a thin trail of smoke. 'And you know why that is?' he said.

'Why what is?' said Matthew.

'Why you's still alive.'

The silver case was somehow familiar – but he couldn't – not for the life of him – think from where. He shrugged. 'Let me guess,' he said. 'Because of you?'

'Me, sir? Oh no, sir,' said the man. 'I was just the . . . how can I say?' He frowned harder, as if searching for something; then, again, he brightened, shifting the rifle to his spare hand. He raised up his shooting hand, first finger extended. 'No, sir,' he said. 'I's just the one with my finger on the trigger, see? I ain't the man that made that trigger *possible* – no, sir, uh-uh. *That* man's the man you want to thank.'

'I don't know what you're saying,' said Matthew.

'You don't? Well, I guess you ain't never heard of Mr Zee –'

'Mr who?'

'Which is why you ain't no businessman. To be a businessman like me you gotta *know* stuff. You gotta *see* stuff. It ain't just about giving people what they want – no, sir. That's the easy bit. Way before that, you gotta show people who's been livin' for centuries what they can't live one more day without.' He lifted the rifle. 'Like this little baby. People don't *need* this – they only *need* it when they *got* it. And when they's got it, well, that's history. You think it's Mr Grant in his White House that's in charge of things out here? No, sir. He's just decoration. Manifest destiny and all that shit. No, sir, it's Mr Zee as rules the fuckin' plains, and then folks like me. This war ain't about the rights of white people – it's about business. And you know what? The army wins or loses – it don't matter. The government wins or loses? Don't matter. Only thing that matters is business – and business never loses.'

Matthew shook his head. He looked about him. 'You're saying *this* is business?'

'Sure it is. It's the *only* business. Well, nearly. War and haircutting. Them's the only businesses to be in. People always gonna kill each other and hair always gonna grow.'

'*Their* hair ain't gonna grow,' he said.

The man shrugged. 'I guess not.' He shook his head, looked about him. 'Fuckin' savages,' he said. Then he smiled.

'What's so funny?'

'Ah, nothin'.'

'Then why are you smiling?'

Another shrug, another drag on his cigarette. 'I guess I was just thinking of them old boys' faces when they saw their first repeater. Holy Jesus, you'd have thought they was seeing some kind of fuckin' miracle! *Again*, they kept saying, *again*, *again*, until I don't know how many rounds I must have wasted just shootin' at that tree – in fact, I'd probably still be there now if Crazy Horse himself hadn't shown up when he did –'

'Crazy Horse? You've *seen* Crazy Horse?'

'Seen him? Seen him? *Sure* I seen him. It was me what told him about our friend Mr Custer. "Look, now," I said, "there's just one thing you need to know about old Mr C – and that's what he's holding in his hand – and I don't mean his dick! I mean," I said, "he may be one mighty fine officer – not to mention a gentleman of the highest order – but unless he gets his hands on these here babies before you do then he better start shaving that head of his before you boys do it for him!" Well now, that was it. I couldn't have got rid of them rifles quicker if I'd given them away for free! No, sir. I tell you, those boys – Jesus, you'd have thought it was Christmas the way they was whooping and hollering – in fact they got so damned lively, what with shootin' them rifles and drinkin' that celebrating whiskey I sold 'em, that I don't mind telling you I was mighty glad to get outta there when I did before they started practicing on me!' He frowned, dropped the cigarette in the dust. 'Say – what's the matter with you?'

Matthew shook his head. He couldn't believe what he'd heard. He felt sick. He looked up. 'Do you know what you've done?' he said. 'Do you have any idea?'

'What I've done? What d'you mean, what I've done? *I've* made me a profit – that's what *I've* done. Which, in case you've been wondering, is the American way.'

'But –'

'But what?'

'Ah, Jesus, you've betrayed your own people – your own *kind* –'

'*My own kind?* Fuck my own kind! They ain't *my* people. My people's the people who's gonna *survive*. And besides, you think any one of these bastards ever gave a shit about me – huh? Well, do you?'

'Well –'

'Well, no, sir. They did not. And let me tell you, *mister soldier-boy*, if they's so dumb as to march into somebody else's country and say *This is my country now, so you can all just git*, then they ain't learned nothin' and they ain't *never* gonna learn nothin' neither – 'cept of course what it feels like to suck dick – not to mention getting yourself a haircut so close that you ain't gonna never need no barber again.'

'But you said yourself they're savages –'

'Of course they's savages, the goddamn bastards! But you think you ain't – just 'cause you got them fancy uniforms? No, sir – I seen what you Sherman boys done in Georgia. I seen women so wasted by the rapin' you boys gave 'em that they's beggin' me to cut 'em so they can't feel no more. No, sir. Don't you talk none about savages.'

Matthew opened his mouth to speak, but no words came.

The man looked about him. 'Now I'm gettin' out of here,' he said. 'You want a ride?'

'What?'

'Or is you plannin' to stay here and bury the dead? 'Cause if you is, then I strongly advise you fix yourself a hole too, as them red boys ain't never gonna let you get away –'

'Then what about you?'

'Me? Oh, they ain't gonna kill *me*. No, sir. I's the golden goose. And besides, who else is gonna scare the Yankee shit out of Custer by tellin' him the Sioux got their hands on repeaters?'

'But if *they* don't get you – the *general* will, for sure –'

'You reckon?'

'Jesus – you've been sellin' arms to the enemy!'

'*Me*, sir? *No*, sir! I ain't *seen* they got them guns, I just *heard*. And besides, me being such a democrat, you think I ain't gonna help out my brothers? You think I ain't gonna even things up?'

'What do you mean?'

The man shook his head. 'Jesus, you really ain't no businessman.' He cocked his head to one side. 'Now tell me,' he said. 'What is it the army's gonna need when old Crazy Horse and his boys come at 'em with repeaters, huh? You think they gonna be happy with them old single-shot?'

'Jesus,' said Matthew.

'No, sir,' said the man. 'The name's Jimmy, and I ain't dying on no cross. No, sir. When I die I'm gonna slip away real quiet in my bed.' He straightened up. 'Now, you comin' or what?'

'No, I ain't coming.'

'Please yourself.'

He picked his way, then, through the bodies to his wagon. The wagon was open, heaving with wooden boxes and all kinds of other things, all of it rope-tied and secure. He climbed up onto the board, picked up the reins. 'You sure now?' he said. 'Ain't nobody else comin' through here.'

Matthew said nothing. Instead he looked away, out across the plains to the far-distant hills. *I strongly advise you fix yourself a hole.* He turned back. The wagon, already, was growing smaller, already disappearing in the dust from its wheels.

141

In those days, Fort Abraham Lincoln (in what is now North Dakota, but was, then, simply *out* there) was the last chance for a man to sleep sound in his bed, or to eat at a table, or to shelter, in summer, from the burning western sun, or the snow, in winter, that climbed over your boots and then over your belt – freezing your bones until your very soul was chilled – until, in the end, you'd forgotten what heat was, or the comforts to be had in simply being alive. Moreover, the fort, in those days, was the last hope a man had outside of his dreams to hear with his own ears the voice of a woman as she laughed with her husband (always an officer – but *still*), or to bathe in the pallor of her smooth marble skin, or to watch her – see the twisting of her skirts – as she crossed the parade ground on some lady's errand, her face cast cool in the shadow of her parasol. In those days, indeed, though primitive and harsh, the life of the fort was, to many (and, indeed, would become so for many more), the last of life itself – for beyond it lay a wilderness of vast untold miles – of day after day of hard-riding plains, of the fear on every rise of some sleek silhouette, and in every night-time wolf's-howl of some secret coded call that was nothing more nor less than the broadcast invitation to a slaughtering.

'And your business is?'

'My business, soldier, is with the general.'

'I see. And yours?'

Already down from the wagon, Matthew Princeton saluted. 'My business is to fight.'

'Fight?' The sergeant at the gates turned to his companions – a motley-looking group lounging outside in the shade of the fort's wooden walls. 'Man here says he's come to fight,' he said. 'You boys know anything about that?'

'Fight?' said one of the group – a thin boy with a face raw with acne. 'No, sir – don't know nothin' 'bout no fighting.' Those around him sniggered; he himself beamed, pleased to have so amused his elders.

The sergeant turned back. 'Look, lieutenant, sir,' he said, 'I think you got the wrong army. We ain't doin' no fightin' today.'

Matthew frowned – he was weary from the ride and didn't need this kind of shit. 'No, *you* look,' he said; he could feel his heart-rate rising. 'You open these gates right now –'

'Or what?' said the sergeant. Again he turned, smiling, to his companions in the shade, then back. 'You gonna have me court-martialed? And then what? They gonna send me out here to this fuckin' place?' The smile bled away. He stepped forward, until he was nose to nose with Matthew. 'I got news for you, lieutenant. I'm already here. I ain't got *nothin'* more to lose.'

From above, then, the double-click loading of a Remington repeater. 'You got your balls, ain't you?'

The sergeant looked up, shielding his eyes against the sun. 'Say what?' he said.

'I said,' said Jimmy Forder, 'you got your balls to lose.' Squinting, he aimed the thing with care, dropping the barrel's end lower and lower until it was pointing directly at the area just below the sergeant's buckle. Jimmy smiled. 'Or maybe you ain't,' he said, still squinting. 'Maybe when I shoot this thing I'm gonna find I shot me a pussy.' He looked up from his aiming. 'Now then,' he said. 'You gonna do what the nice lieutenant says, or shall I make you another hole so big between your legs that you can take all your buddies on at once?' He glanced to the group in the shade; to a man they were staring, the tongue lolling out of the acne-boy's mouth like he was some weird kind of two-legged cow.

For a moment, then, a stand-off – just the far-off sound of voices from inside the fort. Then, stiffly, his eyes still considering the rifle, the sergeant turned his head, barked out an order. He turned back, staring hard and with venom at a smiling Jimmy Forder, as the great wooden doors opened up and the wagon rolled in, its journey for the moment complete.

142

'So where the hell *is* everybody?'

'Sir?'

Matthew Princeton was standing by the flagpole in the center of the open parade ground, scanning the scene, his eyes screwed up tight against the sun.

'The general – the Seventh. Where are they?'

'The Seventh, sir? Why, they've gone, sir.'

'Gone?'

'Yes, sir. They left for the west four days ago, sir.'

'*Four days?*'

'Yes, sir.'

He pointed to a half-dozen high-polished cannon lined up outside the low wooden armory block. 'No, sir,' he said. 'This cannot be –'

'But, sir, I assure you –'

He lowered his arm, turned to the corporal. 'Are you telling me,' he said, 'the general left without his guns?'

'Well, yes, sir. I believe he said they'd slow him down.' He paused. 'He sent back the sabres, too.'

'The sabres?'

He pointed to the boxes like small coffins being unloaded from a wagon just inside the gates. 'He said even his old single-shots was gonna be all he needs against bows and arrows –'

'Oh my Lord,' said Matthew.

'Sir? Is everything alright, sir?'

'When did you say he left?'

'Er, four days ago, sir. Heading for the Big Horn river, sir. Sir?'

'What?'

'Well, I was wondering, sir –'

'Wondering what?'

'Well, sir, if your friend might be carrying any vegetables –'

'My friend?'

'With the wagon, sir. Would you know if he's carrying any, say, potatoes?'

Matthew was staring back out through the gates and across the open plains, as if he were trying to see there General Custer and his regiment of men.

'Sir?'

'I'm sorry,' he said. 'What were you saying?'

The corporal sighed. 'Oh, it don't matter, sir,' he said. He cleared his throat. 'If you'll excuse me, sir?'

'What?'

'I'm on duty, sir –'

'Yes, of course.' Matthew waved the man away. The man paused a few steps off, turned.

'Sir? Will you be requiring quarters, sir?'

Matthew shook his head. No, he said, he wouldn't be requiring quarters. All he'd be requiring was a good horse and rations.

'Very good, sir.'

'And a soldier,' he said. 'Someone to watch the wagon.'

'The wagon, sir?'

'My friend,' he said. 'He and I are going riding. You too – if you choose to.'

'Me, sir?'

'You, sir,' said Matthew. 'Or perhaps you'd rather stay here.'

'Here, sir? *No*, sir.'

'Good,' he said. 'Good. Now – my friend. Did you see where he went?'

143

'Sir, I believe he's with the general's wife.'

'*What?*'

'Mrs Custer, sir. I understand he said he had some business to attend to –'

For a man to find himself thinking again – or, indeed, acting – in a way that he'd come to think impossible is unsettling – particularly so when he'd come to believe such thoughts and actions gone forever – that they'd passed away with the passing, forever, of innocent youth.

'Business?'

'Yes, sir.'

Matthew crossed the parade ground, heading for the general's house. Reaching the steps, however, he paused. It was unnerving to feel suddenly this old twist of conscience (what, after all, was Custer to him? Well, nothing now, of course, nothing), and it made him feel a little dizzy. He grasped the wooden rail, as the sound of a man's voice drifted out through an open, first-floor window. He closed his eyes. Oh, for sure it was crazy, all crazy. What could such a man mean to him now? Now – after all that had happened? He shook his head. Nothing is what – no, sir. For God's sake, all those years ago now, had *Custer* ever cared for anybody but himself? No, he had not. It had always been Custer for Custer – always *his* glittering career that counted – the career of a bone-headed West Point no-hoper (for heaven's sake, there had even, lately, been talk of him for President in the fall) built entirely on the backs of fallen comrades, their lives so carelessly, so *enthusiastically* spent – and all for what? For *him* – always for *him*. No, sir, the glorious slaughtering of Antietam, the Wilderness, even Gettysburg itself – all of it nothing but the willful, profligate sacrifice of others – and always all to that great god, General George Armstrong Custer.

Again the sound of voices. He looked up. *Custer.* He turned away. *Let him ride,* he thought, let all of them ride, let them ride as good as naked into that savage, raking fire. Let them all die, and let their deaths be a lesson to all in the future who would follow such a madman –

His boots slowed in the dust. *A lesson,* he thought, *to fools such as I.*

Closing his eyes again, he held back his head, felt the burning again of the spiteful noon sun.

'Sir? Are you alright, sir?'

He lowered his head, opened his eyes.

'Did you find him, sir?'

'Find him?' he said.

'Your friend, sir.'

Antietam, the Wilderness, Gettysburg.

'Sir?'

He nodded. 'Yes, I found him,' he said.

'Then we ride, do we, sir?'

He hesitated a moment, but then shook his head. 'No, corporal,' he said. 'We don't ride. Not today.'

'Sir?'

He unhooked the sabre from his belt, unbuttoned his tunic. 'Now,' he said. 'Those quarters you mentioned. I assume they're still available?'

'Why, yes, sir. But –'

Matthew raised a hand. 'I'd be obliged,' he said, 'if you'd just point the way. It's been a long ride and I've a need to rest up. Also whiskey,' he said. 'I'd be obliged if you'd bring me a bottle. Can you do that, corporal?'

'Yes, sir,' said the corporal. 'This way, sir.' He turned, then, and Matthew followed him, aware as he did so of the movement around him like some slow, seductive dance, of his harsh black midday shadow.

144

H e lay still. He closed his eyes, but couldn't sleep. One of maybe forty in the long barrack-room, the bed was hard, the mattress meager. He turned onto his side, gazed along the two opposite lines. Each one of them, now – each bed – was unoccupied, its resident gone, perhaps never to return. On each, instead, as if it were some kind of reminder, some kind of hostage, perhaps, guaranteeing a return, sat a neatly folded blanket; above each, on the wall, was fixed a small iron hook, now empty.

Again, he closed his eyes; but, again, sleep would not come. He turned over, lay on his back. He lay quiet, barely breathing, just listening to the sounds of the day.

The journey's beginning seemed so long ago now – Miss Eliot, the whorehouse, the governor and his pictures, all just like memories from some other, past life. And Clare, and the baby – *his* baby: for a while, she at least had meant *something* to him – his shame at selling images of her unprotected body so sharp within him that he felt like he'd swallowed some spiky kind of creature which would never pass through him like so much had passed through him. But even that – that pain – had been smothered in time by the numbness – that unfeelingness – that had come then to claim him – that had come to protect him with insulation so thick, so impenetrable, that nothing – not even joy – could any longer get through.

Not, of course, that it mattered anymore. No, sir. She was gone – *they* were gone – slain by some madman, while he – their protector – had stood aside, just looking away, just waiting for that freedom the deed would surely bring.

Freedom.

Some freedom.

Oh, how could he have been so foolish? How come he hadn't known that in a human man there can be no freedom from the censure of conscience, and that life without conscience – without the reassurance of its borders – would, anyway, not be a life lived in the absence of chains, but a life lived out in some vast open prison, where no extreme is extreme enough, where no night is dark enough, no day bright enough, and no kind deed the act of a friend, but always the sly, grotesque posturing of an enemy wreathed in smiles.

He lifted his good arm, covered his eyes. Faces moved in the darkness, drifting off, coming closer. *Are you happy, Matthew Princeton?* He lowered his arm, opened his eyes. One face in particular – her face – would not be vanquished, even by the light. *Will you love us, now that we're two?* He sat up – he was sweating – set his boots on the floor. *Are you happy?* He was breathing hard, his chest fighting for air. He stood, unsteady – he had to have air. He turned to the window. Barred. *Oh Jesus*, he whispered (though there was no one there to hear it), *oh merciful Jesus, help me, I'm drowning* – Then, groping like a blindman, he made his way between the beds, the sweat streaming in his eyes, until he somehow found the door, the cool brass of a handle, and was moving, then, stumbling, out into the light.

145

M inutes passed then, slow as hours. He stood in the dirt, staring out toward the flagpole – looking toward it alright, but not seeing it. Neither was he seeing the empty stables beyond, nor the rising in the distance of brown baking hills, nor, indeed, the sky, nor, beyond that, the heavens. No. It was nothing Matthew Princeton was considering – complete, perfect emptiness – that which, now with the good grace of life in his lungs, he knew filled his heart as surely as a canteen held down below the surface of a creek will expel all its air and replace it in moments with clear, neutral water.

'Lieutenant?'

Reluctant, finished, he turned.

'Have you come with news?'

'News?' he said.

'Of my husband.'

'Your husband?'

'My husband, the *general*, sir. Were you perhaps dispatched with a letter?'

He shook his head. 'No, ma'am.'

Libbie Custer looked down at her hands, started picking at the lace of one gloved hand with the other. Even against the fort's squat buildings, which themselves were dwarfed by the vast surrounding lands, she seemed tiny, her waist no bigger than that which a man could circle with his thumbs and, perhaps, second fingers.

Matthew looked away. Once it would have thrilled him to be in the presence of such a beauty (her eyes were so dark, for sure a man could not stand long in their gaze without dreaming of death and some new life with her to come); once, but so long ago now. 'I'm sorry, ma'am,' he said. Now, for so long untouched, he fancied he'd become untouchable.

'Sorry?' she said. 'Why, if there's no letter there's no letter, and that's an end of it.' She half-turned, paused. 'Have we met, sir?'

'Met, ma'am?'

'*Before*, I mean.'

'I think not, ma'am.'

She frowned. 'But you know the general?'

'Indeed, ma'am. Everyone knows the general.'

'Quite so.' She turned away again; again she paused. 'Would you care for some tea, sir?'

'Tea, ma'am?'

'I've just purchased some – I'll admit from a very unpleasant fellow – and I'm simply longing to try it. Will you not sit with me? It's so sad, I always think, to take tea alone. The President says not a soul does in England –' She paused, gave a sigh. 'But then, I suppose, the world's drinking habits are something of a *hobby* for Mr Grant, are they not?'

'I couldn't say,' said Matthew.

'Well, *I* could,' said Libbie. She smiled; the smile paled. 'Though I don't suppose I shall. After all, Mr Grant has his spies everywhere, does he not?' She cocked her head, brighter. 'Are *you* a spy, lieutenant?'

'A spy, ma'am?' said Matthew. 'No, ma'am. I believe I should not find employment with Mr Pinkerton and his friends.'

Libbie frowned. 'No, sir? And why is that?'

'Well, ma'am, I believe I am too –' He hesitated, trying to isolate something in his head.

'Too *what*, sir?'

'Too . . .'

'Honest, perhaps?'

'Ah, no, ma'am –'

'Then you are *dis*honest?'

He shook his head, looked away. 'I believe I am neither, ma'am,' he said. 'I believe . . . I believe I am too . . . *weary*, ma'am, for either.'

'Weary?'

'Weary, ma'am.'

Libbie nodded. 'Well, in that case,' she said, 'I believe I have the answer.' A rustling of skirts; Matthew turned.

'The answer, ma'am?'

'Yes, sir,' she said. 'According to an *acquaintance* of mine – a very *recent* acquaintance, mind, and to be sure a most *unpleasant* one – the answer to everything that might ail any kind of living creature is the same.'

'Tea?' said Matthew.

'Indeed,' said Libbie, and she smiled, and – seeing her smile – Matthew smiled too.

'Ten minutes, then,' she said.

He nodded, bowed. 'Ten minutes, ma'am,' he said.

They sat in the cool of the parlor, awaiting tea. The only sound, beside the occasional creaking of their stiff-backed, upright chairs, was the dull tick-tocking of a grandfather clock.

'Well now,' said Libbie.

Matthew looked away from the window. 'Ma'am?' Outside, on the parade ground, the remainder of the garrison (aside, that is, from those too sick to ride) were lining up in the heat for inspection.

Libbie looked down at her hands, laid palms-down in the lap of her skirts. She lifted one hand, placed it gently on the other. She looked up. 'I believe, sir, you're a photographer,' she said.

'*Was*, ma'am,' said Matthew.

'You are no longer?'

'I am a soldier, ma'am.'

'Yes, of course.'

Silence. Muffled calls from the parade ground. He cleared his throat. 'You've a fine room,' he said.

Libbie nodded.

He looked about him.

'Do you not miss it?'

'Miss it, ma'am?'

The parlor was a long room with a high-polished floor, in the center of which, but a little to one side, sat a large dark piano.

'Photography.'

Above the piano, in pride of place, was a photograph of General Custer's favorite general – himself.

'No, ma'am.'

'Not at all?'

'Not at all, ma'am. It was so –' He stopped.

'Lieutenant?'

'Long ago, ma'am. It was so long ago.'

A rattling of cups, then, on a tray, the clipping of footsteps approaching.

'So you gave it up for soldiering.'

'I was always a soldier.'

Dismissing the servant-girl with a wave of her hand, Libbie lifted the teapot's lid and peered inside. 'Always?' she said.

'Since the war, that is, ma'am.'

She replaced the lid. 'You knew the general in the war?'

Matthew nodded.

'You served with him?'

'I served with him, ma'am.'

The tea was rich and dark and left a stain like a shadow on the fine china cups. When he was through drinking, Matthew rose. He cast a glance outside. The parade ground, now, was empty, the only movement that of the flagpole's ropes as they drifted to and fro in the usual late-afternoon breeze. He turned back. Mrs Custer was, again, looking down at her hands, but with an unblinking stare that made you feel that the subject of that stare was so far away now as to be beyond sight – to all, that is, but her.

'Ma'am?'

She blinked, looked up, pitched up a smile. 'You're going, lieutenant – so soon?'

'I must, ma'am.'

'You've orders?'

'Orders, ma'am? Well, no –'

'Well then, lieutenant. It seems the army can spare you. I, however, cannot.'

'Ma'am?'

Matthew felt his heart sinking as the general's wife rose. She stepped with a swish of her long, stiff skirts between the chairs, and clipped on tiny shoes across the high-polished floor. Once at the piano, she gathered her skirts and sat. She lifted the lid. Then, without introduction, she began playing – first, 'How Great Thou Art,' then, 'Nearer My God To Thee.'

'Do you play, lieutenant?' she said when she was through, the last chord fading.

Matthew shook his head. He opened his mouth and was about to somehow insist on his leaving, when the wife of the general stood up abruptly. For a moment, then, she seemed incredibly fierce – as if she might send the piano's lid crashing down. Matthew braced himself; but, as swiftly as it had come, the moment of crisis passed. She lowered the lid with exaggerated care. Without looking up, she said, 'More tea?'

Matthew shook his head. 'Thank you, no, ma'am.' He studied Libbie's face, tried to find in it some clue as to what she was thinking. He found none. It was as if that part of her – the part, perhaps, that made her whole – were absent.

'I want to ask you something,' she said.

'Ma'am?' said Matthew, though he knew what was coming. He'd seen it before – that look. It was the look of someone who, in the absence of another, is only half alive. It was the look of a child who looks out between his fingers and still cannot see in the darkness of night that long-promised, overdue, slow-rising dawn.

He shook his head. 'I cannot, ma'am,' he said. 'I no longer have the skill.' He turned toward the door, though he knew he was doomed. He reached, without hope, for the handle.

146

'**P**lease – you must be still.'

Collodion, bromide, iodide of potassium, ammonia, cadmium, gun-cotton, sulphuric ether, alcohol, nitrate of silver: these the substances, these the smells – these and other things – glass-plates and lenses, telescoping legs and a once-polished but now scuffed and dusty wood and brass box, a curtain of thick purple velvet – these – all this – just to freeze faces in a smile, or to capture for all time (or for at least as long as the image doesn't fade) a solemn group of soldiers with their muskets and their uniforms, and their childlike, staring eyes –

'Ma'am, I said *still* –'

– pleading eyes, eyes already doomed, eyes set blankly in faces already half-dead.

'May I not *breathe*, sir?'

Stepping back, ducking, withdrawing thus from his heavy velvet shroud, Matthew Princeton straightened up. He sighed. 'Ma'am,' he said, regretting already how easily he'd let himself agree to all this. 'If you cannot sit still, then I cannot do my work.'

Mrs Custer was frowning –

'Ma'am?'

– staring hard at the photograph over the piano. 'Do you think he is well, sir?' she said.

'Well, ma'am?'

Matthew followed her gaze. The picture was the famous one – the one copied by artists for all the eastern papers – the great Indian fighter in three-quarter profile, hair flowing down from beneath his cavalry hat, mustache neatly groomed, cool, determined eyes fixed on some far-off quaking foe.

'Well, do you, sir?'

Matthew turned his weary head. Libbie Custer, now, was looking right at him – looking hard, now, as if she half-hoped to find there some news – some news, or at least some encouraging lie.

'Well, sir?'

Again, he turned to the photograph, aware of the eyes upon him.

'Do you not feel it?'

He shrugged. He wanted to say, *But it's only a photograph – only a lie masquerading as truth*, but something inside of him would not permit the heresy. 'Really, ma'am,' he said, 'I'm sure the general is quite well.' He paused, then, let his gaze rest respectfully a moment on the general's boyish features; then he turned away, turning back to the matter in hand. 'Ma'am?' he said. 'Shall we continue?'

Libbie nodded. 'Of course,' she said, and she tried a smile. Then, settling herself, she straightened her shoulders, preparing herself as well as she was able to sit in their parlor below her husband's fearsome gaze quite as still and as rigid as a corpse.

147

B odies mangled, twisted; bodies crying out, silent, in frozen, painless pain; sleeping bodies that will never again in this life awaken; limbless bodies; bodies without heads; the comedy of heads without bodies: these and more – much more – are his memories now. The sights – and then the smells: the sweet, acrid stink of swelling, rotting flesh, the sourness of gangrene in an untreated wound. Oh, the sights, the smells, and, of course, the sounds.

The silence.

But not silence. The distant moaning of men not dead, yet, but dying; the gnawing of rats at a cold blue carcass; the whistling of thieves in the dusk.

Stillness.

But not stillness.

A tapping on the window.

Even in the vast, misty fields of death, already the grotesque sounds of life re-emerging.

'*Hey, mister lieutenant* –'

The appalling joy of birdsong in the trees, the curling and twisting of worms in the earth.

More tapping, harder. He opened his eyes.

'*Hey* –'

Slowly, reluctant, he lifted his head. Bleary-eyed, he looked about him. The barrack-room, as before, was deserted; the beds, as before, neat and empty.

'Hey, soldier-boy! Wakey-wakey!'

He twisted round, toward the window. *Oh Jesus*. He sighed a heavy sigh. He swung his legs round, set his boots on the rough, wooden floor. 'What do you *want*?' he said. His head was still blurry from his dreaming.

Jimmy Forder motioned for him to open the window.

'Fuck you,' said Matthew, cradling his head, but Jimmy Forder just smiled, dipped down. In a moment he was lying on the next bed to Matthew's, his hands behind his head, and smoking – no hands – an enormous, cheap cigar. Squirreling the thing to one side of his mouth, he said, 'Well?'

Matthew lifted his head. 'Well, what?' His dreams, this time, had been oh-so-acute that it was tough, even now, to believe that dreams – the mind's make-believe – was all they were.

'The picture,' Jimmy Forder said, beaming. 'You did get it – didn't you? The photograph, lieutenant mister sir, of the sad but remarkable widow?'

'What?'

He raised his hands, squared up before him an imaginary newspaper. '*The Widow Mourns*,' he said grandly, thumbs and first-fingers already blocking the text.

Matthew squinted hard. 'What the fuck are you talking about?'

Jimmy Forder sat up. 'I'm *talking*, lieutenant, sir, about *business* –'

'Business? What business?'

He blew out his cheeks. 'Fuck, man,' he said, 'you's hard work. Ain't you never heard of the people's right to know? And ain't you never heard neither of Jimmy Forder's right to let the people know what it's their right to know?'

'You're crazy,' said Matthew.

'You think so, colonel?'

'It's lieutenant.'

Jimmy Forder raised his eyebrows. 'For now, maybe,' he said.

'What do you mean?'

'What I mean, lieutenant, is no way the American people gonna stand for the man who tried heroically – though, sadly, unsuccessfully – to rescue General George Armstrong Custer from getting blown to pieces by savages with superior fire-power, being anything less than a *colonel* –'

'You *are* fucking crazy.'

'Maybe even a *general*!' Jimmy Forder sat forward. 'Just think of it, lieutenant. Our next likely President, President God-help-us-all-Custer, sadly – but gloriously – fails to return. So, then, the nation weeps, and, while they're weeping, who should come along but *another* brave soldier – a soldier, that is, with a tear in his eye and four-stars on his shoulder – a hero reluctant, of course, in fact, *absolutely determined* he ain't good enough to serve, but who, in time, pushed forward by the popular will, reluctantly relents – then bingo!'

'*Bingo?*'

'Bingo! I give you the nineteenth President of the United States – President – President – what's your name?'

'Princeton,' said Matthew.

'Perfect! President Princeton! Hail to the Chief!'

Matthew shook his head.

'What's wrong, Mister President?'

'Me. When I said you were crazy *I* was wrong. You're insane – completely fucking insane. I ought to get someone to shoot you –'

'What?'

'Before you start frothing at the mouth.'

'But, Mr President –'

Matthew stood up sharply. 'Stop calling me that!' he said. He felt a little dizzy. He took a few steps, breathing deeply. Slowly, he regained his balance. He turned. 'Look,' he said, forcing himself to stay calm. 'I don't know why you won't leave me alone – but I wish you would –'

'Ah, now, Mr *President* –'

'And you want to know why? *Because*, you pathetic, vicious, low-down piece of shit, I detest you. You are *nothing*. You are *scum*. You make your foul living by profiting from the death of others – brave men, who are trying to do nothing but defend you and your country from a bunch of fucking savages – and what makes me even sicker than just *looking* at you is how you seem to be *proud* of it. Jesus Christ, you're not a *man* – you're some kind of . . . some kind of . . . *fucking whore*. Now, get the fuck out of here –'

'Now?' said Jimmy Forder, sitting back and relighting his cigar.

'Yeah now –'

'Or you'll what?' he said, blowing out a great cloud of smoke. He sat forward. 'You'll shoot me again?'

'What?' said Matthew.

'Well, go on, then.'

Matthew shook his head. 'I'm not gonna shoot you,' he said.

'So what *are* you going to do?'

Good question: Matthew hadn't a clue.

'*Well*, lieutenant?'

148

'You must reach him, lieutenant. Warn him.'

'Ma'am, I cannot.'

'Cannot?'

'Besides, the general said himself that with the Seventh alone he could whup the whole Sioux nation –'

'But you must,' said Libbie. 'You are the general's friend –'

'I am hardly that, ma'am –'

'But you served in the war –'

'I did, ma'am. Antietam.'

Libbie brightened. 'Antietam?'

'Yes, ma'am –'

'Then you'd know my husband's bravery. You'd know how he suffered for the cause –'

'Ma'am?'

Libbie frowned. 'What is it?' she said.

Matthew looked away.

'Lieutenant?'

'It's nothing, ma'am. Look, please don't excite yourself in this way. The general will soon return victorious. I am sure of it.'

Saying nothing, Libbie crossed to the window. For days now she'd felt it – felt something – a feeling – nagging at her. But only this morning had the feeling coalesced into something she could see. She could see it now.

'Ma'am? Won't you sit? Can I ring for some lemonade?'

It was a corpse, white as bone bleached in the sun, a pair of blue eyes gazing up to the heavens. She shook her head. 'No, sir,' she said. 'You are wrong.'

'Wrong, ma'am?'

She turned. With her back to the light, her figure dropped dark into shadow, as if she were suddenly dressed in the deep black of mourning.

'Ma'am? Should I perhaps fetch the fort surgeon?'

'The surgeon?' she said. 'What for?'

'Well, you seem a little . . . a little, well . . . unsteady.'

As if, then, to challenge this, she moved away from the window, made her way between the chairs and crossed to the piano. This she circled, pausing then, looking up at the picture of her husband. 'Did you know, lieutenant,' she said, 'that the general was once promised a bear?'

'A bear, ma'am?'

'From some count or other. A Russian. It was during the war. The man said he would send it. Said it would be a gift from the people of Russia. "A gift of admiration" is what he said. I remember it distinctly. "A gift of admiration." Of course it never arrived. For a year we waited for it – but nothing.' A pause, then, 'Did you know that the great Russian bear has a memory better than an elephant? And they're loyal, too. The general said he was told that such a bear will never forget if its master's badly treated, and that one day – when everything's been forgotten – it'll strike in revenge. That's why some people say they're cunning, and others say they're just vicious.'

'*Ma'am* –'

She turned her head. 'Did you know that, lieutenant?'

'Ma'am, I really think you should try to calm yourself –'

She frowned. 'Calm myself? But I am perfectly calm. It is you, sir, who should perhaps see the surgeon –'

'Me, ma'am?'

'Or perhaps you already have –'

'Ma'am?'

'Perhaps you are *sick*, sir?'

'Sick? No, ma'am, I am well – quite well –'

'Then, perhaps, sir, you are a *coward* –'

'*What?*'

Libbie Custer was breathing heavy, clasping her gloved hands together. 'Or perhaps . . .' she said, stumbling, her eyes darting this way and that, searching the floor as if for some fast-moving spider, 'perhaps . . .' Suddenly, then, she looked up. 'Will you not go, sir? she said. 'Will you not go?'

Matthew shook his head.

'But the general must be warned –'

'I am no coward, ma'am,' he said, aware as he did so that a coward was precisely what he'd been for so long – and what he was still.

'What?' said Libbie.

And he thought of the whorehouse, of Clare and their child. 'I said, ma'am –' he started – but he couldn't repeat such an obvious – such a wretched – lie. 'Look,' he said instead, 'the general has scouts – Bloody Knife . . .' The general's wife, though, was already halfway across the room. 'Ma'am,' he said, 'I'm certain that if the general requires any intelligence –'

She stopped before her French writing table, from which – from a secret, hidden drawer – she withdrew a folded slip of paper. This she studied a moment, turning it over and over in her hands, as if she were satisfying herself as to its authenticity.

'Ma'am –'

Then she carried it, cradling it in her palms, like some ancient, priceless jewel, to where Matthew was standing.

'Look, ma'am, I'm sure the general is safe,' he said, though of course this, too, was a lie (for how *could* he be sure, for God's sake, when he knew the truth – when – thanks to that lying, threatening piece of shit Jimmy Forder – he knew the real danger?) – 'in fact I'm certain of it –'

Slowly, then, and with infinite care, Libbie Custer unfolded the paper. 'Look,' she said. 'Do you see?'

Matthew looked down. Lying in the center of the paper was a single lock of pale yellow hair.

'He cut it,' she said. 'That morning. All of it.' She looked up. 'Of course he told me not to worry,' she said. Then she shook her head, looked away, still frowning. 'But I heard him –'

'Heard him, ma'am?' said Matthew. 'What do you mean, you heard him?'

'What he said. I heard what he said to his brothers. To Tom. He didn't think I heard him, but I heard him –'

Just then, the muffled sound of a shot, another. 'What was that?' said Libbie. She rushed to the window, drew back the lace curtain. There was nothing, however, to see – just a few bored cavalrymen throwing horseshoes in the dirt. She let go the curtain. Her shoulders dipped. She sighed. 'So that's your final word, then?' she said.

Matthew looked down at his boots. *Do you love me, Matthew Princeton? Will you love us still, now that we're two?*

Libbie turned.

He looked up. 'I cannot,' he said.

'Then, sir,' she said, 'I shall detain you no further. You may go.'

Matthew turned, made his way to the door.

'Oh, lieutenant –'

He stopped.

'I'd be obliged if you'd deliver me the photograph. I shall find someone else to deliver it to the general.'

'Very well, ma'am,' he said, and then soon he was out of there, walking slow, across the parade ground, his limbs stiff and heavy, like those of a prisoner who is walking in chains on his way to a date with the gallows.

149

So slowly the image comes: a figure – a woman – emerging from a fog. He leans over, so as to take a better look. Eyes now, now hair – a dark halo, now a brooch, a hand, the sweep of a skirt. He squints, waiting for the moment (the image left a little too long in the darkness means an image that's perfect in the light); he runs his tongue slick across his lips.

And he waits, his heart thumping.

More – just a little.

Wait for it, wait –

With the ease of an expert, he lifts out the paper – finger and thumb (be careful – no smudges, now) – holds it over the tray to drain. One, two, three seconds – count to ten, fifteen – then into the fixer, then step back, wipe your hands, breathe again.

He strikes a match, gropes for the candle, lights it, then stands – blinking like a newborn – in the fort's cramped paper-store. He rubs his eyes with the back of his sleeve. He leans back against the bench, closes his eyes.

Do you love me, Matthew Princeton?

What once was refuge is refuge no more. He opens his eyes. *Will you love me still when we're two?*

He pushes up, pulls on his jacket. There is nowhere to hide now. Everything is breached – all earthworks, all defenses. He is naked now, entirely unarmed – at the mercy, now, of savages. *Oh Lord, give me strength.* He's been dying for so long, and can no longer fight it. The will for it's gone. Dying for so long, that he longs, now, for death's last embrace.

Unseen, he moves out of the store-room, moving slow like a man in a dream. Like a man in a dream, then, he pulls out his pistol. The pistol is heavy in his hand. He smiles at the coolness of the barrel on his cheek.

150

Whether or not Jimmy Forder would have left Fort Lincoln when he did, and whether – *had* he done so (which, frankly, I doubt) – he'd have headed west toward the grasslands of Montana, and not east toward Toledo and that motley group of losers he was pleased (but not often) to call his family – whether or not he'd have done such a foolish – not to say reckless – thing – had there not been the pointed end of a Smith and Wesson thirty-eight pushing hard, though unseen – but anyway persuasively – against the base of his spine, will never be known. Neither will it be known (no reference having been made to the event in any of her personal memoirs) whether Elizabeth Custer, née Bacon, was standing, still, at her window when the great gates were opened and a wagon rolled out, two gentlemen on the springboard and a heavy load of boxes stacked behind. About this – these – one can only speculate.

However.

About another matter one can be sure. One can be certain, indeed (thanks to a note in those memoirs just mentioned), that when – some hours following the wagon's departure – Trooper Dooby (whose trampling, ironically, by the hooves of a horse had caused him – it has to be said, with few regrets – to miss out on the great and glorious expedition) stole into the stables to find a quiet spot for an undisturbed snooze – that when, to his horror, he found all fifteen or so of the regiment's remaining horses either dead or dying – each one from a gunshot to the head – one can be certain that he let out a shriek so loud and so terrifying that it caused, in turn, such a panic in the fort as had scarcely been witnessed on the frontier before – a panic, indeed, so wild and swift to spread that it made, in days, the eastern papers and led, as a consequence, to a sudden dip of confidence in the Grant administration and a disastrous (albeit temporary) drop in value of the dollar . . .

But hey.

I jump ahead.

Back, for a moment, to that wagon, those gentlemen, that stack of slim, coffin-shaped boxes. Back, for the purposes of this story (for that is all it is), to that photograph.

This photograph.

What I've told you of its history is not history at all, but speculation. Or maybe not even that. In fact it isn't, really, a picture of Libbie Custer at all. It is, of course, far more precious to me than that, which explains why I've carried it with me all these years, and why I still have it today as I wait here on this rise. It is, of course, a picture of you – that picture of you snapped that first summer, when you first wore Libbie's dress and did your hair like she used to, and I first wore the uniform and boots of the general. You know, sometimes it's hard to credit it. You look at me, smiling, and yet you cannot see me. And all because of *him* – all because of what he made me – of what he handed down.

Well, no more.

Here is where it ends. Here, on this rise, in this infernal heat, is where the circle will at last be broken.

Part Five

LAST STAND

Eddie

151

'Are we nearly there?'
'Oh, for Christ's sake, how would *I* know?'
'Well, you *have* got the map –'
'Okay – if you think it's *easy*, you read the fucking thing –'
'Hey, I only asked –'
'Children, *please* –'
On the afternoon following the morning of his release from the
Florida State Penitentiary at Titusville Point, Eddie Reno was sitting in a
bar just outside of town called the Top Toto Lounge – just trying to
work up the courage to go home to his wife – when two things (or,
perhaps, more accurately, three things – if, that is, a thought can be a
thing) occurred. That the first two, at least, happened simultaneously
was, at the time, something of a blessing – each one, as it did, lessening
the individual blow of the other – except, of course, to those poor souls
directly involved.

And they were?

Well, in order of national importance, they were: one, the assassina-
tion in the kitchen of a California hotel of Robert Francis Kennedy,
brother of the late President, and, two, the explosion, due to the
unfortunate juxtaposition of three bottles of (totally redundant anyway,
this being Florida, the Sunshine State) automobile anti-freeze and an
over-zealous water-heater in a house in a suburb of Gainsville, the result
of which was the death due to head injuries of the woman whose heater
it was – injuries sustained when she was catapulted upward from her
toilet to a height of approximately seventeen feet, then, consequently,
dropped down hard onto the hood of her neighbor's Buick pick-up –
not to mention the house's (of course) almost total destruction, and the
resulting entirely random distribution around the neighborhood of all
kinds of inappropriate personal items blown this way and that by the
force of the blast. All of which – the explosion, that is – though it meant
nothing to Eddie at the time of course (nor, indeed, to the rest of
America), came – an hour or so later, when, propelled by grief and a
need for big hugs – to mean a great deal, when he at last – having found

the courage required by his conviction – turned the corner of Mason Street only to find the street choking with all kinds of flashing, wailing vehicles and the ghastly acrid stink of burning paint in the air.

'Well, he *started* it –'

'I said be quiet. Didn't you hear me say be quiet?'

'But –'

'Just drive, will you?'

Well, of course that day he just ran – just ran and ran, his eyes streaming in the smoke as he dodged the arms that meant to hold him back – running and running until suddenly there he was, standing, chest heaving, on the sidewalk, unable to believe his eyes.

'There! You see that?'

'See what?'

'The sign, dummy –'

'What sign?'

'Oh Jesus. Now we missed it. Now we have to turn round –'

It had been hard to believe, that day – standing there, just looking at the rubble and the broken sticks of furniture and the glass everywhere – hard to believe how something as safe (as safe as houses, ha-ha) – something as *secure* – as a house could be there one minute and gone the next, and he was just standing there, mute, turning this over in his mind, when they'd brought out the body of Mrs Whitman, and one of the paramedics had asked him if he was a relative.

Well, to start with he hadn't been able to speak, but then his breath had returned and he'd told them. '*No*,' he'd said, '*thank God*,' and they'd looked at him strange. '*You see, on the way over I thought it was my wife.*' He'd pointed, then, to his own house next door. '*I thought it was my house went up.*' They'd taken her away, then – Mrs Whitman – and he'd stood there awhile longer until the police had moved him on, and he'd made his way slowly up the path next door and then – eschewing the use of his key (somehow it hadn't seemed right after so long) – he'd stuck his thumb on the buzzer and waited.

And waited.

And waited.

He'd waited an hour, then another; the third he'd spent sitting on the porch. It was dusk when her car pulled up in the drive.

'Love?' he'd called out.

'Who's that?'

A man's voice. The barking of a dog. *But we don't have a dog*, he'd felt like saying, affronted rather that she should have unilaterally changed, in his absence, their certain, collective decision.

'Who the hell are you?'

The man had had a mean face – though his dog's face had been meaner.

'Well –' he'd started weakly, 'I live here –'

'Live here?'

'My wife –'

'Your what? What the fuck are you talkin' about?'

The man, then, had set down his groceries; beside him, the dog had started growling.

'Well, I've just been, well, away –'

'Yeah? For how long? A fuckin' light year?'

'Four years –'

'Four years?'

'And thirty-two days.'

The man, then, had shook his head. 'You're crazy,' he'd said. 'I've been here for four years, see? And I ain't seen no wife –'

'Oh Lord.'

' 'Less you mean that skinny bitch with the fuckin' dirty hair. The one thats husband got killed by that tow-truck –'

'Killed?'

'Same one whose kid ran off. Jesus, she sure was one skinny bitch. Say – you alright?'

'What?'

'You look fuckin' awful –'

And then, like he was struggling through quicksand, he'd turned away, not bothering to listen to how the woman with the husband and the hair had just moved away one day – one morning she was just gone – moved away without telling a soul where she was going, or even bothering, properly, to close the front door.

'There – you see it this time?'

Eddie nodded, turned the wheel.

'Hallelujah!'

In his mind's eye, even now – even after so long – he could still see the pattern of the stones on the sidewalk, then the cars racing by on the highway – still hear the shouts of the drivers in their cars as they passed him, missing him by inches sometimes, still smell that bitter ash in the folds of his coat.

The place was so popular – so choked-up with cars and people – elderly women walking slow like they were drugged, men with great paunches and new-polished side-arms, parents with picnics and strollers with parasols attached – that they had to park maybe half a mile away, in a fenced-off area a short walk from the visitors' center.

Eddie switched off the engine. They'd been driving for hours by now, and though his clothes were ringing with sweat, he just couldn't rake up the energy to move.

'Well now, boys –'

No, all he could do was just sit there, the strangest feeling drifting over him like a shadow – a sense that there was maybe something ahead he hadn't bargained on.

'Right now,' said Danny Sundance. 'You boys set to go?'

'Fuck off,' Peter Frampton whispered low.

'What was that?'

'Nothing,' he said.

'Hey, what about you?'

Eddie shrugged. It was like, somehow, he'd been brought here deliberately – like there was something here waiting for him – something that would maybe, at last, put an end to it all.

Interview

152

Mrs Custer, may I ask you some questions?

That's what you're here for.

Quite. So. (Clears his throat.) Well. Already they are calling it the Great War – the War to End All Wars. How do you feel about this?

How do I feel? I feel as any student of history feels – that there will always be war.

But Colonel Patton said –

I don't care what Colonel Patton said. Just because of those wretched *tanks* of his, he thinks he's invincible.

Surely the point is, Mrs Custer, that he thinks he's your husband. That he is the general's reincarnation –

Is that the point? Excuse me, sir, but I believe the real point is that Colonel Patton is mad.

Because of his believing himself to be your husband reincarnated – or because he still believes that Benteen and Reno were responsible for the general's death?

Oh, I see. I should have known. You don't want to ask me about Colonel Patton at all.

Oh no. On the contrary, ma'am –

Well, sir, for your records, let me just say this. Let me just say that, yes, I still believe – as any true history will show – that the general was abandoned to his fate on that rise, and that those two gentlemen –

gentlemen whose names I have vowed never to repeat – were indeed, amongst others, through their cowardice responsible –

Amongst others, ma'am?

That's what I said.

Then you still believe, also, that they acted on orders from Washington? That it was all a conspiracy – one that reached all the way up through General Sherman to the White House?

I still believe that, yes.

And you still feel your husband was betrayed as – in your memorable phrase – 'a necessary martyr'?

Yes.

Yes?

That's what I said. And, before you ask me, yes, I still believe, also, that such a sacrifice as my husband's was demanded by the banks and money-lenders.

You mean Wall Street.

I mean, sir, what I say.

That unless progress in the west was speeded up – the Indians once and for all destroyed and their land released – then these banks and money-lenders – in other words, Wall Street – would call in their loans and the Government collapse?

Yes.

And that only a defeat – a glorious defeat – could shore up the American people's dwindling appetite for such a policy of slaughter?

I thought this was an interview.

It is, ma'am.

Not a retrospective of my work. Now. (She looks about her, seeking the eye of a hotel porter.) If there's nothing more –

Just one more thing, ma'am.

Very well.

Well, I was wondering how you feel about this sudden enthusiasm for re-enactments –

Re-enactments?

Shiloh, Gettysburg, the Little Big Horn . . .

I know nothing about re-enactments. The past is the past and cannot be recovered. Justice, however, is eternal.

Eternal?

It means it lasts forever.

Quite. Then that means you'll continue with your crusade?

It is no crusade, sir. Merely a wish to establish the truth.

The truth as you see it.

The truth, sir, as God sees it. The truth is His truth. The truth is indivisible. Now, sir, if you don't mind, I have a luncheon appointment.

Of course. (He starts to rise, but then pauses.)

What is it now?

Well – (He looks to another man. This man is standing in the shadows with a camera.)

Oh very well. Where, pray, would you like me to stand? I am, as you know, sir, entirely at your disposal. Here by the window? No, sir, I will not smile. Only the young have any cause to smile.

Eddie

153

O f course he'd gone to look for her – just as, years ago, he'd gone searching for his son. Oh yes, he'd gone to the corner and all along Dixon Street as far as the gas station, then out all the way to Seahorse Lake in case she'd decided to throw herself in. She hadn't, of course – so, his having sat awhile and stared out across the water (there was a building across on the other side, all tumbledown now, that had been spared by Sherman on his Civil War march – although why, nobody knew), he'd made his way back home and waited for the man with the dog to leave. Using his key this time, he'd let himself in. He'd stood, then, in the light from the ice-box and considered the full-stocked shelves.

It wasn't that he hadn't wanted to find her – no, sir. It was just that not finding her meant not finding her and not having to explain something that in four years he'd not once been able to explain to himself. Oh Lord, how many times during those years had he sat in his cell or stood in the yard, looking down at his hands like they were the hands of a stranger and nothing to do with him? And then, how many times had he tried unsuccessfully to feed them like letters into the franking machine, before at last he'd succeeded (but only with his left hand) and at last he'd seen his skin and all the blood, bone and sinew all mangled up and ghastly – so ghastly, in fact, that he'd fainted dead away?

'Hey, you coming or what?'

He opened his eyes. He was leaning back against the Toyota, just letting the sun and the voices all around him wash over him. 'Do I have a choice?' he said.

Danny Sundance shrugged.

'Oh, *sure* you do,' said Peter Frampton. 'You think our friend here brought us all this way just to let us go now we're here?'

'Well?' said Eddie.

'Sure,' said Danny Sundance.

'What do you mean?'

'I mean,' he said, 'that sure you boys can go now if you want to.'

Peter Frampton screwed up his face. 'Oh yeah?' he said. 'And get a slug in the back?'

'A *slug*?' Danny Sundance laughed. 'This ain't some movie, you know. And anyway –' Withdrawing the pistol, he opened it up, spun the barrel.

Empty.

For a moment, neither of his captives could speak. Then Eddie said, 'You mean . . . all this time . . . it was . . . *empty*?'

'I do.'

He shook his head, disbelieving. 'Then why –'

'Because I needed a ride.'

'You *what*?'

Danny Sundance spun the pistol, set it back in his pocket. Then, stepping forward, he extended his hand. 'Crazy Horse,' he said. 'Pleased to meet you.'

'Oh, fuck,' said Peter Frampton. Reluctantly, limply, he let his hand be lifted, shaken. 'So what was all that shit about the photograph – how you were coming along to stop me? What about spirits and shadows, for fuck's sake?'

'Bullshit, all of it. If you find a picture, good luck to you. You won't, of course.'

'Why not?' said Eddie.

'Because it's a fake.'

'What's a fake?'

'That so-called "journal" of yours. It ain't real. Well, it's *real*, I suppose – it just ain't genuine.'

'Of course it's genuine!'

'Oh yeah? Well, whoever heard of somebody's pen *running out* in eighteen seventy-six? What do you think this Matthew guy's using, for God's sake? A fuckin' ballpoint?'

'You're crazy,' said Eddie, though conviction within him was already slipping.

'Really,' said Danny Sundance. 'Okay, then. How did you come by it?'

'What?'

'Where did you get it?'

Eddie felt himself flushing.

'It's an heirloom,' said Peter Frampton, sensing victory. He turned to Eddie. 'Go on,' he said. 'Tell him. Tell Mr *Fake* here about your granddaddy's granddaddy and all that shit. Tell him how it's been handed down. Go on – tell him –'

Eddie bit his lip.

'Go *on* –'

'I can't,' he said.

'What do you mean, you can't? Just tell him!'

He sighed. 'I can't – because it's not true.'

'What?'

'It's not an heirloom at all. In fact, I'd never laid eyes on it –' he paused '– until it turned up in the mail.'

Peter Frampton felt his mouth drop open. 'The mail?' He said. 'What the fuck are you talking about?'

'I'm talking about how one day it just turned up. I went to my box as usual on my way to work – and there it was. Addressed to me – but nothing else. No clue as to who sent it.'

'And so you read it,' said Danny Sundance, 'and followed it, hoping to find that photograph –'

'Well, yes,' Eddie stumbled. 'I mean, *no* –'

'So which is it?'

Another sigh. It all seemed so long ago now that he could barely remember the sequence of events. 'Well, I wasn't *going* to,' he said, 'but then, well, something happened. Something bad –'

'And so you ran. Using the book as a blueprint?'

'Well, yeah –' Put like that it all sounded quite reasonable.

'So are you going to tell us?'

'Tell you what?'

'This bad thing. The thing that got you so spooked that you just dropped everything to follow in the footsteps of some guy in a book you'd never seen before – a book that just turned up in your mailbox with no return address?'

Eddie flicked a look to Peter Frampton. Peter Frampton had been watching the exchange, his mouth still wide open and his head moving to and fro like a man watching tennis from the stands. 'Well, kinda,' he said.

'Jesus,' said Peter Frampton at last. 'I should have known. I knew the first time I laid eyes on you you were trouble – you and that I'm-too-good-for-this-kind-of-shit look on your face –'

'I'm sorry,' said Eddie.

'Sorry?'

'And I'm sorry I hit you.' He lifted his busted hand, shook his head, turned, then, at the sound of laughter. Peter Frampton turned too.

'What the fuck are you laughin' at, Tonto?'

'Well,' said Danny Sundance. 'It's just occurred to me – that's the bad thing, ain't it? *You* hitting *him* on the head. So it was *him* you were running away from all the time.'

Eddie nodded. *Amongst others*, he thought. He thought again of that cinema, then that full-up, humming ice-box. He watched, then, quite numb, as Danny Sundance, still laughing, turned away.

'Hey, where are you going?' said Peter Frampton.

Danny Sundance turned. 'I gotta get changed,' he said.

'But what about us?'

'What *about* you?'

'Well, Jesus – I gave up my job! What do I do now?'

Danny Sundance shrugged. 'Well, the cavalry's recruiting – I know that for sure.' Then he smiled – though not with his eyes. 'Think you're stupid enough for the glorious Seventh?' he said. 'Think you've got what it takes to die crying on your knees?'

Josh

154

S o.
      Sprung.
      Okay – so it was me. I faked it – the whole thing. So what?
Anyway, is it really any business of *yours* if I did? It is not. I mean, for
God's sake, you sit there in judgement (I bet you're comfortable, too,
probably sitting in some nice comfy chair – while I'm up here sweating
my ass off in this grass) – sit there shaking your head and saying *What
the fuck is all this about?*, when you really don't know the first thing
about my life – except, of course, for the bits I've told you. Which, I can
tell you, ain't the half of it. For instance, did I tell you that when my
father quit 'searching' for my mother (some search: three blocks, max),
he was so upset – having failed to find her – that that very afternoon he
went down to the bus depot and bought himself a ticket one way for
Miami, and later that day he was gone.

I mean, Jesus – *that very same day.*

Oh, and another thing.

What kind of idiot's so screwed on a name that, when one Clare
walks away from him, he goes and gets himself another one? I mean,
what the fuck's *that* all about? Is it in any way healthy? No, sir, it is not.

Jesus.

And you wonder why I'm so fucked.

I feel inclined (for no particular reason that comes to mind, mind you) to
report a certain restlessness up here on the rise. Okay, it's fucking hot,
and Crazy Horse and his buddies way down there across the river *do*
seem to be taking an almighty long time to decide to come up here and
finish us off (somebody said that the Big Chief himself only just showed
up – but who knows? Come to think of it, about the only thing that
hasn't changed around here, what with the monument and all, is the
standard of intelligence) – not to mention the fact that there must be five
thousand people – maybe more – all licking their ice-creams and, no
doubt, starting to get real, real bored.

But hey.

That's not it.

Not the *real* problem.

The *real* problem up here right now is politics. By which I don't mean *regular* politics – no, sir. Nothing so predictable round here. No. The dispute on this rise (a dispute, incidentally, about which I couldn't give a shit, and so have not been taking part) is – yet again – whether Custer didn't hang around as instructed and wait for reinforcements from Crook (who wasn't coming anyway, having been defeated on the Rosebud) and Terry because he wanted to wrap the whole thing up on his own and in time for news of his victory to get back to Washington for the fourth of July – and so help launch his campaign for President – or whether he was just some vainglorious idiot.

Well.

Blahblahblah.

Who, anymore, gives a shit? You'd have to be some kind of real sick obsessive to still be stuck on *that* one –

Yeah, yeah – I know what you're thinking. Takes one to know one – right?

Wrong.

Why?

Jesus. I don't know. Just leave me alone, will you?

Yeah – same to you, buddy.

Anyway, time's up. From the look of things – all that running around and shrieking down there – I don't have much longer. So you'd better quit bugging me and get out of here.

Matthew

155

'**Y**ou mean you're *serious*?'

'Sure I'm serious. Anyway, why not?'

They were sitting, the two of them, in the heat and the dust in the middle of the plains, the wagon and its contents of long wooden boxes having been brought just that minute to a juddering, unexpected halt.

'Why not? *Why not*? Because there's fuckin' Indians out there – fuckin' thousands of them – that's why not!'

'Thousands? I thought you said there was maybe two hundred –'

'Well –'

Jimmy Forder felt the prodding of the pistol in his back.

'Well *what*? Are you saying you were lying?'

'Lying?'

Another prod. 'Yes, *lying*. Are you saying that when you saw them – when you went to the village – there weren't hundreds of them – but thousands?'

He shrugged, expecting, any minute, a bullet in his spine.

'Well?'

'Well, kinda,' he said.

'Jesus Christ.'

He half-turned. 'That mean we're goin' back, lieutenant, sir?'

'Going back?'

'Seeing as how there's so many –'

Matthew shook his head. 'No,' he said. 'We ain't going back.'

'We ain't?'

'No, sir. We're just going faster.'

156

Of course he was crazy – he knew that. Had to be. Why else, for heaven's sake, would he be out there, right in the middle of those never-ending, rolling grasslands, sitting side by side with just about the foulest man he'd ever had the misfortune to meet – not to mention sitting side by side with such a ghastly, shifting group of smells, and in such a desolate place – *and* heading straight into just about the largest group of Indian fighting men ever gotten together in one place at one time in the history of the whole stinking world?

Yup.

Crazy as a loon.

He cocked the pistol –

'*Okay! Okay!*'

– then slowly withdrew it, setting it, then (his hand still gripping it tight, just in case), back in his lap. He eased back on the hard wooden seat. He tried hard to think up a plan.

'So you got some kind of genius military plan?' said Jimmy Forder.

'Just be quiet and drive, will you?'

He shrugged. *Soldiers*, he thought, raising up a spitball, then sending it, hard as a bullet, out into the breathless, dusty air.

'And you can quit that too.'

'Quit what?'

'Thinking how if you just turn this thing around real easy then I won't notice.'

'I don't know what –'

'Is that a yes?'

'Jesus.'

'I'll take that as you agreeing,' said Matthew, as the wagon rolled on – he, involuntarily, rocking this way and that with the hard jarring motion of its wheels.

There was one other thing, of course – one element of all that was happening that was the biggest mystery of all – something that simply *proved* beyond any kind of doubt that he *had* to be crazy. Precisely, it was this: if Custer *was* responsible for so much slaughter (and, oh, he

was, he was – how could anyone forgive Antietam, for Christ's sake?),
then why on earth was *he* – Matthew Princeton – trying so hard to get to
him – to save him? For God's sake, why not just let the man die? Why
not just let him get a taste of what for so long he'd handed out?

'Hey, lieutenant –'

And why *oh Lord* wasn't he – that same Matthew Princeton – just
lying somewhere in some huge dipping bed – just drinking real deep
from a bottle and letting everything go by?

'I was thinking –'

Jesus, he had to be some kind of a fool. Either that or there was
something else going on in his head.

'Maybe you was right –'

'Stop,' he said sharply. But what?

'What?'

'I said *stop* –'

'Hey, I was only saying –'

'I mean, *stop the fucking wagon* –'

'*What?*'

Dropping the pistol at his feet, he grabbed the reins, pulling hard. The
horses objected; the wagon skewed, stopping hard in a cloud of choking
dust.

'What the *fuck* are you doin'? You gone fuckin' crazy or somethin'?'

'We're going back,' said Matthew.

'We're *what*? But you said –'

'I know what I said.' He snapped the reins, pulling hard on the left.
The horses moved on, turning at once in a wide, sweeping arc.

'But what about your buddy Mr Custer?'

'Fuck him,' said Matthew.

'*Fuck him?*'

'You heard me. Anyway, it's what you wanted, isn't it?'

'Well, yeah –'

'So quit complaining – alright? Just drive.' Matthew thrust the reins
hard against the other man's chest.

'I ain't drivin'.'

'What?'

The reins hung limp; the horses slowed.

'I said I ain't drivin'.'

'What do you mean, you ain't driving? It's what you want –'

'*Wanted*,' said Jimmy Forder. He sat back, just letting the reins go. He
folded his arms across his chest. 'I changed my mind,' he said.

'You what?'

'I said I changed my mind. I ain't goin' nowhere unless it's to save the
poor general.'

'You're crazy –'

'Yes, sir. If you say so, sir.'

'Oh Jesus.'

'No, he ain't gonna help you, sir.'

'But *why?*'

'Well, I believe he's real busy, sir –'

'Oh, for Christ's sake, I mean why won't you go back? What about the Indians?'

Jimmy Forder shrugged. 'I ain't scared of no Indians.'

'But you said –'

'Fuck what I said. What I'm sayin' now is either we's goin' straight ahead or we ain't goin' no place.'

Matthew reached down for the gun.

'You lookin' for this?'

He turned, felt the cool circle of the pistol's barrel on his forehead. He frowned. 'But –'

Jimmy Forder smiled. 'You can call it a trick, if you like, Mr Lieutenant, sir,' he said. 'But I *prefer* to call it magic. Now –' He lowered the gun, passed over the reins. 'If you'd be so kind –'

Matthew picked up the reins. 'You're crazy,' he said.

'Yeah, you said.'

'We're gonna be killed – you know that –'

But Jimmy Forder just smiled.

'What's so fuckin' funny?'

'I was just thinkin', is all.'

'Jesus.'

Another smile. 'Not exactly,' he said, then he eased himself back, stretching out his legs, and pulled down the brim of his dark, sweaty hat.

Danny

157

For sure it was a good day to die.

Danny Sundance sat still on his horse in the shade by the river. His horse dipped its head to drink. Behind him, all was ready – two hundred or more young men from the cities, towns, from the reservations – Sioux and Cheyenne in Reebok trainers, Black Foot in Nike. For hours, now, there'd been nothing but talk – a buzz in the camp, the sounds of radios and laughter, the hiss-release of ring-pulls – but now there was silence. Only the breath of the warm breeze off the river and its whispering in the trees, quiet and calm like the breath of ancient ancestors.

He touched the rope reins; the horse lifted its head. The horse was sweating, and with more than the heat. *A horse senses death*, Crazy Horse had once said, *long before a man fears it*. Danny Sundance reached down, laid a hand on the animal's neck. A pulse – he could feel beneath his fingers the throbbing of life. He sat up. He let his eyes close.

What's the matter, sergeant? You know, them's just gooks – so burn 'em, okay? And that's an order.

All his life he'd been waiting for this – and long before. Lying in a foxhole in the mud of Vietnam, all he'd been able to think of as he'd waited in terror for the crack of a twig or in hopes of the *whup-whup-whup* of Hueys above the dense, dripping, strangling trees, had been the day – *oh please let it come, let it come* – when he'd sit there – *here* – on the back of his horse, squinting up through the trees toward the soldiers far away on that sun-glaring rise.

All, then – all, *now* – he'd been able to think of was this moment, this day, this ancient, sacred task.

Which was?

Well, killing Custer, of course.

He reached up a hand, touched the smooth pebble tied loose behind his ear. He ran his fingers light across his face, traced the red flash of lightning painted there. *Every Sioux must kill Custer.* For so long he'd thought it just some old fool's rambling – thought them just the words of an old man too old and too scared to really grasp his freedom – the words of a dead or dying past made as nothing at last by the words of John Kennedy and the shelves stacked high with food at the Seven-Eleven, words negated by those of Mr King – by the Promised Land that was coming and all, then, that would follow in its wake.

But it didn't come – hadn't come still.

But there's always hope, people say.

White people.

Well, fuck hope.

And fuck America.

He opened his eyes, saw her again, her sweet face. '*Will you take me to America?*' He sat a moment, entirely, perfectly still.

You know them's just gooks.

Slowly, he raised an arm, rifle in hand.

Every Sioux.

He drew a long, shallow breath. Then, gripping tight to the reins, he touched the horse's flanks with his knees.

Interview

158

I'd like to ask you, if I may, about your lovely home. Do you like it?

Oh, indeed I do, sir. (Looks around, obviously impressed.) So many treasures!

Yes. I've traveled widely. Just last week I was in Russia. I played polo with the Tsar.

The Tsar! Gracious!

(Mr G. stands, moves to the fireplace, where he leans elegantly against the marble surround. He smiles, but as if at something distant.) You wanted to ask me about my house.

Yes . . . yes, quite. (She clears her throat.) It belonged, I understand, to an industrialist. A Mr . . . (She consults her notepad.) . . . A Mr Zeitezmann . . .

Yes. He failed in business. I believe he went to the west coast. I understand he lives in a sanitarium.

Oh *my* –

Did you notice my swimming pool?

Why, yes. (Turns to look. The pool, however, is obscured by fluttering curtains.) Do you swim?

I have a pool, don't I? (He frowns, as if annoyed at his lack of control.) I'm sorry. I *do* swim, yes. I was awarded this . . . (He pulls something out of his pocket. It is a medal on a red-and-white ribbon.) . . . in

Sweden. At the Olympic Games. (He offers the medal for inspection. She takes it, but doesn't know quite how to hold it.) Do you?

Me, sir?

Swim.

Alas, no.

You should learn. Everyone should learn. Especially the women.

(She lays the medal down on the seat beside her.) Does your . . . *wife* swim?

I think that's *my* business – don't you?

Yes. Of course. Excuse me. Er . . . (Again, she consults her book. She is blushing.) Ah, yes. Er . . . the horse . . . (She looks up.) . . . the famous horse . . .

You mean Comanche.

Comanche, yes. Could you tell my readers something about him? I understand he looks, well, almost *alive* –

He needed a home. So I gave him a home.

And the Keogh family?

They already have a home.

(She smiles, but a weary smile. This is not going quite as she'd hoped.) I meant weren't they sorry to let him go?

I imagine so. But they couldn't keep him. He needs – needed – expert care. He had been badly wounded. Only Mr Rothstein could save him.

Mr Rothstein?

Of the Rothstein Institute in Gstaad, Switzerland. I had him stay with me. So he could attend to the animal day and night.

So he was with him when he died?

Who?

Mr . . . Rothstein. With Comanche.

No. *I* was with him when he died.

(Her composure regained, she nods. She is sincere.) It must have been so . . . moving, to be so close to history . . .

History?

I mean . . . to be in the presence . . . of the only survivor of the famous battle.

Yes.

To be close to someone . . . some*thing*, at least . . . who was there . . . (She looks at her notes, then sits forward, as if she is about to tell a secret.) I believe Mrs Custer is petitioning the Government. She believes there should be some sort of . . . inquiry . . .

So I understand.

Do you think she's right to do so? Or should this be a case of letting sleeping dogs lie?

I have no opinion on the matter. It is something for the Government to decide.

But I thought . . . with your connections . . .

What do you mean?

Well, in . . . business. And what with your having been a soldier yourself . . .

I was a captain. I wasn't a general. (He smiles.) And now I'm a private person. (He curls the fingers of a hand, makes a fist.) And as far as . . . *business* is concerned –

Yes, of course. I'm sorry. It's just I heard she's been mentioning your name. In connection with Mr Zeitezmann . . .

I think you should leave now.

And there's this rumor, of course, that he's at that sanitarium at your expense . . .

I want you to go. (He moves away from the fireplace. He is angry, a sweat gathering on his temples.)

And that in Turkey today . . . (She resists as her arm is lifted roughly. She tries to release herself, but he pulls her up, starts dragging her toward the door.) . . . eastern front . . . American weapons . . .

Here the interview was terminated. Readers of the Long Island Enquirer *will be glad to know that our reporter was unharmed. She is, however, today preparing a charge of assault against Mr G. As for Mr G. himself, we understand he has not been seen recently on the Island. His whereabouts, currently, are unknown.*

Matthew & Josh

159

'So why are we stopping?'

'Why do you think?'

'But the canteens –'

'Not for *you*, asshole. For *them* –' Holding onto the reins, Jimmy Forder twisted round, dropped down, then, to the ground. He beat the dust from his pants with the brim of his hat.

'So where are we?' said Matthew.

'Fuck knows.'

They were in some kind of dip. To the right was a slow-rising hill; to the left, close by, bush-scrub, then a group of shady trees. Beyond the trees was a wide, shallow river.

'I thought you said you knew this country.'

Jimmy Forder moved around to the front of the horses. He started unbuckling the harnesses. 'What I *said* was I knew where this country *was*. And I do.' He looked around him. 'Yup,' he said. 'Reckon it's here alright.' Released, then, from its shackles, the first horse stepped forward, started moving down the slope toward the trees.

'Jesus,' said Matthew. 'So what are you saying? Are you saying we're lost?'

Working on the second harness, Jimmy Forder paused. He looked up, squinting in the sun. 'Not lost, I wouldn't say. No, sir. Not lost.' He went back to his work. In a moment, the second horse was following the route of the first to the river.

'So?'

'So what?' he said.

'So where *are* we then?'

He glanced at the trees, the river sparkling beyond. 'Well now,' he said, frowning. 'That there body of water could be the . . . Rosebud, maybes, or maybes it's the Little Big Horn. It's real hard to say.' He turned back. 'Of course,' he said, he was smiling now, 'it *could* be the fuckin' Hudson. But I doubt it.'

'Great,' said Matthew. He watched as Jimmy Forder made his own way to the river. He leaned forward, then, held his head in his hands. He looked down at his boots. His boots were dusty and worn. He tried to figure how he could have come so far in this life, but, at the same time, have gone no distance at all.

160

I t was a question that took some thinking about, to be sure – that, and just what was going on with Jimmy Forder. He hung his head lower, meshed his fingers together on the back of his neck. Particularly what he couldn't figure was how one minute he was begging to go back (and, indeed, would only go *forward* thanks to the encouragement of a thirty-eight Smith and Wesson), then the next there he was, plain refusing to do anything *but* go on. It was a mystery Matthew Princeton could not seem to solve.

He lifted his head, looked down toward the river. *Maybe*, he thought, *there is no mystery. Maybe it's just human nature.* The horses were grazing, having drunk their fill. And Jimmy Forder? Matthew squinted. No sign. His heart leapt. He stood up. He scanned the trees. Nothing. He searched the river. Nothing. He turned, and in one move jumped down from the wagon, twisting his ankle as he fell. He rolled onto his back, the pain shooting through his leg.

He lay a moment, still, his ankle throbbing, then something moved overhead – a shadow. He lifted his arm, shielding his eyes from the burning sun. 'That you?' he said. He could hear a buzzing suddenly in his ears, feel the cool drip-drip of water on his face.

Jimmy Forder was laughing. 'Who the fuck did you think it was?'

Matthew pushed himself up. 'I thought you were down by the river,' he said.

'I was. I came back. Hey – what do you make of this?'

Jimmy Forder dropped to his haunches. In his hand he held a sodden, cream-colored glove. He turned it over.

'It's a cavalry glove,' said Matthew.

'And look.'

'What?'

'Just here.'

Crossed swords, a flag, the number seven.

'Jesus,' said Matthew. 'Where did you find it?'

'In the river.'

He took it, turned it over. 'Anything else?'

'Like what?'

He shrugged. 'I don't know.'

'You mean like a . . . *body* maybe?'

'Look. There's blood on it.'

Sure enough: the leather was a rich dark crimson – almost black – on the palm.

Matthew pushed himself up, standing unsteady on his one good ankle. 'We have to go look,' he said.

'What do you mean, go look?'

'Maybe the other one's there, too. Maybe –' He paused.

'Maybe what?'

He turned sharp. 'Look, *I* don't fucking know – do I? I'm just saying, we have to go see –'

'Alright, alright. Keep your fucking hair on. So we'll go look.'

It was a struggle (an ordeal, in truth, for both men – for the first, the weight of the second; for the second, the smell, at close range, of the first), but together they made it to the water's edge. Matthew slumped down on the bank. 'Okay,' he said. 'Show me where.'

'What do you mean?'

'What do you think I mean? Where you found the fucking glove.'

'It's a *river*, lieutenant – in case you hadn't noticed.'

'Yeah – so?'

'Well, rivers *run*. They don't stand still.'

'Jesus. Alright. Which way was it going?'

Jimmy Forder shook his head. 'Fuck me,' he said. 'They only run *one way* –'

'What?'

'Rivers. They only go one fuckin' way.'

'*Shit.*'

'Didn't you even know that?'

'No – look –'

'Where?'

'Over there. The other side. On the bank.'

Jimmy Forder squinted hard. 'What is it?'

'I don't know. It sure looks like *something*.'

Whatever it was, it was dark, blue, about the size of a plate.

'It's a cap,' said Matthew.

'Oh yeah,' said Jimmy Forder.

'What the fuck's going on?'

He shrugged. 'Well, whatever it is, it sure ain't healthy.'

'You have to go take a look. Look around.'

'What?'

'We have to know what's going on.'

Jimmy Forder raised his palms like a man surrendering. 'No chance,' he said. 'I ain't goin' fuckin' nowhere –'

'But you have to –'

'*You* fuckin' go –'

'I can't move. Besides, I thought you weren't afraid of no Indians –'

'Well I *ain't*. But I ain't *stupid* neither.'

'Look –'

'No, *you* look –'

'I'm *ordering* you –'

'You can't fuckin' order *me*! In case you hadn't noticed, I ain't in your fuckin' army!'

'Alright. Let's both of us calm down. What do you say you just look over that rise? Just climb up and take a look –'

Jimmy Forder set his hands on his hips. He looked away, gave a great and weary sigh. 'Ah, *fuck* it,' he said.

'Then you'll go?'

'I said fuck it, didn't I?'

'Good.'

Jimmy Forder paused.

'What is it?'

'You know I never was in the army,' he said.

'What?'

'I never was no captain –'

'What are you talking about?'

He shrugged. 'Ah, nothin',' he said. 'Just talkin'. I guess it's time to go. Wish me luck.'

'Fuck it,' said Matthew.

'Yeah, fuck it,' said Jimmy Forder. He turned, then, and started walking.

Matthew turned back to the river. It was flowing fast, scooting over the rocks with the out-of-time urgency of spring. With difficulty, he pulled off his boot. His ankle was already swollen, the flesh already tinged with blue. He pushed himself up, hobbled to the water's edge, dropped down.

The water was cool on his ankle, slightly numbing the pain. He closed his eyes, felt the sun on his face. He was just playing back in his mind what Jimmy Forder had said before he'd left, when something made him open his eyes. The light flared, his pupils shutting down. He sat forward, dipped his hands in the water, so as to massage his foot.

The water.

He squinted, frowning.

Red.

The water was red.

For a moment, then, he couldn't figure what it was. But then it came to him – '*Jesus Christ!*' – and he pulled out his foot, scuttled fast up the bank.

Slightly raised, he could see the whole river's width. 'Oh Lord,' he whispered, unheard but by Him, 'oh my sweet, sweet Lord –' He felt his stomach churning, something rising in his throat. Retching hard, then, he covered his boots, coughing hard, then, in a while, was quiet. He looked again at the river. It was like seeing something from some future, crazy world –

Or maybe from a time already passed.

Antietam, Antietam.

He pushed the thought away, pushing himself up. Hobbling, then, he made his way slow along the bank. The further he went upstream, the redder was the river.

At first he didn't hear the call, but then –

'*Hey, lieutenant –*'

He turned sharp. Back down the river a way, in the shade of the trees, Jimmy Forder was standing stiffly straight like a soldier on parade. His pale face was red, as if smeared with blood, his bulging cheeks sucking hard on the end of a Remington repeater. Either side of him, attracting, now, a whole army of flies, lay the bodies of the wagon's two horses.

'What the hell –' said Matthew.

Awkwardly, then, Jimmy Forder tried a smile.

'Hey –'

Then he closed his eyes.

161

T̲he following, from the *New York Times*, dated June 25th 1997:

Holiday turns to tragedy
Jeremy C. Poolman, Bismark, ND

The annual re-enactment of the Battle of the Little
Bighorn – the engagement known throughout the
world as *Custer's Last Stand* – turned to tragedy
today with the death of Mr Neil R. Sansum, 21, of
Belle Fouche, SD. Mr Sansum, a history major at
Black Hills State University, who, perhaps ironically, had this year taken the role of the famous
general himself, was fatally wounded by a stray
live round during the 'hand-to-hand fighting' that
every year follows the storming of Custer Hill.
The tragedy was compounded by the confusion
following the victorious assault by the 'Sioux' and
'members' of other Indian tribes, during which
the extent and gravity of Mr Sansum's injuries
remained unknown. Eventually, however, he was
transferred by air ambulance to Grace Memorial
Hospital, Bozeman, MT, where, following emergency surgery, he was pronounced dead.

Montana State Police immediately began enquiries, hoping to discover the source of the fatal
shot (live rounds are strictly prohibited within the
boundaries of Custer State Park), and will shortly
be issuing a further statement. It is understood,
however, that no one has yet been detained – a
situation which one unofficial source claimed was
'likely to be maintained'.

Mr Sansum, a keen cyclist, leaves a wife, Clare,
and a baby daughter, Laura.

162

For a while he seemed rooted to the hard ground, while all was swirling round him – the trees, the sun, the river's fast-moving water. And then, suddenly, he was moving – dragging his ankle, the whisper of dry grass beneath his feet, the pounding of blood through his veins – moving, moving, barely wincing at the pain, until he was standing in the coolness of the trees, looking down upon the body of what had once been a man.

Flies.

Already, flies – a thousand of them.

He struck the corpse with the toe of his boot; a great buzzing black shroud rose as one, its constituents for the moment dispersing. *Oh Jesus, Mary and Joseph*. Matthew's stomach rose again, but there was nothing, now, within.

The blast had removed the man's head entire – blown it apart into such tiny pieces that surely even the Maker Himself – had He the will – could not have reassembled it. Indeed, so suddenly, so shockingly, absent was it, that it made what remained – a man's torso and limbs – seem, unharmed as it was, a most curious thing – as if a hurricane had swept without warning through a sleeping coastal town, only to devastate one single, solitary house and leave all the rest untouched.

Wish me luck.

Matthew turned away, hobbled over to the nearest of the two slain horses. Quiet now, unmoving (and with the knowledge seeping out, from somewhere within its form, that it would never move again), it seemed huge – a great, sweating, gathering of flesh – so much bigger, so much heavier, than it had ever seemed in life. From this, in time, he turned away too – for he knew that to look upon death too closely and for too long is to learn for certain that death is indeed, as some say, a beginning – not an ending – but the beginning, not of some new light-filled life, but of nothingness – of an endless emptiness – just as the end of the pier is the very beginning of the endless, empty sea.

*   *   *

When at first he saw the footprints, he thought little of them, thinking them just the marks in the earth of prairie dogs or perhaps a coyote; it was only when his eyes for distraction followed their progress up the rise and over in the direction from which Jimmy Forder had come, that the regularity both in their size and the distance between them (about, something told him, the length of a man's leisurely stride) made him take a closer look. He eased down onto his knees, reaching out the fingers of his good hand, touched the grass where the imprint lay.

Wet.

He touched it again, drew the tips of his fingers to his nose.

Footprints.

He pushed himself back up.

Footprints in blood.

Again, he studied their route.

Then, hobbling, his heart thudding, he moved to the foot of the rise.

163

Well, all I can say is it all happened so fast. One minute there they were streaming out of the trees, really getting into this whooping Indian thing, while we were on the rise really – and I mean *really* – getting into the scared-shitless thing (I tell you, officer, there's something about that hollering that gets to you, even when it's coming from a bunch of accountants and department-store clerks), then the next, well, the place was just buzzing with you guys. I mean, there wasn't even much slaughtering and scalping got done before all those squad cars turned up and ambulances and whatever, and the day, to put it mildly, started turning out really weird. And then when somebody said it was Custer got hurt, well, the whole thing got just too surreal for words. And then when they said he was *dead* – well, I just couldn't believe it. Still can't really.

Anyway.

Yes, it's true I didn't have a pass, and that, strictly, speaking, I wasn't supposed to be there. But what does that prove? All it proves is that, as a former Custer myself, maybe I haven't moved on as much as I should have – which, while I'll agree it's maybe a little sad – is hardly a hanging offense now, is it? All of which is not to say that I'm unaware that what I did was wrong – I'm just saying that maybe you can understand. I don't know whether you're a married man – you are? – well, then, I guess you can imagine how you'd feel if your wife – do you have kids? You do? – if your wife and your kids crashed and burned in an automobile accident, having got themselves into a car that was unsafe to drive in the first place? Oh, I know – you're telling me. Anyway, what I'm saying is, what with the anniversary coming up and all, I guess I just got a little crazy – you know what I mean? And I'm sorry. I really am. And if I can help at all –

The shotgun.

Right.

No, it's not mine. It's my brother Davie's. He kind of, well, *indulges* me when I get a little – what can I say? – a little, well, down.

Oh, no, sir – absolutely not. No way was I gonna be carrying shells. I

466

mean, for one thing, well, Davie'd go crazy if I'd even asked him for some – yes, sir, he's got a real thing about loaded firearms – and, for another, well, I'm a Buddhist.

That's right.

Buddhist.

Yup. Like Richard Gere.

No, I don't. Never have, I'm afraid. Mind you, there *are* a lot of us about. Like the Mormons – that's right. But different, yup. Anyway –

Sure. Ask away.

Did I see anybody? You mean, like, with a *gun*? Well, sure – *everybody* had guns. Sure. A loaded gun. Well, not really –

I mean, well, no. I mean, can you spot a loaded gun – just by looking at it?

Well, maybe. But *I* can't. No, sir. Me, I've hardly spent any time around guns. That's right. From the east. Well, originally Florida, but lately – yup, you guessed it – New York.

Well, I'm an actor.

Yup, like Richard Gere again. Yup, I guess that is some coincidence.

No, you wouldn't know me. I do small stuff – commercial mostly.

You do? Well, maybe I'll come see it sometime. *As an elephant's eye* – yup, that's right. No, I never did see the movie.

Winona Ryder?

I don't know. I guess she *could* be. Yup, I guess she probably *does* know Richard Gere. Yeah, them both being short I guess helps. She is, yes.

Anyway, officer –

Watt, right.

Yeah, good to meet *you*.

Lord – will you look at the time? I really should be going – if you don't need me anymore, that is –

Sure. What is it?

Well, I don't know . . . Like I say, there are a lot of us. I mean, there's pretty much the whole of China –

Okay, okay. I'll try. But I can't promise anything. Sure. Next time I see him, I'll ask.

You're welcome.

Er . . .

Well, it's a favor, really.

Do you think so? Are you sure that's okay? I mean, I did leave my car there. If you could, I'd be most grateful. Sure. I'll wait outside.

No, I won't forget. Next time I see him, I'll ask.

164

They were white – so white, in fact – so tiny, so pure and still in the hard-beating sun – that at first, from such a distance, he felt certain that they couldn't be men, no, sir, but each one a small thicket of beautiful white flowers, dotted sporadically, with all nature's guile, in the dip below, then growing more concentrated as the hill gently rose, until – at its modest grassy summit – they were growing in such abandoned profusion that you'd swear that some strange reverse spring had come by mistake to the plains in midsummer – that the world, indeed, had lost its grasp of nature's cycle, and that following this springtime would be winter, then fall.

For a moment, this fantasy – but only for a moment, for then he saw the horses. They were lying on their sides, as if sleeping, in a ring below the summit – all but one of them unmoving –

He turned his head sharply as something – something moving, far off – caught his eye. He squinted out, away, away, far beyond the dip, beyond the hill, far out over the endless, arching, grassy plains. He raised up his hand against the sun.

Something moving.

A horse?

Yes, a horse, far off and running – raising a great cloud of dust from its hooves – turning and turning in the middle of nowhere in an ever-tightening circle – turning and turning until suddenly it stopped, and then, with immeasurable casualness, dipped its head to the ground – suddenly as serene – suddenly as sane – as the sanest, the serenest, of its brothers back east who have known only thick grass and peace.

He looked back to the rise.

Really, ma'am, I'm sure the general is quite well. Unseen except by God, he frowned, thinking suddenly of a photograph on a wall, then the face of a widow framed in his camera.

A widow.

Really, ma'am.

He closed his eyes. Only now – standing on that other rise – alone but not alone – did he let himself see what he'd seen that day – what he'd seen on so many days before –

But no.

He opened his eyes.

Of course it was foolishness to believe such nonsense. He shook his head. I mean, for heaven's sake, what are photographs but the children of chemicals and glass? What are they but the image of life rendered dead? What are they but portraits come from science? And what is science if not the slaying of myth and mystery? No. They are just moments of the past caught in nets, stilled in ether. They are hearts in a jar in a darkening room. They are silent. They tell us nothing. They smile at us – but stiffly. They are corpses suspended; they are judges, stern and stoic, passing sentence of death upon those who stand before them.

A voice.

A phantom.

Again, he turns, looks down upon the river. Far away, beyond the river, beyond the great mass of trees, a vast rolling darkness is moving slow now, thick like a shadow across the land –

The village. He is sure of it. Their task completed – their victory won – they are moving on. He watches them go – thinks he hears their distant calls – until they melt into the far-distant blueness, and are gone from his sight.

He stands.

Too late.

Always too late.

Do you love me, Matthew Princeton?

Now he is kneeling.

Will you love us when we're three?

Now, like some beast, he is pawing the ground, breaking his nails, bloodying his hands –

She and that whore-child –

Now he is bunched-up tight and crying like a baby.

Now he is longing for the blindness of the womb.

He sits up.

Now he knows why he's here.

165

D id I mention I saw them?
Well, I did.
Oh yes – I saw them alright. Not, of course, that I've told a
soul – except you. I certainly wasn't going to say anything to the police.
No, sir. I mean, for one thing they'd have thought me even stranger than
they already did (any stranger and for sure you can bet I'd be helping
them still with their enquiries) – and for another, well, what would have
been the point? As far as I know they haven't done anything wrong (you
know I mean wrong as in illegal), and besides, it's me they've come to
see (at least one of them has; God knows who the weedy little guy is, but
I guess I'll find out), and I wouldn't want to disappoint. So, no, all the
time it took to get back up here in the squad car I just spent describing
the dinners I've had with Richard Gere (he just wouldn't believe the
truth, so I thought *what the hell*) – not to mention Winona Ryder –
which nonsense seemed to satisfy him.

Cops. Jesus. Who said you had to be smart?

Anyway, I'm here now. And fuck me if it isn't already getting dark.
Jesus, I thought this was supposed to be summer. And with it getting
dusky, it's sure getting spooky too, I can tell you. I guess it's being up
here all alone now, when only a few hours ago you couldn't *move* for
people. Still, a few spooks never hurt. And besides, I have things to do
up here – one thing in particular that if I don't get done soon – well,
soon it's gonna be too late. By which, of course, I mean those shells. I
sort of figured when I buried them that they'd be kind of easy to find,
them being buried (or so I thought) just outside the railings around
that fucking awful memorial. But was I wrong. Maybe in all the
confusion I buried them someplace else – but I don't think so. Carry on
looking is what I have to do. Sure you can sit there if you want. I don't
care. You could maybe keep an eye out. After all, I *am* expecting
company.

Well, it's nearly eight o'clock now and still no luck. You know, I'm
starting to think that maybe I never will find them and I'll wind up

throwing stones instead – which I suppose would just about be the appropriate crowning moment of this whole ridiculous charade.

Oh, and one other thing. Is it getting cold out here or is it me?

Okay, so if you knew where they were all the time, why the hell didn't you tell me? I mean, Jesus Christ. You're supposed to be my fucking wife. You're supposed to be on my fucking side.

Okay, okay. Like you say, no harm done. And yes, you're right – I should concentrate on the job in hand. Well, I'm trying – believe me. It's just this cold's started to get to me. I mean, look at my hands – they're fucking shaking.

But, no. You're right. Stay calm is the thing. Just break the gun and slip in the shells.

Like so.

You know, I was thinking it's some weird kind of coincidence or something that that cop should have mentioned Winona Ryder. I mean *Winona Ryder* of all people – considering, I mean, how she looks so much like you. You know, it never really occurred to me until just now – but Jesus it's true. Thinking about it now, you could be sisters. In fact –

No.

No more letters. No more letters that get no reply.

Oh Lord, I'm cold.

Oh Lord, I'm so cold and you know I'm so tired of being without you.

Eddie

166

'What do you mean, you don't want it?'
  'I *mean* I don't want it.'
  'But you *must* want it! *I* want it!'
'Well, you go get it then.'
'But –'
'But what? The car's there. You can have it. Just turn it around and go.'
'But I *can't* –'
'Why not?'
'*Because I quit!*'
Eddie sighed. 'So you quit. Lots of people quit. Just go tell them you changed your mind.'
  '*Please*,' said Peter Frampton, dropping suddenly to his knees, '*oh please* –'
'Oh Lord,' said Eddie, looking anxiously about him. 'For God's sake, get up, will you?'
  They were standing (kneeling) in the small, glass-walled museum in back of the visitors' center. The only two remaining of that busy day's two thousand-odd visitors, they'd been stood before the general's favorite full-dress uniform for close to two hours now, one not caring if he never left the scene, the other quite desperate to go.
  'Look,' said Eddie (the man on the door was starting to stare), 'just get up and we'll talk, okay?'
'Promise?'
'I promise.'
Slowly, Peter Frampton rose to his full five foot six. Still tearful, he tried to smile – an aspiration, though, that was well beyond him, thanks to his schoolboy's wobbly lip.
  'Now,' said Eddie. 'You know this is crazy, don't you?'
Peter Frampton shrugged.
'Well, don't you?'
'But –'
'I mean, first you take my car without my permission, and then, when I *give* it to you, for God's sake, you won't *take* it –'

He shook his head.

'What now?'

'You don't understand,' he said.

'Well, you're right there,' said Eddie.

Peter Frampton sighed. 'I mean, you don't understand that, well, I can't go back without you –'

'You what?'

'*Gentlemen, please,*' said the man on the door. Eddie turned to him, sort of nodding, turned back.

'Well, you see, I . . . I sort of told them that, well –' Pausing then, Peter Frampton looked about him, as if searching the cabinets for a new source of courage.

'Told them *what*?'

'Well, that you and I . . . that is to say that we . . . *oh Lord . . .*'

'Oh, for God's sake –'

'*Well, that you were my father* –'

'What?'

'And that, well, you were kind of *sick* –'

'*Sick?* What do you mean, *sick?*'

Again, Peter Frampton looked away. He mumbled something entirely unintelligible.

'*What* did you say?' said Eddie.

Again, the mumble.

He gripped the little man's lapels. 'Look, you –'

'Okay! Okay!'

Then released them, took a breath.

Peter Frampton cleared his throat, flicked his eyes to the man on the door, then back. He leaned forward, whispered low.

Eddie blanched. 'You said *what*?'

'I didn't mean to,' said Peter Frampton.

'You didn't *mean* to?'

'It just sort of came out.'

Eddie shook his head. There were times, like this, when doubting his hearing led to doubts – quite persuasive – about his very sanity. He took a breath. 'So,' he said. Another breath. 'Let me get this straight. What you're saying is that not only are they under the absurd impression that I'm your father, but that they *also* believe – as if *that* weren't enough – that I'm suffering from something called . . . let me see, what did you call it? . . . *Castro*something –'

'Itis,' said Peter Frampton. 'Castroitis. It means, well, it means you think you're –'

'*Castro*, by any chance?'

'That's right!'

474

'Jesus Christ.'

'Only –'

Eddie felt his spirits drop even lower. 'What now?' he said.

'Well –'

'Oh, come on, come on,' he said wearily. 'Can this get any worse?'

Peter Frampton swallowed hard, once again dropping his voice to a whisper. 'Well –' Again he cleared his throat. 'I said they were *looking* for you. I *had* to –'

'Looking for me? Who?'

On tiptoe, he raised his lips until they were real close (too close) to Eddie's ear.

Again, Eddie stepped back. 'The *FBI*?' he said.

'Sssh!'

'You told the K-Mart head office that the *FBI's* looking for me?'

'On account of your beard –'

'My *beard*? But I don't *have* a beard!'

Peter Frampton frowned. 'Sometimes you do. When you feel like it. You keep it in your carpet-bag –'

'My what?'

'Carpet-bag. You pull it out and stick it on every time you do them liquor stores –'

Eddie covered his old-man's weary eyes. *Any minute*, he thought, *I'll wake up.*

'Which is why they're looking for you –'

He lowered his hand. 'Okay,' he said. 'Now I know this isn't happening – I know it's just some real weird dream – and I know I'm going to regret even saying this, but can I just recap? Okay. So. So far – as far as K-Mart's concerned – I'm your father, I'm mad, I think I'm Fidel Castro, and the FBI's looking for me on account of my robbing some liquor store –'

'*Stores*,' said Peter Frampton.

'Right. Stores.'

'And it's not a dream.'

'Sure it is.'

'No, it ain't. And anyway, it's on account of your beard, really –'

'What is?'

'That they're looking for you. The liquor stores are nothing. It's your *beard* they want – seeing as how it's special. Which is where I come in.'

'Of course you do.'

'You see, I'm the only one that can track you. Being your son and all. It's a kind of father–son thing, you know? It's like I know what you're thinking, sometimes even before you do –'

'You do?'

'Yes, sir,' said Peter Frampton. There was pride in his eyes.

'Okay,' said Eddie. 'What am I thinking now?'

'Now?' Peter Frampton closed his eyes. There began, then, in his throat, a low humming.

'What's that noise?'

'Ssh! I'm tracking.'

'Oh, I see.'

The humming stopped. The eyes opened. He smiled.

'Well?'

'You're thinking –' Suddenly, he was blushing. 'You're thinking, *oh gosh*, about *me* –'

'Correct,' said Eddie.

'You're thinking how proud you are at the way I've turned out –'

He shook his head.

Peter Frampton's face fell. 'You're not?'

Again, Eddie Reno grasped the little man's lapels, pulled him up with a strength he didn't know he possessed, until they were nose to nose. 'No,' he said. 'I'll tell you what I was thinking. I was thinking that if you don't walk away from me right now and forever – if you don't take the car and keep driving anywhere but here – then I shall push you through this plate glass and you will go and join the general –'

'But –' said Peter Frampton, the word a little strangled.

'But *nothing*,' said Eddie. He pushed his new burden hard up against the glass. Across the room, the doorman started moving.

'*Hey!*'

'Okay?'

'Okay!' said Peter Frampton.

Eddie let the man down.

'What the hell's goin' on?' said the doorman.

'Ah, nothing,' said Eddie, brushing the little man's shoulders. 'Just call it a family dispute,' he said. He looked at Peter Frampton. 'That's right, isn't it, son?' he said.

Peter Frampton said nothing.

'I *said* that's *right* – didn't I, son?'

'Yes, Dad,' he said.

'Good,' said Eddie. He turned to the doorman. 'I wonder,' he said, 'if I might have a word –'

'About what?'

He moved him away, dropped his voice to a whisper. It was a delicate matter, he said – something that had baffled all the doctors. The problem, he said, was a fault in the mind that had led to the boy's poor behavior. It was, he said, entirely regrettable, but he knew it was his duty to report the poor boy missing.

'Missing?' said the doorman.

Eddie raised a hand, one finger extended, circled that finger about level with his temple. 'Bellevue,' he whispered, then he whispered 'reward'; then, stepping aside, he gave the man with the handcuffs room so he could go do his work.

167

Not once during the entire journey north had Eddie thought of Angelia. Not once, in all that time, had he wondered how she was, or stopped, once, to wonder if she'd thought about him. Not once – until now. Now, as he stood in the shadow of the trees beside the visitors' center, watching the tail-lights of his car disappear, he thought of her absolute, unwavering love for the country to which she knew she would never return, and he smiled. He smiled, too, when he thought of her never-loaded pistol, and how she'd hide every morning in the bar beside the cigarette machine – and how, one day – some anniversary day (which anniversary he could not now remember – there were so many) – she'd drunk enough tequila to liberate her tongue, and how then she'd whispered in his ear that, though her kind of Cuba was surely gone forever, her kind of America was the next best thing. 'And what's that when it's at home?' he'd said, talking over the buzzing in his head. Well, she'd just looked at him then and kissed him, and laid her hand on his heart. '*Libertad*,' she whispered, '*Freedom*'; then, with the word like a lantern hanging still in the air, she'd led him upstairs to his room.

A breeze shook the trees; he pulled the doorman's heavy coat about him. He watched the man approaching.

'You okay?'

'Sure,' said Eddie. 'I'm okay.'

'You know you can't stay here. I gotta close up. You want a ride into town?'

He shook his head.

'Suit yourself – but I gotta lock the gates. You comin'?'

It was warm in the man's car, the seats thick and furry. He started her up, flicked on the lights. He pushed the shift to Drive, paused. 'Say, that guy,' he said, 'he really your boy?'

'No,' said Eddie.

The man laughed. 'Yeah, I figured. Just crazy, huh?'

'Just crazy,' said Eddie. 'Thanks for scaring him off. With the cuffs.'

The man touched the gas. The car moved off. 'Ah, it was nothin',' he

said. 'You should see the *wife's* face when I pull those puppies out.'
Again, he laughed. This time Eddie joined him.

He dropped him on the roadside just outside the gates, leaning over,
then, his face glowing yellow from the dash. 'You sure you're okay?' he
said.

'Sure,' said Eddie. 'I could do with the walk.' He waved, then, as the
man pulled away. Then, when the car was safely out of sight, he turned
to the gates, drew a breath and started climbing.

Matthew

168

W hat with carrying most of his equipment (not to mention his busted, burning ankle), it sure was a struggle (the great box camera he balanced on his back as if he were some kind of packhorse, the wood and brass three-legged stand he clasped as tight as he could beneath his arm), but somehow he made it back up that rise – where, panting hard, his body running with sweat, he set it all down. He stood for a moment, then, doubled over, nearly retching with exhaustion, unaware that his efforts – such a wanton waste of a man's sparse resources, especially in such heat – had been observed from afar, and were being observed still.

In a while, his pulse settling, he eased himself upright, set his hands on his hips.

Too late, too late –

Like a dog trying to shake off its fleas, he shook the words from his ears, stared down for distraction at the dusty and travel-worn tools of his trade. The stand that, previously (in that now far-off other life of Clare and Miss Eliot and that New Orleans whorehouse), had been smooth to the touch – its brass so high-polished that it glowed in the last of the sun like candles on a table set for dinner – was now so scuffed, its metal dull, and the camera box itself – once so clean – was so chipped, now, and dirty –

He looked up as something sharp – a light flaring in the distance – caught his eye. He raised his arm against the slow-sinking sun.

He waited.

There.

And again.

He squinted, tried to see what it was – was someone signaling? – but it was way too far off for thirty-year-old eyes as old as his.

A last trick, he told himself, of a sullen, failing sun.

He swept his gaze to the rise where the soldiers and their horses lay dead. He stared, unblinking, a blindman's stare. Still he couldn't quite believe what his eyes were telling him; they were, it seemed to him, looking out upon the landscape of some other, dream-like land. They were, it seemed to him, guilty of some childish – some harmless – deception. He smiled, then, at the failure of their efforts to deceive him – just as, once, long ago now, he had smiled at Clare's lies when she'd stroked the pale flatness of her belly and whispered low about a future sure to come.

He closed his eyes tight, opened them.

Will you love me, Matthew Princeton, now that we're three?

'Oh Jesus,' he whispered, as a cool breeze swept over him. How could he have been so blind? How come it had only been when – all that time ago – she'd appeared upside down in the blackness of his darkroom, that he'd known those sweet lies for the truth they really were? How come it had been only then?

Too late, too late, always too late.

He knelt, eased the camera box onto his shoulders and thrust the stand beneath his arm. Slowly, carefully, his face wracked with pain, he pushed himself up. He stood a moment, then, swaying gently; then, gingerly, first with one foot, then the next, he made his way slow down the dip.

169

The first to fall; the lies of silence.

Working expertly (for what was he if not an expert – an expert in cool death's recording?) – his eyes closed easy like a sleeper's eyes – he spread the stand's legs, set the camera upon it. Then, his fingers moving swift like those of a widow in some cool, spartan parlor, he hitched up the curtain, paused a moment (so as to heighten, in that moment, the relief of release), then ducked down beneath it and gathered it about his shoulders.

Slowly, he counted to ten.

He opened his eyes.

The First to Fall, he would title this picture, and again he saw himself in a room somewhere smiling, while those all around him queued to slap him on the back and shake his brave hand – to flatter him, and to tell him *Thanks to you, now we understand death, and no longer fear it*.

He blinked hard, tried to focus through the sweat. He squirreled his arm beneath the thick velvet cloth, rubbed his eyes with the tips of his fingers.

We understand death.

In the eye of his mind again, they were walking arm in arm along some leaf-strewn autumn street, he dressed calm in a gentleman's Sunday suit, she in a fine dress and parasol, whilst, exactly twelve steps ahead of them (so often had he pictured this splendid scene that he'd long ago counted and double-checked their number), a short woman in black was pushing a baby carriage that was decked-out in fine Charlotte lace, within which lay little Matthew, their dearest summer boy.

He screwed up his eyes.

We understand death.

He frowned, watching hard, as if for some movement. Lord, how comic the man seemed, suspended upside down! How – as ever – like a father pulling faces for a child! He reached beyond the curtain, and, blind, turned the brass of the focus-ring, so sharpening the man's smile.

His teeth.

Find his teeth.

Trapped in his silence, the man, already, was just the image of himself – the image on a wall in a frame somewhere of a fellow caught in song, or calling out across a field –

Except, of course, for the blood.

We understand death, sir.

Oh, the blood.

Matthew searched in the darkness for the wound that had killed the man, scanning the body for that tell-tale bullet blast, or the slit from which gray guts were spilling, or that blunt severed limb, the stump of which, now, was just torn flesh and gristle –

But nothing.

Squinting harder, he looked again – starting, again, at the head and moving down.

Then he stopped, moved back up.

Ears.

The man had no ears.

And no eyes.

He had no eyes.

No head, in fact.

Lord, the man had no head.

Matthew licked his dry lips. *The First to Fall, I call it*, said a voice – just a whisper. *Do you see how the fellow has no head?* Carefully then, holding his breath, he lifted the shutter, counted seconds, let it fall.

Thanks to you, sir, we understand death, and no longer fear it.

He stood a while then, smiling politely as the mayor of some city back east shook his hand. Then slowly, closing his eyes in preparation for the light, he eased himself back, away from the camera, let the curtain drop away.

Then he counted to ten.

He opened his eyes.

There's a history to whistling in afternoon graveyards – just as there's a history to whistling on now-silent battlefields. They whistled, the women, on the fields of Waterloo as they rifled through pockets and severed ringed fingers. They spun their tunes, too, in the woods of Virginia – gay little tunes rising up through the trees as the southern boys tugged at the boots of their now-silent brothers, then, later by firelight, laughed at the photographs of pale, hopeful girls, and the letters that began *My dearest darling love* –

Hey.

A History of Whistling.

Now there's an idea.

But, no.

Back to that day – back to Matthew and his tunes on that failing afternoon, as – seen from on high – he moved like a beetle from corpse to bloody corpse, ducking each time beneath the safety of his thick velvet hood, there to marvel at the selflessness, the wild generosity, with which the ghastly grace of death, and, beyond that, mutilation, had been given free of charge from one man to another – and all in the name of freedom.

Freedom and liberty.

He paused in his whistling as he lifted the shutter, exposing the plate, *here*, to a man whose slitted thighs and busted knees would prevent him, in any further life to come, from ever again mounting his horse, then, *there* – a few yards away up the rise – to the ruin of a man whose hands had been hacked from him in order that no more would he hold a gun in anger, nor touch his mother's face, nor hold a child close in his arms.

He dropped the shutter, crept, then, in a moment, out into the light.

He turned his head sharp.

There it was again – that glinting. He studied the hills that rose beyond the river. *Someone's watching me*, he thought, and the thought made him glad. He raised a hand high in a wave, cupped his hands, then, to his mouth and called out, 'HULLOOO' – listened, then, for some call in response.

None came.

He shrugged his shoulders.

He turned back to his camera. Shouldering it, then, he moved onto the next corpse – rising slowly, with every one, up the steepening hill.

It was six o'clock, maybe seven, by the time he reached the general. The general was lying on his back on the hill's low, grassy summit, his shoulders propped up against the body of a horse, his head thrown back, his blue eyes staring, frowning, upward as if he were searching the heavens for something that the heavens refused to reveal. He was naked save for one single sock, his flesh pale, his cropped hair touched golden in the last of the sun's rays.

And the wound? The fatal shot?

Matthew tracked his eyes slow down the general's muscled torso – down to his waist, his hips, his penis, his thighs – down further, then, to his knees, his calves, his feet, the one sock.

One sock.

He frowned, thinking hard. Had whoever stripped him been called away suddenly? Or did it *mean* something – this one item? Was it some kind of message? He shrugged. It didn't matter now. All that mattered now was the picture. All that mattered was that he capture for all time such fine, exquisite work – that he capture for the mayor of that small eastern city how fine is a man when he's fought hard and died for his nation – how beautiful, how *noble* he is when his thighs have been slashed, his hands and his feet removed, his penis severed and shoved in his mouth, his ribcage pulled apart and his beating heart removed, his jaw smashed to pieces and his ear-drums split with arrows in *this* world so he'll not be so deaf to wise counsel in the next. That was all that mattered now – the lies of silence and how – ironically, perhaps – they can never be heard, but only ever seen. So he reached his hand around, feeling for the shutter – but feeling only, in that moment, a sudden searing pain shooting up from his leg. He twisted, his leg twitching, the muscles failing; he tried to hold on, but the camera and his curtain fell with him to the ground.

He lay then, for a moment, quite still, staring up at the sky, at the first stars emerging, blinking, then, at the sound of horse's hooves, far off but getting nearer. '*Oh Lord,*' he whispered, '*Oh Lord, please forgive me,*' as the hooves ceased their pounding, were replaced by the light pad of footsteps. He lifted his head, reached his hand for the arrow, but before he could grasp it, another found its target and he howled like a dog at the moon. A third, then, then a fourth; again he raised his head, searching the darkness for the shape or the shadow of a man.

A lightning flash, suddenly – dark on a face; the glint, then, of a knife drawing closer, its blade cool and precise. He reached out a hand, felt the smooth wooden sides of his camera. *So smooth*, he thought, and he thought for the last time of Clare. He thought, in that moment, of all he'd never once told her – and now never would. He closed his eyes, and closed his heart. He lay still on the cooling earth, waiting – so calm now – for the final release of silence.

Eddie

170

A nd so he's dead. Alongside his busted camera. How neat. Of course, those eagle-eyed amongst you will have spotted already that this isn't the ending I chose for the journal – because, of course, had it been so, he'd have been in no position (his being dead) to *write* the journal in the first place – not to mention the fact that pretty much the whole *point* of the journal was the photograph of Crazy Horse, which, of course, he never quite got around to taking – except (of course) in the journal.

Oh, and one other thing.

Before all you sad photography buffs out there (God help you) start writing me letters and sending me e-mails and faxes on the subject of how I've got all the details of late nineteenth-century photography all wrong, well –

I *KNOW* – OKAY?

– and, what's more, I couldn't give a flying fuck. This is my story – not yours, okay?

Good.

So.

That, for what it's worth, then, is that; this, meanwhile, is emphatically this. By which I mean this cold, ever-dampening grass, this wind and that wretched starry sky, those gravestones in the moonlight, this fence, that fucking awful memorial which not even nightfall can improve.

171

I *f all that is seen is, in the very moment of its seeing, gone, then*
  where lies the present – that place, here and now, that landscape,
  those colors, that seem so eternal – where, except in the chemical
graveyard of a photograph?

It had been this – this childish, sub-Sartre, sub-*anything* question –
that had, throughout his life, bothered Eddie Reno far more than any
other. The fact that he'd discovered it – all those years ago now – written
at eye-level in a neat upright hand on the wall of a men's-room cubicle at
the humanities faculty of the North Carolina State University at Raleigh
had troubled him not one bit. No, sir. In those days, to Eddie Reno, a
truth was a truth was a truth, regardless of where or how that truth had
been revealed. To him, in those days (we're talking late fifties here), the
message was all, the messenger immaterial. Hence, then, how that
message – however trite, however bone-headed – had stuck, and had
not, in the years ahead, been shifted. Indeed, from that moment of
revelation in North Carolina, to this moment on a slow-rise in eastern
Montana, it had worried him, really – this whereabouts of the present –
far more than it should have done, causing him, at times, such distress
that, as still a young man, free now of his father's absurd performing
and of the rigors of college, he had, on scant advice, made the long jump
with some ease from aspirin to Percatol, and thence to Biazadol, then
finally, today and many days previously, to the great big granddaddy of
them all, Dizoprenoprophrin – a drug expressly contra-indicated (except in the mind of Doctor Silver) in the case of a man of Eddie's health
and age, due to the greatly increased likelihood of his suffering – if not
now, then one day – a probably terminal stroke.

All of which, of course – as he paused that night in his cowboy suit in
the blue moonlit grass behind the visitors' center, before beginning the
rise to the top of the hill – crept through his old-man's battered mind,
reminding him again, though only fleetingly, of all in his life that had
gone before. For a moment, as his hands wrestled clumsily with the
bottle's child-proof (Eddie-proof) push-and-twist top, he pictured that
other man he once had been – the man, who, without so much as a

single second thought, had talked his way into (God knows how now) that house up in Oak Park, only to find himself stood the next morning, his hair all adrift, staring down at what remained of poor Papa's head, but with no thought in his own but quite how he would frame it – the man who, when faced with the beautiful, helpless, blank-eyed Marilyn, had sought so to capture her death fast-approaching that, in so doing, he'd eschewed his one chance of maybe barring – for a little while at least – its arrival. And then, of course, there was Elvis. Oh, Elvis. Why had he not left his camera in its bag and just *looked*? Why had he not rid his ears of those songs and just *listened*? Why had he still played mortician, when he could, perhaps, have played friend?

At last the bottle opened – the top spinning way off into the darkness – followed – *Jesus Christ* – by the tiny white peace-pills inside.

Man, they did it – they really did it. They went and screwed the President –

Down on his knees, then, he was patting the grass in half-circles with his palms, his search not aided by the clouds drawing slow now across the huge Montana moon, nor, indeed, by the blindness of tears welling up in his eyes, then dropping heavy like rain upon the parched, bloodied earth.

His fingers found something tiny, something hard. He lifted it up, held it close, turned it over, round and round in his fingers.

A bullet.

It was a bullet, for sure.

He touched the once-sharp but now-flattened tip.

Then a sound.

Slowly, pushing up on aching knees, he stood, the bullet clasped tight in his hand. He looked about him. Nothing. Nothing to see but the blue-tinged prairie-grass rising slow up Custer Hill to the needle of the fallen man's memorial. He looked back to the center. The center was dark now, a huddled mass in the dip. He turned back, looked again to the hill. For days, now, he'd known that all his traveling, all the miles, all the years of his fake life, had been leading to here, to now. For days he'd known it (*how* he'd known it, he couldn't have said, but he'd known it alright) – for days he'd felt the pull of salvation. He closed his eyes a moment, let his weary bones rest. Just another few steps, he knew, and all would be resolved. Just another few steps and the cycle of wounding that had been for so long so strong would finally and forever be broken.

Part Six

THE CAGE

172

My dear Angelia,

If you're reading this, then it means that I won't be coming back. I wish there was some other way to tell you – but there isn't. Please forgive me for any shock you feel. (I know this would be bad for you right now.) Forgive me also for leaving like I did – without saying goodbye, I mean. I did try to phone you once, but the number was busy. Fate, I suppose.

Anyway, how are you? Are you feeling OK? I suppose mornings are not the best time for you now. I remember how Clare used to get so sick. Anyway, I hope the sickness doesn't last too long.

All of which brings me to what I really wanted to say. What it is is I hope you'll forgive me not only for not saying goodbye, but also for not saying that I knew about the baby. I'm just a coward, you see. It's difficult to explain, but it was like if you knew that I knew, then I'd somehow be a part of the future – a part of her future (don't ask me why, but I've a feeling it's a girl) – and I just couldn't bear that. I couldn't bear to see another life ruined like I've ruined so many already. I hope you will try to understand that it's not that I don't care – but because I do that I have to go. Anyway, I know with you as her mother she'll be just fine. Maybe one day when she's grown you'll show her my picture and try to explain. Or maybe not. Maybe it's just best to forget. Do whatever you think. I know you'll make the right decision.

Finally, I have something to ask of you. Please, if my son should ever find you, would you tell him (I don't know how, but please tell him) that I always held a hope in my heart that we'd meet again one day, and that I feel now – as I write this letter – that day is coming soon. Also, please tell him that (thanks to our friend 'Doctor' Silver) I shall be ready to accept my punishment – that by the time the end comes I shall, as they say, be no trouble.

Well, dearest Angelia, that's just about all I have the energy to say now. Please know that I embrace you, and hope with all my

heart that your dream of returning to your homeland comes true.
Who knows, maybe one day our daughter – half-American, half-
Cuban – will bring freedom and light to the darkness?
  Again, please forgive me.

Yours ever,
Edward.

173

I f I'm honest (now *there* would be something), I'll admit that this room is a little smaller than I'd anticipated. Also, whoever built this place put the window in so high that all you can see (unless you stand on something) is the sky, maybe the tops of the trees. And the bars – well, not even a baby could get out of there.

But still. Nothing, as they say, need be forever. It just *seems* like it is sometimes, ha-ha. Anyways. Having paid so much already, I guess another few bucks won't hurt, if it means lowering the window and maybe getting a look at the lake.

On the subject of which.

Yesterday, when the cops came by (just introducing themselves, they said – being neighborly – though I'm not so sure), one of them mentioned about the lake not having any kind of boundary around it, and how, what with that being the case, a child could easily fall in and drown. *Like that Lindberg kid*, the other one said, which I thought was a little unnecessary. (Not to say completely inaccurate – but that's another story.) Anyway, I said if there ever *was* a child in the house then I'd certainly think about it, and thanked him for his concern. Before they left, of course, they couldn't resist saying how sorry they were about my daddy and all (nobody can), and so I nodded and had to listen yet again to all the same old stuff everybody comes out with – what a tragedy it was and how that doctor should be busted. Ah well. People mean well, I guess. It's just that sometimes, like yesterday for instance, I could do without it. I mean sometimes I'm so fucking tired, what with the book still not coming, not to mention this hand of mine that's already clawing-up, that I just feel like sitting down in the TV room and letting go.

Which reminds me: a note to myself. Next time I get to town, I simply *must* see about getting cable out here. I cannot begin to tell you how sick I am of *I Love Lucy*. I guess if you *do*, it's okay. I just don't happen to. In fact I can't stand the woman.

But where was I?

Oh yes, this room. For sure as a games-room it wouldn't cut it; as a child's bedroom, though (once that window's fixed, and I might change the bars after all, I don't know), it's just about perfect. There was even this bed in it when I bought the place. Sometimes I can't help thinking maybe someone was expecting us. On the subject of which, I did think once that maybe the child's mother might have bought it and smuggled it in somehow – but then I remembered how of course she's back in Havana now (ha-ha), thanks to the Bearded One finally snuffing it (the cause, I like to think, being he choked on his beard), and so it's pretty unlikely. I mean, I know things have changed there since they started on that long road to statehood, but I reckon they must still be fucking hard and for a woman who works in a bar (nice touch that, don't you think?) to find the cash for a bed, and to then pay for its transportation to the US of A, would be pretty much out of the question. I guess all I can ever realistically expect from her are those cards she sends now and then. They're addressed to me, of course – but only for politeness' sake. It's the child she's *really* talking to.

But hey – listen to me, will you?

The child.

For one thing, she's not just any old child – she's *blood*. And for another, she *does* have a name. When she was born, I believe her mother called her Isabelle, which is a nice enough name, I guess – although – seeing as how *I'll* be raising her – I've decided on a change.

A change to what? you say. (I think I hear you.)

Oh Lordy – you mean you can't guess it?

Jesus Christ. You people. You're all dumber than I thought.

A NOTE ON THE TYPE

The text of this book is set in Linotype Sabon, named after
the type's founder, Jacques Sabon. It was designed by Jan
Tschichold and jointly developed by Linotype, Monotype
and Stempel, in response to a need for a typeface to be available
in identical form for mechanical hot metal composition and hand
composition using foundry type.

Tschichold based his design for Sabon roman on a fount
engraved by Garamond, and Sabon italic on a fount by Granjon.
It was first used in 1966 and has proved an enduring
modern classic.

Interesting Facts About the State of Arizona   Jeremy Poolman
£6.99   0 7475 5402 1

Winner of the Commonwealth Writers Prize

A story of death and life, of love lost and found, of chances squandered and second chances, of dust and heat in the American South-west.

'Wonderfully original, dotty and ultimately romantic first novel' The Times

'A delight to read ... the tenderness of the writing triumphs, infusing the whole book with humanity and optimism' Guardian

'Offbeat and original ... evokes a world straight out of the all-American canvas of Edward Hopper or the films of David Lynch' Literary Review

'Poolman's oddballs are a warm bunch, his askance vision and dialogue close in tone to the Coen brothers or Hal Hartley' Sunday Times

'Poolman's loopy humour is truly his own, and quite infectious' Daily Telegraph

To order from Bookpost PO Box 29 Douglas Isle of Man IM99 1BQ www.bookpost.co.uk
email: bookshop@enterprise.net fax: 01624 837033 tel: 01624 836000

bloomsburypbks

bloomsburymagazine.com

Skin Jeremy Poolman
£14.99   0 7475 5344 0

Janek Janowiec is awaiting trial. In his cramped attic apartment in Krakow he has decided to set straight the record of his life, and yet he is wracked by the guilt and knowledge of a number of terrible secrets. What happened to his friend, the charismatic revolutionary leader, Fredzio? Where do the bodies that wash up on the banks of the river come from? Where is his wife Rachel? And will their daughter Ewa ever return from her shopping trip ...?

With Janek himself telling the story the answers can never really be known — glimpsed, hinted at, slowly revealed perhaps, but solid facts disappeared from his life many years ago.

In a Nabokovian narrative, *Skin* casts a revealing light on many of the neuroses of the late twentieth century, looking into the dark and chilling mind of a man whose lies, obsessions and madness spill shockingly across every page.

To order from Bookpost PO Box 29 Douglas Isle of Man IM99 1BQ www.bookpost.co.uk
email: bookshop@enterprise.net fax: 01624 837033 tel: 01624 836000

bloomsbury pbks